I0664273

NEWFOUNDLAND

NES

ELITE SECURITY

NES * SERIES

Risky tango

RHONDA BREWER

Acknowledgments

So many people have made my writing and publishing journey possible. A simple thank you never seems like enough to convey my gratitude.

To the extraordinary ladies who helped me make my stories better, Amabel Daniels, Michelle Eriksen, and Abbie Zanders, I don't know what I would do without your advice, suggestions, keen eyes, and encouragement. Thank you for always being there when I need you, Jackie Dawe Ford, Nancy Arnold-Holloway, and Karie Deegan, as my dedicated betas and dear friends. Thank you, Corey Majeau of Majeau Designs and Golden Czermak of Furious Fotog, for making my covers amazing.

Last but not least, thank you to my wonderful husband, my beautiful children, and grandchildren. Without your love and support, I would never be able to do what I love. You all mean the world to me, and I love you with all my heart.

Dedication

This book is dedicated to the incredible readers who patiently waited for this book release and encouraged me to push ahead during a tough couple of years.

I love you all.

This book is fiction. Names, characters, places, and incidents are products of the author's imagination and are not to be taken as real. Any resemblance to people living or dead, events, location, or companies is purely coincidental.

This is the original work of Rhonda Brewer.

All rights reserved. No part of this work can be reproduced in any way without written permission from the author.

RISKY TANGO@2022 Rhonda Brewer

All Rights Reserved

Prologue

Fifteen years ago…

"I don't understand why you would want to move away," his mother said with a hitch in her voice.

"Mom, I'm not teaching dance forever. I know you think I was born to be a dancer but come on, the most I've done with my skills was teach a bunch of oversexed women who only come to class to gawk at me," Hunter Crawford complained as he continued to pack his suitcase.

Camilla Lacotte-Crawford winced at his words, making him feel horrible for reminding her of the spectacle Shelby Skiffington made two weeks earlier. The woman was close to his mother's age, married, rich, and sexy as hell. She'd stayed after class to ask for Hunter's help with some dance positions. He didn't mind until he realized Shelby had more than dance on her mind.

When she started to rub herself against him, he sidestepped, but she followed. When Hunter refused her advances, she grabbed his face and slammed her mouth against his. He pushed her away, but the woman thought it was a game. Hunter had to put a table between them for her to realize he was in no way interested.

It didn't bother him that she was older. It was the fact she was married. Hunter heard rumors her husband knocked Shelby around, and she'd come into the studio with bruises a few times. Hunter wasn't about to get in the middle of such a volatile relationship, although he hoped she'd leave before her husband killed her.

That day he decided he needed to find another career path. He loved dancing, but he didn't see doing it for the rest of his life. His mom was a former dancer with the New York ballet. She moved to Ontario to teach at The Ontario School of Ballet when she retired. The art was in her blood.

After his parents married, she became pregnant with Hunter. His dad moved the family to his home province of Newfoundland. That was when she opened Madam Lacotte's Dance Studio to teach young dancers the art she loved.

From the time Hunter and his sister could walk, his mother encouraged them to learn, but not just ballet. Hunter and his sister also trained in tap, jazz, and ballroom dancing. Ballroom was probably his favorite, but he practiced ballet to help with flexibility.

His mother wanted them to choose a path they loved, but his sister was the only one to embrace dance as a career. She danced with the Toronto Ballet for four years, but a knee injury ended that. She returned home to join their mother at the studio. Hunter always felt there was more for him, and he'd find out what it was.

"Well, do you blame them? You're very handsome, like your Papa." His father chuckled.

Reed Crawford had an ego the size of the province of Newfoundland. He'd worked as a model in his younger years, then a successful freelance photographer. He'd been all over the world, but his father couldn't wait to hang up his camera to spend the rest of his days with his wife.

"God, Dad, do you need to give him a head as big as yours?" Hunter's younger sister groaned as she walked into the room with an empty box.

"Zara, leave your Papa alone," his mother said in her fading French-Canadian accent.

Hunter loved his family with all his heart, but at nineteen, it was time he stopped using his looks and body to make money. Sure, he was teaching dancing, but he also performed as an exotic dancer once a week at the club where he worked part-time security.

He'd been hesitant to perform at first, but when he saw some of the guys who danced on ladies' night, he knew he'd make just as much as the idiots shaking their asses on stage. At least he could dance.

The short gig gave him enough savings to take off to the west coast of Canada, where he had an interview with a very reputable security firm. *After a telephone discussion, the owner asked Hunter to come for an in-person interview.*

"What if this fella doesn't hire you?" His father's expression was serious.

"I'll find something else, or I'll come back. Dad, I need to do this. I've got all the credentials they want. I've trained in martial arts, sure I'm not a black belt, but I can take someone down if I have to. I've completed firearms training, and I've passed the psychological exam. I'm confident I've got this," Hunter assured his parents as he closed his suitcase.

"You'll always have a place here at home." His mother wrapped her arms around him.

He could hear the emotion in her voice, and as hard as it was to leave, hopefully, it was for the best. After all, he wasn't a kid anymore. Growing up meant making a life for himself.

"Mom, for heaven's sake, he's not going to war." Zara rolled her eyes.

"I can tell you're going to miss me." Hunter chuckled.

"Like a hole in the head." Zara smirked.

"Well, I can't watch you leave. I have a young lady coming for an interview. She's going to take over some classes. I'm going to say goodbye here." His mother hugged him again.

For a few minutes, she held him, then stepped back. The tears in her eyes were killing him, but it wasn't like they'd never see each other again. He decided to hit her with what she told him every time he said the words "good-bye."

"Goodbye is forever, Mom, remember. Let's say see you later." Hunter smiled.

"Throwing my words back at me." His mom smiled as she cupped his face.

"Of course," Hunter teased.

"Je t'aime, mon bébé," she said in French, meaning 'I love you, my baby' "Be safe and call us every day."

"I will." Hunter kissed her cheek.

He'd be in Yellowknife, Northwest Territories, hopefully with a new job within twenty-four hours. He grabbed his case off the bed and made his way out of his bedroom.

After a lengthy discussion with his dad, Hunter finally convinced him it was better to take a cab to the airport. When he arrived at the terminal, someone tapped him on the shoulder. He stepped back as he looked into the face of an angry stranger.

"Where is she?" The brute narrowed his eyes.

"I'm sorry, you have the wrong person." Hunter braced himself in case the guy tried to hit him.

"Where is Shelby?" the man shouted.

"How would I know?" Hunter replied.

"Where is she?" The man repeated.

"Whoa, I don't know where she is." Hunter stepped back.

"She told me she was going with you." The man growled.

"Sir, I don't know what she told you, but I'm leaving for a job. Alone," Hunter assured the man.

He glared at Hunter for several minutes before he stepped back, and his rage slowly disappeared. The man looked frantic and rubbed his large hands over his head.

"If she leaves, she'll screw up everything," the man murmured.

"I don't know what to tell you. I hope you find her." Hunter stepped back. "I need to catch my flight."

The man stood on the sidewalk as Hunter made his way inside the airport. He had no idea where Shelby was, but he wasn't about to stick around to find out. It was none of his business.

Twenty-nine hours later, Hunter pulled into the parking lot of a hotel where he also had the interview. A two-hour plane delay caused concern he wouldn't make his interview appointment.

He hadn't had time to shave or shower but managed to change at the airport, so he appeared somewhat presentable. The icy roads made him anxious, but what else did he expect moving so far north?

He sat in the lobby of the Explorer Hotel, waiting for his interview. The open area was bright, and he could see the beautiful scenery through the large windows. He smiled as he eyed the large stuffed polar bear on one side of the foyer. It was huge, and after staring at it for so long, it was as if it was watching him.

"Yep, don't want to run into one of them," Hunter muttered to himself.

The friendly woman at the reception desk asked Hunter to sit in the lobby while she called to let Mr. O'Connor know he was there for the interview. She explained the owner of the security firm had several interviews scheduled for the day.

Hunter wasn't sure if he actually had the job, but he told his parents if Keith didn't hire him, he'd find something else. That could be a huge problem because he didn't know what kind of employment opportunities he'd find in Yellowknife.

He sat on the uncomfortable armchair, drinking ice water he'd gotten from the bar. He was crunching on a piece of ice when a large bald man walked up to him.

"Are you Hunter?" The man's deep voice made him sound like James Earl Jones.

"Yes, sir." Hunter shot to his feet.

The piece of ice slipped down his throat, but luckily it melted quickly, so he didn't look like a complete idiot. As he shook the man's hand, he tried not to wince when the guy squeezed it roughly.

"I'm Dean Nash, but everyone calls me Bull." Bull motioned for Hunter to follow him.

"Bull?" Hunter muttered under his breath.

"Yeah, it's a nickname I got when I started working with Rusty. He said I looked like the big guy from the old show Night Court." *Bull chuckled.*

"Rusty?" Hunter raised an eyebrow.

"It's what we call Keith." Bull shrugged.

"Well, at least they didn't call you Kojak." Hunter smiled as he popped another piece of ice in his mouth.

Bull narrowed his eyes as they stepped on the elevator, causing Hunter to stop chomping the ice. His heart began to pound as he bit down on the cube nervously. He probably shouldn't have said something so disrespectful.

"Sorry," Hunter muttered.

"Don't worry about it. I'm bald. Don't sweat it, Crunch." Bull grinned.

"Crunch?" Hunter asked in confusion.

"In the five minutes since I introduced myself, you've been crunching on that ice. So, congrats, you've been nicknamed." Bull grinned as they stepped off the elevator.

"Umm…thanks?" Hunter said with uncertainty.

It probably wasn't a good impression to chomp down on ice when he was going in for an interview, but it was something he'd done his whole life. His mother used to get upset with him because she was afraid he'd ruin his teeth.

Bull led him down the corridor to a room at the end of the long hallway. When he opened the door, the guy motioned for Hunter to go ahead of him. A large man with red hair greeted them, and Hunter understood why Keith was called Rusty.

"Keith O'Connor, Hunter Crunch Crawford," Bull introduced them.

"Crunch?" Keith chuckled as he shook Hunter's hand.

"He likes to chomp down on ice cubes. I figured Crunch sounded better than Chompers." Bull shrugged.

"Works for me, but for God's sake, don't do it in front of Sandy. You'll get your ass handed to you." Keith motioned to one of the chairs next to a large table.

"Sandy is one of our computer analysts," Bull interjected.

"Is Sandy his nickname?" Hunter asked.

Bull and Keith broke into a fit of laughter, confusing Hunter. Keith composed himself when he noticed Hunter's discomfort. The guy placed a pen on top of some papers then pushed it across the desk.

"What's this?" Hunter asked.

"It's the papers we need completed to put you on staff, and Sandy is a woman. Her name is Alexandra Churchill but don't ever call her Alexandra." Keith smiled.

Hunter tried not to let his surprise and excitement show, but it was difficult, considering he just walked into the room. Still, he had to verify he'd heard Keith correctly.

"You're hiring me?" Hunter asked.

"Is there a reason we shouldn't?" Bull raised an eyebrow.

"No. I thought this was an interview..." Hunter's voice trailed off.

"Crunch, trust me, Sandy did a very detailed investigation, and we know everything about you." Bull smirked.

"Everything?" Hunter hadn't put his exotic dancing on his application.

"We strip everything down before we hire people," Bull deadpanned.

"Welcome to the company." Keith held out his hand.

Hunter shook hands with his new boss. His life quickly headed in a better direction, and he couldn't wait to see what the future would hold.

Chapter 1

Five years ago…

She stood in the nursery gazing down at the sleeping baby in the crib. Her baby girl, and nobody would take her away. Sabrina Burke wouldn't allow the death of her fiancée to prevent her from giving their daughter the best life possible.

Two weeks earlier, she'd kissed Easton Thornton when he left her to head home after the birth of their daughter. They'd spent the whole night choosing a name, and by daylight, they decided on Charlotte Victoria Thornton.

By lunch, Easton was in the intensive care unit fighting for his life. Somehow, the carpet on the steps at his family home came loose, causing him to trip. Easton fell backward over the steps and landed on the tile floor, causing a fatal brain injury.

She'd held out hope for several days, but his family made the final decision. Nobody asked Sabrina's input, but she was relieved she didn't have to make that choice.

Charlotte squirmed for a few seconds, then sighed as she seemed to find a comfortable position. Barely two weeks old, and she no longer had a father. Sabrina blew out a shaky breath as a tear slid down her cheek.

"Your daddy will always be watching over you, Charlee," Sabrina whispered and ran her hand gently over the baby's soft dark hair. "He loved you so much. Daddy talked to you every night while you were still in Mommy's belly. I wish I'd recorded it for you to hear."

"You should probably let the child sleep," an annoying female voice whispered.

Grant hired Vanessa Boyle to help Sabrina with Charlotte. It was as if the woman didn't want Sabrina to touch the baby at all and constantly stuck her nose in where it wasn't wanted.

"She's sleeping fine," Sabrina retorted.

Vanessa was an uptight snob who thought she knew everything about children. Sabrina didn't know how, since the woman was in her late forties, never married, and had no children of her own. Vanessa reminded Sabrina of the woman in the Nanny McPhee movie, but more attractive with better teeth.

"Babies need to rest undisturbed. You may think you're being gentle, but touching her will stimulate her, and she won't get a restful sleep." Vanessa switched off the light.

"Why are you here at ten in the evening?" Sabrina asked.

"Mr. Thornton asked me to stay in case the baby needed something," Vanessa whispered as she pointed to the open door.

"If Charlee needs anything, I'm here to get it for her. I'm her mother. You can leave." Sabrina sat in the plush rocking chair in the corner of the room.

"I take direction from Mr. Thornton, and he wanted me to stay." Vanessa pointed to the open door again.

"Look, this is my house, not Grant's. Either you leave now, or I'll call someone to have you removed." Sabrina tried to calm her voice as she shot to her feet.

Vanessa didn't seem concerned about Sabrina's outburst. The only way to get the woman to leave was to have Grant tell the bitch to go. She hoped he wouldn't give her a difficult time and make her feel less than adequate because she was still mourning Easton.

According to Grant, Sabrina should be moving on by now. She didn't know how the man's brain worked. The only time she saw any emotion from him after Easton's death was the day of the funeral, and even that looked forced. Grant returned to regular life like nothing happened.

Sabrina stomped out of the room and made her way to the master bedroom, where she'd left her cell phone. She snatched it off the nightstand and immediately placed a call to Grant. The phone rang several times then went to voicemail, and she cursed under her breath

Sabrina tapped his number again, ready to leave an angry message, but he picked up after the second ring. Sabrina took a deep breath before she attempted to start a conversation. She didn't want to take her anger out on Grant because he thought he was doing this to make things easier on her. At least that was what he told her.

"Grant Thornton," he said in his usual business tone.

"I want that woman out of my house," Sabrina said louder than she'd intended.

"Sabrina?"

"Yes, it's me. I want that pickle-puss woman out of my house. Now." Sabrina didn't even try to lower her voice.

"You mean Ms. Boyle?" Grant chuckled.

"Yes. I don't need her here all the time. I don't need her here at all." Sabrina glanced toward the doorway of her bedroom.

Vanessa stood outside the room staring, and it only enraged Sabrina more. How dare that woman listen to a private conversation. Sabrina stomped to the door and slammed it in the woman's face. It gave her a tiny morsel of satisfaction, and she locked the door.

"Sabrina, you're grieving and with a new..." Grant began the mindless dribble he'd said the day Easton died.

"No. I want her out," Sabrina barked.

Grant sighed, and she closed her eyes, expecting him to tell her she was acting like a spoiled brat. Since Easton's death, he was helpful and even agreed to meet with the lawyer to read the will. That was another thing making her edgy.

When she found out she was pregnant, Easton insisted they prepare legal wills in case something happened to one of them. She never thought they would have the wills read so soon. It had been *pretty straightforward; they were each other's beneficiaries. The only thing that was different on Easton's will was he had to name someone to take over his position in the Thornton family business.*

Sabrina had assumed it would all revert to Grant, but Easton had left that portion to his mother, and she'd take his position at the company or name a successor. He'd asked Sabrina not to say anything to anyone about that portion because he didn't want to upset Grant.

Sabrina asked him why he wouldn't put Grant in charge, but Easton simply said his brother already had enough on his plate and wasn't qualified to be put in the position of Chief officer of Thornton Group. It seemed odd, but she didn't know much about that world or question it further.

She didn't understand why they had to go through a formal will reading or why Grant had to be there. Not to mention that their original lawyer had given everything to a new guy, and she didn't know him. The whole thing was another reminder that Easton was gone.

"I'm coming over." Grant sounded irritated.

"I don't need anyone to come over. I want that woman out of my house. Tonight." Sabrina wasn't allowing Grant to talk her out of this.

Over the last two weeks, he'd convinced her to do a lot of things she didn't feel comfortable with. First, he talked her out of allowing her younger brother to move in. His excuse was she couldn't push her problems on Colt. He was young and starting a career as a system analyst with the school board.

Of course, Grant was right, but when she told her brother she'd changed her mind about him moving in, Colt seemed suspicious with her sudden change of heart. Her brother didn't make any bones about how little he trusted Grant.

Then there was the argument over having an autopsy done on Easton. Grant told her it was a waste of time since they knew what happened. After a long, loud discussion, Grant convinced her it would be less stress on the family.

Now, she was dealing with a nanny she never wanted. He wasn't changing her mind this time. If she was going to prove she could take care of everything, then Sabrina had to put her foot down.

"Sabrina, calm down. Do you want me to call my doctor?" Grant asked.

Sabrina clamped her teeth together and tried to control her rage. The last thing she needed was Grant's doctor giving her something she didn't need. His answer for women who were not agreeable was to provide them with something to 'calm their hormones.' Usually, something that would knock out a horse.

"I don't need your doctor. I've got one. I need that woman out. So, either you call her and tell her to leave, or I'll contact the police and have her removed." Sabrina wouldn't do that, but she was desperate.

There was nothing but silence on the phone, and Sabrina looked at the screen to see if Grant hung up. When she saw the call was still active, she put the phone back to her ear.

"Grant," she shouted.

"I sent her a text, and she's leaving now, but tomorrow you and I need to have a long talk. The lawyer sent me a copy of the will, and I didn't expect this." Grant sounded so cold.

"I've read the will. We had them drawn up together," Sabrina told him.

"This is an updated one. Easton changed it the week before the accident," Grant said.

"What?"

Sabrina's legs buckled, and she dropped onto the bed. Easton hadn't told her he was making changes to the document. She assumed he added Charlee, but it was peculiar for him not to mention it to her.

Then she remembered what Grant said. Easton changed it right before his death. Charlee was born the day of Easton's accident. She didn't know a lot about legal things, but she remembered the lawyer saying they couldn't add the baby until after she was born.

"Fine. Come over in the morning, and we'll go over it." Sabrina sighed.

"I'll tell Vanessa to be there first thing in the morning." Grant hung up before she could respond.

"Shit," Sabrina mumbled under her breath.

She didn't want to see Vanessa at all, and she certainly didn't want to see her first thing in the morning. The woman treated Sabrina like an idiot and always seemed to be eavesdropping on phone calls.

Sabrina should have ignored Grant's concerns and allowed Colt to move in with her. At least she'd have someone on her side, and that woman wouldn't have to be there every day.

Sabrina made her way to the door of her bedroom, expecting to see Vanessa looming outside. When she didn't see pickle puss in the hallway, she tiptoed to Charlee's nursery to see if Vanessa was there, but the woman was gone.

"Thank God the witch is gone."

Sabrina walked into the baby's room and smiled down at her daughter. Charlee was sleeping soundly with her pacifier next to her little hand. Sabrina made sure the blanket was tucked around her daughter and quietly left the room.

She needed to figure out what to do with everything Easton left her. She wasn't sure she could remain in the house without him. Sabrina still hadn't been able to go into his parents' house, knowing it was where he fell.

Grant wanted her to move into the Thornton estate so she wouldn't be alone, and when she declined, he seemed surprised. She didn't know why he'd think she could feel comfortable staying there.

"Easton, what am I going to do without you?" Sabrina whispered into the space of the bedroom they once shared.

He was her rock for more than four years. Easton helped her through her parents' deaths and celebrated when her brother graduated from university. He made her smile and filled her life with happiness. She needed his strength to get through tomorrow and prayed his spirit was with her.

After a sleepless night, Sabrina sat in her bed, feeding Charlee. She chose to breastfeed because she wanted a close bond with her daughter, and it was better for the baby. Grant told her she should bottle-feed, or the baby would tie her down.

Before Easton died, Grant hardly spoke to her when she was in his presence. It was as if she was some sort of annoyance that he had to tolerate. After that horrible day, Grant inserted himself into her life, and as much as she appreciated his help, it made her uncomfortable.

"Don't you think you should bottle feed?" A male voice startled her.

Sabrina looked up to see Grant in the doorway leading to her bedroom. He propped his shoulder against the door frame and smirked as his gaze dropped down to her exposed breast. She quickly yanked the baby's blanket up over herself.

"Do you mind?" Sabrina motioned for him to turn around.

"I don't mind at all," Grant said.

He straightened, and instead of leaving, walked further into the room. Grant stared like a wolf ready to pounce, and she wanted to escape.

"Grant, I'd like some privacy while I feed my daughter. I'll meet you downstairs in a few minutes." Sabrina glared at him.

Grant stared for what seemed like forever and then rolled his eyes. When he left, Sabrina placed the baby on the bed and hurried to the entrance of her room. She slammed the bedroom door and locked it, then went back to feeding Charlee. She didn't like the way he walked into her home like he owned the place. It wasn't that Grant wasn't attractive, intelligent, and successful. He was all those things, but there was something else about him that she couldn't put her finger on. Something sinister.

An hour later, she sat in a large office with Grant, and his mother, waiting for a lawyer she didn't know. It wasn't the same one she and Easton had used, but Grant said the guy handled all the legal business for the Thornton family.

"I still don't know why I couldn't take the baby with me," Sabrina complained to Harriet Thornton.

"I'm sure Grant thought the little darling might be a distraction from what we're doing right now." Harriet reached over and gently tapped Sabrina's knee.

"I guess." Sabrina forced a smile.

Easton's mother was the sweetest lady she'd ever met, and Sabrina thought the world of her. Harriet wasn't five feet tall and always spoke with a soft tone. She was a complete contrast to her husband, Bennett Thornton.

Easton's father was brash and loud. He was the type of man who entered a room, and everyone noticed. He was also mysterious *and would disappear for weeks at a time. When he'd return, he was exhausted with no explanation of where he had gone. Harriet never questioned him, and once when Sabrina asked about it, she said he was taking care of things.*

When he left, Easton stepped in to take over his father's duties. Grant didn't like it because he believed the oldest son should take care of the company in Bennett's absence. It made it appear as if Grant couldn't do the job, and it was always a point of contention between the brothers.

The week after Easton's funeral, Bennett was off again, and Grant was concerned with Easton's estate. He'd spent hours searching through papers and practically torn Easton's home office apart. Sabrina asked what he was looking for but told her it was business stuff and nothing she'd understand.

Sabrina didn't know a lot about Thornton Group, except they owned one of the biggest department store franchises in the country. She knew there was stock trading and real estate, but that was the extent of her knowledge.

With Easton gone, Bennett had no choice but to put Grant in charge when he was gone. She didn't understand how the company worked, and she didn't care. She was a dancer who'd dreamed of performing in the New York Ballet, but after her parents died, she couldn't leave her brother alone.

Until three years earlier, she'd taught ballet at Madam Lacotte's Dance Studio. It was her dream job, especially since she got to work with one of her idols, Madam Lacotte. Before that, she managed a retail store that belonged to Easton's family. It was how they met.

Sabrina wanted to open a dance school, and Easton supported that endeavor. He had several real estate investments around St. John's and allowed her to use a building he'd recently acquired. It was the perfect property to start her business. Thanks to Madam Lacotte and her daughter, several students signed up for classes. When she got pregnant, she hired another instructor to help when Sabrina got too big to plié.

"Finley will be with us shortly," Grant told them as he tucked his cell phone into the inside pocket of his suit jacket.

"Grant, I do wish you wouldn't call him by his first name. Have some respect for your elders. It's Mr. McDonald, and I don't understand why we can't wait until your father comes home," Harriet chastised her son.

"Mother, Finley works for us. I'm not going to call him Mr. anything. Sabrina needs to get this all out of the way and get on with her life. We never know when Dad will return." Grant rolled his eyes.

Sabrina bit her tongue to keep her thoughts from flying out of her mouth. It enraged her the way Grant spoke to his mom. It was as if she was nothing more than dirt under his shoe. Sabrina's parents were deceased, and she envied anyone who still had mothers and fathers. Grant didn't know how good he had it.

Sabrina could see the hurt in Harriet's eyes when Grant treated her this way. Sabrina reached over and grasped the woman's hand. It was the only way she knew how to let the sweet lady know she wasn't alone. Grant would be sorry one day when his mother was gone.

The office door opened, and a tall slim man with thinning hair walked into the room holding a thick folder. Before he sat down, he cast a nervous glance at Grant. Something about the man's demeanor said he wasn't a confident person.

"Sorry for the delay. I had to make sure all the papers were here." Finley held out his hand to Sabrina. "I'm Finley McDonald. I'm sorry for your loss."

"Thank you." Sabrina shook the man's clammy hand.

"Yes, yes. Can we get on with this? I've business to attend to," Grant interrupted.

"Yes, sorry." Finley sat down and opened the large folder.

Sabrina felt a gentle squeeze on her hand, and she glanced at Harriet. The woman looked ready to burst into tears, and who could blame her. She was about to hear the last will and testament of one of her children.

"So, this is pretty straightforward, and I don't want to bore you by reading all the legal jargon," Finley said as he flipped through several papers.

"They probably wouldn't understand it anyway," Grant scoffed.

"I understand more than you think," Sabrina retorted.

"Still, let's make this short and sweet." Grant glared at her.

"Yes." Finley cleared his throat.

"Well, I'm not sure if you're aware, but three weeks ago, Mr. Easton Thornton came to me to redo his will." Finley's eyes flicked up to look at Sabrina.

"I didn't know," she replied.

"I'm sorry he didn't tell you, but he changed it drastically. He's left his entire estate to his brother," Finley told her.

"What?" Harriet gasped.

"I don't understand," Sabrina whispered.

"That doesn't surprise me," Grant said.

"Why would Easton take Sabrina out of his will? He was going to marry her. They have a child." Harriet sat up straight.

"I don't know, but he did. There is a trust for the child, but Grant will be the Trustee." Finley held out some papers to her.

Sabrina reached out with a shaky hand and looked down at the formal documents. It was the same as they'd drawn up together but dated the week before Easton's death.

"So, I guess there isn't any need to sit around here. I'll set up a meeting with you later this week to go over everything. Let's go." Grant shot to his feet and buttoned his suit jacket.

"Again, I'm sorry." Finley held out his hand to Sabrina, and she handed him back the papers.

On the drive home, Sabrina was confused. Harriet was quiet but clung to Sabrina's hand as if she was waiting for her to disappear. Grant now owned everything, including the house and studio. She was numb and didn't know if she'd ever feel again.

"Don't worry about anything, Sabrina. I'll give you plenty of time to find a new place to live before I sell the house," Grant said casually.

"What?" Sabrina gasped.

"I need to clear up Easton's assets to pay off his debts," Grant told her.

"What debts?"

"My dear, my brother was up to his ears in debt. I guess it's why he changed his will. He didn't want to leave you with all that worry." Grant shrugged.

Sabrina couldn't respond. She was about to be homeless with a tiny baby and nothing else. What was she going to do?

Chapter 2

In the fifteen years Crunch worked for Keith, there were several changes to the company. His boss moved the business back to Newfoundland and changed the name to Newfoundland Elite Security or NES.

The provincial government contracted NES for all security needed for diplomats entering the province, as well as politicians and their families. The company became government accredited, and all employees benefited from the changes. Keith and Bull introduced profit sharing, which meant Crunch and his co-workers were making more money.

Crunch was glad he'd taken a considerable risk all those years ago. His life changed for the better, and he made great friends, not to mention he was back in his home province again.

When he returned, his parents were thrilled to have him back but annoyed he didn't stay in St. John's. Crunch moved about ten minutes outside the capital city. When Keith and Bull decided to move back to the province, they based NES in Hopedale, a quaint little one-stoplight town where Keith grew up.

Keith purchased a large acreage at the entrance of Hopedale to build his home and a base for NES. Everyone in the town referred to the property as The Compound. His house sat at the area's entrance, and he lived there with his wife Emily and their kids.

The offices and conference rooms for NES and Keith's construction company were in the two-story building on the other side of the property. Keith also stored all weapons, Kevlar vests, and ammunition inside a large vault in the structure's basement. Another building housed a state-of-the-art gym and a gun range.

At the back of the property stood a client safehouse and bunkhouses for staff to reside. A ten-foot fence surrounded the entire property with a security gate at the area's entrance.

Crunch lived in one of the bunkhouses for a while, but he wanted his own place. Many of his co-workers bought homes around the small town because it was impossible not to fall in love with Hopedale and want to settle down.

He found a small house not far from a couple of his co-workers. Hope Road was close to The Compound, and there were several homes for sale on the small street. The house needed a ton of renovations because it had been vacant for years. It took a lot of work and money to make the place liveable. Keith gave him some professional opinions when he needed it, but Crunch did most of the renovations himself.

He finished his house less than a year earlier and moved in. The only thing left to do was put the siding on the shed in the backyard. All Crunch needed was someone to share his life with, but until then, he was content with Crash as a roommate.

Brent 'Crash' Adams was in the process of renovating a house of his own on the same street. It was more convenient to live with Crunch until he completed the renovations. Crunch was happy to have company, so he didn't go crazy talking to himself.

Bruce 'Hulk' Steel and Ben 'Trunk' Murphy also lived within a one-block radius, and when they weren't working, the group would get together frequently to watch a game, play cards, or toss back a few cold ones. Although since Hulk and Trunk had gotten bitten by the love bug, they didn't have as much time for guys' nights.

Crunch glanced at the woman on the other side of the table. She was looking at him as if she were starving and he was a thick juicy steak. He wasn't egotistical, but he was aware women found him attractive. Crunch took care of his appearance, dressed well, and had several tattoos. It didn't usually bother him, but how the woman sized him up made him uncomfortable.

She was an exotic dancer who witnessed a murder at the club where she worked and was testifying against the killer. The guy threatened her life when he realized she was the crown attorney's witness. She was in protective custody at The Compound until the court date, and Crunch drew the short straw. The prosecution team was extra careful since the killer was a suspected hitman for a criminal organization.

He didn't mind the work, but Diamond Starr wasn't shy about letting the guys know she wouldn't be opposed to a good fuck if they were so inclined. Crunch wasn't, and in the three days he'd been assigned to her, she'd tried everything to tempt him into her bed. It didn't work.

"You know, we could find something else to do while you guard my body," she purred.

"I'm watching television," Crunch told her.

"I could teach you some dance moves."

She leaned across the table, which practically pushed her oversized breasts out of her skimpy tank top. Crunch almost laughed at the offer, but he kept his composure and his expression blank.

"I don't need any lessons, Ms. Starr." Crunch leaned back in the chair and glanced at his watch.

Diamond would be attractive if she didn't cake so much makeup on her face. She'd told him all about how her mother thought her name was perfect for someone famous. Crunch doubted her mom wanted Diamond to take off her clothes and prance around naked for a living.

"Come on, everyone likes to learn to dance," she cooed.

"My mother is a former New York ballet dancer. I learned to dance a long time ago," Crunch informed her.

"Maybe you can teach me a few moves." Diamond ran a long red nail down his forearm.

"Ms. Starr, as I've told you numerous times, I'm here to keep you safe and nothing else. I suggest you stop trying to get more out of me." Crunch stood up and walked to the window.

"I knew it," Diamond scoffed.

"What?" Crunch sighed.

"You're gay." She smirked.

"No, I'm not gay. Not that there is anything wrong with that. I'm simply not interested. I'm doing my job." Crunch blew out a breath of annoyance.

He looked out of the window when he heard someone stomp up the steps. Crunch was never so glad for a shift to end, and he sighed when he saw Rex. Thankfully, he was about to be free of Ms. Diamond Starr.

"Hey," Rex greeted him.

Caden 'Rex' Dixon was hired a year after Crunch. He was originally from Georgia and former United States military. Rex was pretty quiet and didn't talk much about his past. He was probably the perfect one to stay with Diamond. There was no way in hell she'd seduce him.

"Hey." Crunch stepped back for Rex to come inside.

"Everything okay?" Rex asked.

"Yes, but since this is your first shift with her, I feel I should give you a heads up. She's a huge flirt and looking for a roll in the hay," Crunch whispered.

"Lawd, will she be wastin' her time with me," Rex's southern accent was more prominent since his return from a visit to his hometown.

"Good luck, Rex." Crunch chuckled as he pulled on his jacket.

Crunch glanced at his watch and grinned. He had plenty of time to make it to Jack's Place before she finished her shift. He'd made a habit of rushing there to catch a glimpse of the first woman to make him want to think about settling down.

Keith's aunt Alice owned Jack's Place. The main entrance opened into a large foyer, to the right was the pub entrance, and to the left was the best diner in the province. Crunch loved the place but made a point to go more often since Alice hired Sabrina a few years earlier.

Sabrina Burke was a tiny woman, and he wanted to wrap her up in his embrace and take care of her. The problem was she didn't seem interested. She tended to shy away and avoid him. Especially after Keith's aunt Cora practically insisted Sabrina needed to take time to spend with Crunch.

Everyone knew Cora Nightengale and how she could tell when a couple should be together. Over the years, she'd matched up couples as far back as her own brothers. He'd seen it with Keith and his brothers, cousins, and as of late, two of Crunch's co-workers found happiness after she'd demanded they listen to her. Cora was never wrong, according to most everyone.

Crunch didn't know if it was true, but a small part of him hoped so. He had a massive crush on the pretty waitress, and something deep down told him Cora wasn't wrong this time either.

As he pulled into the parking lot of Jack's Place, his phone chirped before he had a chance to shut off his truck. He pulled it out and smiled as he put the phone to his ear.

"Hi, Mom," Crunch answered.

"*Mon chéri*, I hate to bother you at work, but your sister is in trouble." His mother sounded panicked.

Crunch didn't like the thought of his younger sister being in any kind of a mess, and his body tensed at the sound of his mother's ragged sigh. Zara could take care of herself, he'd made sure she knew self-defense, but sometimes things happened.

"What's wrong?" Crunch sat up straight.

If his baby sister needed him, he'd be there in a second. Zara was dating a new guy, and if the asshole hurt her, Crunch would make the piece of shit wish he were dead.

"Zara sprained her knee, and she needs someone to take over her classes. I'm taking the ballet sessions, but she has a tap class I can't cover. These are little children, Hunter. They love the class, and…" his mother wasn't going to take no for an answer.

"When is the class, Mom?" Crunch interrupted as he tipped his head back and closed his eyes.

"It's at six this evening," she said with a sigh of relief.

"Mom, I'm a little out of practice, but I'll do my best. How old are these kids?" Crunch asked.

"They're between four and six," she told him.

"Great," Crunch said.

Small children were hard to wrangle together at the best of times, but they were deafening when they got those taps on the bottom of their shoes. Crunch never taught dance to kids before but helped his mom when he was younger.

"They'll love you," his mother assured him.

"I'll be there at five, so I can prepare," he told her.

"Good. *Merci ma chérie. Je t'aime*," she said.

It never made sense how his mother would speak mainly English, but when she called them by pet names or said she loved them, she always reverted to her native French-Canadian. His mother never harped on Crunch or Zara to learn the language, but they did so they could speak with his mother's family. Both were fluent, although he didn't need to use it since he returned to Newfoundland.

"Love you too, Mom," Crunch responded, and she ended the call.

Crunch couldn't remember the last time he'd stepped foot in his mother's studio. There was no point since he wasn't teaching, and honestly, he didn't want to get roped into the older women's classes again. When he'd returned to Newfoundland, his mother suggested he take over the group.

Crunch refused because not only was he too busy with NES, but Zara told him Shelby still took classes with the other male instructor. He wasn't about to deal with her again, especially after that one encounter at the airport.

He had no idea what happened when he left all those years ago, but something must've convinced her to return to the guy. Considering the rumors, the man probably bullied her into going back. Crunch didn't know and didn't care.

He shoved the phone back into his jeans and got out of the truck. His mind was going a mile a minute until he heard someone calling his name. He turned as he hit the top of the steps and waved to one of his co-workers.

Trunk had married two weeks ago and returned from his honeymoon a couple of days earlier. Abbie was the perfect match for Trunk. In mid-August, Crunch had to attend another wedding for Hulk and Caroline. Hopefully, by that time, he'd have a date.

"How did the shift go?" Trunk asked with a smirk.

"Fine," Crunch grumbled.

"How long did it take before she hit on you again?" Trunk dropped his hand on Crunch's shoulder as they walked into the diner.

"About twenty minutes." Crunch motioned toward his usual booth.

"This thing really comes in handy." Trunk wiggled the finger with his new wedding ring.

"Yeah, maybe I should buy one to use when I've got to deal with clients like her." Crunch waved to Alice.

"Why don't you ask Keith to put someone else on her?" Trunk asked.

"The Crown Attorney's office specifically asked for me for the job. I guess because I've been on so many of these types of jobs." Crunch shrugged.

The Crown Attorney is the representative for the Crown because Canada is part of the British Commonwealth. The lawyer serves as the prosecutor in court, but Crunch didn't know much about that part. He was only involved when the attorney needed security for witnesses.

"I heard this new Crown is a hard ass. I know the assistant Crown isn't a fan." Trunk smirked.

According to the people under him, when Saul Dean got promoted to crown attorney of St. John's, he showed no mercy. The lawyers hated him because he didn't take any shit. One of the assistants, Declan Hill, told Crunch the judges also didn't like how Saul ran his office.

It didn't matter to Crunch, he was doing a job, and thankfully, that would end when Diamond testified. That day couldn't come soon enough.

Crunch glanced out at the fishing boats docked in Hopedale Harbor as they slid into the booth. It was a busy time with the fishery, and workers filled the docks unloading the catches. He never liked fishing, but he respected the hard work of the men and women who risked their lives to make a living on the rough Atlantic Ocean.

Crunch picked up the menu but didn't need to look at it because he knew it by heart. It was something to do while he scanned the cheerful diner. He tried to look as if he wasn't hoping to catch a glimpse of Sabrina.

"Looking for someone?" Trunk asked as he slid into the seat across from him.

"No," Crunch answered far too quickly.

"She asked to leave early today." Alice O'Connor smiled as she placed two cups of coffee in front of them.

"Who?" Trunk picked up one of the small creamers and poured it into his coffee.

"Sabrina." Alice winked at Crunch.

Alice knew he was interested in the sweet waitress, which annoyed him slightly, but he'd never say anything to the woman. No, she was one of the many people who believed Cora and did everything to help her sister-in-law's predictions come true. Alice was married to the love of her life because of Cora.

Kurt O'Connor would move heaven and earth for Alice, and when they were together, it was as if nobody else existed. Kurt was well-respected, not only in Hopedale but the entire province of Newfoundland. He was a highly decorated police officer who made his way through the ranks to become Chief. He retired several years ago then became Mayor of Hopedale, and Alice stood by his side for all of it.

Crunch spent a lot of time with the O'Connor family since coming home to Newfoundland. If they embraced you, you were part of their family, and when Keith moved the security firm back, the entire staff became an extended family.

Alice treated her staff the same way. She didn't care that she owned Jack's Place. The woman still worked in the kitchen, served customers, and cleaned the same as her employees. She respected them and wouldn't expect them to do anything she wouldn't do herself.

Alice also had a soft spot for people in need. She seemed to have a sixth sense for hiring people who were down on their luck. Alice told Keith's mother the girl needed a fresh start when she hired Sabrina, but Crunch never found out why.

Although, he didn't know when the woman had time to sleep, because Sabrina also did nightly cleaning at Snippy Gals, the beauty salon owned by Keith's wife, Emily. She worked several shifts at Cupid's Closet as well. Cora's daughter Pam and Emily's sister, Elaine, owned the small boutique.

Crunch grew more concerned about Sabrina over the last several months. She was slim, to begin with, but seemed to have lost weight. Sabrina looked barely eighteen years old, which was why he felt like a pervert when his attraction started, but Sandy found out Sabrina was only two years younger than him.

At thirty-five, Crunch was ready to settle down and stop dating the wrong women, not that he'd been dating much. He couldn't remember the last time he spent time with someone he wanted to see again. He knew in his heart it wouldn't be that way with Sabrina because simply seeing her pretty face was more stimulating than time with the most exciting woman in the world.

"I'll tell her you were asking about her." Alice smiled as she pinched Crunch's cheek.

"I wasn't asking. Trunk was the one who asked." Crunch pointed at Trunk.

"Oh, stop it, you need to ask that sweet girl out before she wastes away to nothing." Alice grabbed Crunch's chin with her thumb and index finger as she bent down to look into his eyes.

Clearly, he wasn't the only one who noticed Sabrina's weight loss. Maybe she was ill or working so much she had stopped taking care of herself. He had no idea why she worked so much, but he certainly would like to know.

"Alice is right." Sandy slid into the booth next to Crunch.

Crunch suddenly wished he'd gone to the dance studio when his mom called. At least he wouldn't be stuck in another conversation with Sandy about his non-existent love life and how he needed to bite the bullet with Sabrina.

Sandy didn't pull punches. Crunch learned it the first time he met her. Sandy mellowed a little since coming back to Newfoundland, especially since she married Keith's brother, Ian, but she liked to put in her two cents when it involved other people's love life.

"You should invite her to Hulk's wedding as your date," Sandy suggested.

"We haven't had a cup of coffee together, but you think it's a good idea to ask her to a wedding. That's not a disaster waiting to happen." Crunch didn't even try to hide the sarcasm.

"You could help with the Canada Day celebrations. She's volunteered to work the booth for Jack's Place," Alice recommended.

Crunch glanced at Trunk for some support with the women harassing him, but the smirk said the ass wasn't going to help. Crunch wanted to ask Sabrina out and came close a few times, but she always shied away, and after several attempts to start a conversation, he assumed she wasn't interested.

"I could ask her for you," Sandy offered.

"No," Crunch practically yelled.

"Spoilsport." Sandy pouted.

"Leave him alone, Sandy. I'm sure he'll grow a set of balls someday," Trunk said after Alice walked away from the table.

"That's funny coming from the man who took ten years to admit he belonged with Abbie," Sandy deadpanned.

She didn't care which one of the guys it was, she'd get her digs in whenever the opportunity arose. She was like the sister none of them wanted, but they would all give their lives for her.

"Fuck off." Trunk narrowed his eyes.

"Nice come back, Chrome dome." Sandy snorted.

Crunch didn't even try to hide his amusement at Sandy's nickname for Trunk and Bull because they were bald. She continued it because it annoyed them. Crunch was relieved the focus had temporarily shifted from him.

The truth was he didn't want to get into the whole *I hate rejection* excuse. Crunch promised his mother he'd be there in less than two hours, and he needed to eat before he made a fool of himself in front of a bunch of hyper kids.

Thirty minutes later, he headed out of the diner and rushed back to his house to get a shower and grab his old dance bag. He kept it in the back of his closet, still packed with his tap shoes and ballet slippers. He still practiced some ballet positions to stay flexible and toned. Sure, he went to the gym six days a week, but ballet was a way to stay limber.

The fifteen-minute drive to St. John's was uneventful, and he made a couple of calls while he drove to the studio. All hands-free, of course, thanks to the Bluetooth in his truck. By the time he arrived, he'd checked in with Keith, made an appointment for a haircut with Emily, and set up a time to drop by Cupid's Closet for a tuxedo fitting for Hulk's wedding.

"Hulk's wedding." Crunch shook his head.

Another fucking night in a monkey suit as one of his friends took that long walk toward happiness. Crunch liked Caroline and never doubted for a minute she and Hulk were perfect together, but it was hard when Crunch didn't believe he'd ever be with the woman who made his heart skip with a simple smile.

He made it to the studio a little before five. Tap dancing wasn't his strongest skill, but with a bunch of kids, all he had to do was make it fun. Hopefully, there was only one class to teach, although he'd be guilted into helping until Zara was back on her feet.

Crunch stepped into the foyer of the dance studio, and the familiar scent of sweat, wood, and rosin made him smile. As strange as it was, the smell reminded him of his childhood and the hours he spent with his mother and sister. It was as if he was home, and the feeling increased when he eyed his mom through one of the large glass entrances of a ballet room. She was smiling at someone as she walked toward the door.

He was always awed how she remained so patient with the little girls and boys. Even when he was young, he couldn't ever remember her yelling in anger. It was probably how he learned to stay calm in stressful situations, at least most of the time. He did get angry with himself when he made stupid mistakes.

He was reaching for the handle of the door when it opened, and a woman walked through. Crunch froze.

Chapter 3

"Sabrina, thank you so much for taking over this class on such short notice." Camilla hugged her.

The woman never learned personal space boundaries, but it didn't bother Sabrina. She met Camilla fifteen years earlier, and they'd hit it off right away. When Sabrina's parents died in an accident, the sweet woman cried with Sabrina. It was why she felt so awful for not keeping in contact after Easton's death.

Sabrina reconnected with Zara when she came into Cupid's Closet for a dress a few months earlier. They were shocked to see each other but quickly picked up where they left off. Zara told her she was also meeting her older brother for lunch since he lived in Hopedale.

It was hard to believe she'd worked in Hopedale for so long and never met Zara's brother. She remembered the pictures on Camilla's walls and was sure she'd recognize the slim man with shoulder-length curly hair if he'd come by.

The men she met in Hopedale were hot, muscular, and way out of her league. None of them looked remotely like the guy in the pictures. Some of the women seemed to think one of the guys was interested. Anytime she saw him, she felt like a teenager and tried to avoid him. The last thing she needed was to make a fool of herself.

"I'm glad to do it, although I haven't been practicing much lately." Sabrina's muscles were angry with her, but it felt incredible to feel them again.

"I saw you dance, *mon chéri*. You've not lost your grace and talent." Camilla took Sabrina's hands and gave them a gentle squeeze.

"I'm so glad I dropped by this afternoon to ask about classes for Charlee," Sabrina admitted.

"Me too," Camilla said with a smile.

Sabrina glanced back toward the small ballet class to check on her daughter. Charlee had a huge grin that lit up her sweet face. The young ballet instructor helped show the first five positions, and Sabrina's daughter was soaking it all in. Charlee was as fascinated with the art of ballet, much like Sabrina was as a child.

Ever since Charlee started watching *The Wiggles*, she became obsessed with ballet. It was a children's show from Australia, and one of the characters was a dancer. Charlee would imitate the movements every time she watched.

Harriet noticed Charlee's obsession and called Sabrina to suggest enrollment in a ballet class. Sabrina hesitated because she knew it was a cost she couldn't take on, but the older woman insisted on paying for the lessons. When Sabrina declined the offer, Harriet wouldn't take no for an answer.

Not many people in Hopedale knew about Charlee, mostly because she didn't want them asking questions about how she worked so much with a child. She already got enough grief from her brother about the number of hours she worked.

The truth was, she was still paying off debts she'd built up after Easton died. She'd taken out a couple of loans so she could survive and get a place to live. Nothing was cheap, and she wasn't about to move somewhere she didn't feel safe.

After a year of trying, she finally got an apartment in a secure building in the city. She had a feeling the landlord had been impressed with having Harriet as one of her references. Since the Thornton name was well known, Harriet's recommendation probably sealed the deal.

The rent was steep, which was why she worked three jobs, but since Colt moved in with her, things were a little less stressful. She felt horrible for accepting money from her brother, but he refused to move in unless he paid half the expenses. It didn't matter that he was a grown man who made his own money. He was still her baby brother.

Since she knew Madam Lacotte's Dance Studio was the top one in the city, she and Harriet decided Charlee should take lessons there. Sabrina asked Alice if she could leave early to do some personal business, and her boss didn't hesitate. It was a ten-minute drive from Hopedale to St. John's, where the daycare and the dance school were.

When Sabrina picked up Charlee from daycare and told her where she was going, her daughter squealed almost the whole way to the studio. The light in Charlee's eyes was worth every penny the lessons cost.

"She's so much like you." Camilla smiled as she wrapped an arm around Sabrina's shoulders.

"I see a lot of Easton in her." Sabrina swallowed the lump in her throat.

Since Easton's death, her life spiraled into working more hours than one person should, rushing home to try and spend what little free time she had with Charlee, not to mention trying to keep Grant out of her hair with his unreasonable requests. All because Easton left her penniless and homeless without an explanation.

Her emotions were conflicted when she thought about Easton. She missed him, and her heart still hurt over losing him, but she was angry. How could he not tell her he accumulated so much debt and change his will without discussing it? He must've known she'd never move into the mansion because she'd refused when he'd suggested it after their engagement.

Harriet wanted to take her in, but Sabrina wouldn't feel comfortable in the house where Easton died. Not to mention dealing with Grant every day. A year earlier, Bennett left on one of his mystery trips, and his plane went down in the Atlantic Ocean. They never found him or the pilot, and after Bennett disappeared, Harriet couldn't stay in the house. She moved to a condo, leaving Grant to rattle around in the family estate. From what Sabrina heard, he didn't exactly spend his nights alone.

Grant had a line of women who shared his bed and never tried to hide it. He practically bragged about it, making it difficult to understand why he still constantly pursued her. Then there was his decision to hire Vanessa as a house manager. Sabrina would lose her mind living in a house with that woman. One of the other staff quit because Vanessa treated the staff as if they were below her.

Holly Peddle was a housekeeper for the Thornton family when Sabrina started dating Easton. The two women hit it off and would get together often. Grant suggested she not associate with the help if she was going to date a Thornton. Easton told her to ignore him, and she did. Holly was a friend, even if they didn't get to see each other often.

Holly helped Sabrina find work and even let Sabrina stay with her for a few months. Thankfully, she overheard some women at a coffee shop talking about a diner in the town of Hopedale who was hiring. She'd immediately looked up the place and called the owner.

Sabrina was never in the small town but was thrilled when Alice told her to come right away for an interview. By the end of the evening, Alice hired her. Over the next several months, she took on two other part-time jobs, and things started to look up.

Sabrina was exhausted most of the time and missed out on time with her daughter. Charlee spent most days with Harriet, and although she was thankful to have someone in her life to help with childcare, Sabrina shouldered a lot of guilt because she missed so much of Charlee's childhood.

Harriet offered to help Sabrina financially, but there was no way she could accept. Especially when Grant made a point of accusing Sabrina of using his mother, it was why she found it so strange he wanted to marry her.

"I'm going to change, so I'm ready when Charlee's class is over." Sabrina pulled open the door and blew her daughter a kiss.

She stepped into the hallway, and the door closed behind her. Her eyes locked with the last person she expected to see in Madam Lacotte's Dance Studio. Her heart jumped as it always did when she saw him, and her palms dampened. No man, not even Easton, affected her in the same way.

Crunch was the most beautiful man she'd ever seen. His skin always appeared slightly tanned, and thick, dark lashes surrounded the intense sea-green eyes. Crunch kept his hair cut short on the sides but longer on top, and her fingers itched to run through it.

He was over six feet, all hard muscles, tattoos, and would kick any woman's libido into overdrive. He was a walking sexual fantasy come to life.

He seemed stunned to see her. As his gaze took her in, she suddenly felt self-conscious in only a leotard, ballet skirt, and tights. She used to be proud of how her body looked but working so much and not eating a lot, Sabrina had lost a lot of weight. She'd been surprised by how loose her old ballet attire fit when she'd put it on.

"Sabrina?" He was the first one to speak.

"Hi." She almost choked on the word.

"What are you doing here?" Crunch asked.

Before she could answer, Camilla glided out of the room and immediately wrapped her arms around Crunch. Sabrina had no idea how they knew each other, probably something to do with Hopedale. After all, Zara said her brother lived in the small town. They probably knew each other.

"Right on time." Camilla smiled up at Crunch.

"Did I have a choice?" He smirked.

When his eyes found Sabrina again, his smile disappeared. She figured he was probably taking dance classes since Camilla said she had a private student coming that evening. Maybe he was embarrassed Sabrina had seen him.

"Oh goodness, where are my manners. I forgot you two have not met. Although, I don't know how you could be in the same town and never bump into each other." Camilla tugged Crunch further into the foyer.

Sabrina folded her hands together in front of her. The whiff of his usual scent enveloped her senses, and she had to force herself to stop the sigh. She didn't know what kind of body wash he used, but the smell was clean, fresh, and intoxicating. It was some sort of citrus but woodsy at the same time. She loved it.

"Do you remember the instructor who took over when you left for Yellowknife?" Camilla asked Crunch, and he nodded. "This is her."

"I see." Crunch raised an eyebrow.

"Sabrina, this is my very handsome son, Hunter." Camilla grabbed Crunch's chin and kissed his cheek.

"Your... your son?" Sabrina stumbled over the words.

"Yes," Camilla said as she gazed lovingly up at Crunch.

"He's the one in the pictures in your office?" Sabrina asked.

She didn't know how the slim ballet dancer caught mid-air in a photo could possibly be the broad-shouldered man in front of her. Camilla always raved about her son, but Sabrina had only seen pictures of him dancing.

"They were taken a lifetime ago," Crunch said with a soft chuckle.

"He was so talented. Still is if he'd put more time into his dancing." Camilla sighed.

"I didn't forget how to dance, Mom." Crunch rolled his eyes.

"It was nice to meet you. I should go change." Sabrina tried to sound casual as if she'd never met the man before.

"Charlee is going to be another half hour. Could you please help Hunter set up the tap room?" Camilla asked as she waved to a young woman coming into the studio.

"I... umm." Sabrina bit her lower lip.

"I can manage on my own." Crunch sounded annoyed.

"It's been a while for you, and Zara showed Sabrina where everything is." Camilla waved her hand and then walked over to meet the student.

Sabrina watched her walk away and wondered why Camilla was under the impression Sabrina knew anything about the tap room.

Zara showed her the room, but they never went inside. Before she could explain to Camilla, she'd run off.

"I guess I'm helping." Sabrina smiled nervously.

"It's okay. You don't have to." Crunch adjusted his knapsack on his shoulder.

"I don't mind," Sabrina said as she headed toward the vacant studio.

They moved around the room in silence for several minutes, clearing away things and pulling out benches. Sabrina cleaned the mirrors as Crunch set up the music. When she turned, he was staring at her.

"All this time, I didn't know you were a dancer." He tilted his head.

"I didn't realize you were Madam Camilla's son." She raised an eyebrow.

"Why didn't you tell her we knew each other?" Crunch asked

"Why didn't you?" Sabrina returned.

Crunch glanced back over his shoulder and smiled but didn't say anything as he moved around the room. There were six studios in the building but only one room for tap classes. Sabrina remembered Camilla saying she didn't want her floors scratched up by the tap shoes.

"Is Charlee your boyfriend?" Crunch asked as he walked away from the entertainment unit.

"No," Sabrina answered.

"Oh?" he stopped and looked at her.

"Charlee is short for Charlotte." Sabrina smiled.

"I didn't know. Well, I'm glad I didn't make a fool of myself." Crunch muttered.

"What do you mean?" Sabrina walked toward him.

Crunch didn't look at her as he pulled off his jacket and tossed it on the bench. He sat down as he dug through his knapsack and pulled out a pair of black shoes before he finally looked up.

"Everyone kept telling me to ask you out. I would've been a little embarrassed if I asked, and then you tell me you have a girlfriend." Crunch shrugged.

Sabrina stared at him for a moment, and when it registered what he said, she laughed. He thought Charlee was her girlfriend and the confusion in his expression only made her laugh harder. She dropped down on the bench across from him until she could control her giggles.

"Charlee isn't my girlfriend," she said, trying to catch her breath.

"Oh?" he tilted his head.

"She's my four-year-old daughter," Sabrina told him.

"Daughter?" Crunch stopped tying his shoe.

"Yes." She smiled.

"I didn't know you had a child. How come you never bring her to the diner?" Crunch seemed genuinely interested.

"I only work in Hopedale. We live in St. John's, and that's where her sitter is." Sabrina shrugged.

"Is she in this tap class?" Crunch asked.

"No, she's a ballet fanatic," Sabrina replied.

"Like her mom." Crunch pointed to the point shoes on her feet.

"It is my first love, but Ballroom is a close second."

"Ballroom is a favorite of mine too."

He met her gaze, and for a moment, time seemed to freeze as she stared into his eyes. She couldn't believe they had this in common. She could talk to him about her love of dance.

She stood up, feeling a little uncomfortable with how intimate the thoughts in her head seemed. She grabbed the window cleaner and tucked it away in the closet with the roll of paper towels. When she turned, he was clicking his taps against the hardwood floor.

"I haven't done this in so long I don't know if I even remember." Crunch chuckled.

"It's like riding a bike." Sabrina smiled.

"I hope you're right." Crunch crossed his fingers.

"Just have fun," she suggested and walked to the door.

Sabrina left the room, but before the door closed, she heard the rhythmic clicks of his shoes. She peeked through the small window and watched as he leaped and shuffled across the floor. Before she could look away, he was dancing around the room as if performing on stage.

"He's amazing, isn't he?" Zara's voice startled her.

"Yes, he is," Sabrina replied.

Crunch's grace and rhythm were impeccable. There wasn't any music, but with the way he tapped rhythmically across the floor, she could practically hear the song in her head. It was beautiful, and it surprised her because in the past, she'd always found tap annoying.

Zara stood next to Sabrina, gazing through the window at her brother. Anybody could tell she looked up to him and was proud of his talent. Zara leaned on the crutches, and Sabrina looked down to see the woman's knee wrapped up tightly.

"Mom always said he should've been on Broadway, but Hunter had other plans." Zara smiled.

"He works for Alice's nephew." Sabrina glanced back into the room.

"You've met him before?" Zara asked.

"Yes, he comes into the diner all the time. I had no idea he was your brother." Sabrina glanced at Zara.

"You're the waitress." Zara gasped as if she'd finally figured out some big secret.

"What?" Sabrina was confused.

"Oh, nothing." Zara started to move away from the doorway.

"What did they say about your knee?" Sabrina asked.

"Doctor said it's Patellar Tendonitis which basically means it's inflamed and irritated. I've got to restrict using it, use ice, and ibuprofen for pain. This wasn't the time for this to happen. I'm short-staffed, not to mention the fundraiser is in a couple of months." Zara sighed as she hobbled toward the change room.

"I'd love to take over some classes for you, but I'm working three jobs now as it is." Sabrina couldn't afford to lose one of them.

"Honey, you need to slow down. Pam told me you work practically every day. You look exhausted, and you've gone away to nothing." Zara motioned to Sabrina's trim waist.

"I'm fine. Really." Sabrina lied.

She wasn't okay. Between the exhaustion and long hours, she didn't take the time to eat properly. If she continued to lose weight, she wouldn't have any clothes to wear. Harriet constantly told her she was concerned, and Colt threatened to tell her bosses she wasn't taking care of herself.

Alice, Emily, and Pam already brought up her weight loss. It wasn't that she was starving herself because she'd never do something like that. She was very health-conscious, but she put most of her money into keeping a roof over her daughter's head, keeping Charlee healthy, and paying bills.

Easton left her with nothing, and she was working her ass off so Grant wouldn't take Charlee from her. She still shuddered every time she recalled the conversation with him a week after the will reading. It was the one time in her life she was truly terrified and enraged at the same time.

Four years ago…

Sabrina walked into the Thornton estate, dazed as if she was in the middle of a dream. She didn't understand why Easton would leave her with nothing.

Grant sauntered in behind her as if nothing happened and asked to speak with her privately. She walked into the den and sat on the dark leather couch against the far wall. She heard Grant say something to his mother and then enter the office, closing the door behind him.

"I know how you must feel." Grant pushed off the door and sat next to her.

He placed his hand on her knee and squeezed. She was uneasy with the way he seemed overly comfortable touching her. She didn't know what to do and hoped he was going to tell her he'd fix things.

"I don't understand," Sabrina whispered.

"I didn't either, but we can't change things now. There is a solution to make sure you're financially secure." Grant leaned closer.

"What do you mean?" Sabrina instinctively pulled back from him.

"You know what I'm talking about, Sabrina." Grant ran his hand up and down her thigh.

"Grant, you're making me uncomfortable." Sabrina pushed his hand away, shot to her feet, and moved to the other side of the room.

"If you don't want to end up living on the street and losing your kid, you need to get over that." Grant stood and stalked toward her.

"Stay away from me." Sabrina's voice quivered as she backed away.

Before she could leave the room, Grant pinned her against the wall with his body. She struggled to push him off, but he was almost double her size, and he had her arms behind her.

"Grant, let me go." She turned her head as he tried to kiss her.

"I know you want this. You've been teasing me since the day you walked in here with Easton. Parading that sweet little body in front of me," Grant whispered into her ear.

"I wasn't teasing you. Get away from me." Sabrina cried out as he bit her neck.

"Don't fight me, Sabrina. I can give you the world, or I can take everything away. Would it be so bad to have someone like me ravishing you?" Grant grabbed the bottom of her skirt and struggled with her to pull it up.

"Get off me," Sabrina shouted.

Grant stepped back a little but still kept her firmly in his grasp. She couldn't believe he was doing this to her barely a month after his brother died. She never gave him any reason to think she'd be interested.

"Don't fight me, Sabrina, because you'll never win," he whispered as his hand slid up her thigh under her skirt.

"Grant, for the love of God, let the girl go." Harriet's voice startled him.

He released Sabrina and stepped back, freeing her to adjust her skirt into place. Grant scared her, but the hatred in his eyes when he glared at his mother was terrifying. Grant always seemed to strongly dislike Harriet, but Sabrina had no idea why.

"Fine, if this is the way you want it, Sabrina. I'll give you one month to get out of the house, and don't think for a second I won't have Charlee taken away if I find out you're living on the street." Grant leaned in until he was close enough she could smell the whiskey on his breath.

"Grant, why are you doing this to her? Easton wouldn't want you to treat her this way." Harriet shook her head.

"Easton isn't in charge anymore, Mother. I call the shots. Sabrina, you've got a week to decide if you want to save yourself from a life of poverty and marry me. Otherwise, be out of the house in a month." Grant stared at her for a second and then marched out of the den.

Harriet stared after her son while Sabrina rubbed her arms where Grant grabbed them. There was no way she'd marry Grant, but he was right. She needed to make sure she and Charlee had a roof over their head.

"Sabrina, are you okay?" Zara's voice pulled Sabrina from the memory.

"Yes, sorry. What did you say?" Sabrina smiled.

"I said there's always a spot here for you. I'm so sorry your studio didn't work out. You know that building is still boarded up.

58

Some guy keeps offering to buy this building from Mom, and she thought about selling and buying a bigger place. She looked at your old place but couldn't get in touch with the owner." Zara told her.

Sabrina walked by her old studio almost every day when she brought Charlee to daycare. Plywood covered all the large windows around the front of the building, and thick chains secured the doors. The place appeared abandoned, but Grant was supposed to sell the site to cover Easton's debts.

"I don't know what the owner is doing with it." Sabrina shrugged.

What bothered her the most was the house was still vacant as well. Sabrina didn't know what Grant wanted to do with the property, and neither did his mother. He told his mother it was none of her business when she asked about it.

Sabrina wouldn't ask because she didn't want to deal with him at all. The problem was, Grant still called her at least once a week, but there was something weird in the last conversation. It was as if he gave her an ultimatum. He said she had until Canada Day to decide.

She didn't know why he wanted to marry her or why he thought she'd change her mind. He still harassed her even four years later. Grant was up to something, but she had no idea what.

"Mommy," Charlee squealed, bringing Sabrina out of her thoughts.

"Hi, cutie. Did you have fun in your class?" Zara asked as Sabrina lifted Charlee into her arms.

"It was so much fun, Miss Zara." Charlee's grin was so big that it was contagious.

"Do you want to come back?" Sabrina asked, knowing the answer already.

"Oh yes, Mommy. I really, really want to dance again," Charlee responded.

Before Sabrina could say anything, Charlee was distracted by the tapping from the room. She leaned closer to the window in the door before turning to her mother.

"Who is he?" Charlee asked.

"That's my big brother, Hunter," Zara replied.

"His shoes make a lot of noise." Charlee watched as Crunch slid across the floor.

"He has taps on his shoes," Sabrina explained.

"Like Emma Wiggle has?" Charlee asked, referring to a character from her favorite show, *The Wiggles*.

"Yes." Sabrina smiled.

"He's also going to hear it from Mom if he continues to slide across the floor. That's the one step she hates. I keep telling her we need to put a different type of flooring in there, so it doesn't scratch." Zara laughed.

"You could get some tap mats and place them around the room. Give each student their own mat," Sabrina suggested.

"That's a great idea," Zara said.

Charlee wiggled in her arms until Sabrina released her. Charlee stepped into the room and stared in fascination as Crunch glided across the floor.

The slight smile on his handsome face showed he enjoyed the freedom of dancing around the room, lost in the music. Charlee clapped her hands frantically when he stopped, and Crunch spun around.

"You were so good," Charlee praised.

"Thank you." Crunch smiled as he moved toward Charlee, his shoes clicking with each step.

When he crouched in front of the little girl, Sabrina stepped into the room. Crunch met Sabrina's eyes as she moved behind her daughter. Charlee looked at him as if he were the best person in the world and who could blame her.

"Wasn't he good, Mommy?" Charlee said excitedly.

"Yes, he was," Sabrina agreed.

"It's always nice to receive high praise from a beautiful lady, but when two of them agree, it makes a guy feel great." Crunch gave Sabrina a sexy wink.

"Hear that, Mommy, he called us beautiful." Charlee looked up at her with a huge grin.

"Well, you're beautiful. I keep telling you that." Sabrina gently cupped her daughter's cheek.

"You are too, Mommy," Charlee told her. "Right, Hunter?"

"Charlee, it's Mr. Lacotte to you," Sabrina told Charlee.

"Lacotte is the name my mom uses professionally. My last name is Crawford," Crunch corrected and then moved his attention back to Charlee. "But my dad is Mr. Crawford, and all my friends call me Crunch."

"Crunch?" Charlee tilted her head and stared at him.

"It's a weird name, isn't it?" He laughed.

"Yes," Charlee agreed.

"It's a nickname. My friends gave it to me because I like to crunch down on ice cubes." Crunch chuckled.

"Mommy, can I call him Crunch?" Charlee asked.

"If it's okay with Hunter." Sabrina shook her head in amusement.

"Okay, I'll call you Crunch." Charlee quickly made her choice.

"It's nice to meet you, Charlee." Crunch said.

"Sweetie, I think we should go and leave Hunter to prepare for his class," Sabrina interjected.

"Aww, I wanted to watch more," Charlee complained.

"We need to get home and get supper." Sabrina urged her daughter toward the door.

Sabrina tried not to notice how sexy Crunch looked when he stood up wearing a black tank top and grey sweatpants. His tattoos ran from his fingers up to his shoulders on both arms, and she could also see more ink across his chest, and her fingers itched to pull down the neck of his shirt to get a better look.

She knew he had them, but it was the closest she'd ever been to seeing how beautiful they were, or maybe it was because they were on Crunch. He was so damn sexy, and she didn't understand how he was single. Sabrina wanted to give in to her attraction, but it was impossible.

"Yay, Mommy, you make the best pizza. Wanna come to our apartment for pizza, Crunch?" Charlee squealed excitedly.

"Umm… Charlee, I think Hunter is busy." Sabrina took her daughter's hand proceeded to pull her out of the room.

"Thanks for the invite, but your mom is right. I've got to teach a class and then get some sleep for my job tomorrow." Crunch smiled at Charlee. "But thanks for the invite. Maybe another time."

His gaze locked with Sabrina's as if he expected her to agree. She couldn't do that. She simply waved as she pulled Charlee out of the room and hurried to the dressing room. The last thing she wanted to do was to drag the sensual Hunter Crawford into her complicated life.

Chapter 4

Two weeks flew by since they ran into each other at the studio. Sabrina was more at ease when he came into the diner and would talk to him about the classes. He was almost glad Zara was out of commission because she hired Sabrina to teach evening groups, and Crunch would drop by to help anytime he had free time.

Since she started at the studio, Sabrina only worked one shift a week at the diner and a couple of mornings at Cupid's Closet. She gave up her hours at Snippy Gals as far as he knew. There was a new light in her eyes, and it was evident how much she loved to dance. He caught her several times in between classes, dancing alone while she waited for students.

Crunch was in awe of her talent. She was graceful and elegant and got lost in the music. She easily incorporated ballet with modern, as well as some jazz. It was incredible to watch. She was beautiful but in the middle of a crowd laughing as she chatted to people around the booth, she looked mesmerizing.

In the more than ten years since Crunch moved to Hopedale, he volunteered during the Canada Day Celebrations because it was a huge charity event. Keith's family was heavily involved in the festivities and recruited everyone they knew to pitch in.

All the businesses in Hopedale erected booths the entire length of the beach to sell food, drinks, or offer games. The money raised was put into a fund to keep the Hopedale community center running.

It was the first year he didn't mind spending the day on Hopedale Beach in the heat surrounded by thousands of people because he got to spend almost the whole day with Sabrina. She smiled and enjoyed interacting with the people who came by for food. He'd never seen her so relaxed, and she even teased him because he broke one of the soft drink dispensers.

"You don't have to be rough with it. Gentle. Like this." Sabrina smirked as she pulled the lever lightly.

"You're very good at that." Crunch grinned.

"Thank you." She handed him a filled cup and nodded toward the person waiting for their drink.

During the midafternoon, her brother dropped by and brought Charlee to the festivities. Crunch liked the guy immediately, and when Charlee begged to play some games, Alice gave both Crunch and Sabrina a break.

Crunch chatted to Colt while they walked the length of the beach. He never looked around in previous years, but with Sabrina, he enjoyed it as if for the first time. He managed to win a stuffed ballerina bunny for the little girl, and she was so excited she practically leaped into Crunch's arms.

"Well, you certainly won over my niece." Colt chuckled.

Colt Burke was a pretty laid-back guy who obviously adored his sister and niece, but who could blame him. According to Sabrina, Colt worked in the IT department for the school board in the city. She'd beamed when she talked about her intelligent brother.

"Kids are easy to win over. It's the adults you need to work at." Crunch couldn't keep his gaze from moving to Sabrina.

"She's guarded," Colt whispered.

"As a single mother, she has to be careful." Crunch didn't blame her.

"That's part of it," Colt mumbled but didn't elaborate.

Crunch watched Sabrina lift Charlee to show her a boat sailing by the beach. The sun hit her face, making her skin glow in the light, and it was as if someone punched him in the stomach knocking all the wind out of him. His heart pounded, and when her eyes found his. Crunch swallowed hard. What the hell was happening to him?

"You might want to start breathing before you pass out." Colt nudged him, breaking the spell. "Wow, you've got it bad for my sister."

Crunch narrowed his eyes and playfully shoved Colt. It only made the guy laugh harder as they walked behind Sabrina. She turned around and raised an eyebrow as if to ask why Colt was laughing, but Crunch distracted her when he pointed to another game booth.

They made their way back to Alice's area, hitting most of the game booths on the way. Sabrina chastised both him and Colt for all the money they spent to win prizes for Charlee, but all he said was the money was going to a important cause. Charlee was asleep on Colt's shoulder by the time they got back where they started. He offered to take his niece home but only if Sabrina agreed to stay and enjoy herself.

As usual, the people of Hopedale flocked to the diner's booth, making it difficult for him to talk at length with Sabrina. As the sun set, the crowd headed to the large bandstand at the top of the beach. It gave them time to clean up the area before the entertainment started.

He glanced toward the stage where *Rockin' The Law* got ready to entertain the crowd. Keith's brothers, John, Mike, Nick, and Aaron, together with Cory Fleming and Jason Brenton, were members. All except one were police officers, and the other was a lawyer.

They weren't professional musicians, but they helped raise money for charities all around the province. They were talented and could probably make a career out of it, but they kept it a hobby. Each of them loved their jobs and were damn good at what they did.

Sabrina leaned on the wooden partition when the music started to echo through the speakers around the beach. Crunch stood next to her, paying more attention to her than the entertainment. She unconsciously moved to the upbeat country tune, and he couldn't help but smile. He recognized "She's Got the Rhythm" because he'd heard the band perform the Alan Jackson song on many occasions.

She smiled, and it gave him a boost of courage to snatch her hand and spin her around. Her sweet laugh was like music to his ears, and he was surprised how easy they moved together. She had no issues keeping up with the quick beat of the country tune, not that he thought she would.

"Look at you two." Alice stepped into the enclosure.

"Sorry, we kind of got into the music." Sabrina's cheeks turned pink, and she stepped away from Crunch.

"It was my fault," Crunch admitted.

"Don't be silly. I've had my share of spontaneous dancing in my lifetime. Kurt and I still like to turn up the radio and have a scuff around the kitchen." Alice grinned.

A *scuff* was a Newfoundland term for dancing. Newfoundlanders had a language all their own, and sometimes it was difficult to understand. The accent compared to Irish, and the dialect changed depending on the area.

"And when you know how to dance the way you two do, it's even better." His sister's voice echoed in his ear.

Crunch smiled at Zara and his parents. It was the first time they attended the Canada Day event in Hopedale. They would head to Montreal every other year to spend the holiday with Crunch's grandmother, but she'd passed away before Christmas. His family decided to stay in Newfoundland for the celebrations.

"You two should head out to the dance area and show everyone how it's done." His dad smirked.

"Why don't you and Mom show them?' Crunch returned.

His father could never keep up with Crunch's mother on the dance floor. He said he'd been born with two left feet and only enjoyed dancing when he could hold his wife close. Crunch figured it was because his dad didn't have to do more than sway during a slow song.

"We will when they play a little romance." His father grinned.

"I never married your father for his dancing skills. It was his pretty face." His mother winked.

"And my charm." His father grinned.

Crunch loved the respect and honesty between his parents. They weren't perfect and had disagreements that usually ended with his dad giving in first. Crunch wanted that kind of relationship with someone. A partnership where he could spend the rest of his life with the woman of his dreams. Could he have that with Sabrina?

Crunch helped pack up the leftover supplies and equipment to transport back to Jack's Place as the festivities started to wind down. The crowd slowly thinned, and soon the only people left on the beach were volunteers. Alice told Sabrina to go home, but she insisted on staying.

Sabrina told him Zara offered her a full-time position at the studio as they made their way back to the diner. She was thrilled but said she'd miss the people in Hopedale. Crunch could relate because when it came to the residents of the tiny town, they were like one big family.

They chatted about the classes, and Crunch admitted he enjoyed teaching the kids more than he expected. The little boys and girls were honest, fun, and made him feel like a hero with how they thanked him for being the best teacher. It was difficult not to feel a hundred feet tall when they looked up to you like that.

As they headed up the steps of the diner, Crunch saw something move out of the corner of his eye. He sent Sabrina and Alice inside so he could check the permitter of the building. It was close to midnight, and if someone was slinking around, they weren't up to anything good.

Crunch made his way around the side of the building, doing his best not to trip or bump into anything. Several trees enclosed the back, so none of the light from the parking lot reached the area, and the crescent moon didn't help. He used the light on his phone to scan the area but only saw garbage bins and propane tanks.

He spotted something but couldn't be sure if it was a person or an animal looking for a meal. Crunch scanned the area one more time before giving up and making his way to the parking lot. When he rounded the corner of the building, he spotted Alice's husband walking across the parking lot.

"Hey, Crunch." Kurt waved.

"What are you doing here so late?" Crunch asked.

"Dropped by to walk Alice home." Kurt held open the door.

"I could've walked her home." Crunch stepped inside.

"I don't mind. I've been walking my wife home since I was nineteen years old, and I intend to do it until I can't anymore." Kurt smiled.

Kurt was in his mid-sixties and could be a serious person, but his face lit up when he looked at Alice. They were still so deeply in love even after all their years together. The couple was certainly what every couple should aspire to be.

Alice locked up the diner while Crunch escorted Sabrina to where she parked her vehicle. They strolled back to the beach in comfortable silence while he tried to build up the courage to ask her out.

"You didn't have to walk me back to my car." Sabrina broke the silence.

"It's late, and Alice would skin me alive if anything happened to you. So would my mother," Crunch said.

"They're like mother hens." Sabrina chuckled.

"Undeniably." Crunch nodded.

A warm breeze from the beach swirled around them, and the waves rolled up on the shore. The small beach rocks crackled as they rolled under the weight of the water. The sound usually calmed him, but her car was less than fifty yards away, and he swallowed nervously. She hit the button on her key fob, so he knew it was now or never.

"Sabrina, I know you're busy, but would you like to meet for coffee sometime?" Crunch held his breath as she stopped in front of her car.

It may have only been a few seconds before she responded, but it seemed like an eternity to him. He was ready to have his heart shattered by her rejection, but when she turned, she was smiling.

"Tomorrow is my last day at the diner, and then I'm teaching two ballet classes. I only have a couple of hours in between. If you don't mind meeting me at the diner." Sabrina pressed her lips together.

"I don't mind at all. Tomorrow is perfect," Crunch assured her.

"I'll see you at three." Sabrina pulled open the car door.

"See you at three," Crunch replied.

Grinning like an idiot, he waved as she drove off. When she was out of sight, he made his way home. It was a warm evening, but the fog rolled in across the harbor. As he crossed Sandcastle Road, a vehicle took the corner jumping the curb. Crunch dove out of the way as the car whizzed by, barely missing him. By the time he jumped back on his feet, the only thing he could see were taillights disappearing onto Main Road.

"Fucking lunatic," Crunch grumbled as he dusted the dirt off himself.

Without further incident, he made it home and decided not to let a crazy driver ruin his good mood. Hopefully, tomorrow would be the start of something special with Sabrina. Sure, it was only coffee, but he had to start somewhere.

The next day seemed to drag on, and by the time Rex arrived, Crunch had paced for over an hour. He'd asked Rex to relieve him early because he had an appointment. Nobody needed to know it was a coffee date with Sabrina.

When Crunch arrived at the diner, Sabrina was about to finish her last shift. She pointed to a booth next to the large picture windows, and he sat down with hands folded on the table. His leg bounced as he tried to hide his nerves. By the time she joined him, he'd managed to calm down most of his restlessness.

"Sorry about that," she said as she placed a steaming cup of coffee and a piece of blueberry pie on the table.

"No problem. Where's your coffee and pie?" he asked.

"I hate coffee, and I'm not hungry." She looked down at her hands.

"Tea?" Crunch suggested.

"No." She shook her head.

"Okay. It's not exactly a coffee date if you aren't drinking anything," Crunch teased.

"I know. I'm weird." She lifted her beautiful eyes to meet his.

In some lights, he couldn't tell if they were blue or violet, but they certainly took his breath away. He'd been so curious about the eye color he'd looked it up and found out it was rare, and she shared the same eye color as Elizabeth Taylor. Crunch thought Sabrina was more beautiful.

"Not at all. I'm glad to have your company," Crunch told her honestly.

"Thank you," she replied with a shy smile.

It took a few minutes of awkward conversation before it became a more natural discussion. It was a little different from the previous evening at the beach. They chatted about Hopedale, his job, friends, and family, but he realized she didn't say much about herself other than dancing and her daughter.

"What about you?" Crunch leaned back and sipped his coffee.

"There's not much to tell." She shrugged.

"Where are you from?" Crunch pushed.

"St. John's," she replied.

"Colt is your only sibling?" Crunch continued.

"Yes, and since my parents passed away, he's the only family I have now, besides Charlee." She smiled.

"I'm sorry about your parents," Crunch said.

"It was a car accident about eight years ago. We were driving home from a weekly family dinner. Dad decided to take the highway, and it started to rain. He hit a rut in the road and…lost control of the car." Sabrina's eyes dropped down.

"You and Colt were in the car?" Crunch asked.

"Yes. The car went into the back of a transport truck stopped on the highway. My parents died on impact. Colt's leg was broken, and all I got was a few scratches and the inability to bend my finger."

Sabrina held up the index finger on her right hand. She made a fist, but the pointer stayed straight. She looked slightly embarrassed and then dropped her hands to her lap.

"Thankfully, I'm left-handed, so it doesn't impact much." Sabrina smiled.

"Cool, that's something else we have in common." Crunch grinned.

The more they talked, the more relaxed she seemed, but a few minutes later, her laughter died as she glanced over his shoulder. She shifted uncomfortably, her face paled, and her eyes widened to almost twice their size. The hair on the back of his neck prickled, but before he could ask what was wrong, someone stepped next to the booth.

Crunch glanced up at the intruder and locked eyes with a man. The guy didn't appear threatening dressed in a black business suit, but his cold glare told Crunch to stay alert. Especially when the guy blatantly let his gaze travel down over Crunch's attire. From the way he snubbed his nose, the snob didn't appear to like the jeans and t-shirt combination.

The man turned his attention to Sabrina and smiled. He looked as if he'd caught her with her hand in the cookie jar, but her expression was unreadable when she raised her eyes to glare at the man.

"I thought I'd find you here," he said with a wide grin that reminded Crunch of the cat from Alice in Wonderland.

"It's where I work. You wouldn't have to use much brain energy to figure that out," Sabrina said flatly.

Although she tried to appear annoyed, Crunch could hear the quiver in her voice. At first, he thought she was scared of the arrogant intruder, but her clenched jaw and narrowed eyes said she was pissed.

"I expected a waitress to be serving customers, not joining them for a meal." The man glanced at Crunch.

"I was taking a break." Sabrina tried to slide out of the booth.

Before she could, the man took a seat, halting her exit. She blew out an annoyed breath and moved as close to the window as she could get.

"You must think I'm very rude." The man smiled, and the words Cheshire cat popped into Crunch's head. "Grant Thornton."

"Hunter Crawford." Crunch shook the guy's hand.

"Are you from this… town?" Grant asked with a hint of disdain when he hissed the word *town*.

"I wasn't born here, but I've lived here for about ten years. It's the greatest place in the world." Crunch sat back and glanced at Sabrina.

Anyone who glanced at Sabrina could tell she was uncomfortable with Grant. When the asshole slid closer, she sat with her back rigid and her hands clasped in front of her. When he draped an arm around Sabrina, Crunch wanted to rip it off and beat Mr. Money Bags to death with it.

"I have to say I'd rather the city, but I guess I can see the appeal. Maybe after we're married, we could get a place here since you like this town so much." Grant muttered.

Sabrina's eyes grew as wide as saucers, and when Grant cupped her cheek, she flinched away. It was as if she didn't want him near her, and if what he said was true, that didn't make sense.

Crunch's heart sank, and for a moment, he thought it had stopped beating. He hoped he'd heard incorrectly, but from the intimate way Grant touched Sabrina, something was going on. Although, she wasn't as relaxed with Grant as Crunch.

"Married?" Crunch locked eyes with Sabrina.

"Yes, Sabrina and I are engaged." Grant grinned.

Sabrina glared at the man and her face flushed red as she pushed Grant's hand away. She blew out a slow breath as if she needed to calm herself before she exploded.

"Grant, I need to talk to you. Outside. Now." Sabrina pushed his shoulder.

He didn't seem concerned by her sudden change in demeanor as the corners of his lips lifted in a sly smirk as he stood up. The guy's smug attitude made Crunch dislike the jerk even more, and it had nothing to do with the fact that Sabrina was engaged to the guy.

"Well, it was wonderful to meet you, Howard." Grant held out his hand.

"It's Hunter, and back at ya." Crunch extended his hand.

He knew it was childish, but he squeezed the asshole's hand harder than was necessary. Crunch took pleasure in the slight wince on Grant's arrogant face. It also took all his restraint not to punch the asshole when he pulled out a handkerchief and proceeded to wipe his hand.

"Excuse us, Hunter. I'll be back in a few minutes." Sabrina called behind her.

Sabrina practically shoved Grant toward the exit and glanced back once before she followed behind her future husband. Luckily, Crunch could see the entire parking lot and kept his eyes on them as they stepped next to a black Lexus RX 350.

Grant said something that appeared to set her off on a tirade. Crunch smirked as her hands flew into the air. Grant looked concerned for a split second, but as she gave him an earful, the guy pulled a phone out of his pocket. After tapping the screen a few times, he held the screen up to Sabrina.

She froze. Crunch couldn't see her face, but she dropped her hands to her sides. Grant said something, but when she responded, he grabbed her arm roughly. Crunch sprang to his feet and was out of the diner in less than sixty seconds.

He practically ran down the steps but stopped halfway across the lot when Grant pulled Sabrina into his arms. A knot formed in Crunch's stomach as he watched the asshole press his lips to Sabrina's mouth. He was about to turn away until he noticed Sabrina struggle against Grant's hold. He continued toward the couple and stopped next to the car.

"Is everything okay?" Crunch asked.

"Yes, only a little tiff between lovers." Grant didn't bother to look in Crunch's direction.

"Sabrina?" Crunch wasn't going to take the word of the asshole.

"Everything's fine," Sabrina said as she wiped her arm across her mouth.

She was uneasy, and that didn't sit well with Crunch. He didn't care if the guy was engaged to her, the asshole had no right to mistreat Sabrina. Crunch watched her more intently, and she didn't act like a woman committed to the love of her life.

"Thanks for your concern, but you should probably stay out of other people's business." Grant glared at Crunch.

"It's in my nature to check on my friends when they appear in distress." Crunch met Grant's glare with one of his own.

"Sabrina, are you distressed?" Grant touched her cheek.

Sabrina slapped his hand away, and Crunch bit back a chuckle at the surprised expression on Grant's face. Sabrina shook, but she wasn't letting this asshole have his way, and Crunch couldn't be prouder as she straightened her shoulders.

"I'm fine. Let's go back inside," she said, then scowled at Grant. "Goodbye, Grant."

"Okay. We'll chat later, darling." Grant tried to lean in for a kiss, but Sabrina spun around and walked away.

Grant chuckled as if he took pleasure in Sabrina's discomfort. Crunch wondered if the guy got off on it. She didn't deserve a prick like him. Sabrina needed someone to treat her like the treasure she was.

"Don't worry. She'll be like a wild tiger when we make up later." Grant smirked.

"I'm sure." Crunch tried not to punch the guy in the teeth.

As the vehicle drove out of the lot, Crunch stepped back and watched the car disappear down the road. Sabrina sat at the booth as he made his way into the building. She stared out the window, and he was sure he could see tears in her eyes.

"Fiancée. Fucking great," Crunch mumbled to himself as he shuffled toward the booth.

That would be his luck, falling for a woman who wasn't available. He couldn't wait to see Cora and tell her she was wrong about him and Sabrina.

Chapter 5

Sabrina stepped into the diner trembling with a blend of anger and panic. Usually, the delicious aroma that greeted her when she entered Jack's Place put her at ease. It was like walking into a huge hug, but after the encounter with Grant, she felt sick. How could he stoop to blackmail to get her to marry him?

She couldn't refuse when he had something like that. If he sent that photo, she'd never be able to show her face again. It would haunt her for the rest of her life and ruin any chances she had with Crunch.

A picture of her laying on her bed pleasuring herself was the last thing she wanted to be made public. She wasn't embarrassed about masturbating. Since Easton, Sabrina hadn't been with anyone, and she was only human. It was natural to ease that tension when she'd gone so long without sex. She thought it was done in the privacy of her bedroom.

Grant said the picture was a still shot from one of the several videos he acquired. He only grinned when she asked how he got them. Now, she was terrified to go back to her apartment because she didn't know who was inside. It seemed as if the image came from her bedroom window, but the blinds were always closed, so how was it possible to record her?

"Are you sure you're, okay?" Crunch eased into the seat across from her.

Sabrina blew out a ragged breath and managed to force a smile. What was she supposed to tell him, that she hated Grant with every fiber of her being, but she may have to marry him, so he didn't release a humiliating video? A video of her probably fantasizing about Crunch because he starred in all of them.

"Yes," Sabrina answered.

"Is he always rough with you?" Crunch rested his forearms on the table.

Sabrina shook her head. The truth was, she avoided Grant as much as possible. Her dilemma wasn't his demeanor but his underhanded manipulation to get what he wanted. She may have to go through with a marriage that would make her miserable.

"No, he isn't." Sabrina didn't want to talk about the jerk.

"I didn't know you were engaged. I mean, you don't wear a ring." Crunch motioned toward her hand.

Sabrina instinctively touched the finger where she once wore the ring Easton gave her. Sabrina took almost a year to remove it, and now it sat in a safe deposit box Easton suggested she get. She was surprised Grant hadn't taken the ring, along with all the other things Easton owned, but he never even asked about it.

It was all she had left of Easton. That and the few things she'd managed to stuff into her storage locker at the apartment building. She hadn't been able to go through the boxes because it was too difficult to see his things, but they were there for Charlee.

"I...We..." Sabrina wrapped her arms around herself.

She couldn't lie to Crunch when he looked at her with such concern, and it was tough not to spill everything. Grant had tried to push her to marry him for way too long, and she had no idea why. It wasn't like it would be a marriage of love.

Crunch reached across the table and took her hand. It warmed her chilled fingers almost instantly, and the heat radiated through her body. Sabrina raised her gaze to meet his sea-green eyes. She could get lost in them, but how could she when Grant was about a second away from ruining her life?

"Are you regretting saying yes to marrying him?" Crunch asked.

"No." Sabrina closed her eyes for a moment, and when she opened them again, she shook her head. "I'm not engaged to Grant."

Crunch furrowed his brow and tilted his head. He was so handsome, and with his attention focused on her, it was difficult to calm the flutter in her stomach. Sabrina didn't mind being the center of attention if she was performing, but she'd rather be a wallflower any other time.

"Why would he say you were?" Crunch questioned.

"It's a long story." Sabrina pulled her hand away.

"I'm not going anywhere, and I love long stories." Crunch tucked his fists under his chin and gave her a sexy grin.

Sabrina couldn't tell him what was going on, could she? If Grant hadn't shown her the picture, she'd open up to Crunch, but Grant could destroy her. He wouldn't hesitate to make the videos available to anyone if she pushed him.

"I was engaged to his brother," Sabrina said before she could stop herself.

"Was?" Crunch pushed.

"Easton fell over the stairs at his parents' home the day after our daughter was born. They couldn't help him and took him off life support." Sabrina blinked back the tears that always formed when she thought about that day. "We buried him two weeks later."

"I'm so sorry, Sabrina."

"He kissed Charlee and me when he left the hospital and said he'd be back in a couple of hours. I could still smell his cologne when Grant came to tell me Easton was in the hospital. It was a freak accident. Loose carpeting. Do you know how often he walked up and down those steps? Thousands of times. He grew up in that house. He never got to know his little girl." Sabrina swiped her fingers across her cheeks to wipe away the tears.

"It doesn't make sense, does it? How someone with everything to live for gets ripped from the world. I'm so sorry," Crunch said.

"At first, I didn't think I'd survive the pain, but I had a little girl who needed me. I couldn't let her down," Sabrina whispered.

"So, Grant thinks you should marry him. Why?" Crunch asked.

"I guess he thinks I'd be better off if I marry him because he's rich. Easton changed his will before he died and left everything to Grant for some reason. Grant is offering to take care of us if I marry him. His mom thinks he's up to something." Sabrina mimicked Crunch's position and rested her arms on the table.

"His mom doesn't trust him? That's never a good sign." Crunch shook his head.

"Harriet is a wonderful person, and I wonder how she could birth two such opposite personalities. Easton was different from his brother." Sabrina lowered her eyes and focused on one of his arms.

"He couldn't be too different if he didn't make sure you and his child would be taken care of." Crunch sounded angry.

"I don't know why he changed it, but Easton was an amazing man. There had to be a reason. I never found out what it was." She shrugged as her attention moved to the beautiful art on his arms.

Crunch had a sleeve of tattoos from his fingers up the length of his arms. She wasn't a huge fan of ink, but it suited him and made him that much sexier. She wondered what other parts of his body he had covered, and her cheeks warmed at the thought.

"You miss him," Crunch said.

"I do, but I have Charlee, and she helps me remember all the good times. She's a lot like him." Sabrina smiled.

"She's like you too." Crunch winked.

"Why would you say that?" Sabrina never thought Charlee looked anything like her.

"I've seen her at Mom's dance studio. She's picking things up quickly," Crunch told her.

"She does love it," Sabrina admitted.

Charlee fell in love with ballet and was constantly watching videos of dancers. It was a struggle to get the little girl to wear anything but leotards and tutus since she started classes.

"You're an amazing dancer, you know." Crunch lowered his voice to a tone that made her break out in goosebumps.

"Thank you, but I'm an amateur compared to you and your family." Sabrina smiled.

"Mom and Zara are the dancers. It was never a career goal for me." Crunch sat back in the seat.

Sabrina tilted her head and studied him for a few minutes. She knew many people in Hopedale, but nobody mentioned Crunch trained professionally in dance. Not even Sandy, who loved to tease and torture the men she worked with.

"Is it a secret that you're teaching classes for Zara?" Sabrina lowered her voice.

Crunch slumped in the seat and blew out a breath. He could be embarrassed about that aspect of his life. Some men thought dance was a girl thing. She wondered why Zara, Camilla, or his father never went to the diner, or at least not while she was on shift. She remembered Zara called her brother almost every day when he was in Yellowknife.

"It's not a secret, per se." Crunch shrugged. "Some people like to tease when you do something out of character. When Sandy found out that I was an ex… A dancer, she tortured me for months," Crunch grumbled.

"She didn't tell anyone?" Sabrina asked.

"No. Sandy's a pain in the ass, but she's loyal. Trust me, Sandy knows things about all of us she'd never divulge unless we said it was okay," Crunch said, and she could tell he didn't doubt Sandy's trustworthiness for a second.

"I like her," Sabrina admitted.

"Most people do." Crunch chuckled.

"Most people?" Sabrina couldn't think of anyone who disliked Sandy.

"Several years back, someone wanted to kill her," Crunch told her.

"Why are you talking about me?" Sandy appeared as if the mere mention of her made her materialize.

"If you weren't eavesdropping, you wouldn't know we were talking about you." Crunch rolled his eyes.

"If I'm not eavesdropping, how can I keep everyone on their toes?" Sandy ruffled Crunch's thick curls.

"Damn it, leave the hair alone," Crunch complained.

"He hates when anyone messes up his hair." Sandy snickered.

The pretty dark-haired woman was a huge personality. She was brilliant, and according to people around town, Sandy was one of the top computer analysts in the country. She worked for the Newfoundland Police Department as well as NES.

A sudden realization hit her that maybe Sandy could help. Sabrina needed to know what would happen if Grant decided to betray her and put her video on the world wide web.

"No, I hate when you do it because you do it all the time." Crunch pushed Sandy's arm when she tried to mess with his hair again.

"Sandy, I was wondering if I could ask you a computer question." Sabrina tried to sound casual.

"If it's about computers, I'm your girl." Sandy moved around the booth and pushed in next to Crunch.

"You can't answer her from your own seat?" Crunch grumbled.

"Nope, besides, I hate sitting by myself." Sandy winked at Sabrina. "What do you need to know?"

"Is it true if something is uploaded to the internet, it will be there forever?" Sabrina folded her fingers together, trying to keep her hands from shaking.

"Well, for the most part, yes. Think of it this way, the internet is like a huge spider web interconnected. If you upload something to one website, someone could get the content and save it to their server in seconds, not to mention backups. As much as sites try to prevent people from copying content, there's always a way," Sandy explained.

"What about if it's on one computer or phone?" Sabrina inquired.

"That's a little different. You can delete content from a single computer or phone. Sabrina, is everything okay?" Sandy asked.

"Oh... yeah. It was a discussion I was having with my, umm... brother," Sabrina lied.

She hated dishonesty, but since Grant interrupted her day, she seemed perched on a ledge over a pit of deceit. The acid in her stomach bubbled up, reminding her how disappointed her parents would be with her for lying. Still, she couldn't confess because she was too embarrassed to admit what Grant did.

"Well, if you need any more lessons, let me know. Now, I need to get home to my hot doctor. All the kids are gone for the night, and I've got him all to myself." Sandy wiggled her eyebrows. "I think it's a nice night to see how many rooms we can—"

Before she could finish, Crunch covered her mouth with his hand and shoved her off the bench seat. When Crunch pulled his hand away and wiped his palm with a napkin, Sabrina laughed.

"That's disgusting. What are you, eight?" Crunch grumbled.

"If you don't want me to lick it, don't put it near my mouth." Sandy winked.

"How does Ian put up with you?" Crunch shook his head.

"I keep Dr. O'Connor very happy." Sandy stood up.

"Go home." Crunch pointed to the exit.

"Sabrina, if you have any other computer questions, give me a call." Sandy headed out of the diner, waving to some people as she left.

"That woman is a handful." Crunch chuckled.

"But you'd step in front of a speeding car for her," Sabrina interjected.

"I would but don't tell her that, for Christ's sake." Crunch sat back in the seat. "Is your brother in trouble?"

"Why would you think that?" Sabrina didn't have to worry about Colt.

If anything, her brother was on a better path than she was. He had a new girlfriend and a great career. That was one person she didn't need to lose sleep over, at least not unless Grant ruined her life.

"The questions you were asking Sandy." Crunch shrugged.

"Oh. He's fine. It was just a discussion." Sabrina glanced out the window.

She had a feeling if she looked into his eyes, he'd know she wasn't truthful. For a split second, she thought about spilling her guts and telling everything, but as much as she wanted to confide in him, she didn't know him well.

"I should probably go. I have to pick up Charlee at Harriet's." Sabrina stood up.

"Would you mind?" Crunch held out his hand.

Of course, she wouldn't mind holding his hand. She wanted to stay with him for a lot longer, but she needed to get back to her apartment. Sabrina needed to check her bedroom and find the damn camera. Still, she put her hand in his, and he chuckled.

"I do like holding your hand, but I wanted your phone to add my number. Maybe you could call when you've more time to talk." Crunch smiled.

Sabrina's face warmed and was probably scarlet red. She pulled her hand from his, and after unlocking her phone, she gave it to him. When he finished, he pulled out his cell.

"I sent myself a message, so I've got your number as well. I hope that's okay?" Crunch asked.

"Of course." Sabrina adjusted her purse over her shoulder. "Thanks for this."

She couldn't say thanks for the coffee because she didn't have any. The truth was she didn't have any extra money, and she wasn't sure if he'd pay. So, she decided to opt for nothing.

"You didn't have anything. Maybe next time we could actually have a meal together." Crunch smiled.

"I'll think about it." Sabrina wished she could give him a less evasive answer.

"That's all I can ask for. May I walk you to your car?" Crunch stood up.

Sabrina nodded, and they headed out to the parking lot. She didn't miss the smiles from some customers familiar with Cora the Cupid and her matchmaking habits. Cora told Sabrina she should take a chance on Crunch, and she wouldn't be sorry, but Grant made it impossible.

She had to deal with that problem before considering a future with Crunch. The issue was she didn't know what she could do to stop the storm that was closing in on her.

Chapter 6

It was obvious Grant scared Sabrina when they were in the parking lot, but she wouldn't open up. It wasn't going to stop him. He'd find out exactly what the egotistical prick was up to and why he was trying to push Sabrina into an unwanted marriage.

There was nothing he hated more than entitled people who thought they could intimidate others. If Sabrina needed help, he'd do the same thing he did to the asshole who was harassing his mother and sister because the guy wanted her to sell the dance studio.

Nigel Greenwood sent several different men to talk to his mother, and when she refused to sell, Nigel showed up at the studio himself. According to Zara, the guy was a cocky bastard who didn't seem to understand the word, no. He'd left his card in case Crunch's mother changed her mind. Crunch took the card and went to see the guy.

Like most people who thought his money could get him whatever he wanted, Nigel sat in a corner office of one of the tallest office buildings in downtown St. John's. Walking into the man's office, the only thing going through Crunch's mind was how Nigel seemed to be overcompensating for something he was lacking.

Of course, the guy tried using charm, but when he realized it wasn't working, he used threats. Crunch bent over the desk and made sure Nigel understood his mother wasn't selling. Crunch warned him to back off but didn't wait for an answer and stalked out of the office.

Crunch and Sabrina stopped on the bottom of the steps for a woman nobody ignored. Everyone loved and respected Nanny Betty, as did anyone else who met her. She was linked with her husband as they walked together.

Elizabeth 'Betty' Roberts, previously O'Connor, was Keith's grandmother and the matriarch of the O'Connor family. When her husband, Jack, died, she was lucky enough to reconnect with her childhood sweetheart, and they got married a few years earlier. Tom was a wonderful man, and they were so cute together

"Well, look wat we have here, Tom," Nanny Betty said with an Irish Newfoundland lilt.

"Hello, Nan." Crunch leaned down to kiss the cheek of the octogenarian.

To Nanny Betty, people she liked were family, and she became their grandmother, which was why practically everyone called her Nan. People she disliked simply received opinions on what she thought about them.

"It's nice to see you, Nan." Sabrina hugged Nanny Betty.

"I see ya finally took my Cora's advice," Nanny Betty said.

"We… umm… had coffee and pie," Sabrina stammered over her words.

"Dat's a start." Nanny Betty gently patted Crunch's arm.

"Let's let the youngsters finish their date, my love." Tom motioned to the steps leading to the diner.

"You two have a nice night," Crunch said as he and Sabrina stepped back for them to proceed.

"I love that woman." Sabrina smiled.

"Everyone does," Crunch agreed.

"Thanks for walking me to my car, but it wasn't necessary." Sabrina pulled out her car keys.

"Necessary or not, I wanted to make sure you got to your car safely." Crunch pulled open the door.

"That's twice you've done that. Thank you." Sabrina looked into his eyes.

"No need for thanks. It's a selfish reason." Crunch stepped closer to her.

"Selfish?" Her voice was barely audible.

"It means I get to spend a few more seconds with you." He tucked a piece of her hair behind her ear.

"Every second counts." She smiled.

"With you, it does," Crunch whispered as he leaned forward.

Sabrina's eyes closed, and he swallowed hard. He wanted to kiss her plump pink lips because it wasn't a regular date, but to him, it was as close as he'd gotten with her. So, being the gentleman, he kissed her cheek then stepped back.

Sabrina's eyes fluttered open, and she smiled. Crunch moved around her and held open her car door. She eased into the seat, and he closed the door. She started the car and lowered her window.

"Bye." Sabrina pulled out of the parking spot.

"Night." Crunch waved.

As she drove out of his field of vision, something in the back of his mind told him Grant had something on her. He needed information on that asshole, and if Sabrina got hurt, Crunch would make sure the guy paid. He pulled out his phone and called the one person who could find anything.

"This better be good. I'm kinda busy," Sandy practically growled into the phone.

"Shit, I forgot. I'll call you tomorrow." Crunch was about to end the call.

"No, because if you don't tell me now, I'm not going to be able to enjoy my evening. Spill it," Sandy ordered.

"I want you to find out all you can about Grant Thornton." Crunch said.

"Why am I doing this?" Sandy asked.

"It's a long story, and I'll tell you about it tomorrow. Please find out if this guy is trouble or not." Crunch knew Sandy would dig up every little dirty detail on Grant.

"Do you have anything more than his name?" Sandy asked.

"Besides the fact that he's an arrogant prick?" Crunch scoffed.

"Yeah, I'd have to narrow down the parameters a little more than that. Arrogant prick could bring up eighty percent of the population in the world." Sandy chuckled.

"All I know is he lives in the city, he had a brother named Easton who died four years ago, and his mother's name is Harriet," Crunch said, remembering some of the information Sabrina had revealed.

"Got it. I'll get back to you tomorrow. Now I've got to go give this man hunk of mine a—"

He ended the call before she could finish. Sandy could find out what Grant was up to. Crunch only met the man for five minutes, but he knew the guy couldn't be trusted.

He was almost home when his phone buzzed. As great as Sandy was, there was no way she'd gotten any information that quickly, and he knew her well enough she wasn't going to work on one of the rare nights alone with her husband.

Still, he was slightly disappointed to see it wasn't Sandy calling. He wasn't sure he wanted to deal with his sister because she'd been harping on him to perform for a charity event put on by several dance studios around St. John's. His mother hosted it every year, and the money raised helped fund arts programs in schools around the city.

Zara was supposed to perform a ballroom dance with one of the other instructors, but since her leg was injured, she couldn't do it, and the guy backed out, so they were down two dancers instead of one. Crunch hadn't been in front of an audience in a long time, and the last time he did, he was only wearing a black G-string full of five-dollar bills.

"Ah hell." Crunch sighed as he put the phone up to his ear.

"Nice way to answer the phone, Hunter," Zara said sarcastically.

"I knew it was you," he replied.

"Then you should have answered with, hello my beautiful sister, how can I make your life better today?" Zara's sing-song tone made him laugh.

"Yeah, okay. Why don't you hold your breath, hang up and call again?" Crunch chuckled.

"I'm too young to die," she scoffed.

"So, what do I owe the pleasure of this call?" Crunch asked.

"Have you thought about what I asked you yesterday?" She sounded so hopeful.

"You mean what you asked yesterday, the day before, the day before that, and the day before that," Crunch teased.

"Yes, and I'll ask again and again until you give me an answer," she told him.

"Zara, I don't know. I haven't done that shit in a long time. I mean, I need a partner who knows what they're doing because I'm not teaching anyone." Crunch sighed.

"I've got the perfect partner." Zara wasn't going to give in.

"You do?"

Crunch wracked his brain, trying to think of someone from the studio he'd be willing to perform with. All the instructors at his mother's studio were either barely out of high school or only trained in ballet. The only other person trained in ballroom dance was his mother.

"Yes," Zara said.

"I'm not dancing with Mom." Crunch laughed.

"It's not Mom. It's Sabrina. She'll pick up a routine quickly," Zara pushed.

Crunch's heart jumped when he heard Sabrina's name. He wasn't sure if he was good enough to perform a routine with her. He'd seen her a couple of times dancing while she was waiting for her daughter. She was incredible.

"She's a ballet dancer." Crunch tried to sound casual.

"Yes, she's trained mostly in ballet, but she's done ballroom as well. When you left to go to Yellowknife, she helped with those classes, and to be honest, she's terrific," Zara explained.

The thought of holding Sabrina in his arms made his heart jump in his chest. Ballroom was a series of different dances such as the Waltz, the Rumba, the Cha-cha, the Tango, and the Foxtrot. He pictured himself holding Sabrina as they performed the Tango and smiled. He was smiling to himself when he heard Zara shout his name.

"Hunter," she yelled.

"Sorry, I was driving and just pulled into my driveway. What dance will we be performing?" Crunch asked.

"We were going to do an old-fashioned waltz to a George Strait song," Zara told him.

"What song?" Crunch was familiar with the country artist.

"'You Look So Good in Love.' I knew the song would piss off Wesley," Zara said with a snicker.

Wesley Williams was supposed to perform with Zara, and although Crunch didn't know the guy well, he found him to be a bit of a snob. He was a great instructor, and the women loved him, but he always seemed to have his nose in the air.

"Nice song," Crunch said.

"I can send you the video of us practicing. You don't have to do it the same, but you'll get the idea," Zara pushed.

"Okay, I'll watch it and let you know," Crunch responded.

"You're going to do it because you don't want to ruin Mom's event." Zara sighed.

His sister knew exactly how to push the right buttons. She was right, the event was important to their mom, and it helped a lot of children who wouldn't be able to participate in arts programs if it wasn't for the fundraiser.

"Send me the damn video," Crunch grumbled and ended the call.

A few minutes later, a message popped up on his phone. Watching his sister perform with Wesley didn't do the performance justice. Not that they both weren't amazing dancers, there simply wasn't any chemistry or passion.

Crunch didn't know if he could do any better, but he'd definitely be feeling passionate if he was dancing with Sabrina. With everything going on in her life, maybe she may not have the time or interest to practice.

He was lost in thought when a text startled him. He looked down and shook his head at the message on his screen. His sister had sent a string of emojis with praying hands and question marks.

Crunch: I'll do it, but only if Sabrina agrees and not because you bullied her into it.

Zara: I don't bully. I nudge aggressively.

Crunch: Let me know.

Zara: Love you.

Crunch: Love you too.

Crunch shoved his phone in his pocket as he entered the bright foyer of his home. A stack of mail sat on the entrance table next to the wooden bowl where he dropped his keys and wallet. Crash always left it there for Crunch to sift through in case something important showed up. He shuffled through the bundle until he came to a dark blue envelope.

He flipped it over when he noticed the only thing written on the front was Hunter Crawford. When he tore it open, he found a folded piece of black paper inside—a sentence written on it in thick red letters.

"Back off or pay the price," Crunch read the warning out loud. "What the fuck?"

He didn't know who'd send a mysterious note, and it didn't seem like Nigel would stoop to that level. Before he could try to determine where the mysterious message came from, the front door opened. Crash strolled into the house with a toolbelt hung low on his hips and what looked like drywall dust covering his clothes.

"Hey." Crash tossed his keys in the bowl.

"Oh, yeah. Hey," Crunch muttered.

"You look confused," Crash said.

"You look filthy." Crunch nodded to his friend's dusty clothes.

"Dad and I got most of the sanding done today. I wanted to get it finished. Keith has me starting a new client tomorrow, and I didn't want Dad to do it all," Crash told him.

"Hmm," Crunch answered while he stared at the paper in his hand.

"We'll start painting over the weekend," Crash continued.

"Hmm," Crunch repeated.

"Then I'm going to stick glitter all over the floor." Crash raised his voice.

"Sounds nice," Crunch responded. "Wait, what?"

It took him a second to realize what his friend said, and his head snapped up to see an amused expression on Crash's face. He'd only heard half of what the guy told him. Crunch sighed and dropped the paper on the table.

"What the hell are you looking at?" Crash grabbed the paper.

"That was in the mail on the table," Crunch explained.

"Was this what was in that blue envelope?" Crash asked.

"Yeah, but there's no return address on it," Crunch responded.

"I came home after the gym, and it was on the step. I thought it was an invitation or something. I was kind of pissed because I never got one." Crash chuckled.

"Guess you're glad now," Crunch scoffed.

"Who would send this?" Crash held the note up.

"I don't know, but I'm not going to worry about it." Crunch shrugged. "Go get cleaned up, and I'll toss a couple of T-bones on the grill."

"Crunch, you should show it to Rusty or the police." Crash picked up the paper again.

"It's probably some kids fucking around." Crunch headed into the kitchen.

He wasn't worried about the cryptic note, but he also wasn't going to take it with a grain of salt. He had a meeting with Keith in the morning, and he'd mention it to him then. It probably had something to do with the job he was on or a previous one.

While preparing the steaks, he thought about what had happened with Sabrina earlier. Was the note connected to her? Grant seemed annoyed that she was sitting with Crunch, but the guy wouldn't know where Crunch lived. Plus, he drove off in the direction of the highway leading out of Hopedale. Crunch's house was in the opposite direction.

No, it had to be something to do with one of his jobs. That was the only logical answer.

Chapter 7

Sabrina asked Harriet if she could watch Charlee a little longer, making an excuse about having to run some errands. The truth was, Sabrina wanted to examine her bedroom and find the damn camera. A shiver skittered down her spine, and her heart raced at the thought of someone watching her. She had no idea what other things Grant recorded because it wasn't like she kept herself covered in the privacy of her bedroom.

She sighed as she pulled into the parking garage of the apartment building. It was a nice place, and yes, the rent was a little high, but she wanted a decent roof over her daughter's head. It was a little easier since Colt moved in and shared the expenses. Her brother took a lot of financial pressure off her shoulders.

She hopped out of her car and headed to the elevator. The hair raised on the back of her neck, and she spun around to scan her surroundings. She didn't see anything out of the ordinary, but she quickened her pace to the elevator. It was a secure area for the tenants, but she didn't feel less nervous.

She frantically hit the button for the third floor in an attempt to get the doors to close quicker. She blew out a shaky breath when the elevator started to head up. It was the first time since she moved into the building that she felt unsafe.

Her phone rang as she closed the door of her apartment. She was disappointed when she didn't see Crunch's name on her screen, but she was happy to see who was calling.

"Hi, Holly." Sabrina tried to sound upbeat.

"Hi, Sabrina. I was thinking about you today and realized we haven't talked in a while." Holly always sounded like she was in a hurry.

"I know, and I keep meaning to call, but life is so busy I barely get time to do anything but sleep." Sabrina sighed.

"You have to slow down before you work yourself into an early grave," Holly said.

"I am actually going to be down to two jobs by the end of the month." Sabrina walked further into the apartment.

Walking into her apartment was worse. She felt violated and sick to her stomach. She wanted to grab all her things and get the hell out of there, but she couldn't. Unless she wanted to live in her car, there was nowhere else to go.

It was as if she was walking into a place she didn't know. Not the same haven she'd lived in for a couple of years, it felt eerie and unsafe. This didn't feel like home to her and all because Grant had somehow breached her home, but she didn't know how.

"Sabrina?" Holly's voice brought her out of her head.

"Sorry, I just got… home and..." Sabrina stopped. "Sorry."

"You sound strange. Is everything okay?" Holly asked.

"I'm fine. Tired and hungry," Sabrina lied.

"Well, why don't we meet for a late supper?" Holly suggested.

"I'd love to, but I still have to go to Harriet's and pick up Charlee. Rain check?" Sabrina felt horrible for neglecting her friend.

"Okay, but I'm holding you to it. Call me next week."

"Definitely, thanks, Holly." Sabrina ended the call.

She wanted to turn and run away from her place. She could ask Harriet to stay with her, but then she'd have to explain to her brother why she suddenly wanted to leave. Colt would ask questions, and she wouldn't feel comfortable telling her little brother Grant had videos of her.

Sabrina made her way to her bedroom and pushed open the door as if something would jump out at her. Everything looked the same as it had that morning. Her bed was still not made, her nightshirt was on the floor, and her laundry basket was still overflowing with clothes, but somehow, the room changed. It didn't feel like the warm cozy place where she relaxed and slept. It seemed dark and sinister.

As always, the curtains were closed, and the blinds were down. Sabrina scanned the curtains, but it was the same thick drapes she'd put up the day she moved in. She checked the blind, again nothing. She examined the window frame with her fingers, expecting to find something but much to her dismay, there was nothing out of the ordinary.

When her efforts failed, she plopped down on the bed and blew out a puff of air. Had Grant removed it already? If so, how did he get into her apartment? It was a secure building, and he would've needed to check in with the security desk.

She knew Grant had friends who would be considered shady. Easton told her it was one of the reasons his father wouldn't give Grant control of the company. Bennett didn't trust his son. She'd overheard Easton on a phone call the week before his death, saying Grant may be associating with criminals. The news continued to talk about different criminal organizations with ties to the province. It wouldn't surprise her if Grant mixed himself into the groups.

"I'm not going to be able to sleep in here until I know for sure the camera is gone," she muttered to herself.

Sabrina stood up, and as she turned to leave the room, something caught her eye under the windowsill. She crouched to get a better look. An outlet sat under the window, but the screw holding the plate looked as if it had backed out.

She leaned closer. Something was different about this outlet. The screw appeared larger than usual, but she checked other outlets in the room. She was afraid to touch it, and her first thought was to call her brother. After all, he was an IT guy. She didn't know what to tell him, and she'd need an explanation as to how she discovered it. Unless someone was looking for it, they would never see it.

The first step was to make sure Grant couldn't record anything else. She wasn't sure how to disconnect it, so she moved a side table in front of it and stepped back.

It wouldn't be able to record her, but she was still uncomfortable knowing it was there. Asking her brother to remove it was out of the question because even if she lied and said she didn't know where it came from, Colt had skills and would do some internet search to find some kind of address.

Sandy would know how to get rid of it, but she may ask too many questions. After all, the woman was known for being nosey but not in a bad way. Then there was the possibility Sandy would tell Crunch, and then Sabrina would need to explain why she was looking for the thing in the first place.

"God damn you, Grant," Sabrina ground out through clenched teeth.

"What did that son of a bitch do now?" Colt's voice startled her.

"I didn't hear you come home." Sabrina forced a smile.

Colt crossed his arms and narrowed his dark blue eyes. He wasn't about to let her dodge yet another incident with Grant. Colt despised the man and believed Grant convinced his brother to write Sabrina out of his will. He'd even suggested Sabrina talk to the lawyer they'd used with the first will.

At the time, she didn't care about anything and simply tried to live life without Easton. It was too difficult to believe the man she loved left her without anything to look after their daughter.

"What did he do?" Colt pushed.

"It's nothing, Colt." Sabrina pushed past her brother and headed to the kitchen.

"Is he still trying to bully you into marrying him?" Colt was like a dog with a bone.

"I said it's nothing. It's not like he'll ever force me to do it." Sabrina picked up her purse and hung it over her shoulder.

"I don't trust him, Sabrina. I think it's about time I talk to him." Colt's large arms flexed.

The last thing she wanted was her brother confronting Grant. She didn't want her brother's life ruined because he tried to protect her. Grant was sly enough to do something that would probably land Colt in trouble. Plus, she didn't want to give Grant a reason to release the videos.

"Just leave it. He'll give up eventually." Sabrina headed to the door and stopped. "I've got to get Charlee. Do you want me to pick up supper on the way back?"

"Sure, but we're not finished with this conversation, sis. Maybe if he thinks you're with Crunch, he'll back off," Colt said.

"I'm not with Hunter. We had coffee, and I doubt there will be a second time." Sabrina walked away before her brother could say anything else.

By the time she arrived at Harriet's condo, she'd worked herself up so much that her heart was racing. Sabrina wouldn't put the older woman in the middle of everything. No matter what an ass Grant was, he was still Harriet's son and the only child she had left.

On her way to the elevator, she waved to several of the residents gathered in the lobby. She didn't know them but saw them every time she came to see Harriet. She stepped on the elevator and tried to calm the anxiety as she rode to the top floor.

"Hello," Sabrina called out when she stepped into the spacious apartment.

She heard Harriet laugh and followed the sound to the kitchen. When Harriet moved into the building, she gave Sabrina a set of keys so she wouldn't have to worry about buzzing in.

"Hello," Sabrina said a little louder.

"We're in here," Harried called out.

Sabrina found Charlee and her grandmother covered in flour and placing round mounds of something on a cookie tray. Charlee's face lit up like a Christmas tree as she placed the tiny balls of dough neatly in a row.

"We're making peanut butter cookies, and Nana pulled the bag of flour down on top of us." Charlee giggled.

"That's because I didn't close it the last time we made cookies." Harriet smiled down at Charlee with the love of a grandmother glowing from her eyes.

As Sabrina stepped into the large kitchen, she glanced down at the floor. She chuckled at the dusting of flour all over the black marble floor. Her first instinct was to grab the broom from the pantry and clean up the mess.

"Don't worry about that. I'll get that cleaned up later." Harriet took the broom and handed Sabrina a cup of tea.

"It's no bother." Sabrina reached for the broom again.

"Sit down and drink your tea while I put these in the oven." Harriet motioned toward the small dinette on the other side of the kitchen island.

Sabrina sipped the hot tea while watching Charlee jump down from the stool and clapped excitedly when Harriet closed the oven door. A lump formed in her throat as she tried to hold back the tears. The thought of her daughter being tainted by Grant possibly releasing the video made it hard to keep her composure.

"Charlee, why don't you go watch television while the cookies are baking? Mommy and I can have a chat while they bake," Harriet said as she sat across from Sabrina.

Charlee didn't need to be told twice and skipped out of the kitchen as Harriet reached across the table. Her soft hand rested on Sabrina's arm, and she gave it a gentle squeeze.

"Do you want to tell me what has tears in your eyes?" Harriet whispered.

"I don't have tears in my eyes," Sabrina tried to force a smile.

"My darling, I've known you long enough to know when you're about to burst into tears," Harriet pushed.

Sabrina blew out a shaky breath and stared into the cup on the table. She always felt close to Harriet and knew she could tell her anything, but to tell her what Grant was doing may upset her. Wouldn't it?

When Sabrina lifted her head to look at Harriet, she couldn't stop the tears from spilling over. The older woman quickly pulled a napkin from the holder and handed it to Sabrina.

"My goodness, my darling, what's wrong?" Harriet's eyes filled with concern.

"It's been a hectic week." Sabrina used the napkin to wipe the tears from her cheeks.

"What has Grant done now?" Harriet sighed.

"Why would you think he did something?" Sabrina asked.

"Because the only time you get upset like this is when he has harassed you. What did he do?" Harriet pushed.

Should she tell her? Maybe she could convince Grant to delete the video and save Sabrina the humiliation. Could she possibly convince her son to leave Sabrina alone? It hadn't worked over the last four years.

"It's the same old thing. He wants me to marry him." Sabrina wasn't lying.

"That boy has always wanted what he couldn't have. He has been that way since the day Bennett brought him home." Harriet stopped, and her face paled.

"When Bennett brought him home?" Sabrina asked in confusion.

"Oh… I meant… when we brought him home." Harriet shifted uncomfortably in her chair.

"Why do I get the feeling that's not true?" Sabrina pushed.

Harriet rose to her feet and hurried across the kitchen as the buzzer on the oven sounded. She pulled the cookies from the oven and placed them on the counter with her back to Sabrina. Harriet was trembling as she lifted the cookies onto the cooling rack.

"Harriet, is there something you aren't telling me?" Sabrina moved across the kitchen to stand next to her friend.

Harriet placed the spatula on the counter with a huge sigh and dropped her head. This was something Harriet never told anyone before. Harriet walked toward the large floor-to-ceiling window that looked out over the city. The older woman wrapped her arms around herself.

"Harriet?" Sabrina hated to push the issue, but she did. "Tell me."

"Nobody knows this. Not even Grant," Harriet said after a couple of minutes of silence.

"Knows what?"

"Grant isn't our biological child." Harriet turned to Sabrina.

"He's adopted?" Sabrina was surprised, but it made sense.

Grant didn't look anything like Easton or his parents. He had dark hair, whereas the rest of the family had blond. He was the only one with brown eyes, and he had a darker complexion than the rest of the family. Of course, she'd never said anything in the past, but she'd always suspected that maybe there was some sort of affair or previous relationship.

"Yes," Harriet whispered.

"Why didn't you tell him?" Sabrina asked.

"It's a long story, but his birth mother had an affair with a married man. The man was mixed up with some hard people, and she didn't want him raised in that life. She worked for us as a maid and went to Bennett to ask for help. Grant was barely a week old when we got him." Harriet walked back to the chair and sat down.

"That's a good thing, Harriet. He may have ended up with a terrible life." Sabrina sat next to her.

"We tried. We tried to have a child for a long time, and I'd given up. When she approached Bennett, he thought it was a gift for both of us. I was thrilled to adopt Grant." She smiled.

"Was Easton adopted too?" Sabrina asked.

"No, we conceived him all on our own. He was a miracle." Harriet swallowed hard. "Grant was barely a year old when I got pregnant, and as they grew up, we used to tell him what a great big brother he was."

"You said he always wanted what he couldn't have," Sabrina reminded her.

"Even as a child, if he wanted something and didn't get it, he'd have a tantrum to the point of making himself sick. When he got older, it got worse. He was and still is a huge handful." Harriet sighed.

Having a secret like that must've been hell to keep from people. Especially the child, but there had to be a reason, or they wouldn't have done it.

"It doesn't mean I love Grant any less, but I'm starting to believe maybe he inherited his biological family's criminal tendencies. I know that sounds insane. His mother was a sweet girl who got caught up with a man who could be charming." Harriet wiped a tear from her cheek.

"Was?" Sabrina handed a napkin to the woman.

"She was killed in a fire about three months after we adopted Grant. They thought it was arson but couldn't be sure. Two other women died in the fire as well." Harriet sat up straight. "I need you to keep this to yourself. Grant can't know."

Sabrina would never break Harriet's confidence, but a little piece of her pitied Grant because he didn't know the truth. Although, why she felt empathy for him, she'd never know, especially considering what he was doing to her.

"I won't say a word," Sabrina assured the older woman.

The problem was all this new information didn't help with her dilemma. She was still in the same predicament she'd been in when she arrived. How was she going to get out of this?

Chapter 8

The following week, Crunch walked into the courthouse behind Rex and Diamond Starr. They escorted her to a secure room until she needed to testify. The Crown Attorney wanted to make sure she arrived safely.

"This stupid thing is so uncomfortable. It's flattening my tits," Diamond complained as she squirmed in the Kevlar vest.

"It's better than getting a bullet in the chest," Rex deadpanned.

"Both of you wear them, so why don't you wrap those hot bodies around me? Then I'll be covered." She winked at Rex.

Diamond's flirtation annoyed Crunch more than if a bee was buzzing around his ear. She was about to stand in court and testify against a man believed to be a hitman, but she acted like she was going to a dinner party.

While they got ready at the safehouse, Rex mentioned the woman was too calm for someone about to testify against a murderer. He wasn't wrong. Although people had different ways of dealing with stress or fear, Diamond seemed relaxed.

"You'll be safer with your own vest," Rex told her with a dismissive wave of his hand.

"I can't wait for this to be over. I'll be on a beach in Cancun with all the money and freedom I could ever want," she said, but it mainly seemed to herself.

Crunch locked eyes with Rex. They didn't know she was going into witness protection. If Diamond thought that was what they did, she'd be sadly disappointed when the time came. If she were going into the program, she certainly wouldn't have all the money she could ever want.

"I hate this island. Newfoundland sucks." She pouted.

"As someone who wasn't born here, I'd take this island over some of the places I've been." Rex seemed pissed.

Crunch didn't know much about his co-worker except he was former American military and from Georgia. He never talked about his family or his hometown. He was a nice guy, but he kept to himself, and Crunch could count on one hand how many times the guy had been out on a date.

"You must've been in some pretty shitty places if you'd rather be here." Diamond twirled her overbleached hair around one of her fingers.

Before Rex could respond, someone knocked. Crunch opened the door, and the bailiff informed him it was time for Diamond to testify. For a split second, Crunch thought he saw a hint of fear in her eyes, but she fixed her skirt and straightened her shoulders. As she sashayed by Crunch, she smirked and blew him a kiss.

"Maybe we can celebrate after all this is over." Diamond purred as she ran a finger down the front of Crunch's shirt.

"Let's go." Rex grabbed her elbow and guided her out of the room.

"Are you this rough in the bedroom?" Diamond asked.

"You'll never know," Rex responded.

The courtroom was small with only the defendant and his lawyer, the judge, the Crown Attorney, the assistant crown. Diamond was escorted to the stand after, and she fixed her oversized breasts when they removed her vest. Crunch slid into one of the seats behind the prosecution, and Rex sat next to him.

An uneasy feeling came over Crunch as he scanned around the almost empty room. Rex nudged him and inconspicuously pointed toward the defendant. The man focused on Crunch and didn't attempt to divert his eyes when Crunch saw him.

It would be intimidating, but given the man's size and shackles, Crunch wasn't exactly in danger. Igor Voznesensky didn't look like a cold-blooded killer. He looked more like a teenager who still hadn't hit a growth spurt.

Igor's long brown hair was pulled back into a slick ponytail that hung down below his shoulders. He was skinny with beady wide-set eyes. His overly large nose looked out of place on his slim face, but he'd broken it once or twice. Still, there was something in the guy's expression that said he'd slit Crunch's throat without flinching.

"He seems to dislike you," Rex whispered.

"Maybe it's you he doesn't like," Crunch replied.

There was no mistake. Igor's attention locked on Crunch, but why? It didn't matter because Diamond was about to help put the guy away for a long time.

Saul seemed to want the assistant to take over questioning Diamond. Crunch got to know both Declan and Saul over the years because of NES's relationship with The Public Prosecution Service. The security company was hired frequently over the years as security for witnesses. Keith's brother Mike also knew Declan from law school.

Declan was a nice guy, but he was somewhat shy outside of court. Mike said the guy was always self-conscious about the sizeable wine-colored birthmark covering his cheek and neck. Although when the guy was in court, he was a different person and fought hard for victims. It wasn't surprising he'd left his firm to work as a prosecutor.

Saul only took over when things became more political. Keith believed the only reason the guy stayed in office was so he could get his face on the news so often. From what Crunch saw with this case, Keith wasn't wrong.

Declan stood up after the bailiff swore in Diamond. She looked confident and smirked as she glanced at Igor. She didn't seem scared of the guy, which was odd since he'd threatened her life. It was the reason Crunch and Rex escorted her to court.

Declan asked several questions about the night of the murder, and Diamond spoke with clear, concise answers. The problem was she continued to flash a flirty smile at Igor, not that the guy seemed to be affected by it. Then Declan asked the big question.

"So, Ms. Starr, you were at the club when the owner was shot, is that correct?" Declan asked.

"Yes." Diamond nodded.

"Can you tell us what you saw that night?" Declan continued.

"Well, I was in the dressing room counting my tips. I made a bundle that night." Diamond glanced at Igor. "The club had just closed, and the only one out front was the owner."

"You're referring to Mitch Snider, the victim," Declan confirmed.

"Yes. One of the other dancers waved as she left through the staff door, and I was putting on my coat when I heard shouting."

Declan looked confused but allowed her to continue. Diamond glanced at the defense lawyer and then went on.

"I heard Mitch scream something." Diamond shook her head as if the memory disturbed her.

"What happened then?" Declan pushed.

"How would I know? I ran out the back door." Diamond shrugged.

"You didn't go out to the front of the club and see the defendant shoot Mr. Snider?" Declan looked frazzled.

"Objection, the Crown is leading the witness." The defense lawyer stood up.

The judge agreed with the defense and warned Declan to change his line of questioning. Saul sat up straight and began to write on a notepad frantically. Crunch glanced at Igor, and although it was barely visible, there was a grin on his face.

"She lied," Rex whispered.

"What the hell is happening?" Crunch muttered.

"Ms. Starr, the night of the shooting, didn't you tell the police you saw Mr. Voznesensky in the club?" Declan asked.

"Yes, I did see him. He was sitting right at the front of the stage." Diamond tilted her head.

"Didn't you also tell us you saw him shoot Mr. Snider?" Declan raised his voice.

"How would I see that if I left?" Diamond snorted.

"You realize if you lie under oath, it is punishable by up to fourteen years in prison?" Declan threatened.

"That's why I'm telling you the truth, duh." Diamond crossed her arms.

Declan placed a piece of paper in front of her, then went back to the desk. His birthmark was darker, and his lips were in a thin line. His shoulders tensed as he shoved his hands into his pants pockets.

"Do you recognize that piece of paper?" Declan asked.

Diamond leaned forward and looked at it for a few minutes before sitting back and shaking her head. Declan dropped his head and blew out a breath as if he wanted to calm himself before he continued.

"Ms. Starr, that is a statement you signed saying you saw Mr. Voznesensky shoot Mr. Snider," Declan said through clenched teeth.

"I don't remember doing that. I can't see how I would. I can't read." Diamond gave the lawyer a smug smile.

"Your Honour, can we approach the bench?" Saul shot to his feet.

The judge nodded, and all three lawyers walked up to the large wooden desk. While they were talking, Crunch noticed Diamond give a little wink to Igor. The man smiled and glanced back over his shoulder at the exit.

Diamond was the prosecution's star witness. If she took back her statement, it could screw the case. It would be a stain on the Crown Attorney's career if he allowed an assassin to go free.

After several minutes, Declan stepped in front of Crunch and Rex. The man looked ready to explode, but Saul was stoic. The Crown Attorney was probably waiting to get back to the office to lose his shit.

"Did she call anyone?" Declan asked.

"Not while I was there. She asked to use my phone a few times, but I told her she wasn't permitted," Rex told him.

"She never asked me, and it was always in my pocket, so there was no way she could've used it," Crunch confirmed.

"Then how did they get to her and make her change her testimony?" Saul raised an eyebrow.

"I have no idea," Crunch replied.

"It's days like this I wish I'd stayed in private practice," Declan grumbled.

"It's days like this I realize we may be on the wrong side of the courtroom," Saul grumbled.

The judge told Diamond she was free to step down after the defense confirmed she'd not seen anything. She strolled down to sit next to Rex and gave him one of her flirty smiles. Rex simply rolled his eyes and proceeded to find his fingernails suddenly interesting.

Declan adjusted the collar of his robe as he glared at Diamond. It always seemed weird to Crunch that judges were not the only ones to wear robes in Canadian courts.

"You're free to go, Ms. Starr." Saul kept his voice low.

"I know. I'm waiting for these guys to escort me out," she scoffed.

"These men were hired to protect you because we believed you were a witness to a murder. Since you insist you didn't see anything, you no longer need the service. Good day, Ms. Starr." Saul motioned to the exit.

"I need to get my things at that house." She seemed panicked.

"They'll be delivered to your home." Saul sounded cold.

Diamond stared at him as if he'd slapped her. She slowly stood up and nervously glanced around the room. When she locked eyes with Igor, she spun around and hurried out of the room.

"Should we make sure she gets home safe?" Crunch asked Declan.

"No, I've got someone tailing her. She doesn't know, but if someone comes to pay her off, we'll get them." Declan practically stomped out of the courtroom.

Crunch couldn't help but feel bad for Diamond on the way home. She was in a tricky business, and since Mitch Snider was known to be involved with organized crime, chances were, the club's new owner was as well. The authorities didn't know how the hell any of them got to her.

"I guess that job ended abruptly." Rex chuckled.

"Guess so," Crunch agreed.

Since he and Rex were free for the next few days, Crunch decided it was an excellent time to see if Zara talked to Sabrina. Maybe they could schedule some practice. He also wanted to see what Sandy found out about Grant to get rid of that voice in the back of his mind telling him the guy was trouble for Sabrina.

He may be off duty for the next few days, but he wouldn't be bored.

Chapter 9

Sabrina dialed Sandy's number six times but deleted it before hitting send. What was she supposed to say? She couldn't afford to hire anyone else, and it seemed wrong to ask Sandy to keep it private, but she had to do something.

It wasn't like she could run into her at the diner anymore since she had finished her last shift. Sabrina could ask her to have coffee and bring up some hypothetical situations. That wouldn't seem suspicious at all.

"Sandy would see right through that," Sabrina mumbled to herself.

"Like a window?" Charlee asked from the back seat.

Sabrina smiled at her daughter through the rearview mirror. She didn't realize she'd said anything out loud. Her daughter usually got distracted with the iPad, but she'd look up now and then when she heard something interesting.

"Sure, honey. Like a window." Sabrina nodded as she drove into the parking lot of the dance studio.

"Yay, we're here." Charlee squealed.

Sabrina remembered when she felt the same way over attending dance classes. She still loved it, but it was hard to feel anything but anxiety with everything going on in her life.

They stepped into the foyer as Zara exited her office and hobbled toward Sabrina, smiling. It was hard not to see the resemblance between her and Crunch. Sabina was surprised she hadn't noticed it before.

"Just the lady I'm looking for." Zara maneuvered her crutches and linked her arm into Sabrina's.

"Why am I suddenly scared of you?" Sabrina laughed as she helped Charlee into her ballet slippers.

"Mommy, that's Miss Zara. She's not scary," Charlee hugged Zara's leg.

"Exactly, I'm not scary at all." Zara smirked.

"Not scary but sneaky." Sabrina raised an eyebrow.

"Charlee, Miss Ava is about to start class." Zara pointed across the foyer.

Charlee scurried off to join the junior instructor who helped with ballet classes. Ava Mixer was a seventeen-year-old and had been a student with the studio since she was younger than Charlee. Now she assisted the teachers with the smaller kids.

Once Charlee disappeared into the ballet class, Zara practically dragged Sabrina into the office and asked her to sit. Once Zara had herself in her chair and her leg propped on a stool, she smiled at Sabrina.

"So, I need a favor," Zara began.

"I'm helping with as many classes as I can," Sabrina replied.

"Oh, I know. This isn't about teaching. It's about the Performing Arts Ball." Zara smiled.

"Okay," Sabrina said cautiously.

"I usually perform with a partner at the event, but… well…" Zara pointed to her knee.

"You can't do it this year," Sabrina finished.

"It sucks. I only know of one person who can learn the routine in less than two months." Zara smiled.

"Me?" Sabrina asked with a light gasp.

The dance studio had other instructors with more experience who could do it. Why Zara thought Sabrina was the person for the job was beyond her. It had been years since she performed in front of an audience.

"I don't know. Aren't the performances usually couples?" Sabrina inquired.

"Yes." Zara grinned.

"Are you sure Wesley will be okay with me taking your place?" Sabrina didn't like the idea of dancing with him.

"He backed out." Zara held up her finger as her phone buzzed.

Sabrina sighed as she looked at the walls around the office. They contained dozens of photos of Zara's mom when she danced in New York, but the picture that attracted her like a magnet was a young man in mid-air doing Grand Jeté, which is when the dancer did a perfect split while in the air. It was Crunch, and he looked magnificent. It was a shame he hadn't gone further with his talent.

"Okay, that was your partner," Zara told her.

"Who is it?" Sabrina asked with some trepidation.

Before Zara answered, the door opened, and the most beautiful man in the world walked through wearing mirrored aviator glasses and about a day's worth of scruff on his face. Crunch gave her a thousand-watt smile, showing that sexy dimple on his right cheek, and she had to bite back the sigh at the sight of him. He shoved his glasses up as he plopped down on the chair next to her.

"I think you know your dance partner," Zara said with a flourish of her hand.

Sabrina was mute for a few seconds. She expected Sabrina to dance with Crunch? Was Zara insane? This was the man who starred in her fantasies, and she had dreams of being wrapped in his strong arms, but they certainly weren't dancing.

"You're blushing." Zara smirked.

Sabrina instinctively brought her hands to her cheeks. She prayed for the floor to open up and swallow her so she wouldn't have to explain why she was blushing. Even the thought of her desires made her instantly flush. Probably because some of them were things she'd never done with anyone.

"I'm not sure… I mean… He's…" Sabrina pressed her lips together before she put her foot in her mouth.

"I know. I don't do this all the time, but this charity ball is important to my mom, and since Miss Clumsy screwed herself, I agreed to step in. I promise I won't step on your toes." Crunch smiled, showing his perfect white teeth, and there was that dimple again.

How in hell was she going to dance with him and not want to lick him from head to toe? Zara probably didn't realize how sexy her brother was and that Sabrina wasn't blind. Sabrina rationalized that the only reason for the strong reaction to him was because she hadn't been with anyone since Easton died. Then again, Crunch was the only man who caused her body to ignite with a smile.

"It's not that. I don't know if I'll have time to practice," Sabrina lied.

"It's only going to be an old-fashioned waltz, and if you can fit it in, something more upbeat and fun," Zara explained.

Sabrina glanced back and forth between Zara and Crunch. They were both staring at her with such optimistic expressions she couldn't refuse. She wasn't sure how to keep her feelings from getting out of control.

She blew out a long breath. Zara sat with her hands clasped together as if she were praying, and Crunch gave her a reluctant thumbs up.

"Okay." Sabrina sighed.

Zara squealed as she jumped up and hobbled around the desk. She wrapped her arms around Sabrina, thanking her over and over. The whole thing had Sabrina giggling at the overwhelming gratitude.

"So, I don't get any thanks at all," Crunch complained.

"Of course, you do." Zara practically fell on her brother's lap and kissed him on the cheek. "You're both the best."

Before Sabrina knew it, she and Crunch were in one of the studios watching videos of possible routines they could do for the Ball. The old-fashioned waltz was easy, and she liked the song Zara picked. It wasn't typical for ballroom dancing, but people would enjoy more casual music.

"I have to confess; I haven't danced with a partner in a long time," Crunch told her as they clicked the following video.

"Me either. I never danced with partners when I was learning." Sabrina couldn't help watching his arm flex as he moved the mouse.

"We should probably set a practice schedule." Crunch closed the laptop.

"Yeah," Sabrina said as she wondered where she'd get the time.

Crunch took out his phone and was swiping through something on the screen. Sabrina reached in her bag and pulled out her cell, but when she looked at the screen, she stifled a gasp. Grant sent a message with a photo attached. There was no way she was opening anything while sitting next to Crunch.

"Excuse me for a minute. I have to… ladies' room." She hurried out of the studio and practically ran to the bathroom.

Sabrina stepped into one of the stalls and opened the message. A photo of her naked in her room but at least her body was blurred out. Her eyes filled with tears, and she had to blink several times to clear her vision so she could read the message.

Grant: You may have blocked my view of you, but I still have these to keep me hot at night. Still waiting for your decision.

Sabrina wanted to scream, but it wouldn't help anything, and she'd have to explain why she was making such a fuss. She couldn't marry Grant, but if he continued to do these things, she might not have a choice.

"Damn you," Sabrina whispered into the hollowness of the bathroom.

She was startled when her phone vibrated with another message. Grant obviously waited for her to open the text, and she swore under her breath.

Grant: I want your answer by the end of the month, or I'll send these to everyone you know.

Sabrina: Why the hell are you doing this? Why would you want to marry me when you know I don't love you?

Grant: The end of July.

Sabrina angrily wiped the tears running down her cheeks. She wasn't marrying that evil bastard and letting him ruin her life. He had her over a barrel, and she didn't know a way out of her dilemma.

"What am I going to do?" Sabrina sighed. "I need help, but who?"

Crunch's handsome face flashed in her head, and something deep down told her that if there was a way out of this, maybe he could help her figure it out. Did she dare involve him?

Chapter 10

Crunch looked through his schedule for the next few weeks. He had some assigned clients, but he had some vacation time built up, and Keith was on his back about taking it. He never had a reason to take it before, but now he could spend time with Sabrina, practicing. The event was held at the end of September, which meant they had two months to prepare.

Crunch: Hey Rusty, can I drop by to chat about getting some time off in the next couple of weeks?

He wasn't sure if Keith could work the schedule to give him the vacation time, but it wouldn't hurt to ask, especially since his boss was ragging on him about it. Crunch never had a chance to put his phone away when it buzzed in his hand.

Keith: About fucking time. Give me the dates.

Crunch shook his head and chuckled in amusement. Keith was a wonderful boss, not to mention a great friend. It was the main reason Crunch loved his job. He sent back a message explaining the situation and how he'd like the next couple of weeks and the week of the ball.

Keith: Approved and done.

He looked up at the door and then at his watch. Sabrina had been in the bathroom for a long time. He wondered if she was ill because her face seemed to turn especially pale right before she hurried out of the studio.

When another ten minutes passed, and she hadn't returned, Crunch headed out of the studio. He saw her leaving the bathroom looking as if she was ready to throw up. He hurried toward her.

"Are you okay?" Crunch asked, seeing tears in her eyes.

"I'm…fine," Sabrina stammered.

Before he could say another word, she burst into heavy sobs, and he slipped his arm around her trembling shoulders. Crunch pulled her into his side and guided her into the empty studio.

When he closed the door, he pulled her against him and let her weep into his chest. Her body shook as her tears soaked his shirt, but he didn't care if he had to wring it out after. Crunch would do anything for her.

"I got you, sweetheart." Crunch held her tighter and kissed the top of her head.

"I'm… so…sorry," Sabrina sniffled.

"You don't have to be sorry for anything, but I'd like to know what's upset you." Crunch didn't like to see anyone upset, but it hurt his chest to see Sabrina in such a way.

Sabrina pulled out of his arms and dropped down on the bench. She looked defeated, and he wanted to fix everything for her. When he crouched in front of her, he held her hands between his.

"Tell me," he urged.

"I wish I could." Sabrina shook her head.

"Does any of this have to do with the performance?" Crunch had to ask.

People with stage fright could have a lot of anxiety over performing in front of an audience. Maybe it was why she didn't go further with her career in ballet.

"No." Sabrina almost choked on the word as she stifled another sob.

"Please, Sabrina. Tell me so I can help." Crunch cupped her face between his hands. "It hurts me to see you like this."

She lifted her eyes to meet his as tears spilled down her blotchy cheeks. Crunch's heart broke because he could practically feel fear radiating from her. She was terrified of something, and he remembered the last time she had that look.

"Did he hurt you?" Crunch tried to keep a calm tone.

Sabrina looked down, and another sob escaped. Crunch drew her into his arms as he tried to cool the rage growing toward Grant. The guy was an ass and harassing her but to cause her to become so distraught was crazy.

"Talk to me," Crunch whispered against her temple.

"I can't. I can't tell anyone, or he'll…" Sabrina sniffled.

Crunch pulled back and lowered his head until he could see her eyes. His breath caught for a second because even with tears running down her cheeks, puffy eyes, and red blotches on her face, she was still so damn beautiful.

"You can tell me anything. It will remain between you and me if that's what you want, and I'll do whatever I can to stop the person causing this." Crunch used his thumbs to wipe her damp cheeks.

Sabrina took in a shaky breath as she studied him. It was as if she couldn't decide if she could trust him. There was no way to make her see it, and all he could do was wait for her to make a choice.

"He's given me until the end of the month to decide," she finally whispered.

"If you're going to marry him?" Crunch wanted to confirm.

She nodded and took another slow breath before she stood up and moved toward the large window on the opposite side of the room. Her arms around her body as if it would stop her shaking.

Crunch wasn't sure it was the right thing, but he stepped behind her and pulled her back against his chest. Her body relaxed, and she stopped trembling. For several minutes, the only sound in the room was the muffled music from the other studios. Crunch didn't care how long she needed him to hold her because he'd stay there forever.

"If I don't give him the answer, he's going to ruin my life." She sighed.

"I won't let him." Crunch spun her around, so she was facing him.

"You're sweet, but he has the capability to humiliate me." She gazed at him with tear-filled eyes.

"I have the capability to break his bloody neck," Crunch said with a growl.

Sabrina smiled as she cupped his cheek. When she brought her hand down to rest against his chest, he knew she had to feel the way his heart pounded.

"I don't think that would help but thank you for the gesture. I need to decide if I want to call his bluff." Sabrina sighed.

"What is he threatening to do?" Crunch asked.

"He...I can't tell you. It's embarrassing." She tried to turn away, but he stopped her.

"Please, tell me," Crunch pushed.

She pressed her lips together as she stared into his eyes. Maybe he shouldn't push her, but someone had to stop that asshole. Crunch hated bullies.

"He has some... videos... of me." She dropped her eyes from his.

"Videos?" Crunch didn't like the sound of this.

"Yes. In my bedroom." She lowered her head.

"How in the hell did he get those? Wait, not from your fiancée who passed away?" Crunch was starting to dislike her dead husband-to-be.

"No. Somehow he placed a camera in my apartment without me knowing. I've got no idea how he could've gotten it there. He's never been inside my apartment." Sabrina shook her head. "God, I can't believe I told you that."

Sabrina pulled away and ran to where her bag lay on the floor. She hoisted it on her shoulder and started to leave the room, but before she pushed open the door, she turned to face him.

"I think it's better if Zara finds another partner for you. I can't marry Grant, and when I tell him that, he's going to post those videos all over the internet." She started to open the door.

"Let me help." Crunch raced across the room to stop her.

"I can't involve you in this. Thanks for the offer." Sabrina touched his cheek. "I wish things were different."

She pushed through the door, leaving him staring after her. She might not want to involve him, but he wasn't going to let that asshat destroy someone he cared about.

Chapter 11

It took every ounce of strength not to stay wrapped in Crunch's embrace. It was the first time she felt any affection from someone outside of her family in a long time, but she couldn't bring him into her craziness. She cared too much about him and his family, not to mention his job dealt with some pretty influential clients.

She just buckled Charlee in her booster seat when she heard someone call her name. It wasn't Crunch, but the man's voice was familiar. She saw the lawyer who drew up their wills. It wasn't hard to recognize the guy because of the red birthmark that covered his left cheek and down the side of his neck.

"I thought that was you," he said.

"Hi." Sabrina smiled as she shook his hand.

"How have you been?" he asked while Sabrina tried to remember the guy's name.

"I'm good, thanks." Sabrina tossed her bag in the car.

"I still can't believe Easton is gone. I'm so sorry." He sounded so sincere.

"Thanks, I still miss him," she replied.

"I hope the lawyer made everything easy." He glanced at his watch.

"Yeah, it was surprising, to say the least," Sabrina admitted.

"At least you were well looked after." He smiled and pulled out his phone.

Sabrina stared at him in confusion, but before she could ask what he was talking about, his phone rang. He held up his finger and put the phone to his ear.

"Yes, I'm here now. I'll talk to him and ask if he knows anything," he said to the caller.

Sabrina pulled open her car door and gave a little wave to the lawyer as she sat in the vehicle. Before she closed the door, she heard Crunch shouting to her.

"Sabrina, wait." Crunch ran to the car but stopped when he saw the lawyer. "Declan, what are you doing here?"

Declan Hill.

The lawyer's name instantly popped in her head, although she didn't know how Crunch would know him. Then again, between the police officers, lawyers, and the mayor of Hopedale, all part of the O'Connor clan, Crunch probably knew most of the legal staff in the province of Newfoundland.

"I'll call you back," Declan said into the phone. "I came to talk to you about Voznesensky."

"Why? Isn't that case in the toilet?" Crunch asked.

"Not really. We're still trying to get this guy, but we found something I'd like to talk to you about." Declan glanced at Sabrina.

"How did you know to find me here?" Crunch grabbed the top of Sabrina's car door.

"I called Keith, and he said you'd be here," Declan explained.

"I've got to go." Sabrina looked up at Crunch.

"Declan, give me five minutes." Crunch turned back to Sabrina. "Here's the key to my house. Go there, and I'll meet you as soon as I finish here. I can help. Please let me try."

Sabrina looked into his hopeful eyes as she struggled with the decision to take him up on his offer or keep him out of it. She wasn't sure she wanted to involve him, but she sure as hell needed help. Maybe telling him was a good thing.

"Please," Crunch pleaded.

"Okay," Sabrina replied and accepted the key.

She knew where he lived because Alice once asked her to drop off an order when Sabrina went to Cupid's Closet. She didn't realize Cora and her boss had set her up at the time.

"It was nice to see you, Declan," Sabrina said as she closed her door.

Charlee was dozing in the back seat as she made her way to Hopedale. She called her brother to let him know she'd be home later and picked up some fast food for herself and Charlee. When they pulled into Crunch's driveway, she saw a man across the street, staring at the house.

He appeared harmless, but it was odd how he held his phone up as if taking pictures. Sabrina wanted to ask what he was doing, but she didn't know if he was dangerous or a guy site seeing. Crunch's house was beautiful, so maybe the guy liked the style.

"Hi, Sabrina," a male voice said from behind her.

Surprised, she spun around and lifted her fist. Her foot got tangled in Charlee's backpack, and she fell back against the car, almost tumbling to the ground.

"Whoa, careful." Crash caught her arm.

"Sorry, you startled me." She regained her balance. "You'd never say I was a dancer."

"Hey, we're all clumsy sometimes. I came over to help you into the house. Crunch called and said you'd be coming by." Crash grabbed the backpack and the tray of drinks.

"I wish I'd known. I would've picked you up something." Sabrina helped Charlee out of the car.

"Nah, I need more than a McD's burger to fill this gut." Crash slapped his hand against his flat stomach.

Sabrina wanted to tell him about the guy across the street, but the man was gone when she checked over her shoulder. She scanned up and down the road, but he'd disappeared.

"Something wrong?" Crash asked.

"I saw a guy across the street. He looked like he was taking pictures." Sabrina closed the car door.

"Where?" Crash's humorous expression disappeared as he placed the items he held on the car's bonnet. Sabrina pointed to a cluster of trees nestled between two homes across from Crunch's house. Crash jogged across the street and searched while Sabrina helped Charlee out of the car. After a few minutes, he ran back to where Sabrina stood.

"Mommy, I'm hungry," Charlee complained.

"Well, let's get you inside and get you fed," Crash said with a strained grin.

He tossed Charlee over his shoulder with one hand and grabbed the bags with the other. Charlee squealed with laughter as Crash held her on his shoulder while they headed into the house.

"Sabrina, where's Charlee? I can't find her," Crash shouted as he bounced Charlee on his shoulder.

"I'm here, silly," Charlee said.

"Where?" Crash spun around, making her daughter giggle.

"Mommy, he's crazy," Charlee shouted.

"Maybe a little." Sabrina smiled.

Crash pulled Charlee back to the front of his chest and gasped.

"There you are," he said.

"I was hanging over your shoulder, silly." Charlee shook her head.

Crash brought them into the kitchen, and Sabrina situated Charlee at the table with her cheeseburger and fries. She arranged her meal on the table, but her stomach was in knots, so food was the last thing she wanted.

"Crunch said he'll be here shortly," Crash told her as he pulled a bottle of water out of the fridge.

He was glancing out the window toward the driveway, but something told her he wasn't watching for Crunch. A shiver ran down her spine. Something about the man lurking across the street was unsettling, and Crash's reaction didn't make her feel less uneasy.

"Brent, is everything okay?" Sabrina asked using Crash's given name.

Although all the guys who worked with Crunch and Crash went by nicknames, she didn't use them. When she thought about it, besides Sandy, most of the women who knew them used their given names.

"Sure, wondering who the hell was taking pictures." Crash shrugged.

He was a good-looking guy and single, although he spent a lot of time with Aaron's sister-in-law. Allyson was a widow, raising a teenage son, and worked as an emergency room doctor at the hospital in the city.

"I'm going to take a little stroll outside. Make yourself at home." Crash walked out before she could respond.

It was strange being inside Crunch's home without him there, but she felt comfortable and safe. After they finished eating, she and Charlee snuggled on the couch, watching a kid's show she'd found while channel surfing.

Sabrina glanced around the large living room. Nobody would ever doubt only men lived there. The décor of sports memorabilia, pictures of bikes and cars, and the large screen television made it clear it was bachelor central.

Still, she felt at home surrounded by Crunch's things. She looked above the fireplace at several family pictures on the mantle. Crunch valued his family with the way he displayed the photos.

Sabrina kept glancing at her phone, waiting for Crunch to tell her when he was on the way and why he wanted her at his home. She was ill wondering what to do about Grant. She wasn't going to marry him, but how could she keep him from ruining her life?

He wasn't exactly the easiest person to deal with, and when he wanted something, he wouldn't quit until he got it. Harriet wasn't wrong when she said he wanted things he couldn't have. There was a reason he was pushing her to marry him, but she didn't know what he'd get out of it. If by some slim chance she did marry him, they'd be married in name only.

Could Crunch help keep Grant from releasing the videos that could ruin her life?

Chapter 12

Crunch invited Declan inside the studio and asked Zara to use her office. She seemed annoyed but left, giving Declan a quick glance before closing the door behind her. After offering some coffee to the lawyer, he sat down on the small sofa.

"What's up?" Crunch asked.

"Voznesensky is out on bail," Declan replied.

"I don't understand what happened." Crunch shook his head.

"Someone got to Diamond. We found two burner phones under her pillow when we cleared the safehouse. Each phone dialed a different number. She must've had them when we put her there." Declan sipped from the cup.

"She's a piece of work, that's for sure." Crunch stood up.

"The problem is we believe her testifying was a set up to get close to another target," Declan told him.

"That makes no sense. The only people she interacted with during the time she was in protective custody were me, Rex, and you." Crunch spun around. "Are you saying someone is after you or Saul?"

Declan pulled something out of his briefcase and handed it to Crunch. It was a file folder with several pieces of paper inside. He flipped through them, but he had no idea what they were.

"What is this?" Crunch asked.

"They're text messages between Diamond and one of the burner phones. Luckily she wasn't smart enough to delete them." Declan stepped next to Crunch and pointed to something. "They're talking about you, Crunch. Whoever this is, they want you out of the way,"

Crunch took a closer look at the papers. He read through the messages, but he couldn't see why they would think the conversation was about him until he got to the last page.

Diamond: This guy isn't falling for my flirting.

Unknown: Come on, you can turn a gay man straight.

Diamond: Thanks, but neither of these men is taking the bait.

Unknown: I only want that tattooed jerk. I need to keep him busy and away from the target until I get signed papers.

Crunch knew he was the only one between him and Rex who had visible ink. He had no idea what papers they were talking about or why he needed to keep out of the way.

"I thought she couldn't read," Crunch scoffed, remembering Diamond's testimony in court.

"Yeah, that will be my first question when we confront her," Declan said.

"This is weird." Crunch shook his head.

"Do you know what they're talking about?" Declan asked.

"I've got no idea." Crunch closed the folder and handed it back to Declan.

"Saul doesn't think it has anything to do with you, but Keith is worried, and he has his analysts looking into it. The conversation on the other phone suggests the threat be permanently removed. You may be in danger," Declan explained.

"Why the fuck would I have to be kept busy because of some papers? Maybe it's not even me they're talking about." Crunch suggested.

"Do you want to take a chance on that? Voznesensky is out, and if the unknown on the other phone thinks you're going to put a kink in the plans…." Declan stopped.

"Look, I'm a big boy. I'll keep an eye out, but I need to go. I've got to help a friend with something," Crunch explained.

"Are you talking about Sabrina?" Declan asked.

"Yes." Crunch headed out of the office behind Declan. "How do you know her?"

"I met her when she came in with an old friend of mine. They wanted to draw up wills. I'm sure you know he died." Declan stepped next to his car. "That woman will never have to work a day in her life."

"What are you talking about? Sabrina works her ass off. She's worked three part-time jobs for a couple of years, and she works here with my sister now as well." Crunch figured the guy was mistaken.

"Her late fiancée was Easton Thornton." Declan got in his car.

"Yeah." Crunch knew the guy left Sabrina without any financial support.

"I can't talk about it; you know, lawyer confidentiality and everything." Declan started his car.

"Well, I don't know about that, but Easton left everything to his brother," Crunch said.

"Why would you think that?" Declan looked stunned by the news.

"Sabrina told me. She didn't even know he'd changed the will until after his death," Crunch explained.

For a few seconds, Declan stared through the windshield as if he didn't have words to reply. Crunch figured Declan probably didn't know Easton very well since he seemed shocked by the change.

"Wow, I don't know why he'd do that. He was adamant about taking care of Sabrina. He loved her so much," Declan said.

"You knew him?" Crunch asked.

"Yeah, we rowed together in the summer when we were teenagers." Declan ran his finger across the side of his face where the birthmark covered his cheek.

The lawyer did it a lot when stressed or contemplating something. He wondered if Declan even realized he did it.

"So why didn't he go back to you to change it?" Crunch wondered more to himself.

"I left the firm a couple of weeks after I drew up the wills, but Easton would've gone back to that firm to make any changes." Declan narrowed his eyes. "Something isn't right. I've got a friend still there. I'm going to see if he can tell me about the change."

"I don't think it matters to Sabrina." Crunch didn't understand why Declan would be so concerned about it.

"Maybe not, but Easton dropped by the day after to pick up copies. He wanted me to make sure there was no way his brother could contest the will in the event of his death. He said he didn't trust Grant." Declan pulled on his seatbelt. "We weren't close after our last summer of rowing, but he was a friend once, and I need to make sure nothing fishy happened."

"That guy is an ass." Crunch agreed.

"Yeah, from what I remember of him, he's an entitled prick. He only rowed for one year, but he acted like a professional. When the coach suspended him for going against the rules, he tried to have the coach fired." Declan rolled his eyes. "Grant never came back after that."

"Listen, if you find anything, would you let Sabrina know?" Crunch hoped it would help her get Grant to back off. "This is my number and address. She's there right now and possibly for a few days if I can talk her into it."

"Definitely." Declan took the business card and shoved it into his jacket pocket.

When Declan drove off, Crunch ran inside the studio to say goodbye to his sister and gave her a scaled-down version of why

155

Declan was there. As he headed out to his vehicle, he called Keith. He didn't want to worry about his family becoming a possible target. Crunch wasn't about to take any chances with their safety.

Keith assured him someone was on the way to the dance studio as well as his parents' home, but Crunch needed to let them know the guys were coming. He hated to cause stress in their lives, but he'd never live with himself if anything happened to them. He called Zara and explained everything the situation.

"Be careful, Hunter," Zara pleaded.

"Always," Crunch assured her.

"I know I don't tell you this often enough, but I love you, and I'd be devastated if anything happened to you."

He could hear the hitch in her voice, and it made him feel like shit. She was his little sister, and he should be protecting her, not causing her anxiety.

"I love you too, and I promise to be careful," he said as he hugged her.

Keith told him someone was outside his house when Sabrina arrived, but Crash hadn't seen the guy. Sabrina said the guy was creepy. That one word had the hair on his neck stand up on end. Igor Voznesensky was all kinds of scary-looking. It meant the guy had seen Sabrina and Charlee go into the house. That meant they could be on the asshole's radar.

"That's all she needs to worry about," Crunch muttered to himself.

Sabrina had enough stress with Grant harassing her. The last thing she needed to be concerned about was looking over her shoulder because she spent time with Crunch.

When he pulled into the driveway, he texted Sabrina's brother. He gave Colt a watered-down version of the situation and suggested he come to Hopedale after work. He also asked him to pick up some clothes and belongings for Sabrina and Charlee.

Crunch couldn't let her return to the apartment until he was sure it was safe. Between Grant putting hidden cameras in her apartment and some creepy guy seeing her at his home, the safest place for her was Hopedale, or at least that was what he told himself.

He found Sabrina and Charlee curled up on the sofa, sleeping when he walked inside. Seeing them in his home so cozy caused a warmth to radiate through his chest, and he knew this was what he wanted for the rest of his life.

"They dozed off about twenty minutes ago," Crash whispered from behind Crunch.

"Let them rest." He pointed toward the kitchen.

"Someone was staking out the place when we got here." Crash poured two cups of coffee.

"Did you get a look at him?" Crunch's heart pounded in his chest.

"No, I didn't see him. Sabrina did." Crash handed him a cup.

Crunch placed it on the counter because his stomach suddenly felt like it was going to revolt. He knew who was outside his house because Declan warned him. Crunch wasn't worried about himself, but he was concerned about what the guy could've done to Sabrina and Charlee.

"I can see by that expression on your face that it's not good, but we won't let anyone lay a hand on her or the little one." Crash could read him like a book.

"Maybe I can convince her to stay here. At least for a couple of days," Crunch said, thinking out loud.

"You can try." Crash placed his empty cup in the sink. "I need to run by Allyson's place and help her move some furniture. I'll keep my phone close, so if you need me, give me a shout."

"I will." Crunch headed to the living room.

He grabbed a blanket on the back of the couch and quietly placed it over Sabrina and her daughter. He smiled as Sabrina let out a soft sigh and snuggled deeper into the sofa. She obviously felt comfortable in his home, which made him happy.

Crunch locked the windows and doors and set his alarm before heading to the shower. He stepped out of the bathroom as the alarm started blaring. He quickly wrapped a towel around his waist and ran to the front of the house.

As he stepped into the foyer, he stopped cold. Sabrina stood in the open front door with her hands over her ears, looking completely flustered. Crunch punched the code into the security pad, and the alarm instantly stopped.

"I'm sorry, I woke up and wanted to go outside for some fresh air. I didn't realize I was in Fort Knox." She dropped her hands.

"Don't be sorry. I was in the shower and wanted to make sure everything was locked up. Crash told me someone was outside earlier." Crunch closed and locked the door again.

"I can't believe that didn't wake Charlee. She sleeps like a rock sometimes." Sabrina's voice was soft.

Sabrina's eyes moved down his body, making him suddenly aware he was only wearing a towel. When she lifted her gaze to meet his, her cheeks flushed.

"You've got a lot of tattoos," she said, barely above a whisper.

"I like ink." He swallowed hard as he struggled to keep his dick from showing how much he wanted her.

"It's beautiful." She took a small step toward him.

"Thank you," he whispered as he moved closer.

"I've always wanted to get one, but I've been too scared of…" Sabrina traced her finger across the words on his chest.

The ink on his chest was special to him. Whenever his father wanted to encourage them to take a chance, he'd lift his fists in the air and shout the words, *Carpe Diem*. He decided it would be perfect to put on his chest.

"Seize the day," she murmured.

"Yes," he replied.

"I've never been a Carpe Diem person." Sabrina stepped closer, and he could feel her warm breath across his chest.

"Why do you think that is?" Crunch's breath hitched as her hand smoothed across his left pectoral.

"I don't know." She lifted her gaze to meet his. "Are you that type of person?"

"I am in some ways, but in others, I tend to be more cautious." Crunch lifted his hand and tucked a piece of her hair behind her ear.

She smiled as her fingertip lifted the small ring on his right nipple. Crunch also liked piercings and had several, including his nose and both ears. There was still one he wanted to get, but when he looked up how it was done, he decided it wasn't worth it.

"You like piercings too," Sabrina murmured.

"Yeah," he whispered.

He cupped the side of her head, and she leaned into his touch. She moved her cheek against his palm, and her eyes fluttered closed as she lifted her other hand to rest against his chest.

"What things are you more cautious with?" She opened her eyes.

"With you," Crunch admitted.

Crunch swallowed as he rested his other hand on her hip and moved closer. Her chest touched his, and his cock jerked as the sweet scent of strawberries filled his senses. He always loved the smell, but on her, it was intoxicating.

"Why?" She ran her hand up his body until it rested against his cheek.

"Because I've never wanted anyone like I want you," he answered honestly.

Sabrina's mouth opened slightly, and her pink tongue flicked out and glided across her lower lip. The moisture made it glisten. It was as if it drew him in like a moth to a flame, and his eyes locked with hers as he lowered his head.

His lips brushed against hers in a feather-like kiss that caused her breath to hitch. Crunch pulled back a little to give her a chance to change her mind. Sabrina wrapped her hands around the back of his head and pulled him down, pressing her lips against his with some hesitancy.

When Crunch backed her against the wall in the foyer, she gripped his hair and tilted her head to give him better access to her mouth. He licked across the seam of her lips, begging to enter, and she opened for him. Their tongues tangled together as he pressed his body against hers.

There was no way he could hide his arousal, and she didn't seem to care. Her moans made him painfully hard, and he almost didn't hear the sound of his phone ringing in the other room.

"Fuck," Crunch growled against her lips.

"What?" She was panting as much as he was.

"That's probably the alarm company. If I don't get it, they'll call the police," he explained and ran to the bedroom.

Crunch grabbed the phone and let the operator know he wasn't in danger. Once he gave them the password, he tossed the phone on his bed and blew out a breath.

The interruption was probably needed because he would've taken Sabrina right in the middle of the entry. He wanted her, but taking her for the first time in the foyer while her daughter was asleep in the next room wasn't his idea of romantic.

Crunch pulled on a pair of his jockstrap underwear and slipped into a pair of track pants. On the way out of his room, he put on a T-shirt. He found Sabrina in the living room with Charlee. The little girl looked up with a smile.

"I had a nap on your couch." Charlee yawned.

"I saw that," Crunch replied.

"I'm hungry, Mommy." Charlee rubbed her eyes.

"Well, lucky for you, I know the best place in the world to get chicken nuggets and fries." Crunch sat next to the little girl.

"McDonald's?" Charlee tilted her head.

"No." Crunch shook his head.

"Where?" She climbed up on his lap.

"My kitchen," Crunch told her.

"You can make chicken nuggets?" Charlee's eyes opened wide with surprise.

"Oh yeah." Crunch stood up, lifting the little girl in his arms. "You can help me make them."

"Yay," Charlee squealed as Sabrina followed Crunch into the kitchen.

He assembled all the ingredients for his homemade crispy chicken burgers on the counter. Instead of leaving the breasts whole, he cut them into small pieces and let Charlee dip them in the coating. She chattered about helping her grandmother make cookies, and then when Sabrina started to prepare the salad, Charlee went off on a tangent about how spinach was disgusting.

Crunch didn't mind the chatty little girl, and when he glanced up, Sabrina was watching him. He wanted to know what was going through her head, but the conversation he wanted wasn't appropriate with a child in the room.

That kiss set him on fire, and he wanted more, much more, but did she want the same? Was she just caught off guard when he appeared in only a towel? She had to be attracted to him to kiss him, right? Cora told him Sabrina was his future, but she was never wrong. Was Cora the Cupid right again?

Chapter 13

Sabrina smiled as Charlee devoured the homemade chicken nuggets. She'd enjoyed them as well but was distracted by the memory of the kiss they'd shared. She made the first move by touching his muscled body because she couldn't help herself.

His body. God.

The man was perfection in every way with his defined pectorals, slim waist, six-pack abdominals, and that V pointing down to what he had hidden under the towel. She felt the hard length of him when he pressed her against the wall and kissed her like she was his only source of nourishment.

If the phone hadn't interrupted them, she probably would've let him have her right in the front foyer of his home. She squeezed her legs together to ease the ache caused by thinking about him. The thought of being naked with him made her body erupt into goosebumps.

"Sabrina, are you okay? Your face is flushed." Crunch pressed the back of his hand against her cheek.

She flinched away and jumped to her feet. There was no way he could tell what she was thinking, but how was she supposed to explain the blushing? Well, it wasn't precisely blushing, it was arousal, and damn, was she turned on.

Sabrina hadn't been with anyone since Easton. Most people wouldn't believe it, but a relationship wasn't her priority. Crunch was the first man to make her think about falling in love again.

"I'm fine. A little warm," Sabrina lied.

"I'll turn up the air a little. July is kind of hit or miss in Newfoundland, as you know. You don't know if you'll need air conditioning or a winter coat." Crunch chuckled.

"Yeah." She smiled.

"Mommy, are we staying at Crunch's house tonight?" Charlee asked as she shoved a fry in her mouth.

"No," Sabrina answered.

"Yes," Crunch said at the same time.

Sabrina stared at him wide-eyed, and her heart thudded against her ribs. She hadn't planned to stay overnight, and she certainly didn't know if spending the night at Crunch's house was a smart thing to do.

"I'm confused." Charlee tilted her head.

"Why don't you take the rest of your supper and go watch cartoons while your mom and I talk." Crunch picked up Charlee's plate and glass.

Charlee scampered out of the kitchen with Crunch behind her. Sabrina sat on one of the chairs and wrapped her hands around the glass of water she'd been drinking.

"I think we need to talk," Crunch said when he returned.

"I can't stay here," she practically shouted.

"If it's about what happened earlier..." Crunch began, but she held up her hand.

"No, that's not it. I need to go home. I don't have clothes for Charlee or me and... other things. I can't leave Colt home alone...I know he's not a kid, but..." Sabrina blew out a breath.

"Actually, I texted Colt. He's coming here when he gets off work," Crunch said.

"You told him about Grant?" Sabrina shot to her feet.

"I gave him a condensed version of the situation," Crunch told her.

"He's going to have an aneurysm when I tell him." Sabrina sighed.

"I told him to bring an overnight bag for himself, you, and Charlee. That way, I can get Keith to send Smash and Sandy over to go through your apartment." Crunch took her hand.

Sabrina knew Smash was one of the men who worked with Crunch and saw him many times when he came to the diner. His real name was Gage Hodder, but like all the other employees of NES, he went by a nickname.

"By the way, Declan told me something I'm not sure you know." Crunch motioned to the chair.

Sabrina sat down and folded her hands in front of her. What would Declan know? She'd only met him the one time and hadn't had any contact with him again until she'd seen him earlier that day.

"Do I want to know?" She sighed.

"He couldn't tell me much for legal reasons, but he did say Easton went back to see him the day after you two filed your wills. Your fiancée was concerned about Grant contesting the will if anything happened to him," Crunch explained.

"Why would Grant contest it if Easton left him everything?" Sabrina furrowed her brow.

"I don't know, but Declan is going to check into it and get back to you. He thinks something weird is going on." Crunch covered her folded hands with his.

The warmth of his touch made her racing heart calm, and she felt safe. How his touch could both calm her and ignite her libido was like some sort of magic. She'd give anything to see where things would go with him, but she couldn't until she had the monkey off her back.

"I've got lots of room here. You and Charlee can take the guest room. It has a bathroom and a great view of the beach." Crunch smiled.

"You're making it hard to say no." She sighed.

"That's what I'm trying to do." He grinned.

Sabrina dropped her gaze to his full lips and smiled at the dab of ketchup on his mouth. Without thinking, she wiped her thumb against his lips, and he caught it before she pulled back.

"You had ketchup on your…" Sabrina gasped when he sucked her thumb into his mouth.

"That's the best ketchup I've ever tasted," Crunch whispered.

His voice was so deep and rumbly she could almost feel it in the pit of her stomach. She bit her lower lip as he placed soft kisses across her wrist then lifted his eyes to meet hers.

"I'm not going to lie, Sabrina. I like you a lot. I have for a long time, but wanting you to stay here has nothing to do with that. I don't want that son of a bitch to be able to get to you or Charlee." Crunch held both her hands in his.

"I like you too, and if it weren't for Grant, I wouldn't hesitate to stay, but I believe he's tied up with some bad people, and I don't want to put you or Brent in danger." Sabrina sighed.

"You let Crash and me worry about that. We're big boys, and trust me, we've dealt with bad people before." Crunch kissed her knuckles. "Stay?"

How could she say no when he was so gentle and caring? Any woman in their right mind would jump into his arms and shout *yes,* at the top of their lungs. He was right, he could take care of himself, and she might sleep better knowing she was in a house with Crunch. Plus, Crash and her brother.

"Okay," she whispered.

"Good." Crunch smiled.

She'd practically had to beg him to let her help clean up after supper. Not that it was a lot to clean up. Once they packed everything into the dishwasher, she wiped down the counters, and he cleaned the stove.

Crash and Colt arrived a short time later, and Crunch let him know he'd made sure to put a plate of food away for him and Crash.

While they ate, the three men talked about the situation with Grant. Sabrina didn't want to hear any more about Grant and went to settle Charlee in bed for the night.

After reading two stories and telling her why they had to sleep in the same bed, Charlee finally drifted off. Sabrina tiptoed out of the room when she heard Charlee's soft snore, telling her the little one was out for the night.

She found Crunch in the kitchen with Declan but no sign of Crash and Colt. They looked at papers on the table and didn't notice her until she cleared her throat. Declan looked up and pulled all the documents together as if he was hiding something.

"Sorry, I probably shouldn't have been showing him this without your permission," Declan said.

"Show him what?" Sabrina sat across from the lawyer.

"This is a copy of Easton's legal will. The only one that was filed and notarized." Declan pushed the papers across the table.

"Everything was left to Grant. I know that already." Sabrina didn't bother to look at the papers.

"No, it wasn't. This will was filed with probate courts and the only legal will." Declan tapped his finger on the paper.

"What?" Sabrina gasped as she picked it up and started to skim through the will.

It was the same as the one she saw when she and Easton met with Declan. How was that possible? She'd seen the other will, hadn't she? Sabrina sat back in the chair. She hadn't seen it because the shock of what Finley McDonald told her was too overwhelming.

"But the lawyer said…" Sabrina whispered.

"This will wasn't pulled when Easton died. My buddy told me you guys didn't even go into the office." Declan looked pissed.

"We didn't go to the office where you worked. Grant said Easton changed lawyers." Sabrina couldn't control the shaking.

"Who was the lawyer?" Declan asked.

"McDonald, Finley McDonald." She was glad she remembered the name.

"Fuck," Declan grumbled.

"What?" Crunch and Sabrina said together.

"Finley McDonald is one of the lawyers tangled up with Mitch Snider." Declan pulled out his phone. "Is this the guy?"

Crunch covered her hand with his. The warmth made her feel better, and she looked up at Declan's phone. She nodded at the picture of a mousy-looking man, and anger began to override her fear.

"To be honest, he looked like he was ready to jump out of his skin at the meeting." Sabrina placed her other hand on top of Crunch's forearm.

"Someone's behind all of these groups. Whoever it is, they manage to keep their hands clean. Nobody is willing to turn over on them. The one person going to give us information ended up dead." Declan seemed frustrated with the whole thing.

"You mean Mitch Snider," Crunch said.

"Yeah," Declan replied.

"I don't understand what any of this has to do with Easton's will." Sabrina sighed.

"Maybe Grant needed money," Declan suggested.

"Grant needed control." Sabrina snapped. "I swear I could kill him for all this."

"Sweetheart, that's probably not a great thing to say in front of someone who works at the Crown Attorney's office." Crunch squeezed her hand.

"I guess not, but what do I do? If this is Easton's legal will, it means everything is mine." Sabrina sat up straight with the realization. "The house and the studio. They're mine. Oh, my God. He made me believe Easton left us homeless and without anything to support us. He basically threw us out on the street. That cold-hearted son of a bitch."

Sabrina jumped to her feet and started to pace the floor. She was furious, and she'd love to have Grant Thornton in front of her at that moment.

Chapter 14

Declan left with a promise to check into how Finley and Grant connected to the group he was investigating. He also promised to have a lawyer from his old firm contact Sabrina and help her fight Grant for what was rightfully hers.

"You know it's not about the money. I could care less about that." Sabrina was ranting.

"I know." Crunch stood in the kitchen, watching her pace.

"Hunter, he made me believe Easton didn't want us taken care of in the event of his death. Grant made me believe Easton never cared about Charlee and me. Oh, he tried to cover it by saying Easton was in a ton of debt and didn't want to burden me." Sabrina blinked to hold back the tears, but the crack in her voice gave her away.

"Sweetheart," Crunch whispered as he walked toward her.

"I told Easton I hated him for abandoning me. I screamed at his headstone the day after I found out. I said he was no better than Grant." Sabrina's lip quivered.

"You didn't know, Sabrina. Grant and that lawyer lied to you." Crunch tried to calm her down.

"Not just me. He lied to his mother. Harriet was there when that damn lawyer told us." Sabrina blew out a shaky breath. "Do I tell her this? Do I tell her what a bastard her son is?"

"I think the first thing you need to do is wait until you can get your head around this. Then we'll talk to the lawyer Declan is getting in touch with. I don't think you should call his mom like this." Crunch finally got close enough to take her hands.

"I… can't." Sabrina pulled away and hurried out of the kitchen.

It was painful to hold back from running after her, but she needed time to process everything. Maybe calling Colt would help. Her brother left to stay at his girlfriend's house and told Crunch to call if Sabrina needed anything. He needed to give the guy a heads up.

He tapped Colt's number on his phone while he scanned the road across the street. He was still wary, especially knowing someone was outside his home earlier. There was no doubt about who it was, but it was a mystery why he was a target for this guy.

Colt answered on the third ring, and Crunch explained everything. He promised the guy Sabrina was okay and he didn't have to drive back to Hopedale.

"I'll kill that son of a bitch," Colt said with a growl.

Crunch didn't doubt he could rip Grant's head off. Colt was a big guy, and he may be Sabrina's younger brother, but Crunch knew how it felt to want a sibling to be happy and safe. If Zara was in the same situation, he knew he'd rip the guy's head off.

"I know how you feel, but that's not going to help Sabrina. Let's wait until we talk to the lawyer and go from there," Crunch suggested, surprising how calm he sounded.

"How are we supposed to trust another lawyer after this?" Colt sighed.

"Declan isn't going to send someone he doesn't trust, and I trust Declan," Crunch said.

"I hope you're right. Take care of my sister. I'm taking a personal day from work tomorrow, and I'll be there in the morning. I can take a couple of days off. I've still got a month before schools open up again." Colt sounded calmer.

"I hope we can convince your sister to take the day off too," Crunch said.

"Isn't she working at the dance studio tomorrow?" Colt asked.

"Yes," Crunch replied.

"Maybe she should go. She always says dancing helps her deal with stress." Colt chuckled.

Crunch smiled because his sister and mother said the same thing, and if he was honest, he found dancing helped him relax when things were getting too much. Maybe if they went to the studio, they could practice the routine. Probably put their spin on it and make it more personal to them. That would get both their minds off what was happening in their lives.

Crunch locked the doors and window, then set the alarm before heading to his bedroom. He stopped in front of the guest

175

room, and he wanted to go inside to check on Sabrina, but it sounded quiet, and he didn't want to chance waking either her or Charlee.

Crunch didn't bother to turn on the light in his bedroom as he closed the door behind him. He pulled off his shirt and tossed it in the basket by the bathroom. As he placed his phone on the nightstand, something near the window caught his attention. He reached for the lamp, but her soft voice stopped him.

"Don't turn on the light, please," Sabrina whispered.

Crunch's hand froze above the lamp. He could make out her silhouette in front of the window. She stood with her back to him and her arms wrapped around herself.

"I was afraid I'd wake Charlee, so I came in here until I could calm down." Sabrina sighed.

"Are you feeling better?" Crunch walked closer and sat down on the trunk at the foot of his bed.

Sabrina didn't say anything for a few minutes, and when she started to speak again, she turned around. The moonlight illuminated the side of her face and around her head, looking like a halo. He didn't think she could look more beautiful, but she took his breath away.

"I don't know how to feel," she said. "I never grasped how angry I was with Easton until I realized I directed it at the wrong person."

"You didn't know. You were lied to," Crunch whispered.

"I was so stupid…" She sat down on the window seat.

"You're not stupid, Sabrina." Crunch immediately knelt at her feet and held her face between his hands.

"I should've read the papers. I should've trusted Easton would never do that to Charlee and me." Sabrina sniffed as tears streamed down her cheeks.

"You were grieving. You shouldn't have to worry about Grant taking advantage of that," Crunch said.

He hated the pain in her eyes and would do everything to make it go away. Crunch wanted to see the same joyful expression she wore at the Canada Day celebrations. He longed to make her smile and put that brightness back in her eyes.

"I'm not going to let him get away with this. He's going to pay," Sabrina said through gritted teeth.

"He won't get away with this, but you've got to promise me you won't do anything until we talk to the lawyer." Crunch placed his hands on her shoulders as he stood up.

"I want to confront him. I want to scream at him and call him a... a... a...I don't know... what do you call someone who would do this?" Sabrina jumped to her feet.

"A lot of things, but I wouldn't say them in front of a lady," Crunch returned.

The corners of her mouth lifted in a small smile. He wanted to make her happy and protect her from any heartache and pain. Crunch wanted to be a hero who could fix everything that took away her smile.

"I'm so sorry to involve you in all this," she whispered.

"Don't be sorry. I'd do anything for you and your little girl. I'll be by your side as long as you need me." Crunch meant every word.

She met his eyes and placed her hand against his cheek. Her touch was warm, and he leaned into her palm. A simple touch from her made his heart race, and he covered her hand with his as he gently brushed his lips against her wrist.

When she leaned forward, he held his breath. Her lips touched lightly against his, once, then again. He wanted to pull her into his arms and devour her mouth. Maybe finish what they'd started earlier, but he couldn't pounce on her like a wild animal.

"Your lips are so soft." She sighed against his mouth.

"Sabrina," Crunch murmured as she kissed him again.

"I want…" She traced her tongue along the seam of his mouth.

He opened to her, and his tongue darted inside her mouth. His arms slipped around her body as he moved between her knees. Her hands rested against the sides of his neck as the kiss deepened. His dick didn't take long to become rock hard, and it pressed against the zipper of his jeans.

When they stood up, Sabrina pressed her body against his as her arms wrapped around his waist. Her hands slipped down and cupped his ass, making him groan involuntarily. Crunch had to stop before things went further. She was vulnerable, and the last thing he wanted was to take advantage of that.

"Sabrina," Crunch mumbled against her mouth.

"Hmm." She gently bit his lower lip.

"We… fuck…we can't…" His words came out like he was in pain.

Crunch was finding it hard to think when Sabrina slipped her hands down the back of his jeans and dug her nails into the bare flesh of his ass. His cock pulsated painfully, and he thrust against her instinctively.

"We need to… stop… Oh, God." Crunch panted as he pulled his mouth from hers.

She hadn't even touched his cock, and he was ready to go off in his pants. He never wanted anyone so desperately, and it was difficult for him to think with her so close.

"I want you," Sabrina whispered.

"God knows I want you too. So damn much, but you're upset, and I don't want you to regret—"

Crunch's words stopped when a small red dot moved up her cheek to her temple. It took him a millisecond to realize it was coming from outside, and every hair on the back of his neck stood up. Almost simultaneously, he took Sabrina to the floor, and the window shattered.

Crunch kept his body over Sabrina like a blanket while a hail of gunfire whizzed over them. It was probably only a few minutes, but it seemed like forever before the popping sounds stopped. He didn't want to get up and look until he was sure Sabrina was out of the line of fire.

"I need you to roll over and stay low to the ground. We're going to crawl out of here," Crunch whispered in her ear.

Sabrina didn't speak but nodded when he lifted his body enough for her to roll onto her belly. They were halfway across the room when his bedroom door flew open, and Crash crouched next to the entrance with his Beretta Model 92 in his hand.

"Get her out of here. I'm going to see if the prick is still out there." Crash moved so they could get into the hallway.

"Charlee?" Sabrina gasped as they exited the room.

"Go check on her but stay low," Crunch warned.

Sabrina opened the door to the guest room, and the little girl was still sleeping contently. Crunch blew out a breath of relief when he saw Charlee was okay, but his body shook with rage, knowing someone scared them.

"Sabrina, take her into the bathroom and sit in the tub. There are no windows in there. I need you to stay there until we come to get you." Crunch crouched in front of them.

When he heard the click of the bathroom door, he headed back to his bedroom. He stepped inside, staying low to ensure if anyone was still watching, they couldn't see him through the now shattered window.

"You think it's the guy who was outside earlier today?" Crash asked as he peeked out the broken window.

"Who else?" Crunch grabbed his weapon from the safe in the closet.

He always had it locked safe unless he was working. Newfoundland wasn't usually a place for drive-by shootings or where people carried guns. Many people in smaller communities still didn't lock their doors, but Crunch discovered danger could come out of nowhere.

"We should probably keep these at arms reach for a while." Crash held up his weapon.

Before Crunch could speak, the blaring of sirens started faint but grew louder as he made it to the front door. He sighed with relief and lowered his weapon. It seemed like someone called the police, which meant half of the town was about to appear on his doorstep.

"Might as well get ready for a crowd," Crash said as if reading Crunch's mind.

"I'll go make sure Sabrina and Charlee are okay." Crunch didn't even wait for a response.

Chapter 15

Sabrina held Charlee tightly in her arms as they sat in the tub. Her daughter whimpered softly in her arms, and she tried to soothe her little girl. It was difficult, considering her heart pounded so hard it seemed as if it would jump out of her chest.

Her legs started to cramp as she hunched down in the tub, and it seemed like they'd been in the bathroom for hours. She could hear the sound of sirens, but Crunch told her to stay until he came to get her. She jumped when she heard a creak outside the bathroom door.

"Sabrina," Crunch called through the locked door.

She climbed out of the tub and hurried to open the door. Charlee clung to her as if Sabrina would disappear. It was hard to steady her legs since she'd sat crouched in the bathtub with forty extra pounds on her lap.

"The P-O-L-I-C-E are coming." Crunch spelled the word *police*.

"Why are the police coming?" Charlee lifted her head off Sabrina's shoulder.

"She's pretty smart," Crunch chuckled.

"Too smart sometimes." Sabrina followed Crunch into the bedroom.

"The police are coming because someone was making a lot of noise and broke some windows in my house." Crunch bent down, so he was at eye level with Charlee.

"It was really loud," Charlee said as she looked down at Crunch's hand. "Is that a gun?"

"Shit." Crunch shoved the weapon down the back of his jeans and locked eyes with Sabrina.

"That's not a nice word. Why do you got a gun?" Charlee wasn't going to give up.

"It's for his job, baby. Why don't you and I lie down?" Sabrina carried Charlee to the large bed.

"Are you gonna lay down too, Crunch?" Charlee asked.

"I sure am. As soon as I talk to the police." Crunch headed out of the room.

"I'll make sure Mommy don't take up all the bed." Charlee yawned as she snuggled into Sabrina.

"I guess I'm sleeping in here," Crunch whispered.

"I guess so." Sabrina held Charlee close to her side.

"I'll be back as soon as I can." Crunch walked out and closed the door.

Sabrina lay in silence with Charlee nestled in her arms. The adrenalin started to fade, and her muscles relaxed as she sank into the mattress. She had never heard gunshots before and didn't want to hear it again. Sabrina had never even seen a gun other than on television, and to see one in Crunch's hand was a reminder that his job could be dangerous.

She always thought of Newfoundland as a safe place. Still, the last couple of years, she'd overheard people in the town talk about kidnappings, shootings, human trafficking, and disturbed individuals looking for revenge. How could anyone be safe?

Once she knew Charlee was asleep, she grabbed the toiletry bag her brother brought and headed back into the bathroom. When she placed her palms on top of the marble counter and stared at herself in the mirror, she gasped. The stress she suffered since Easton's death was hard, but the pressure from Grant played havoc with her, and she looked ten years older.

Then the events of the evening played over in her head. If Crunch hadn't knocked her to the ground, she'd probably be dead. It made all the crap seem small compared to losing her life or losing Crunch.

"He saved my life," she whispered.

Something in her chest seemed to flip, and her eyes filled with tears. He covered her body with his and never hesitated for a second. Crunch didn't consider his safety, he wanted to shield her from danger. Could he protect her from Grant?

Grant had the potential to ruin her life or at least humiliate her, but with the news from Declan, she had the ball in her court. If it was true, the police could arrest Grant for fraud at the least. She should wait to confront him as Crunch suggested, but it was tough to do when annoyed.

"No, I need to face him and tell him I know everything and I'm not afraid of him," Sabrina muttered to herself. "Grant thinks he can control me, but I'm going to fight back. To hell with him."

She had to go to the studio in the morning, but after that, she'd march right to Grant's house and tell him she knew everything. Sabrina had the upper hand because he'd only make himself look worse by releasing them.

As she prepared for bed, she tried to put together a plan of attack. She was a little scared of what Grant would do, especially with everything she'd learned.

She reached into her toiletry bag and pulled out her toothbrush, but her brother had forgotten the toothpaste. Sabrina rolled her eyes as she glanced around the small bathroom. She checked in the line of drawers at the side of the vanity and was about to give up when she found a new tube of toothpaste.

She smiled as her eyes zeroed in on the box of condoms sitting next to some other essential bathroom products. It was nice that Crunch thought of his guests' safety, she thought as she closed the drawer and finished getting ready for bed.

Sabrina carefully crawled into bed next to Charlee and sighed as she closed her eyes. Tomorrow would be the day she made Grant Thornton sorry he was ever born.

Chapter 16

Crunch watched Aaron take a statement from Crash. Keith's youngest brother showed up right as the two police cruisers pulled into Crunch's driveway. Aaron, or A.J. as everyone called him, told the other officers to check out Crunch's bedroom while he took statements.

"Do you know how many rounds?" Aaron asked.

"I don't know. Jesus. All I heard was a bunch of pops and glass breaking. It woke me out of my sleep, A.J." Crash sighed.

"What about you?" Aaron asked.

"At least ten or fifteen. Maybe more. I was more concerned with keeping Sabrina and me safe," Crash told them.

"You were both in your room?" Aaron lifted an eyebrow.

"We were talking," Crash snapped.

"Uh-huh." Aaron dropped his head and started typing something into his phone.

"Declan thinks that fella who shot the strip club owner could be watching Crunch," Crash blurted out.

"You mean the hitman Declan is trying to put away?" Aaron's head snapped up.

"Yeah," Crunch said.

"Why would he be watching you?" Aaron shoved his phone in his pocket.

"Have no idea. According to Declan, the stripper was supposed to get the tattooed guy out of the way. We assumed it was me." Crunch straddled one of the kitchen chairs and rested his arms on the back.

"There was a guy outside when Sabrina got here today, but I didn't get a look at him," Crash said.

Crunch wasn't sure Voznesensky was after him, but it was starting to look like someone wanted him out of the way. The memory of the laser on the side of Sabrina's face made his stomach feel like it was in knots.

He was in full view of the window, so if Crunch was the target, they could've easily zeroed in on him. He saw the red light flickering against her temple, which told him she was in danger.

"I think Sabrina was the target," Crunch said with a hitch in his voice.

"Why do you think that?" Aaron asked.

"The laser was on her. Whoever it was could easily see me. We were both in front of the window. She was the target." Crunch jumped to his feet.

"But why?" Crash asked.

"The only thing I can think of is Declan found out her late fiancée's brother may have stolen her inheritance by passing off a fake document leaving everything to him. According to Declan, Sabrina should have been left a fortune." Crunch was pacing.

"Maybe I should go talk to this guy," Aaron stood up.

"I want to go with you. If this guy tried to put a hit on Sabrina, he's going to be sorry he was ever born." Crunch fisted his hands at his sides.

"Let me check into some things first but keep this under your hat until I get back to you." Aaron started to head out of the house behind the other officers.

They'd collected evidence in the bedroom and told Crunch he should probably sleep elsewhere for the night. There was glass everywhere, and with the windows gone, it was too easy for someone to try again.

"I'll sleep on the couch," Crash yawned. "My bed is covered too. The bastard got almost all the windows in the back of the house. Fucker."

"I think all of you should go to *The Compound* to be safe. At least we know nobody is getting in there," Aaron suggested. "I'll keep a car here all night to make sure the house is secure, but you've got to think about Sabrina and the kid."

"I'll stay in one of the bunkhouses. I'll grab some essentials." Crash ran to his room.

An hour later, they settled Charlee in the biggest room of the safehouse. The little girl still insisted she'd leave room for Crunch when he was ready to go to bed, and then she snuggled against her mother.

Crunch could probably sleep in one of the other rooms, but he wanted to check on Sabrina and Charlee first. He pushed open the door quietly and smiled at the sight in front of him. Sabrina was curled up on her side with Charlee practically spread eagle on most of the queen-sized bed. It looked like the little girl was the one who was going to take up the bed. He pulled the duvet over Sabrina and Charlee, trying not to wake them.

"What time is it?" Sabrina mumbled.

"It's about three in the morning. Go back to sleep," Crunch whispered.

She grabbed his hand and tugged him down next to her. She rolled over and glanced at Charlee on the other side of the bed. When she reached over to pull the little girl to the middle of the mattress, Crunch stopped her.

"What are you doing?"

"When she wakes up, and you aren't on that side of the bed, she'll say I took up too much room," Sabrina said quietly. "Besides, I need to know you're here next to us."

Sabrina gazed into his eyes as she lifted his hand to her lip, and he reciprocated before he walked around the bed. He placed his head on the pillow and faced Sabrina, but Charlee moved, and her hand connected with his face with a loud slap.

"Oh, I'm sorry," Sabrina whispered but let out a little giggle. "She's not exactly a motionless sleeper."

"It's okay. I've had worse smacks in the face." Crunch gently placed Charlee's hand next to her, and Sabrina tucked it under the blanket.

"You may want to watch her—" Sabrina didn't get a chance to finish her sentence.

Charlee shifted on the bed and her foot shot up to his groin. Thankfully, he swung his legs away before she connected with the most sensitive part of his body.

"Feet," Sabrina whispered.

"Would it be wrong to strap her down?" Crunch smirked.

"I think that sort of thing is frowned upon," Sabrina whispered as she tucked a pillow down between Crunch and Charlee.

"You think that will protect me?" Crunch took Sabrina's hand and linked their fingers together.

"I hope so." She smiled as she tucked her other hand under her cheek.

"Goodnight, sweetheart," Crunch said.

"Goodnight, Hunter," Sabrina whispered and closed her eyes.

He couldn't sleep, mostly because he was sick thinking about what could've happened to Sabrina if he hadn't been close by. As the bile rose in his throat for what seemed like the hundredth time, he swallowed it down and watched Sabrina relax as she drifted off to sleep.

The following day, he was tired, not to mention pissed, and the last thing he wanted to do was go to the dance studio, but he needed to keep Sabrina distracted. They went back to his house while Charlee stayed at the safehouse with Sandy. He only got angrier at the sight of the broken glass all over his bedroom.

"I can clean that up," Sabrina said as she glanced around.

"That's okay. Crash is going to make sure it gets done before we get back." Crunch didn't look at her.

He hadn't even asked anyone to clear out the place, but he didn't want her worrying. He'd shoot Crash a text to take care of things before they went back.

He didn't know how long they'd have to stay at the safehouse. Considering Aaron had no idea who shot at them, it wouldn't be safe for any of them to stay there. Obviously, the shooter knew where he lived.

"There's a fair at the community center today. Sandy called and offered to take Charlee. Her older girls are going, and they're taking some of their younger siblings and cousins." Sabrina scanned the room nervously.

"If Sandy is going with them, Charlee will be in good hands. Chances are most if not all of the O'Connor's will be there." Crunch walked toward her. "She'll be safe."

"I know. I need to get to your mom's studio." Sabrina began to turn away from him.

He caught her hand, and she met his eyes. She seemed so small, but there was something in her eyes he couldn't quite figure out. She gently squeezed his hand and gave him a small smile.

"I'm fine," she said.

"I didn't ask," Crunch replied.

"I could see the question in your eyes. I'm still rattled because of last night, but I know I'm safe with you." She lifted her other hand and cupped his cheek. "You saved my life."

"I'll protect you with everything I have." Crunch covered her hand where it lay against his face.

"I wonder if we're ever going to have a kiss that's not going to be interrupted." She took a step closer.

"We keep trying until we do," Crunch whispered as he lowered his mouth to hers.

He moved his hands into her thick tresses and tilted her head to give him better access to her mouth. Sabrina moaned as his tongue glided across the seam of her lips, begging to enter. She fisted the hair at the back of his head and opened for him. Their tongues tangled together in a dance that had him lifting her into his arms and bracing her against the wall.

Sabrina wrapped her legs around his hips and squeezed them, causing his growing dick to press against the heat between her legs. He could feel the wetness through their clothes as he ground against her.

"God, Sabrina," Crunch murmured against her mouth.

"Hunter, don't stop," she panted.

"I don't want to, but…" Crunch's words halted when she nipped his lower lip.

"No buts. I need you, and I want you now." She held herself up with her legs while she pulled her blouse over her head.

Crunch sucked in a breath as she revealed her naked breasts. No bra, just firm, round breasts big enough to fit in his hand, and her hard pink nipples begged for his mouth. He lowered his head and flicked his tongue against one. When he sucked it into his mouth, she gasped as she fisted his hair in her hands.

"Oh… yes," Sabrina whispered.

"So delicious. I could feed on them all day long," Crunch murmured against her breast.

He glanced back at the bed and cursed under his breath. Glass covered the top of the blankets, and he knew even if he threw them on the floor, they could still end up rolling around on shards of glass. Before he could say anything, she slipped down from his arms and picked up her shirt.

"I'm sorry. We keep…" Crunch started to say, but she grabbed his hand and tugged him out of the room.

"No interruptions," she whispered as they moved to the guest room.

"No interruptions." Crunch growled.

She tossed her shirt to the side, and he closed the door behind them. Crunch tugged his shirt over his head as he backed her toward the bed. His dick practically cried out for release from his jeans, but if he finally got to be with Sabrina, he wanted to make it last as long as possible.

"What about Brent?" Sabrina mumbled against his lips.

"He's not coming here today, and there is a police cruiser outside if anyone else decides they want to come in here." Crunch nipped her lower lip.

She smiled and placed soft feathery kisses down his jaw to his chest. She kissed around his pierced nipple then slowly circled it with her tongue. His head fell back when she pressed her lips together and gave the ring a gentle tug.

"Fuck," Crunch growled between his teeth.

"Did that hurt?" Sabrina asked.

"In a good way," Crunch whispered.

Sabrina kissed across his chest and nipped her way up the side of his neck. His body erupted into goosebumps as she stopped at his ear and gently sucked on the lobe. Crunch's cock jumped, and he grabbed her by the ass to lift her into his arms.

"Fuck, I want you so bad," Crunch moaned against her neck as he lowered her onto the bed.

"Take me," Sabrina purred into his ear.

She didn't have to tell him twice. He circled his tongue down the side of her neck, kissed his way to each of her beautiful breasts, and slowly slipped her yoga pants down her toned legs.

The scent of her arousal and the sight of her panties, soaked with her wetness, almost sent him over the edge. He had to taste her, and once her pants were on the floor, he glided his tongue across her stomach. It was flat but showed the marks from when she was pregnant with Charlee. It turned him on even more if that was possible.

He could spend hours kissing every inch of her sweet body but knowing what was waiting for him under her panties had him slip his tongue under the waistband of her underwear. Luckily, God blessed him with a long tongue, and he could taste her sweet juices before he slipped off the barrier.

He continued to remove her panties until she could kick them to the floor. When his tongue gently flicked over her tiny bundle of nerves, causing her to arch off the bed, he grabbed her thighs and shoved them up on his shoulders.

"Hunter," Sabrina cried out as she fisted the hair on the top of his head.

"You taste delectable, baby." Crunch growled against her pussy.

His tongue moved slowly between her folds, devouring every drop of her excitement. Except for a small area of curls, she was bare, and he pushed her folds apart with his fingers. He dropped to his knees and leaned close to her sex. Slowly, he slid his long tongue inside her and swirled it.

"Ah… Oh yes." Sabrina lifted her hips off the bed.

Crunch pushed in and out of her wet entrance and moved his thumb to her clitoris. He used firm, gentle circles to stimulate her while fucking her with his tongue.

His cock throbbed painfully inside its confinement, begging to be set free. The minute he released his dick, he wouldn't be able to hold back from slamming into her.

"Fuck, honey. You taste delicious." Crunch moaned against her sex.

"Don't stop," Sabrina tugged on his hair.

Crunch smiled against her folds, enjoying the forceful way she tried to take control of the way he was eating her. He couldn't disappoint her, and he drove his tongue into her again. He flicked and circled inside her as he continued to stimulate her clit.

He felt her clench around his tongue and moan his name as her body convulsed with her release. He licked and sucked at her until her body calmed and her grip on his hair relaxed.

"Oh, God." Sabrina jerked one more time before finally exhaling a slow, satisfied breath.

"I could eat you all day," Crunch said as he gave her pussy one more flick of his tongue.

"It was amazing, but I want something else." She sat up and reached for his belt.

"We need condoms," Crunch whispered against her cheek as his belt buckle released.

"Fortunately, my host makes sure his guests have everything they need." Sabrina popped the button on his jeans.

Crunch's brow furrowed with confusion when she nodded toward the bathroom, but it could be because most of the blood in his body went south to his dick.

"Did you forget stocking the bathroom?" She slowly lowered his zipper.

"I didn't do that. My sister did when she decorated the room. She said she'd be a frequent guest." Crunch cringed.

Nope.

He couldn't allow thoughts of Zara to ruin things. Sabrina helped when her warm tongue traced the line down his stomach and around his belly button. When he moaned her name, Sabrina smiled. Then she tugged his jeans down his thighs, causing goosebumps to erupt on his skin as her fingers lightly touched his skin.

"I like your style." Sabrina purred as she licked around the thin waistband of his underwear.

"I like the way you lick." Crunch gasped as she flicked her hot tongue against his thick erection through the fabric of his jockstrap underwear.

She might have liked his choice of underwear, but she didn't leave them on for long. She slowly removed them down his legs and released his thick cock.

Without hesitation, she wrapped her hand around the shaft and sucked the swollen head. Crunch almost dropped to his knees at the sensation of her mouth on his member. He closed his eyes and clenched his teeth as he tried to slow the building orgasm that had his balls tightening and his dick throbbing.

Sabrina moaned as she moved her lips down his length, taking him almost to the hilt and then back up to the tip again. Crunch clenched his teeth as his dick jerked in her mouth, and he almost lost it when she used her other hand to massage his balls gently.

"Baby, that feels so fucking good," Crunch groaned as his hips thrust forward instinctively.

Sabrina hummed in agreement, and the sensation traveled from the tip of his cock right through his entire body, making him shudder to ejaculate. As much as he wanted her to continue the amazing blowjob, he wanted to sink deep into her much more.

"Sabrina, I want to be inside you and if you keep… ah fuck… keep doing that, I'm not going to last." Crunch grunted.

Sabrina took him deep into her mouth once more before releasing him, making him almost drop to the ground. He pushed her on the bed and covered her mouth with his as he stepped out of his clothes.

He drew her tongue into his mouth as he cupped her firm breast in his palm. He massaged it, and when he gently squeezed it, she gasped into his mouth, and her hips thrust off the bed.

"Condom," Crunch panted as he pulled his mouth from hers.

"Yes," Sabrina whispered.

"Don't move," Crunch told her.

"Bottom drawer," she called out as he stepped into the bathroom.

Crunch hovered over her again in less than thirty seconds with a condom in his hand. She squirmed on the bed as she watched him tear it open and roll it onto his cock. She cupped her breasts as he knelt between her legs.

Sabrina pushed up on her elbows as he grabbed his cock and guided it to her opening. The sight of his swollen head at her entrance was the hottest thing he'd ever seen, and he took a couple of deep breaths before he slowly sank into her. With a whimper, her head dropped back, and she licked her lips. Crunch groaned as he watched his thick shaft disappear into her completely.

"Sweet fuck," Crunch moaned at the way her body seemed to grab onto his cock. "You're so tight."

"Almost five years," she whispered.

Knowing he was the first man she allowed to touch her in such a long time made him want to beat his chest like a neanderthal and shout to the world that she was his. Instead, he flipped them over, so she sat on top. He didn't know how but the move seemed to drive his cock deeper.

"Ride me, baby." Crunch gripped her hips as she began to rise up and drop down on him.

Crunch wrapped his arms around his waist and focused on her soft breast. He wrapped his lips around one nipple and sucked it into his mouth. Sabrina moaned his name as he bit down gently on the hard nub, then soothed it again with his tongue.

"That's it, beautiful. Fuck me." Crunch grunted against her breast as she bounced up and down.

"Yes." Sabrina began to grind on his cock as she rubbed her clitoris against his pubic bone.

She was trying to get the pressure where she needed it most, and he wasn't about to disappoint her. Crunch slipped one hand between them and pressed his thumb against the swollen bud at the top of her sex.

He grabbed the cheek of her ass with the other, and they rocked together until he felt her clench around his dick. As Sabrina trembled on top of him, she moaned. Hearing his given name come from her lips as she came undone was all he needed. He flipped her over on her back and slammed into her three times. His cock jerked, and his abdominal muscles clenched as his release jetted inside her.

"Fuck, fuck, baby. Sweet Fuck, Sabrina," Crunch called out through clenched teeth.

His legs quivered, and his body shuddered as he emptied himself deep. When his body stopped convulsing, he was able to use what little strength he had left to lift up and gaze into her beautiful face. A slight sheen of sweat covered her face, and he couldn't remember ever seeing anyone look more lovely.

"You're so beautiful." Crunch brushed his lips across hers.

"You make me feel that way," Sabrina whispered.

He hated to break away from her, but he needed to dispose of the condom. He pulled out and groaned at the feeling of not being inside her anymore. When he returned to the bedroom, she was on her side with the sheet covering her naked body.

"Are you okay?" Crunch asked as he lay down next to her.

"Better than okay." She cupped his cheek and smiled.

"Me too." He covered her hand with his and kissed the inside of her wrist.

"We should probably get ready and go to the studio." She sighed.

"We could skip it and practice at the safehouse," Crunch suggested, hoping she agreed.

"Sounds great, but I've got to get all the information for the classes I'm going to be teaching." She snuggled into his chest, but her body seemed tense.

"It will be safe, sweetheart," Crunch whispered and wrapped his arms around her.

"Okay," she murmured.

They lay in each other's arms for a while, and by the time they cleaned up and got out the door, Zara called to make sure Sabrina was still coming. The whole way to St. John's, he held her hand and reassured her his sister wasn't upset with her. He didn't want to stop touching her until he had no choice.

For the first time in his life, he could see himself spending his life with someone. He wanted to wake up every morning and look into her eyes. Sabrina was it for him, and even with all the unknown danger surrounding them, he didn't doubt it for a moment.

Chapter 17

Sabrina was on cloud nine, and it was difficult to stop smiling as she hurried into the studio to teach the intermediate ballet class. Several of the students seemed to notice her giddy mood.

"Ms. Sabrina, you look like someone in love," one of the students teased.

"She really does," another agreed.

"Is he handsome?" a third asked.

"I think you all should concentrate on practice and not the reason for my good mood." Sabrina rolled her eyes.

The students dropped the topic, and she managed to get through the class without more questions. Thankfully, she only needed to teach two classes that day because Zara wanted to give Sabrina and Crunch time to practice for the Ball.

They hadn't had time to perform the routine, but there were several things they'd discussed that wouldn't work for them. They even talked about changing the song and possibly the type of dance. Of course, Crunch needed to talk it over with Zara and his mom before committing to the changes.

During the second class, she was distracted when she allowed her thoughts to drift to Grant's betrayal or what Declan believed he'd done. She was anxious to confront him, but Crunch would never agree to drive her to the Thornton Estate.

Lies were not an option for her, but if she tried to sneak out and not tell him, wasn't that a type of deceit? Either way, she didn't want any of this crap over her head anymore, especially since things with Crunch had taken a giant step forward.

"That's a huge smile," Zara said as Sabrina held open the door for the students to exit the studio.

"I love dancing," Sabrina returned.

"Is that why my brother is in the other room grinning like the cat who ate the canary, too?" Zara asked.

"Maybe he heard a joke." Sabrina chuckled as she closed the studio door.

"Sure, he did." Zara hobbled next to her.

"Did he talk to you about the changes?" Sabrina shifted the subject.

"Yes. Both Mom and I think it's great." Zara stopped in front of the practice room.

Sabrina glanced through the glass and held back the sigh at the sight of him dancing around the floor. He stopped several times to write something on a notepad before turning again and trying something else.

"He could've been a professional," Sabrina said mostly to herself.

"I know. He's amazing," Zara agreed as she pulled open the door.

Crunch stopped and smiled when Sabrina entered the room. She had the urge to run to him but stopped because Zara was next to her, but he crooked his finger, and she made her way to the middle of the room.

"Let's show her what we got." Crunch winked.

Sabrina couldn't contain her laughter when he grabbed her hand and spun her into his arms. When they were in place, he nodded to his sister, and she started the music.

They moved around the floor as if they'd danced together all their lives. It was the first time they'd performed the routine, and Sabrina couldn't believe how easy it was, and except for one slip-up where she missed a spin, it was practically flawless. By the time they finished, Zara stood on the other side of the room with her mouth agape.

"You guys must've practiced that," Zara finally said when the song ended.

"No, this is the first time," Crunch told his sister.

"Liar," Zara scoffed.

"It's true. We only looked at the video and made a few adjustments," Sabrina explained.

"How is that possible? That was practically flawless." Zara was still dumbstruck.

"Well, let's see if this other one goes as well." Crunch laughed as he nodded to his sister.

They'd talked about doing a sexy kind of rumba, tango, and modern rolled into one. Crunch said he could think better when doing it, and Sabrina understood completely.

"Slow Hands" by Niall Horan started with a gentle, sexy beat that fit with the type of routine they'd pulled together. Sabrina began on one side of the room and Crunch on the other. By the time she was in his arms, she was lost in the sensual moves. She almost groaned when Crunch pulled her back into his body and whispered into her ear.

"And I want you, baby," he murmured part of the lyrics before spinning her out again.

The routine ended with her in his arms and their faces practically touching. She was about to lean in and plant a kiss on his lips, but Zara's excited clapping ruined that, and Sabrina stepped back to face Crunch's sister.

"That was so incredible." Zara squealed.

"Yeah, I could practically have an orgasm watching that," Sandy said from the doorway.

"If you nearly got off watching that, then Ian isn't doing it right," Crunch teased.

"Oh, he does…" Sandy began.

"Nope," Crunch shouted over her.

"When did you become such a prude?" Sandy rolled her eyes and walked into the studio.

"Is there a reason you're here?" Crunch took a towel and wiped it down his face.

Sabrina's heart pounded in her chest not only from the exertion but also because if Sandy was at the studio to talk to them, something had to be wrong.

"That little investigation you wanted us to do." Sandy glanced at Zara.

"It's okay. I'm leaving." Zara grabbed her crutches and left.

Sabrina sat down and accepted a bottle of water from Crunch. She knew Sandy had gone to her apartment to find the camera, but who knew what else was there. Her mind was going in so many different directions she almost didn't hear Sandy say her name.

"Sabrina?" Sandy sat next to her.

"Yeah." Sabrina could barely say the word.

"I asked if you were okay." Sandy touched her shoulder.

"Oh. Umm…yeah." Sabrina smiled at her and then picked up a towel to wipe her face.

Crunch met her eyes when she looked up, concern written all over his handsome face. She didn't want to be the person who fell apart at every bit of bad news, especially since getting through some of the roughest times of her life. She could deal with whatever Sandy had to say.

"I'm fine, really." She forced a smile.

"Okay, so the good news is, we only found one camera and removed it." Sandy held up a bag full of shattered pieces of plastic and wires.

"You smashed it." Crunch chuckled.

"Not exactly." Sandy placed the baggy next to her.

Crunch dropped down on the floor and crossed his legs in front of him. When he was comfortable, he motioned for her to continue.

"Well, Smash and I were going through the apartment. Colt came home, and we explained we'd only found one camera. Smash left it on the counter, and Colt used a huge frying pan to turn it into plastic confetti." Sandy shook the baggie.

"Maybe we should start calling your brother Smash," Crunch said.

"He did calm down when we told him there weren't more in the apartment. He was pissed off and said he wanted to kick the shit out of Thornton. Smash took him back to Hopedale to talk to Keith." Sandy told them.

"I can understand his anger. I'd like to have five minutes with that prick myself," Crunch said.

"Yeah, me too, but it's not going to fix anything. Anyway, we're working on hacking into the server, but it looks like it's gone dark. I do have a watch on it, so if someone turns it on again, I got them." Sandy dropped a hand on Sabrina's knee. "I think you should stay at the safehouse for a few more days. At least until the police find out more about the shooting."

Sabrina stared off into space. She didn't want to be a burden to anyone, but the thought of going home made her sick to her stomach. She'd also feel safer with Crunch, and Keith's property seemed like the safest option at the moment.

"We're staying at the safehouse until we know more about the shooting." Crunch met her eyes. "I'm staying with you and Charlee."

It was as if he answered the question before she even voiced it. She wanted him to stay with her, hold her and make her forget everything going on in her crazy life.

She wanted to have a chat with Grant too. She didn't know how to get to the estate without company. Crunch wouldn't like her going alone, but Grant wouldn't do anything stupid, especially in the middle of the day with a houseful of staff.

"Hunter, Mom needs to talk to you about a few things," Zara called from the door.

"Be right there. Keep me in the loop with this, Sandy." Crunch jumped to his feet.

He glanced down at Sabrina and cupped her cheek. She didn't know if she could meet his intense gaze. As she picked nervously at the threads of the towel, she raised her eyes to meet his.

"Why don't you get changed, and when I'm finished with Mom, we'll head back to Hopedale," Crunch told her.

"Okay." Sabrina smiled.

"Charlee is with Lily and the other girls at my house. They're making cookies. I can drop her off after supper." Sandy stood up and lifted the strap of her laptop bag on her shoulder.

"That would be great." Sabrina shot to her feet.

After Sandy and Crunch left her alone in the room, Sabrina grabbed her bag and headed to the dressing room. Taking a shower would only waste time, and the cab would be at the back entrance. By the time she pulled on her jeans and sweater, the cab was outside. She left a short note on the door to the practice room for Crunch.

Hunter,

I'll be back soon. Don't worry. I'm going to deal with something, and I'll be back.

Sabrina.

The estate was less than ten minutes away, and when she arrived, she saw some of the gardeners working on the flower beds. One of the men waved, but the other didn't acknowledge her. Sabrina paid for the cab and stomped up the steps to the front door. She was trying to decide whether to walk in or ring the doorbell when the large oak door opened.

"Sabrina, can I help you?" Vanessa stood in the doorway as stern as ever.

"I need to talk to Grant." Sabrina tried to step into the house.

"I'm sorry, he's with someone right now." Vanessa almost shoved her back.

"I'll wait. It's important." Sabrina shouldered Vanessa aside stalked into the house.

"He might be a while," Vanessa snapped.

"Look, tell him I'm here, and I've made a decision. I'm sure he'll cut the meeting short." Sabrina still wanted to punch the woman.

Vanessa glared at her for several seconds, but Sabrina crossed her arms over her chest and raised an eyebrow. The woman showed a hint of uncertainty for a split second, but she quickly squared her shoulders and walked toward Grant's office.

"I'll tell him, but I can't promise he'll jump because you showed up." Vanessa knocked on the door.

Sabrina could hear muffled voices from inside the office, and they didn't sound happy. When Vanessa knocked, she heard Grant shout for her to enter, irritation evident in his tone.

Sabrina glanced around the large entrance and shuddered. More than four years had passed since she had stepped into the estate, but her anger helped her not bolt back out of the house. Her gaze landed on the marble stairs where Easton fell, and her brain screamed to get the hell out of there, but the office door opened.

"Sabrina, come in." Grant grinned from the doorway of the office.

Before she made it across the foyer, a red-faced man stomped through the door. He narrowed his eyes at Grant and then glanced at Sabrina. The man left the house without another word.

"Vanessa, make sure he leaves the property," Grant told the house manager.

"Yes, sir." Vanessa nodded and left the office with her nose in the air.

"Come in, darling," Grant cooed as he reached to put his arm around Sabrina's shoulders.

"Don't call me darling, and don't touch me." Sabrina stepped into the office.

"So, it's like that?" Grant closed the office door. "Drink?"

"No," Sabrina snapped.

"Tea, coffee, water?" He pointed to the large jug of ice water on the credenza behind his desk.

Sabrina's mouth suddenly felt like it was full of cotton, and the water looked very refreshing, but she didn't want Grant to think this was a social call. She also wanted to make sure he knew she wasn't there to accept his proposal. Maybe if she had a glass of water and sat down, she could swallow the bile rising in her throat.

"Water," Sabrina said as she sat on the large leather sofa across from the desk.

"Water it is," Grant replied.

While he poured the water into a glass, she took the opportunity to look around the room. It used to be Bennett's office, but Grant removed all evidence his father ever used the den. She noticed a picture on the end table of Grant, Easton, and their parents, but it was old and looked like Easton was barely out of diapers.

"That was the day we had a picnic at the park." Grant handed her the glass of water.

He sat next to her with a glass of what looked like whiskey, but she couldn't be sure. She didn't like how close he was and moved further away to put some space between them.

"Grant, we need to talk," Sabrina blurted out.

"Yes, we do." He took a sip of his drink.

Sabrina lifted the glass to her lips and drank two long gulps before placing it on the end table. She was about to speak but decided she needed more water before letting him know she knew everything.

"Thirsty?" Grant chuckled as he took another sip of his amber liquid.

Sabrina downed the rest of the glass before redirecting her attention back to Grant. She wanted to slap the smirk right off his face, but someone knocked before she could say anything. Grant grumbled something under his breath then called out.

"Come in," Grant said with some disdain.

Vanessa walked into the office with a large envelope and placed it on the table next to Grant. He picked up the papers and skimmed through them before putting them back on the table.

"Tell Holly I'll get these signed and sent off," Grant told Vanessa.

"Someone is outside and would like to speak with you, now. I also need to run a few errands," Vanessa said with a harsh tone.

"I'm sorry, give me a few minutes, Sabrina." Grant followed Vanessa out of the office and closed the door.

She was sure he said Holly, but Holly quit working for the Thorntons. It seemed impossible her friend would go back to work with the prune face running the house, and she definitely would've told Sabrina she'd gone back to work there.

About fifteen minutes passed before Grant stepped back into the room and closed the door behind him. As he walked closer,

Sabrina couldn't focus. It was as if the room was underwater, and everything waved back and forth.

"Holly's working for ya 'gain?" Sabrina asked, but she found it difficult to form the words.

"No." Grant picked up his glass and took another sip.

Sabrina's vision blurred, and her body felt heavy. She was nauseous and reached back for the glass of water, but she misjudged the distance, and the glass crashed to the floor.

Grant smiled and moved closer to her. Sabrina tried to get to her feet, but she lost her balance and fell to the floor amongst the broken glass. She lifted her hand and blinked several times.

"Isss… tha… blood." Sabrina could hardly speak.

"Let me help…" Grant reached for her, but he stopped and glanced above her head. "What are you doing here? I said we'd talk… What are you doing? Are you crazy?"

Sabrina couldn't keep her eyes open, and the noise around her faded. She heard some loud pops and then fell backward. She blinked several times as a figure appeared above her, and something cold was placed in her hand. She lifted her head, but everything started to fade, and her head dropped back. The last thing she heard was a shrill scream before everything went black.

Chapter 18

"Yes, Mom." Crunch held back the urge to roll his eyes.

"I know Shelby made you uncomfortable in the past. If she becomes inappropriate with you again, let me know. I told her she is to keep herself under control or she will not be performing with the group." His mother continued as she flipped through some papers.

"Okay," Crunch said.

"You have to understand, *mon chéri*, she doesn't have a steady man in her life anymore. You know how I hate to gossip, but I've heard she has been going through a line of young men. It's why I warned her not to pursue you. She is a wonderful person but never found love. She's also looked into finding a bigger property for the studio." His mother smiled.

"Why are you looking for a bigger place?" Crunch asked.

"I want to take more students, and the area down here isn't like it was when I first opened this place." His mom glanced out through the window in her office. "So many are leaving the area."

"Mom, is that son of a..." Crunch stopped. "Is that guy bothering you again?"

"What? No, I haven't heard from him since you talked to him, but he is quickly taking over this area." She shook her head. "I'm sure the guy feels he's improving the neighborhood. I don't think he'd done it to be mean."

That statement was one of the reasons everyone in the dancing community loved his mother so much. She always saw the good in people no matter what. He aspired to be like her in his life, but it wasn't always easy.

"Well, the one thing you don't need to worry about is me. It's not like I'm helping Shelby's group, but thanks for giving me a heads up. I'll also ask Trunk's wife if she knows of any property that would work for you." Crunch stood up.

"That would be wonderful." She smiled.

Trunk's wife, Abbie, owned a real estate agency and Crunch was sure if he asked, the woman would dig high and low to help Crunch's mom find the perfect place.

He was anxious to get to Sabrina and take her back to Hopedale. Although, it wasn't like she wasn't safe in the studio. One of the guys stayed at the reception desk to keep an eye on Crunch's family as well as Sabrina. Lane 'Shadow' West had been on a six-month contract with a celebrity on tour.

After such a long stint, Keith offered Shadow a few weeks off, but when Shadow found out what happened, he volunteered to stay at the studio to watch Crunch's family. Shadow wasn't a guy who could sit back and take it easy.

Shadow was Sandy's half-brother, but they were nothing alike. Shadow was quiet and kept mostly to himself when he wasn't working. When he was in Hopedale, he lived in one of the bunkhouses.

"Okay, so that's everything I needed. Make sure you and Sabrina drop by to see the lovely Pam for your costume fitting." His mom stood up.

"Yes, Mom. We'll go by there on the way home if that will make you feel better." Crunch draped his arm around her shoulder.

"It would." She wrapped her arms around his waist in a gentle hug. "Zara says you two dance beautifully." His mother looked up at him with a huge smile.

"We do work well together." He kissed her temple.

"She's a wonderful person," she said.

"I know, Mom," Crunch replied.

"Don't you treat her like one of those bam, whack, thank you ma'ams," she warned.

Crunch laughed because he wasn't someone who jumped from one woman to another. There were a couple of relationships over the years, but nothing lasted more than a couple of months. He did have a couple of one-night stands, but he didn't make a habit of it.

"I love you, Mom, but I think you mean, wham, bam, thank you, ma'am," Crunch corrected her.

"Either way, don't do it." She poked him in the chest.

"I don't, and I won't," he assured her.

Crunch made his way to the practice room, expecting to find Sabrina waiting for him. When he walked in, he saw a group of women with Wesley. It was the group he and his mother discussed in her office.

He grabbed his bag from the bench and headed toward the reception area. He was almost through the door when someone called out to him. His whole body tensed as Shelby sashayed toward him like a lioness about to pounce on her prey.

"Hunter," she called.

"Ms. Skiffington," Crunch said, trying to sound friendly.

"My goodness. Haven't you grown. All over," Shelby practically purred as she ran a finger down his bicep.

Crunch stepped back and lifted his bag onto his shoulder. He didn't want to be disrespectful, but the woman obviously ignored his mother's request to be professional. Shelby was a flirt, and nothing anyone said would change her personality.

"Yes, I have. I don't want to be rude, but I need to run. My girl is waiting for me." Crunch pushed open the door.

He wasn't lying. He wanted Sabrina, and after what happened that morning, he hoped things headed in that direction. Plus, maybe the knowledge he wasn't available would make the she-wolf back off.

"What a lucky, lucky girl, but if you ever want to try a—" Shelby stopped as her eyes glanced over his shoulder.

Crunch locked eyes with his mother. The crossed arms, narrowed eyes, and lips pressed tightly together wasn't a good look on his mom because it meant she was trying to control her temper. He'd seen the expression many times when he was a child and misbehaved. He was glad this time she directed it at someone else.

"Hunter, your friend needs to speak with you," his mother said as she glared at Shelby.

Crunch didn't say a word as he squeezed out through the door and headed to the reception desk. He glanced around for Sabrina, but a knot formed in his stomach when he didn't see her. He didn't know why.

"Shadow, have you seen Sabrina?" Crunch asked when he noticed the large man behind the reception desk.

"I saw her go into the change room." Shadow nodded toward the women's room. "But that was a while ago."

"She didn't come back out?" Crunch looked out into the parking lot where he'd parked his truck.

"If she did, it must've been when I was on a call," Shadow told him.

Crunch nodded and headed to the ladies' change room. As he stepped next to the door, it opened. He was about to ask Sabrina if she got lost, but one of the younger students walked out.

"Hey, did you see Sabrina in there?" Crunch asked.

"Nobody is in there." The young girl shrugged. "She might have gone out through the back door."

The exit was on the opposite side of the building and led to the back parking lot where most parents picked up their kids. He made his way toward the back, and when he pushed open the door, he saw a couple of girls on the back step giggling at something on their phones.

"Have either of you seen Sabrina?" Crunch asked.

"She left in a taxi a little while ago," one of the girls said without looking up at him.

"Are you sure?" Crunch asked as panic started to rise in his chest.

"Yeah, I thought it was my dad coming to pick me up, but it was another driver." The girl shrugged.

Crunch spun around and stepped back into the building as he pulled out his phone. He jogged toward the reception desk with the phone to his ear. When the call went to voicemail, he tried again.

"What's wrong?" Shadow was on his feet.

"Sabrina left through the other door in a taxi, and she isn't answering her phone," Crunch said as the voicemail kicked in again.

"Who's not answering their phone?" Sandy walked out of Zara's office with his sister behind her.

"Sabrina. She left in a taxi," Crunch told them.

"What did you do?" Zara glared at him.

"Nothing, I was in the office with Mom. When I came out, she was gone," Crunch defended.

"What taxi did she call?" Sandy asked.

Crunch cursed under his breath at his neglect in asking the girl what company had picked up Sabrina. He headed back to the other door, but both girls were gone. Sandy was clicking on her laptop behind the desk when he returned to the reception area.

"One of the girls said her dad drives for the company that picked up Sabrina." Crunch looked at his sister.

"If it's who I think it is, then that would be *Jiffy Taxi*." Zara reached behind the counter. "I have the number on this book."

"I'm on it," Sandy said with her phone to her ear. "Hi, this is Sergeant Sandy O'Connor with the Newfoundland Police Department. I'm calling to find out if one of your cars picked up a woman from Madam Lacotte's Dance Studio on Hamilton Avenue?"

Crunch drummed his fingers on the counter as Sandy listened to the person on the other line. He had no idea why Sabrina would leave without telling him, but something told him she wasn't heading to Hopedale.

"And where was she dropped off?" Sabrina asked. "I understand, but we need to find this woman immediately."

"Isn't it against the law to impersonate a police officer?" Zara whispered.

"Sandy is a police officer but only works with the department when they need her," Crunch explained.

"Oh." Zara wrapped him in a hug.

"Okay, thank you very much." Sandy ended the call and typed something into her computer.

"Well, where did the cab take her?" Crunch asked impatiently.

"Give me a minute to look up the address," Sandy snapped.

Crunch tapped his fingers on the counter as Sandy's fingers flew over the computer keys. He was screaming in his head for her to hurry up, but if he said it out loud, Sandy would probably throw the laptop at him.

"Got it," Sandy said. "19 Collingwood Crescent."

Sandy wrote the address on a piece of paper, but before handing it to Crunch, she typed something into the laptop again. Her brow furrowed, and she pursed her lips. Whatever she saw didn't make her happy.

"What is it?" Zara practically shouted before Crunch could say a word.

"I knew this address was familiar." Sandy shook her head.

"Who do you know on Collingwood Crescent?" Crunch asked.

"Some pretty prominent families live there."

Shelby again.

"By the way, I found this on the floor in the room. I think it might be yours," Shelby said.

Crunch wanted to groan as Shelby squeezed between Crunch and his sister, holding a piece of paper. When he took it from her, she leaned over the counter and practically purred as Shadow became the object of her ogling.

Crunch opened the paper and cursed under his breath when he read the note from Sabrina. What would she have to take care of on her own? He didn't like it.

"The Smallwoods, the Devons, and the Thorntons are a few of the families that live there." Shelby reached out to touch Shadow. "How did you get such amazing hair?"

"I grow it from my head." Shadow furrowed his brow.

"Aren't you cute. I mean, how do you keep it so thick and luscious?" Shelby tried to touch Shadow's head, but he pulled back.

"I wash it," Shadow deadpanned.

"Wait? Thorntons, as in Grant Thornton?" Crunch grabbed her arm and spun Shelby around to face him.

"Yes. We live a few streets over from him." Shelby leaned closer to him. "Would you like to visit?"

"No," Crunch snapped as he ran out the door.

He knew what Sabrina had to deal with, and he was pissed she'd gone off to do it on her own. He was in his truck and about to drive off when Shadow stepped in front of the vehicle. Crunch slammed on the brakes as Shadow walked around and climbed into the passenger side.

"I'm going with you," Shadow said.

"You need to stay at the studio. You were hired to keep an eye on my family." Crunch reached over and pushed open the passenger door.

"First, I volunteered to care for your family, and second, Sandy is staying until Rex arrives." Shadow closed the door again.

Crunch knew it was pointless to argue with Shadow because the man was a calm, mysterious entity most of the time. The only time he'd ever seen the man lose his cool was when he thought his older sister was missing.

"I saw your face when you read that note." Shadow locked eyes with him.

"She's going to confront Thornton," Crunch said through gritted teeth.

"I'm going to be your backup in case things go wrong." Shadow pulled the seatbelt across his massive chest and folded his hands in front of him.

"Fine," Crunch grumbled as he sped out of the parking lot.

He wasn't familiar with the area, but Shadow plugged it into the GPS. It wasn't hard to see when they'd entered the high-end neighborhood.

The houses were huge and surrounded by high privacy fences. The area was several long streets that intersected with the most prominent estates on Collingwood.

He took the corner onto the street and stopped. Two police cruisers parked diagonally across the road, cutting off access. Crunch scanned the area for other authorities.

"This doesn't look good," Shadow said.

"No, and I've got a bad feeling this has something to do with Grant." Crunch shut off his truck and got out.

He walked toward the police officers next to the cruisers that closed off the street. He didn't recognize them, but the *NPD* had extensive recruitment over the last couple of years.

"Do you think any of the O'Connors are here?" Shadow asked.

Before he could answer, Crunch was interrupted by the vibration of his phone. He pulled it out of his pocket and was tempted not to answer it when he saw Keith's number. He knew if he didn't, his boss would keep calling until he did.

"Rusty, I'm not going to do anything. I just…" Crunch began, but Keith stopped him.

"Where are you?" Keith sounded frantic.

"I'm on Collingwood Drive," Crunch replied.

"A.J. is at the Thornton Estate." Keith cleared his throat. "There's been a shooting."

Crunch's body practically turned to ice as the words echoed through his ear. Sabrina had gone to the Thornton estate, and she probably confronted Grant about the will. If he was desperate enough, he might have pulled a gun on her.

"Crunch?" Keith's voice brought him out of his head.

"Is she okay?" Crunch fisted his hand at his side.

"A.J. is coming to find you. Where on Collingwood are you?" Keith asked.

Crunch explained they were at the barricade, and Keith told him Aaron would meet him there, then the call ended. Crunch put his phone back in his pocket and told Shadow what Keith said.

Crunch paced in front of the cruisers with his hands linked and pressed against the top of his head. It seemed as if time stopped as Shadow nodded toward the end of the road. Aaron sprinted toward them with an expression Crunch couldn't read.

"Tell me she's okay, A.J." Crunch croaked out the words.

"She's on the way to the hospital," Aaron told him.

Crunch didn't need to hear anything else. He spun around and went back to his truck. He was about to climb in his vehicle when Aaron grabbed his shoulder to stop him.

"I need to go to her." Crunch shrugged away from Aaron

"Crunch, there's something you need to know," Aaron began.

"She was shot. I need to go to her," Crunch shouted.

"Sabrina wasn't shot. Grant Thornton was," Aaron said.

"What are you saying, A.J?" Crunch asked.

"It looks like Sabrina shot him."

Crunch stared at Aaron as if he was speaking another language. Sabrina wouldn't hurt a fly. Sure, Grant pissed her off, but there was no way the sweet woman he made love to would shoot anyone.

"Is he dead?" Shadow asked.

"He's alive, but not sure how bad it is," Aaron told Crunch.

"She didn't shoot anyone. Why is she gone to the hospital?" Crunch asked.

"She was found unconscious on the floor." Aaron was all business.

"Then why the fuck would you say she shot that son of a bitch?" Crunch shouted.

"The gun was in her hand," Aaron explained.

"I don't care if she was holding a fucking cannon. She didn't shoot him. Although, I wouldn't blame her if she did. That prick should be in jail." Crunch shoved Aaron.

Shadow stepped in between Crunch and the police officer. It probably wasn't a good idea to assault his boss's brother, not to mention a cop. He glared at Aaron over Shadow's shoulder for a moment and then headed back to his truck.

"I'm going to the hospital." Crunch yanked open the door and got in.

"I'm not the enemy here, Crunch. I'm doing my job, and right now, she's the only suspect," Aaron yelled.

"Fine. Do your fucking job and find out who shot that prick. I'm going to make sure Sabrina is okay," Crunch returned.

"As a friend, I suggest you get her a lawyer," Aaron called out as Crunch and Shadow drove off.

Chapter 19

Sabrina's body felt weighed down, and she had difficulty opening her eyes. She could hear distant beeps and voices, but she had no idea what they were. Why was it so hard to move?

"Sabrina," a familiar voice whispered in her ear.

It was a man, but for the life of her, she couldn't tell for sure who he was. Was it her brother? She fought to open her eyes, but her lids felt like lead. When she finally forced them open, the brightness above her made her slam her eyes closed again.

"Turn off the light," another male voice whispered.

"Sabrina, it's okay. You can open your eyes now," the familiar voice said. "It's me."

When she opened them again, the room wasn't completely dark, but she could look around. It wasn't difficult to tell she was in a hospital room. Her brother stood next to the bed with one of her hands sandwiched between his. Crunch sat on the bed with his hand on her leg.

She lifted her other hand to touch his face, but something rattled, and she wasn't able to lift her arm. Sabrina glanced down at handcuffs with one end around her wrist and the other attached to the bed.

Handcuffs? Why was she in handcuffs?

Sabrina started to struggle to free her hand, but panic started to bubble up when she couldn't. It was hard to think the way her head throbbed, and her stomach churned as if she was about to toss her cookies.

"Sabrina, try to calm down." Colt pushed her back gently.

"Calm down? Why am I handcuffed to a bed in the hospital?" Sabrina tugged at her cuffed arm again.

"She's not going anywhere; can you take them off?" Crunch asked someone behind him. "I'll take responsibility for her."

"I'm sorry, but I can't without Inspector O'Connor's okay," a male said.

"Call him. Tell him Crunch is here, and I'll make sure she stays." Crunch sounded pissed.

Whoever it was left the room, and Crunch placed his hand over her cuffed one. Her brain was foggy, and she didn't understand how she got to the hospital.

"What's going on?" Sabrina looked at Colt.

"You don't remember?" Her brother looked surprised.

"No." She shook her head and then cringed when the pain hit like a sledgehammer.

"What's the last thing you do remember?" Crunch asked.

Sabrina closed her eyes and tried to think. Flashes of memories from the last few days were muddled in her brain mainly because the pain made it difficult to concentrate.

"I remember…" Sabrina glanced at her brother.

The memory of making love with Crunch was fuzzy, but she knew it had happened. She locked gazes with Crunch, letting him know she remembered their lovemaking. She couldn't exactly say the words aloud in front of her brother.

"Do you remember this morning?" Crunch asked.

Sabrina nodded.

"Do you remember going to the studio?" Crunch continued.

"I think so," Sabrina whispered.

"Do you know why you left the studio?" a voice asked from behind Crunch.

Aaron appeared next to the bed and nodded to someone behind him. A young police officer removed the handcuffs, then stepped out of the room. Sabrina pulled her hand to her chest and rubbed her wrist. She didn't remember leaving the studio. She could barely remember arriving.

"Did I hit my head? Is that why I don't remember?" Sabrina asked Crunch.

"Actually, you were drugged," Aaron told her.

"Drugged?" Sabrina gasped out the word.

She pressed her fingers against her temples. She couldn't think with the pain in her head, and she was so confused. Who could've drugged her? She'd only been with Crunch and the people at the dance studio.

"Who drugged me?" She glanced around.

"All we know is we found you on the floor at the Thornton Estate," Aaron explained.

Sabrina didn't understand why she was at the estate. A flash of a taxi, and then she locked eyes with Crunch. She'd left the studio to talk to Grant, but she didn't remember arriving or what happened after she got in the car.

"I'm sure your memory is fuzzy, but we need to ask you a few questions. Do you think you can answer them?" Aaron pulled out a notepad.

"I'll try," Sabrina whispered.

"Why did you go to the estate?" Aaron asked.

"I'm not sure. I may have wanted to talk to him about Easton's will." Sabrina couldn't think of any other reason.

"Did you bring a gun?" Aaron locked eyes with her.

"A Gun? What? No." She shook her head.

Sabrina had no idea what the hell Aaron was talking about. Other than the previous night, the only time she'd seen a gun was on television. The fact that she couldn't remember anything made her anxious.

"Do you own a gun?" Aaron asked.

Sabrina shook her head again and flicked her gaze to Crunch. He glared at Aaron, and his jaw clenched as he fisted his hands at his sides. When she glanced at her brother, he looked as if he was about to explode.

The door to the room opened, and she saw a white lab coat. Her attention landed on a familiar face. Aaron's brother Ian wore scrubs under the lab coat and a stethoscope around his neck. He narrowed his eyes when he saw Aaron, and his smile disappeared.

"I told you to wait until her blood work came back." Ian shook the papers in his hand.

"I only asked a couple of questions." Aaron held up his hands in defense.

"Well, if you're asking her about the last twenty-four hours, you might as well give up. We found flunitrazepam in her system," Ian told his brother.

"What is that?" Sabrina asked.

"You'd probably know it better as Rohypnol," Ian told her as he pulled his stethoscope off his neck and put it up to his ears.

"Isn't that the date rape drug?" Colt practically shouted.

Sabrina's body felt cold, but she broke out in a sweat. Did all this mean she was… raped? Did she shoot Grant because he tried to rape her?

"With the amount in her system, I find it hard to believe she'd be able to lift a gun, let alone fire one," Ian said, then placed the stethoscope against her chest.

"She was holding the gun, and the swabs showed residue." Aaron sounded defensive.

233

"Well, right now, Sabrina needs rest, and she can't do that with you interrogating her." Ian grabbed Aaron by the shoulder and guided him to the exit.

"What the hell are you doing?" Aaron pulled away.

"Protecting my patient." Ian motioned for his brother to go ahead of him.

Aaron glared at his brother before glancing at Sabrina. He seemed to want to say something, but when Crunch stood up, Aaron threw his arms up in the air and headed out of the room with a warning for Sabrina not to leave town.

"Where the hell does he think she'll go?" Colt grumbled.

"He's just doing his job," Sabrina whispered as she lay back on the pillow.

Her head still throbbed, and to make it worse, she couldn't get the thought of being drugged out of her head. It felt like the world's worse hangover, and her brain seemed to block out everything important.

"Try to rest, sweetheart," Crunch whispered as he kissed her forehead. "I'll be right here."

"Okay," she said with a yawn.

Sabrina closed her eyes and let sleep take her. She wasn't sure what would happen, but as long as Crunch was next to her, she'd get through it.

Chapter 20

Sabrina was restless while she slept, constantly moaning, tossing, and turning. She probably wasn't getting a restful sleep with all the moving, but she was alive.

He'd convinced Colt to go to the safehouse with Charlee because Sandy told Crunch the little girl was upset and wanted her mommy. Crunch figured that if Colt was with her, she might settle down a little.

Colt left reluctantly but only after Crunch promised to call him if there was any news. Since Sabrina slept most of the morning, it was reasonably quiet.

Harriet dropped in and was beside herself when she discovered Sabrina was a suspect. She insisted there had to be another explanation for what happened because she didn't believe Sabrina would shoot Grant. Crunch agreed and was determined to find out what happened, but since Sabrina had no memory, Grant was the only witness left.

According to Grant's mother, her son was lucky the bullet missed his heart. He had two wounds, but one of the bullets lodged in his rib. He'd gone into surgery to remove it and was in recovery.

Crunch asked Harriet to keep him posted on Grant's condition because he could clear Sabrina. Hopefully, when he regained consciousness, he'd remember what happened.

He lifted Sabrina's hand to his lips and kissed it. She stirred but didn't wake. Crunch studied her hand and noticed her injured finger didn't bend with the rest, even in sleep. He kissed the tip of the finger and raised his eyes to look at her beautiful face.

"Everything is going to be fine. You didn't do this, and we'll figure this out," Crunch whispered into the quiet of the room.

His eyes popped open when someone smoothed his hair back. Sabrina gave him a small smile, but it disappeared quickly. She looked pale but seemed more lucid than the previous day.

"Where's Charlee?" She sat up a little.

"She's at the safehouse on Rusty's property," he told her. "Colt is with her."

Sabrina nodded and laid her head back against the pillow. She traced her finger across the tattoo on his fingers before she lifted her eyes to meet his.

"Why did you stay all night?" Sabrina asked.

"I didn't want you to be alone," he admitted.

"The police think I shot Grant."

She wasn't asking. It was more a confirmation of what she faced. Crunch grasped her hand and held it between his as she got lost in her thoughts.

"I don't remember shooting him. Wouldn't you think I'd remember doing that?" She glanced around the room.

"You didn't shoot him. I don't believe it for a second. As for your memory, you did have a pretty heavy drug in your system, but you probably don't remember because it never happened. Someone else did it." Crunch was sure.

"What if I did?" Sabrina sighed.

"You didn't," Crunch insisted.

"But what—"

Crunch stopped her words by placing a finger over her lips. He sat on the bed next to her and pulled her into his arms. She sighed and snuggled her face into his neck.

"No, buts. You didn't do it, and when the evidence comes in, A.J. will verify it." Crunch kissed her temple.

"I can't go to jail," Sabrina whispered.

"You won't." Crunch rested his cheek on the top of her head while he held her.

When the doctor released Sabrina from the hospital, the first thing he had to do was make sure she had a good lawyer. He knew Jason Brenton was a criminal lawyer, and since he was a friend of the O'Connors, Crunch knew he made sure his clients got exceptional representation.

Crunch didn't believe Sabrina shot Grant. Something told him someone set her up to take the fall. Considering the number of enemies the man probably had, it could be a long suspect list, not to mention Grant's suspected criminal connections.

"I want to go home." She sniffed.

"Ian should be here soon. It's almost seven in the morning." Crunch gave her his biggest smile.

"Am I going to be allowed to go home, or will A.J. be taking me to jail?" Sabrina's voice cracked.

"You're going home with me, or at least to the safehouse at The Compound," Crunch assured her.

Her body relaxed at his words, and Crunch prayed he wasn't talking out of his ass because the truth was, he didn't know if Aaron would walk in and take her into custody. The man was a friend, but if Aaron arrested, Sabrina it would seriously strain the friendship.

It was a little after nine when Ian arrived and examined her. He gave her a clean bill of health and released her with instructions to take it easy. Crunch's heart was in his throat while they waited for the discharge papers.

Aaron hadn't come to arrest her, but it didn't mean he wouldn't. Although it was only a short ten-minute drive from St. John's to Hopedale, Sabrina dozed off and only opened her eyes when he pulled into The Compound.

"I think that drug is still in my system," Sabrina said with a yawn.

"You can lay down when we get into the house." Crunch reached over and grasped her hand.

He was surprised to see several cars parked in front of the house and was uneasy as he got out of the truck. He opened Sabrina's door and took her hand as they walked to the front door. When he reached for the knob, the door flew open, and Charlee launched herself into Sabrina's arms, almost knocking them down the front steps.

"Mommy. Mommy. You're back." Charlee squealed as she hugged her mother. "I missed you so, so, much."

"I missed you too." Sabrina chuckled.

"Are you all better?" Charlee pulled back and looked into her mother's face.

"I'm all better," Sabrina assured her daughter.

For a minute, Charlee stared at Sabrina as if she was confirming the diagnosis. It wasn't difficult to figure out when the little girl decided everything was okay. She wrapped her arms around Sabrina's neck and kissed her cheek

"I'm so happy you're all better, Mommy," Charlee whispered.

Sabrina was happy to be out of the hospital and relieved Aaron didn't arrest her. The thought of going to jail for shooting Grant made her sick to her stomach. The man pissed her off, but there was no way she'd try to kill him.

Crunch guided Sabrina into the house with Charlee still clinging to her. The kitchen was a bustle of activity with Nanny Betty, Alice, Pam, and Cora preparing something in the kitchen that was sending a mouth-watering aroma through the house.

"I'm going to play with the babies." Charlee pointed to two toddlers.

Pam's twins, Evan and Tara, sat next to the coffee table, eating something out of bowls. They didn't appear to notice anyone as they focused on a children's show. Charlee plopped down next to them with a dish of her own.

Keith, Crash, and Rex were locked in a quiet conversation at the living room entrance, and their hushed discussion made Crunch uneasy. He escorted Sabrina to the kitchen and pulled one of the chairs out for her. As if Alice read his mind, she joined Sabrina at the table and poured them both a cup of tea.

Crunch marched over to join the men, interrupting them. Keith was the first to acknowledge Crunch and crossed his arms over his chest.

"How's she doing?" Keith asked.

"As well as can be expected. She's been told the police think she shot someone, so there's that." Crunch raised an eyebrow.

"There's also the fact that someone shot at her a couple of days ago," Rex reminded them.

"That's a lot for anyone to deal with in a couple of days." Crash glanced over Crunch's shoulder.

"Has A.J. told you anything, Rusty?" Crunch wanted to get right to the point.

Keith shook his head as he shoved his hands into his pockets, but he was holding back. Crunch narrowed his eyes because he knew the men weren't saying something. He didn't like the way they eyed Sabrina.

"One of you spit it out. Now." Crunch tried to keep his voice low.

"She's going to need a lawyer," Keith blurted out.

"Why?" Crunch fisted his hands at his sides.

"She shot a man, Crunch," Crash interjected.

"Shut the fuck up. Sabrina didn't shoot anyone." Crunch practically growled through his teeth.

"Well, if she didn't, someone went through a lot of trouble to make it look like she did. Even as far as making sure she had gunshot residue on her hand." Keith handed Crunch his phone.

"What the hell is this?" Crunch asked, looking at a picture of a police report.

"A.J. sent me this. It says her hand was positive for gunshot residue. That means Sabrina shot a gun." Keith tapped the top of his phone.

"I know what it fucking means," Crunch snapped as he read through the report.

"She was holding the gun," Crash reminded him.

"Someone could've put it in her hand," Rex surmised.

"For what purpose?" Keith asked.

"What else? To set her up." Rex shrugged.

"The residue says she shot a gun," Crash reminded them.

"The shooter may have stood over her," Rex reasoned.

Crunch could hear the conversation, but he was too busy reading the report off the phone. They'd found residue on her right hand, her sleeve, and her blouse.

Wait. Her right hand?

Crunch read it several times to make sure he didn't miss something. He didn't, and if they thought she could shoot a gun with her injured finger, they'd be mistaken. Plus, like him, she was left-handed.

"Someone did set her up, but they weren't smart about it." Crunch lifted his eyes to meet Keith.

"What are you talking about?" Keith asked.

"Watch." Crunch looked around to find something he could toss to Sabrina.

He found a small plastic toy on the couch and walked closer to the kitchen. When he was a few steps away, he called out to Sabrina.

"Catch." Crunch tossed the toy to her.

Sabrina caught the toy in her left hand and stared at him as if he was crazy. When he turned back to his friends, they had the same *what the hell* expression. He probably should have explained his experiment.

"She's left-handed." Crunch pointed out.

"I don't get it." Sabrina held up the toy.

"Me either." Crash shrugged.

"The report says the gun was in her *right* hand. It's also where they found the residue," Keith said as he studied his phone.

"Even if she did hold the gun in her right hand, she wouldn't be able to shoot it." Crunch stepped closer to Sabrina.

"She could be ambidextrous," Crash suggested.

"I'm not," Sabrina confirmed.

"She couldn't pull the trigger." Crunch took her wrist and held it up. "Make a fist."

Sabrina closed her hand into a fist. As he expected, all her fingers curled except the index finger. She looked baffled by the whole thing, but Keith, Rex, and Crash understood.

"Sabrina, what happened to your finger?" Keith asked.

"I was in a car accident about ten years ago. I broke it, and it never healed properly. I haven't been able to bend it since." Sabrina dropped her hand into her lap.

Crunch walked back to the circle of men and motioned to Keith's phone. Without a word, he put the phone to his ear.

"Jason, when can you get here," Keith asked.

A sense of relief washed over Crunch as his boss explained everything to Jason. It was still difficult to get his head around anyone believing Sabrina could try to kill someone. Still, there was a chance people wouldn't think she was innocent.

Crunch glanced over his shoulder. Sabrina was engaged in a conversation with Pam and Alice but continued to glance in his direction. There was no doubt in his mind she was set up to look like the guilty party. Hopefully, Grant would wake up and tell them what happened.

Chapter 21

Sabrina was exhausted and scared all evening. When the lawyer arrived, Pam took the kids to the small playground in Keith's backyard. She knew Charlee wasn't in any danger with the security surrounding the property, but part of her wanted to take her daughter and run away.

Jason was a nice guy, and she felt comfortable with him. He frequented the diner and was always friendly. Crunch also seemed confident Jason could help her if, by some chance, Aaron arrested her.

She shivered at the thought of going to prison for something she didn't do or didn't remember doing. The last thing she recalled was Vanessa greeting her at the door. The rest was a complete blank.

The doctor told her some memory might return, but she might never recall what happened. That scared her more than anything else because she had no idea how she ended up drugged with a gun in her hand.

Sabrina looked down in her lap at her hands. She'd never held a gun in her life, and the only time there was one in her grasp, she didn't remember. There was no way she'd ever shoot anyone, even Grant. Maybe if she felt her life was in danger. There was also the question of where she got the gun in the first place. She definitely didn't bring it.

"Are you okay?" Crunch crouched beside her.

"I don't know. It feels odd missing a whole block of time and not knowing what I did or said." Sabrina sighed as she glanced at Jason.

"Well, if it makes you feel better, I'm going to make sure you have the best lawyer possible," Jason said with a grin.

"I thought you were going to represent her, Jason," a voice said from behind her.

Sandy stepped into the room with a smirk. For some reason, knowing Sandy was there helped Sabrina feel at ease. Sandy wasn't a lawyer, and Sabrina didn't know her well, but it was good to see a friendly face. Crunch might be her rock at the moment, but she was still scared to let herself get too close.

"I am. That's why I said the best possible lawyer." Jason winked at Sabrina.

"I'll hold my judgment until I see the results," Sandy retorted.

"What are you doing here?" Crunch asked.

"I'm here with some news." Sandy held up a box.

"What is that?" Jason looked up from where he was writing.

"This is one of the boxes from Sabrina's storage locker." Sandy placed the box in front of Sabrina.

While Jason dealt with the possibility of being arrested, Crunch and Sandy had tried to find why Easton didn't trust Grant. She'd told them about the boxes in storage and given Sandy the key to access the locker.

She stored a couple of file boxes Easton kept separate from the office. Since Grant never asked about it, she assumed it wasn't important, but Sabrina kept it because several note pads contained Easton's handwriting. She couldn't get rid of it at the time but moved it around wherever she went.

She'd mentioned a box labeled *IOG* to Crunch. He thought they should go through it, although they were probably grasping at straws. She wanted to know if any of the files could tell them why Grant would lie and commit fraud.

Sabrina felt sick. She tried to get her head around Grant's manipulation. It wasn't the money because she didn't care about any of it. Grant made her believe Easton lied about his finances and didn't have her well-being in mind.

Thinking back on it, she was gullible to believe it in the first place. Easton was careful with finances and didn't keep anything from her regarding bills. The Thorntons were wealthy, but Easton said it didn't mean they should be careless with money.

"How could I be so stupid?" Sabrina mumbled to herself.

"You're not stupid," Crunch whispered as he sat in the chair next to her.

"No, I'm not, but there's something wrong with me if Grant could get away with this so easily." Sabrina placed her hand on the pile of papers Sandy placed in front of her.

"Listen to me," Sandy said as she crouched next to Sabrina. "You were grieving, and that can play havoc with your brain. It makes it hard to think rationally. This is on that prick."

"Sandy's right," Crunch agreed.

"She is, but the police could use it against her," Jason interjected.

"She didn't do anything wrong." Crunch shook his head.

"No, but it does give her a motive." Jason locked eyes with Crunch.

Sabrina swallowed the giant lump that formed in her throat as she fought the urge to burst into tears. People would believe she tried to kill Grant over money, and she'd end up in jail. Charlee would be without both her parents.

"Did you tell anyone you were going to see Grant?" Jason asked.

Sabrina shook her head. She didn't tell anyone because she didn't want anyone to stop her. It was probably the dumbest thing she ever did in her life.

"Who was there when you arrived?" Jason leaned closer.

"I only remember Vanessa answering the door and going inside, and… the rest is blank," Sabrina sighed.

"Who's Vanessa?" Jason wrote something on a notepad.

"She's the house manager. Grant hired her as a nanny when I had Charlee, but I didn't like her. She kind of reminds me of an attractive Nanny McPhee," Sabrina said.

"Who is that?" Jason seemed confused.

"Nanny McPhee? You don't know who that is?" Sandy laughed.

"No." Jason shook his head.

"Do you?" Sandy asked Crunch.

"It's a movie, isn't it?" Crunch asked.

"Yes." Sabrina smiled.

Sandy pulled out her phone, and after a few taps and swipes, she held up the screen to Jason. He wrinkled his nose and shuddered.

"How the hell could you make that attractive?" Jason chuckled.

"It's more her personality," Sabrina admitted.

"So, she was the one who answered the door," Jason said, bringing them back to the subject.

"Yes, but everything else is fuzzy." Sabrina shook her head.

How was she supposed to help Jason defend her when she couldn't remember anything? She prayed Grant would fill in the blanks for everyone, but would he tell the truth? Was it possible to use this as another form of blackmail to get her to marry him?

Her memory didn't get any clearer the next day as Crunch helped go over the tower of files Sandy brought. It was difficult to be helpful when she couldn't concentrate, and none of the papers made sense to her. She had to do it to distract herself because Grant woke up, but the police couldn't question him yet.

Grant's mother called to ensure Sabrina was okay and said she knew someone else shot her son. Harriet didn't believe for a minute that Sabrina could hurt anyone. Knowing that made Sabrina feel more at ease because Harriet was like a second mother. The last thing she wanted was to lose that.

According to Harriet, Grant didn't remember what happened, but he was still on medication and sleeping a lot. The doctor said he probably would be more lucid the next day, which meant the police would soon question him.

Harriet asked to take Charlee to the park and out to supper later in the week, which made both of them happy. Charlee missed her grandmother and couldn't understand why they weren't going home, but she loved the large area around The Compound, too.

Keith may have built his property for security purposes, but it was obvious that children lived there. Charlee enjoyed having playmates close, and Keith's three kids were thrilled to have another friend.

Sabrina tossed another file folder onto the growing pile and sighed. She couldn't understand what any of this had to do with what was happening to her. The only thing they learned was Easton didn't trust his brother and planned to have him arrested.

"This is a waste of time," Sabrina complained.

"I know it seems like it, but we need to see if there's anything that would give the police another suspect in the shooting." Crunch took her hands and tugged her into his lap.

"Can't we wait to see what Grant says?" Sabrina touched his cheek.

He slept next to her every night and held her until she fell asleep. They hadn't been intimate since the day at his house, but it was difficult to get an hour alone with people coming and going. Not to mention, Charlee wasn't sleeping well and crawled into bed with them the previous night.

"If you want, we can take a break and go for a walk around the property," Crunch suggested as he kissed her cheek.

"I want to go to the studio and dance." Sabrina sighed.

"We can do that here." Crunch motioned around the open area.

"This is way too small to practice." She shook her head.

"Keith has a huge conference room, and I can ask if we can use that." Crunch picked up his phone.

"Why can't we go to the studio? Am I under house arrest or something?" Sabrina stood.

"No, honey. You're free to leave, but I think we're safe here and considering the shooting at my house as well as what happened at the estate, I don't want to take any chances." Crunch stood and wrapped his arms around her.

"I'm starting to feel trapped." Sabrina leaned against him and rested her cheek against his chest.

"Then let's go be free." Crunch grabbed her hand and practically dragged her out of the house.

They hopped in his truck, and he drove about five minutes before making a sharp left turn. The road was uneven, and if she didn't have a seatbelt on, Sabrina would've bounced off the seat. After several minutes Crunch stopped the truck at the opening of a large field.

They hadn't left The Compound, so they were still inside Keith's secure area. She got out of the truck and took in the beautiful scenery. Tall pines mixed in with some maple trees enclosed the place. The grass looked recently mowed, and a small pond sat on the far side of the area.

"What is this?" Sabrina asked as she moved further into the grassy field.

"Keith cleared out this area to build another home for his family, but Emily loves the house they live in. So, he's trying to decide what to do with it." Crunch stepped behind her and wrapped his arms around her waist.

"It's lovely, but why are we here?" She turned into his arms.

"You wanted to dance." Crunch gave her a quick kiss on the lips and opened the door of his truck.

After a few seconds, she heard music blaring from inside the cab. Crunch left the door open and grinned as he did a little shuffle before grabbing her around the waist and spinning her.

"Hunter." She squealed.

"Let's practice." Crunch placed her on the ground again and took her hand.

The song wasn't what they'd practiced, but she liked the music, and it fit better to the slow sensual dance they were doing. Thomas Rhett was also one of her favorite country artists, and the song "Blessed" was beautiful.

As they danced, she forgot about everything and got lost in Crunch's eyes. She'd never felt more in tune with anyone in her life, and it was as if they could read each other's minds when some of the steps changed. It worked a lot better and felt more natural.

The song ended with him dipping her and pressing his forehead against hers. He held her that way as they caught their breath, but he gazed into her eyes when he lifted his head. Sabrina felt heat in the pit of her belly as he lowered his lips to hers.

The sun started to set behind the trees and reflected on the pond making the whole area glow. When he brought her up to a standing position again, there was a halo of bright orange light behind him. She sighed as he cupped her face between his large hands and gazed into his eyes.

"I've been dying to kiss you for the last couple of days," Crunch whispered.

"Why have you waited?" She slipped her arms around his waist.

"You have so much on your mind, and Charlee had trouble sleeping. She's the priority." Crunch moved back.

Sabrina smiled as her heart swelled, knowing he was distant because of his concern for Charlee. It was difficult not to fall a little more for him when he put her daughter before anything else.

"Thank you for being concerned about her." Sabrina touched his cheek.

"I adore her, Sabrina." Crunch rested his hands on her hips. "I adore you. I'm happy just spending time with you."

Sabrina's mood slipped with the realization of what hung over her head. People believed she tried to kill someone, and she couldn't say for sure that she didn't do it.

"I guess we better spend as much time together as we can because I could end up in jail if Grant doesn't clear me." Sabrina rested her cheek against his chest.

"Don't say that. You're not going to jail because you didn't shoot anyone." Crunch wrapped his arms tightly around her.

If only she could stay in his embrace forever and forget everything. She wanted her world to be Charlee, her, and Crunch. It was too bad life didn't go that way. Sabrina wouldn't be able to live a happy life with her daughter or Crunch until the police cleared her.

"Let's go pick up Charlee, and the three of us will have a movie night. We'll forget everything for tonight." Crunch dipped his head down until he could look into her eyes.

Sabrina nodded. They didn't have to leave the property to get Charlee. The idea sounded great, but she also wanted a night alone with Crunch. Did that make her selfish or a terrible mother?

Chapter 22

Crunch ached to take Sabrina back to the house and lose himself in her, but she was a mom, and her daughter was more important than his hormones. He'd never want her to choose between him and the little girl.

As they walked into Keith's house, he could hear children's squeals from the other room, along with a deep booming voice roaring like a bear. Crunch glanced at Sabrina and smirked. His boss could be a serious man, but he was a marshmallow when it came to his kids. He spent all his free time with them and his wife.

"Who do I see hiding under the table?" Keith growled as one of the kids giggled.

"You know he's a big softy," Crunch whispered.

"He's worse than the kids," Emily grumbled as she meandered around the kitchen.

"Aren't all men like that?" Sabrina snickered.

"That's a smart woman," Emily said as she placed several cups on the counter.

Crunch rolled his eyes and headed into the living room to either save Keith or help him. The kids scampered around the room, hiding behind furniture to avoid the large man clomping around making monster noises.

"Who exactly is the kid here?" Crunch leaned against the archway that separated the living room and dining room.

"When they run around like this, they fall asleep faster, and I get my wife to myself." Keith leaned close to Crunch.

"Your wife looks annoyed." Crunch hitched his thumb toward the kitchen.

"She won't be when they're all asleep by eight." Keith winked and spun around as one of his sons tried to dart past him.

He picked up eight-year-old Noah and tossed him over his shoulder. The boy giggled as his dad spun around before dropping him on the plush sofa. Before Keith could stand up, seven-year-old Patrick, four-year-old Scarlett, and Charlee took the opportunity to jump on Keith, knocking him to his knees.

"You could help me out over here," Keith shouted over the screaming kids.

"Nah, you seem to have it under control." Crunch chuckled.

"I think you need to attack Crunch," Keith whispered to the kids.

Before he had a chance to react, Charlee ran across the couch and launched herself toward Crunch. He caught her mid-air, and she wrapped her little arms around his neck. Her big grin melted his heart as she glanced back over her shoulder at the pile of kids on top of Keith.

"I'll protect you, Crunch." She kissed his cheek.

Crunch knew it was over. He was a complete bowl of jelly with this little girl. There was nothing he wouldn't do to make her happy, and if it meant he was getting on the floor and acting like a bear, he'd do it.

"Let's get outta here," Charlee whispered.

"Come on." Crunch wrapped her up in his arms and darted out of the living room.

"Come on, Mommy. We gotta protect Crunch. Let's go." Charlee squealed.

"What are we protecting you from?" Sabrina smiled.

"Rusty and the kids." Crunch chuckled.

"Oh, then we better run," Sabrina said.

"Thanks a lot. Now you guys are going to leave me with three crazy kids and their father." Emily sighed.

"You married him." Crunch chuckled as they headed out of the house.

"You knew him longer and didn't warn me," Emily shouted behind them.

Crunch laughed as they hopped in the truck. Since they weren't on the main roads, he wasn't worried about putting Charlee in a booster seat, but he didn't move until he checked with Sabrina.

"Is it okay if I sit her on my lap and let her steer the truck?" Crunch asked.

"That's up to you." Sabrina smiled.

"Charlee, would you like to drive the truck?"

The little girl bounced up and down on the seat excitedly. Crunch thought his ears would burst with the pitch of her voice. He pulled the excited little girl onto his lap and showed her how to place her hands on the steering wheel.

"I can't reach the buttons on the floor." Charlee wiggled her feet.

"I guess I'll have to press those buttons for you, and you can steer the wheel because that's the most important part," Crunch said as he pulled the truck into drive.

Crunch kept his hands on the bottom of the wheel, trying to make sure the little girl didn't steer them into the trees. He glanced at Sabrina out of the corner of his eye. She had pulled out her phone and was recording her daughter. He was sure the smile on Charlee's face was big and bright.

"Do we turn here, Crunch?" Charlee glanced up at him.

"Yes, we do," he told her as they slowly guided the truck in front of the safehouse.

"You forgot to turn on the blinker. Mommy always gets mad when people don't do that." Charlee reached for the indicator.

"You're right, Charlee. That's very important." Crunch smirked as they stopped.

"Mommy calls them mor-oon," Charlee told him.

"Mommy shouldn't call anyone a mor-oon," Sabrina sighed. "That's not a nice word."

Crunch pressed his lips together to hide his smile as they made their way into the house. Charlee stopped in the middle of the kitchen and looked around with hands on her hips.

"Why is there no food for me?" Charlee asked.

"There is food in the fridge," Sabrina said.

"But nobody is cooking." Charlee pointed to the stove.

"We just got here, honey." Crunch laughed.

"But the Nannies were cooking the food." Charlee tilted her head and stared up at him.

She'd gotten used to Nanny Betty, Cora, Alice, and Keith's mother, Kathleen, being at the safehouse over the last couple of days. The four women seemed to think they needed enough food for an army, and there were still enough leftovers to feed the three of them for a week.

"I think we can manage to feed ourselves today," Sabrina told her daughter.

"Are you sure you can cook it like the Nannies?" Charlee asked.

"I think so." Sabrina smirked.

"Crunch, maybe we should call them." Charlee looked up at him.

"I'm overwhelmed by my daughter's faith in my ability to heat leftovers." Sabrina opened the fridge and pulled out several containers.

Crunch assured the little girl they could manage and settled her in front of her favorite Disney movie while he helped Sabrina.

For several minutes, they worked in silence, filling plates with roasted chicken, mashed potatoes, and salad. Once it was heated, Crunch carried the meal to the living room, and they sat on the floor around the coffee table.

While Sabrina and Charlee discussed the movie, he remained quiet. He loved this. Just the three of them. As if they were a family, and he could get used to it. He never thought a simple supper on the floor in front of the television could feel so right.

"Hunter." Sabrina waved her hand in front of his face.

"Sorry, I got lost in my thoughts." He smiled at her.

"I saw that. You're worried, aren't you?" Sabrina put down her fork.

"Everything's going to be fine, and right now, I'm simply enjoying having supper with two beautiful ladies." Crunch cupped her cheek.

"It's nice." Sabrina smiled

Charlee was lost in her movie and didn't even notice when he started to clear their empty plates. Crunch nodded his head toward the kitchen, and Sabrina followed him.

"Why are you worried?" Sabrina whispered when they were alone in the kitchen.

"I'm not worried." He pulled her into his arms. "I was simply thinking about how much I like being together like this."

He kissed her forehead, and she sighed. Crunch was worried about who tried to kill her and who shot Grant, but until he knew more, he wasn't going to make her any more anxious than she already was.

"I like being together like this too." She gave him a soft kiss on his lips. "I feel like I'm supposed to be here with you."

"I wouldn't want to be anywhere else," he whispered against her lips.

"What will I do if they can't prove I didn't shoot Grant? I don't even know if I did it." Sabrina rested her cheek against his chest.

"First of all, I don't believe for a second you shot Grant, and A.J. is a good cop. He'll find the truth. I promise," he assured her.

Crunch truly believed what he said, but until they got a statement from Grant that confirmed Sabrina was innocent, her life would be in limbo. With all the staff who worked at the Thornton estate, someone needed to clear her.

Chapter 23

Sabrina woke up in an empty bed and blew out a breath of frustration. She and Crunch spent the previous night with Charlee tossing and turning between them. Her daughter wouldn't settle down until she was in her own bed.

Charlee wasn't a clingy child and only wanted to sleep with Sabrina when she was sick, but since the night of the shooting, Charlee wanted to be between Sabrina and Crunch. Of course, she was probably confused with bouncing around from house to house.

Sabrina needed to find a way to get Charlee around her own things. She sat up in the bed and threaded her fingers through her long hair. When she looked up, Crunch was in the doorway with a tense expression.

"What's wrong?" she sighed.

"A.J. has gone to interview Grant," Crunch said.

Sabrina wasn't sure if it was good or bad that the police could finally speak to Grant. Hopefully, they'd get confirmation Sabrina didn't shoot him and tell him who did. She should be relieved, so why was her heart racing and hands shaking?

"How long until we know?" She sat on the side of the bed.

"He was at the hospital when he called." Crunch moved into the room and sat next to her.

"What if I did—." Sabrina stopped.

"You didn't shoot him." Crunch wrapped her in his arms.

She hated the unknown, but she couldn't remember ever being so scared. If she went to jail, what would happen to Charlee? Her chest hurt to think about saying goodbye to her daughter if the police arrested her.

"Where's Charlee?" She suddenly needed to see her daughter.

"She's trying to explain why Crash needs to watch *Beauty and the Beast*." Crunch smirked.

Sabrina stood up and left the bedroom. She found Charlee on Crash's lap, trying to force him to watch the television, but he pretended he didn't want to see it.

"I can't. That monster scares me," Crash said with an exaggerated gasp.

"He's not scary. He's really not. You gotta watch, Crash. The beast isn't a monster. He's a people. Watch, he's gonna turn into a people." Charlee put her hands on Crash's cheeks and tried to turn his head.

"He's been doing that since the movie started," Crunch whispered from behind her.

Sabrina smiled, but she itched to pick up her daughter and hold her. She didn't know if Grant confirmed or denied that Sabrina shot him. She closed her eyes and pulled in a shaky breath.

"Sweetheart, come here," Crunch said low enough that she barely heard it.

He wrapped his arm around her shoulder and led her back to the bedroom. When they got inside, he closed the door and pulled her into the safety of his embrace. She took several shaky breaths as she allowed his touch to help her calm her frayed nerves.

"I'm scared," she admitted.

"I know, sweetheart, but I'm here, and no matter what Grant says, we'll get through it." Crunch kissed the top of her head.

"I need to make arrangements for Charlee." She lifted her head and looked into his eyes.

"Charlee is fine here." Crunch tilted his head.

"I mean, in case I end up arrested... or..." Sabrina blew out a breath.

Crunch pushed her back and held her face between his hands. She looked deep into his eyes, and her vision blurred. She wanted to look away, but he wouldn't let her, and she couldn't stop the tears as they spilled down her cheeks.

"You're not going to jail for something you didn't do. Do you hear me?" Crunch spoke slow and firm.

"But—" Sabrina choked.

"No buts. I don't believe for a single second that you shot Grant. How many times do I have to say it before you believe it?" Crunch's eyes were intense.

She wrapped her arms around his neck and clung to him. He held her tight against his body until she stopped trembling. Sabrina needed to believe he was right, but she still doubted in the back of her head.

"I told Zara I would go to the studio today and set up for Monday's classes." Sabrina sighed.

"If you want, we can go to the studio today. Emily asked if Charlee wanted to play with Scarlett while Keith took the boys fishing." Crunch pulled back and wiped the tears from her cheeks.

"Is it safe to go?" Sabrina asked.

"I'm taking one of the company vehicles, and Shadow will be at the studio while we're there. It's Sunday, so we'll have the whole place to ourselves, and we can practice," Crunch told her.

"I need to do something, and I made a promise to all the instructors that they wouldn't have to deal with cleaning when they come in for classes," Sabrina whispered.

"We can get everything done, then practice for the Performing Arts Ball." Crunch smiled.

"At least I can forget for a while." Sabrina sighed.

"Mommy, mommy." Charlee skipped toward her.

"What, what?" Sabrina caught her daughter as she launched into her arms.

"I gotta question for Crunch." Charlee tilted her head and looked at Crunch.

"What's your question, my little ballerina?" Crunch tapped her on the nose.

"Are you the prince?" Charlee cupped her hand around her little mouth and whispered.

"What do you mean prince?" Crunch chuckled.

"You know, the prince that gets the princess. Mommy is the princess. Are you the prince?" Charlee was so serious.

Crunch looked like a deer caught in the headlights, and Sabrina pressed her lips together to hide her smile. Charlee stared at Crunch as if he was about to utter the most important words in the world.

"Well... umm... I'm not a prince." Crunch stammered.

"I know you're not a real prince." Charlee rolled her eyes as if to say, *duh*. "But are you Mommy's prince?"

Crunch flicked his gaze at Sabrina as if to ask for some help. What was he supposed to say to a little girl about whether her mother was in a relationship? Were they? They only had one date, sort of, but she felt a connection to him and hoped he was her prince.

"Charlee, do you want me to be Mommy's prince?" Crunch asked.

"Uh-huh, you're the bestest." Charlee grinned.

"Thank you, sweetheart. Here's what I know, I care about your mommy, very much. I'd like to be her prince if that's okay with you and her." Crunch met Sabrina's eyes.

"Mommy, you want Crunch to be your prince, right?" Charlee tilted her little head.

Sabrina smiled at her daughter, and then she glanced at the man next to her. He was as handsome as any prince, sexy as any model, and the sweetest person she'd ever met. Why wouldn't she want him to be her prince?

"I think I'd like that." Sabrina gazed into his eyes.

"Yay. Crunch, you're Mommy's prince." Charlee wrapped her arms around Sabrina and reached for Crunch.

Sabrina giggled as Charlee kissed Crunch's cheek then wiggled to get out of Sabrina's arms. As she ran off, Crunch pulled her into his arms.

"I like being your prince," he whispered and then pressed a soft kiss on her lips.

They walked into the empty studio an hour later and locked the door behind them. Shadow stayed in the vehicle to watch the surroundings because nobody needed to enter the building since the place was closed. There wasn't much activity on the street since most businesses were closed on Sundays, so Shadow would notice if someone were around.

It was strange in the large studio with nobody else. No music playing, no giggling kids or phones ringing. When the light of the main area went on, she turned to see Crunch flicking switches.

"We'll get the rooms done and then use the taproom to practice," Crunch suggested.

They went room to room, cleaning mirrors, mopping floors, and wiping down the ballet bars for a couple of hours. Once they had everything done and the cleaning supplies put away, Crunch smiled at her.

"After you." He waved his arm as he opened the door to the tap room.

She smiled as she headed into the room. She opened her bag and pulled out her shoes while Crunch set up the music. She slipped off her leggings and wrapped her sheer skirt around her waist. When she buckled up her shoes, she stood up.

Crunch was staring at her. His gaze slowly moved from her face, down her body, and then back up. The flare of lust in his eyes made her heart jump in her chest, and she smiled. They'd only been together once, but their chemistry was obvious, and her nipples pebbled, poking against the thin material of her leotard.

"I swear you get more beautiful every day." Crunch started the music and leisurely moved toward her.

He held out his hand, and she met him in the middle of the room. Crunch pulled her against him and deliberately moved them around to the soft music. He grasped her hand and twirled her around twice before bringing her back against his body. They weren't doing the routine they'd practiced, but she wouldn't complain.

"I don't remember this part," she said as he rested his forehead against hers.

"I want to feel your body against mine," he whispered.

"I'm sorry." She closed her eyes.

"Why are you sorry?" He pulled back and met her eyes.

It was difficult for them to get intimate, and they'd been interrupted every night by Charlee crawling between them. She wanted to be with him again, desperately.

"I'm sorry Charlee has been so clingy. She needs me, and I'm all she has," she admitted.

"You don't ever have to be sorry for that. I've told you before, Charlee is the most important thing in your life and very important to me as well," Crunch said.

"Thank you." She raised up on her toes and brushed her lips against his.

When she started to pull back, he tugged her closer and deepened the kiss as he pulled her against his hard muscles. She thrust her tongue into his mouth and swirled it with his, causing a deep groan to vibrate against her lips. Crunch slid his hands down to her ass, cupping both cheeks as he pulled her tight to his growing erection.

"We need to practice. You're not being very princely right now," Sabrina murmured against his lips.

"Mmm, hmm. I'm not trying to be." Crunch kissed across her jaw and down the side of her neck.

"The dance, Hunter." Sabrina giggled as he nipped her ear.

"Dance, right," he whispered into her ear, but his hand glided up her side and cupped her breast.

"Hunter." she sighed when he pinched her hard nipple through her leotard.

"Sabrina." His voice rumbled against her neck.

Crunch pulled down the snug piece of material until he exposed her breast. He gently kneaded it as he kissed down her chest until his mouth was next to her nipple. He circled his tongue around the hard bud several times before gently biting it.

"Ah, yes." Sabrina gasped.

Crunch sucked and nibbled at her breast while he tugged down the other side of the leotard, exposing her other breast. He repeated the attention but continued to massage each mound. He'd lick one, then the other, leaving each nipple wet with his saliva. He blew on them, causing goosebumps to erupt over her skin.

"You have beautiful tits," Crunch whispered with a deep rasp.

He kissed slowly down the front of her body as he dropped to his knees, slipping her leotard down and baring her naked body to his view. He licked around her navel while he pushed her clothes down over her hips. Sabrina closed her eyes as his hands stroked her skin, making every bit of her body tingle with his touch. His tongue lapped against her abdomen and slowly moved lower to where she ached to be touched.

"So damn perfect." He growled against the top of her pussy.

Sabrina braced her hands on his shoulders to steady herself while he slipped his tongue between her folds and flicked it against her swollen clitoris. Crunch gripped her hips as he tasted her aching sex.

"Oh, Hunter," she whimpered and gripped his shoulders.

"You smell delicious. I want to devour your sweet pussy." Crunch hummed against her slit.

While he teased and licked her clit, he tugged her clothes down until they pooled around her heels. He pulled back and took her hands so she could step out of the clothing, and he shoved it aside. He wrapped his hands around her thighs and pulled her legs apart so he could nuzzle her sex. He inhaled, then wrapped his lips around her throbbing bundle of nerves.

Her head dropped back as he sucked her into his mouth. Her pussy clenched as he continued to focus his attention on her sensitive bud. She needed more and thrust her hips forward, causing him to hum against her sex.

She was so close, but he must've sensed it before she could tell him and pushed two fingers inside her. Sabrina hissed as he sucked her clit harder and curled his fingers inside, rubbing against her inner walls.

"Hunter. Yes… God… yes…" Sabrina trembled as her body erupted into a long-overdue wave of pleasure.

Her legs quivered as he lapped at her release, drawing out the climax. When the final tremor ravaged her body, her knees buckled, but Crunch caught her and lowered her to the floor. He grinned as he hovered over her.

"Are you okay?" Crunch whispered against her lips.

"Uh-huh," she murmured.

"Good, because I'm not done practicing yet." He smiled.

Sabrina wasn't having it and pushed him over onto his back. He smirked up at her as she stood over him naked except for her dance shoes. The way he looked up at her made her feel sexy, and she winked as she placed a foot on either side of his body.

"If you want to dance, then get those clothes off," she demanded.

"Bossy, aren't you?" He grabbed the bottom of his muscle shirt and yanked it over his head.

"I can be," she purred as he wiggled out of his pants.

He lay under her in only those hot jockstrap underwear, and she licked her lips at the sight of his cock straining against the material. He tucked his hands under his head and raised an eyebrow as she ogled his body.

"Did you get tired of undressing?" Sabrina asked, straddling his thighs.

"No, you looked like you were enjoying the view." Crunch moved his hand to his covered cock and rubbed it.

"I can help with that if you would like." Sabrina gently scraped her nails down his chest.

"Fuck," Crunch hissed through his teeth.

"We can do that too," she said in a low, husky voice.

Crunch pushed down his underwear, and she lifted enough for him to kick them off. She reached for his shirt and placed it over his eyes. At first, he protested, but she stopped him and bent over, so her lips were next to his ear.

"Close your eyes and enjoy every touch, lick, and suck." She nipped his earlobe.

"Yes." Crunch practically growled the word.

Sabrina moved her lips down his neck and across his jaw, leaving a trail of kisses up to his lips. His tongue flicked out and skimmed across his lower lip. Sabrina brushed her open mouth across his and thrust her tongue into his for a moment.

Crunch whispered her name as she licked along the side of his neck while her nails lightly skimmed down the hard muscles of his chest. The sounds coming from him made her bolder as she traveled slowly down his body.

"Sabrina, I'm going to fucking explode." He gave a needy moan.

"Hmmm, that's the point." She hummed against his belly.

She moved down until her mouth hovered above his thick cock. A drop of fluid seeped out of the tip, and she licked it away, causing his hips to thrust up. Sabrina swirled her tongue around the swollen head as she wrapped her hand around his shaft and took him into her mouth.

"Sweet Jesus," Crunch groaned.

Sabrina moved her mouth down over his length, taking as much of him as she could and then sucking hard on the way up. She cupped his balls with her other hand, and he fisted her ponytail as he lifted his hips.

"Sabrina… feels so amazing," Crunch panted.

"Take the shirt off and watch," she purred.

He ripped the shirt off his eyes and lifted his head. He grunted as she dragged her teeth across the tip, and he tugged her ponytail a little harder. She'd never had anyone pull her hair while giving them a blowjob, but the more Crunch did, the wetter she became. She straddled one of his thighs so she could grind against it and give herself some relief from the ache in her pussy. He must've liked it because he pressed his leg against her.

"I want to fuck you so bad," Crunch grunted through gritted teeth.

Sabrina slowly released his cock with a pop and grinned. Crunch blew out a breath of frustration as she licked her lips and jumped to his knees. When he pulled her forward, he slammed his mouth against her. The kiss was hard, needy, and he shook as he pulled away.

"I don't have a condom. I didn't exactly plan this." He flipped her over onto her back and kissed her breast.

"I'm protected." She squeaked as he sucked her nipple into his hot mouth.

"I'm clean. I haven't been with anyone in a long time, and I'm tested regularly." Crunch lifted his head and looked into her eyes.

"I want you inside me," she whispered.

"Are you sure?" he asked.

"I want you with nothing between us. Just me and you," Sabrina whispered.

Sabrina pushed him over onto his back and straddled his hips. She wrapped her hand around his shaft and rubbed the head between her folds. She was so wet that he slipped inside with no resistance.

"Baby," Crunch cried out as she dropped down, burying him completely inside her.

"You feel so good." Sabrina gasped as she lifted up and dropped down again.

Crunch grabbed her hips as she continued to ride his dick. She laid her hands on his chest to balance herself while she thrust her hips back and forth. The movement put pressure on her throbbing clit, and she trembled as a climax edged its way to the surface.

"Look at me, Sabrina." He lifted his hips, thrusting into her hard. "I want to look into your eyes as I slam into that sweet pussy."

Sabrina was close, and she needed more pressure on her clit. While she gazed into his eyes, she began to slip her hand between them, but he slapped her hand away and pressed his thumb against her bundle of nerves.

"Come, Sabrina. I want you to come around my cock," Crunch demanded.

Sabrina was sure even if he hadn't been stimulating her clit, she would've come from his words. Her sex squeezed around his shaft, and she threw her head back as her body quivered.

"That's it, baby." Crunch thrust up again.

"Yes, oh…" Sabrina screamed.

"Yes, squeeze my cock." Crunch grunted as he slammed up into her one more time. "Yes."

His body convulsed under her as he pulled her tight against him. She could feel him jerk inside her, and he grunted with every pulse. Sabrina's passage contracted, and she shivered.

She dropped down on top with him still deep inside her. The only sound in the room was the soft music and their heavy breathing. Sabrina lifted her head and gazed down at the gorgeous man under her.

"I don't think we can do this routine at the ball." Crunch smirked.

"Yeah, that wouldn't work." Sabrina giggled.

"I swear I didn't plan this," Crunch whispered.

"I didn't either." She pressed her lips against his.

"I'm not complaining, though." He lifted his head and kissed her nose.

"Me either, but maybe we *should* practice a little." Sabrina smiled.

"In a few minutes." Crunch wrapped his arms around her and let out a content sigh.

He held her for a few minutes before reluctantly releasing her and tugged her into the dressing room. They cleaned up, and after a few more kisses, they got dressed again. While she fixed her hair, Crunch said he was going out to switch off the lights, and they'd head home.

A few minutes later, Sabrina walked out of the dressing room. She found Crunch at the studio's back door, crouched next to a box on the floor. He stood slowly and took several steps backward.

"Hey," she said.

Crunch spun around. His jaw clenched, and his eyes narrowed as she started to move toward him. He held up his hand, and she stopped.

"We need to get out of here." Crunch grabbed her hand and pulled her toward the front of the building.

"What's wrong?" Sabrina asked as he dragged her with him.

"I think there—"

Crunch's words disappeared when a thunderous boom erupted behind them. It was as if something picked her up and tossed her across the building. She slammed against something hard and then dropped to the floor. The impact knocked the wind out of her, and she gasped as she tried to get air back into her lungs.

Sabrina groaned and attempted to roll over, but things were falling on her, and it was hard to see. She blinked and pushed up on her hands and knees. Thick dust surrounded her, and debris covered her. She pushed large broken pieces of wood off her and used the wall to help her stand up. She staggered to her feet as she tried to scan the area.

"Hunter," she choked out the name.

When there was no response, she called out again. Nothing. It was almost impossible to see through the smoke and dust flying around. As she took a couple of steps toward what she thought was the back of the building, she froze. Large orange flames licked up the wall, and tiny sparks danced around the floor as pieces of the ceiling fell from above.

"Hunter, where are you?" Sabrina screamed.

She stumbled around what used to be the foyer of the studio, or at least it was where she thought it was. Sabrina shouted out to him again, and the effort caused her to cough as she inhaled smoke. It burned her throat and lungs, but she had to find Crunch. She'd held his hand right before the explosion threw them across the building.

"Hunter, please answer me." She coughed as she dropped to her hands and knees.

Sabrina gasped for air as she pushed splintered pieces of wood aside and continued to search for Crunch. He wasn't answering, and her heart raced as panic bubbled up inside. It was harder to breathe, and the flames quickly moved toward her.

"Hunter," she screamed.

A soft groan to her left had her frantically tossing things aside until she found the source of the sound. She picked up what could only be a melted piece of plastic and blew out a breath when Crunch's eyes stared up at her.

"Oh, thank God. I found you. We got to get out of here." Sabrina continued to pull debris off of him.

"Something's pinning my legs." He winced as he tried to sit up.

"Let me see," Sabrina shouted.

"You need to get out of here," Crunch yelled.

"We will as soon as I get your legs free." Sabrina wasn't leaving him.

Desperately, she flicked off debris that covered him until she saw why he couldn't move. A large part beam lay across his legs, and from what she could see, it wouldn't be long before the rest of the wall would fall on them if they didn't get out of there.

"I need to get this off of you," she shouted.

Sabrina stood up and grabbed the edge of the large steel piece. She grasped the edge of the metal and grunted as she used all her strength to lift the large hunk. It didn't move, and she tried again.

"Sabrina, get out of here," Crunch yelled.

"No," she grunted as she strained to lift the beam.

The smoke was worse, and she pulled her shirt up over her nose and mouth as she glanced around for something to help pry the beam off Crunch. Before she could find anything, he grabbed her hand.

"Sweetheart, please. You need to get out of here. Charlee needs you." Crunch pulled her down as something popped and sparks sprinkled over them.

"I know, and we're going to get home to her. I need something to use as a fulcrum," she said, remembering her high school physics.

Sabrina pulled away from him and frantically scanned for something to help. She prayed her high school teacher knew what she was talking about because she didn't like how thick the air was getting around them.

"Damn it, woman, get the hell out of here," Crunch roared at her.

"Don't tell me what to do. I'm getting both of us out."

She spotted one of the ballet bars sticking out of a studio door. She stumbled over the debris and grabbed the broken piece of wood. She dragged it to where Crunch was still yelling for her to leave. She ignored his pleas and managed to get the bar under the end of the beam.

"I'm going to try and pry this off your legs, Hunter. You need to pull yourself out from under it." Sabrina used all her weight to lift the bar.

After several tries, it still didn't move. Sabrina was on her knees coughing when Crunch grabbed her and pulled her close to him. Tears streamed down her cheeks as the blare of the sirens echoed through the noise of the crackling wood, letting them know the firefighters were there.

"Please, Sabrina. You can get out through there." Crunch pointed to a small area where the fire hadn't reached.

"I'm not leaving you," she sobbed.

"You need to get out and tell them I'm stuck. Go. Please." Crunch pushed her.

She fell back, and for a second, she stared, then before going to the exit, she moved toward him and pressed her lips against his. This wasn't going to be the last time she kissed him. She knew that.

"I'll send them in to get you. Don't you dare give up," Sabrina ordered.

After one more glance back, she stepped over the rubble and headed toward where the door used to be. She shoved her way out of the building until she fell through, landing on the steps outside. Someone picked her up and carried her away from the studio toward the ambulance.

"Hunter is stuck under a beam. You've got to get him out." Sabrina coughed.

"The firefighters will get to him," a deep male voice rumbled.

She looked up as the paramedic placed a mask over her nose and mouth. Inhaling the fresh oxygen caused her to cough, but she grabbed the man who carried her. Before she said anything else, he nodded and rushed toward the building. It was as if he had disappeared. That was probably the reason they called him Shadow.

Sabrina trembled while the young paramedic checked her and encouraged her to take slow, deep breaths. She knew she inhaled a lot of smoke, but she refused to leave until Crunch was safe.

"Does this hurt?" the paramedic asked.

Sabrina looked down at her arm. The skin looked like raw meat, but she was so high on adrenaline she didn't feel it. When she shook her head, the paramedic began to treat the wound while she worried about the man she loved.

The streams of water sprayed over the burning structure, and she managed to calm the coughing a little. She took a deep breath as firefighters moved closer to the entrance, then another explosion.

Chapter 24

Crunch struggled to breathe as he used all his strength to try and free himself. The flames were creeping closer, and the smoke burned his throat as he gasped for air. He pulled his shirt up over his mouth and nose, but it was doing little to help him breathe.

He was going to die. He could feel it. Crunch didn't want his life to end without telling Sabrina how he felt, but he made her leave before he could. He was about to die without telling her how much he loved her.

He slapped his hands against his pockets, remembering his phone. Crunch winced as he pulled it out and opened the camera. If he couldn't tell her face to face, she was still going to hear it from his lips before he died. He hit *record* and pulled the shirt down from his face.

"Sabrina, I'm so sorry I didn't tell you sooner." Crunch's voice was raspy, and he had to take a break to cough. "I don't think I'm getting out of here, and I wanted you to know... I love you."

Crunch coughed until he practically vomited. He gasped for air, but it was harder to breathe. He held the phone to his chest as his breaths got shallower. This was it. He was going to die.

"I'm sorry, Sabrina. I'm sorry, Mom and Dad, I'm not going to get out of here. Zara, take care of—" Crunch coughed.

"You can take care of them yourself. Let's get you out of here," a familiar voice shouted.

Crunch opened his eyes and looked up at the man lifting the beam off his legs. He had to be dreaming. Shadow wouldn't run into a burning building. No. He must be fading into delirium from lack of oxygen.

"Come on, twinkle toes. Get up off your arse," Shadow yelled.

Crunch felt his body dragged up, and his eyes flew open as he looked into the face of his friend. Shadow grinned as he wrapped his arm around Crunch's waist and practically dragged him out of the building.

"Sabrina," Crunch wheezed.

"She's safe. Now we need to get out of here so you can tell her that shit face to face." Shadow nodded toward the exit.

"Okay," Crunch rasped.

They stepped over the broken door, but another explosion hurled them forward before Crunch could thank Shadow for risking his life. Crunch grunted as his head hit something and things around him faded. He managed to open his eyes enough to see a blur of someone running toward him before everything went black.

Chapter 25

Sabrina closed her eyes and tried to erase the image of Crunch and Shadow slamming against the pavement of the parking lot. She thought Crunch was gone, but then she saw them through the thick smoke a second before the explosion hurled them forward.

Shadow managed to catch himself before he hit the side of the firetruck, but Crunch didn't. Sabrina ripped off the oxygen mask and ran as fast as she could to where he lay motionless on the ground. He was so still, and before she could make sure he was alive, she was pulled back for the paramedics to work on him.

Now, she sat in a hospital cubicle waiting for the doctor. She knew she was fine, and except for a couple of stitches, minor burns, and smoke inhalation, she was ready to leave. She wanted to see Crunch, and the doctor wouldn't tell her anything because she wasn't family.

She adjusted the oxygen around her face and under her nose. It was better than the full mask they'd used. At least this didn't make her feel claustrophobic. She glanced at her bandaged arm and sighed.

She didn't know how she'd cut it, but it was deep enough she needed several stitches. She had a couple of burns on her hands, but the doctor said they were minor.

"What's taking so long?" she muttered to herself.

"Sabrina." Her brother stepped into the cubicle and wrapped his arms around her.

"I'm fine. I need to see Hunter." Sabrina couldn't hold back the emotion any longer.

"I don't know where he is. I got a call you were here. What the hell happened?" Colt held her as she cried.

"We were... practicing... dressing room... and then boom," Sabrina whimpered.

"At the dance studio?" Colt pulled back and looked into her face.

"Yes." She wiped the tears with her fingers.

"I don't understand." Colt shook his head. "It's a dance studio. There shouldn't be anything there to cause an explosion."

Sabrina didn't know what had happened. The only thing she knew was Crunch saw something and suddenly became in a huge hurry to get out of there, but it was too late.

"I need to make sure he's okay, Colt," Sabrina whispered.

She sat up and tried to get out of bed, but the oxygen tube pulled her back. Colt helped her lay back into the bed and handed her a tissue to wipe her eyes.

"I need to know, Colt." Sabrina stared up at her brother.

"Look, I'll see what I can find out, but you need to stay there until the doctor comes and I get back. Got it?" Colt held her hand between his.

"Got it," she whispered.

Colt hurried out of the room, and Sabrina closed her eyes. She reached for the blanket at the foot of the bed and pulled it up over her body. The paramedic wrapped it around her when the ambulance brought her in. Now she felt like she needed it around her again.

She closed her eyes and curled up on her side as she waited for someone to tell her Crunch was okay and that she hadn't lost another man she loved. God, she wouldn't live through that again.

She was startled when someone touched her leg. Her eyes flew open, and she looked up at a tearful Zara. Sabrina felt a weight on her chest as she sat up slowly.

"No," Sabrina hiccupped. "He's got to be okay."

"He's… alive." Zara dropped her gaze to the floor.

"Alive, but," Sabrina pushed.

"He hit his head, and he hasn't woken up yet. They're sending him for a scan." Zara sniffed.

It was as if someone poured a jug of ice water down over her, and she got thrown back four years earlier when the doctors said the same thing to her about Easton. It couldn't be happening all over again.

"Sabrina, I'm so glad you're okay." Zara hugged her.

"I need to see him," Sabrina sobbed.

"He's in ICU right now," Zara told her.

"Can I get in to see him?" Sabrina wasn't family.

"Of course, but your brother said you need to wait for the doctor." Zara sat next to her. "I need to get back with Mom and Dad, but as soon as the doctor says you're okay, come find us."

Sabrina nodded because she couldn't speak. What was she supposed to say? She barely held back the tears long enough for Zara to leave the cubicle. She rocked and cried for the man who helped heal her heart.

Hysterically crying was how Colt and Shadow found her a few minutes later. Her brother immediately wrapped his arms around her and held her until she could pull herself together again.

"Sabrina, it's going to be okay," Shadow said in a soft, soothing tone.

"He's not awake. Zara told me." Sabrina looked up at the man.

Then she noticed Shadow's arm was in a sling and a bandage on his forehead. He'd gotten hurt, and she didn't realize it. She'd been so concerned about Crunch she never asked about the hero who saved the man she loved.

"You're hurt," Sabrina whispered.

"Nothing bad. Strained shoulder and a small cut. I've had worse." He winked at her.

"Thank you," Sabrina said.

"For what?" Shadow tilted his head.

"For saving him." Sabrina swallowed hard.

"He's family, and I do anything for family." Shadow nodded.

The curtain to the cubicle opened, and a man walked in with a smile. He was probably in his early forties, with greying hair and about a day's worth of beard. He nodded at Colt and Shadow as he stepped next to the bed.

"Hi, Ms. Burke. I'm Dr. Cramer, but I tell everyone to call me Adam." He held out his hand to her.

"Nice to meet you," Sabrina replied.

"I wish it were under better circumstances, but thankfully all your X-rays came back fine. I want to keep you overnight because you inhaled a lot of smoke. It's simply a precaution to make sure there are no complications and—"

"I can't stay. I have a daughter at home and—" Sabrina interrupted the doctor.

"And I'll look after Charlee," Colt cut her off.

"Well, looks like that's settled." Adam pulled his stethoscope from around his neck. "I want to recheck your lungs."

She lay back and let him examine her, but the whole time she tried to convince them she was well enough to leave. The truth was she needed to see Charlee and hold her. She knew her little girl would be fine with Colt, but it wasn't the same.

"Adam, have you seen Crunch?" Shadow asked.

Adam tilted his head as if trying to figure out if he knew the large man asking about Crunch. Sabrina could see the exact moment the doctor recognized Shadow.

"Jesus, I didn't recognize you with your hair longer. The last time I saw you, it was buzzed off." Adam checked Sabrina's blood pressure.

"Yeah, I've had it long for a while and cut it off but letting it grow back again." Shadow threaded his fingers through his shoulder-length hair.

"Crunch was sent down for an MRI, but he's under the ICU doctor's care now." Adam turned back to Sabrina. "We're going to keep you on the oxygen and redo the blood work in the morning."

When the doctor left, a nurse came in with a bag to put her smoky clothes in. They'd removed them when she arrived and put her in hospital scrubs. She rolled on her side and gagged as her hair fell over her face. The smell of the smoke was sickening, and she wanted to take a shower.

"He's going to be okay, Sis." Colt crouched next to the bed.

"How do you know?" Sabrina whispered.

"I just do." Colt pushed her hair back from her face.

For several hours, she tossed and turned. It was impossible to get comfortable with the Iv in her hand and an oxygen tube in her nose. Then there was the fact nobody came to tell her any news about Crunch, and she lay alone since her brother went home with Charlee.

She must've fallen asleep at some point because the next thing she knew, she heard people outside her cubicle. She sat up as Sandy and Shadow walked through the curtain.

"How's Hunter?" Sabrina said and winced at the raspy sound of her voice.

"He's stable," Sandy told her.

"He hasn't woken up?" Sabrina's voice cracked.

"It's only been a couple of hours, honey." Sandy sat on the bed next to her.

"I couldn't… he was stuck…" Sabrina pressed her lips together to keep the sob from escaping.

"He's alive," Shadow interjected.

Sabrina nodded. She tried to take a deep breath, but it made her cough. It wasn't as bad as when she first arrived, but she did have a headache.

"Colt asked me to let you know Charlee is fine, and he'll be by in the morning." Sandy handed her a piece of paper. "Charlee said this picture will make you better."

Sabrina unfolded the paper and smiled at a drawing of three stick figures and a big yellow sun at the top. She clenched her daughter's artwork in her hands and blinked several times to clear the tears that formed.

"She made one for Crunch too," Sandy said as she held up another folded paper.

"She loves him," Sabrina whispered.

"I don't think she's the only one." Sandy smiled.

Sabrina sighed and was about to admit it when her curtain opened. She was surprised to see Aaron walk in with another police officer behind him.

"Really, A.J. Can't this wait until she leaves the hospital?" Sandy snapped as she stood up.

"Stay out of this, Sandy," Aaron warned.

"What's going on?" Sabrina looked from Aaron to Sandy then to Shadow.

"A witness gave us some information on Grant's shooting, Sabrina." Aaron stepped closer, but Sandy stood in front of him.

"She's not going anywhere," Sandy snapped.

"Stop interfering. I don't want to do this any more than you want me to." Aaron looked pained.

"What's going on?" Sabrina asked.

"Sabrina, the witness said you shot Grant," Aaron told her.

Sabrina shook her head.

"Grant said I shot him?" Sabrina's voice was barely audible.

"Actually, he doesn't remember anything. We have another witness." Aaron met her eyes.

"You're arresting me." Sabrina closed her eyes.

"No, he's not," a booming voice echoed from behind the curtain.

Everyone watched as the curtain opened, and two men stepped into the cubicle that was getting more crowded by the minute. One of the men may have grown a beard, and his hair was longer, but she'd recognize him anywhere.

"Bennett?" Sabrina gasped.

Chapter 26

Sabrina stared at Easton's father with wide eyes and disbelief. They thought he died four years ago and suspected his body taken out into the Atlantic Ocean after the plane crash. His family grieved for him.

"I'm sorry, who are you?" Aaron asked.

"If you're asking who I am now, then you can call me B.K. but if you want to know who I was before I had to go undercover, my name is…"

"Bennett Thornton," Sabrina whispered.

"*The* Bennett Thornton?" Sandy asked.

"Yes." Bennett nodded at them.

Sabrina glanced from Bennett to Aaron and then the man next to him. He looked familiar too, but she was having difficulty placing him. He was mean-looking but stood in silence in the middle of the discussion.

"You… the crash…" Sabrina ripped off the oxygen tube.

"I can't talk about it, but I didn't get on that plane." Bennett turned to Aaron.

"This will prove she did not shoot my son." Bennett handed a flash drive to Aaron.

"What is this?" Aaron asked.

"It's video surveillance of my office the day Grant was shot." Bennett stepped next to Sabrina. "Whoever did this will not get away with what they did to you and your friend."

"B.K., we need to leave," the other man said quietly.

"Give me a minute, Skiff," Bennett snapped.

"Bennett, you need to let Harriet know you're alive." Sabrina grabbed the sleeve of his sweater.

Bennett smiled and sat down on the bed next to her. He nodded to the other man who walked outside and closed the curtain behind him. She still couldn't shake the feeling she knew the guy, but right now, she needed to get her head around the fact Bennett was alive.

"Would you mind if I spoke with the young lady alone?" Bennett asked.

"This is a police—" Aaron said.

He stopped when his phone buzzed. Sabrina watched as he read something on the screen and then lifted his eyes to look at Bennett. Without a word, he nodded and motioned for everyone to leave.

When Sabrina and Bennett were alone, he smiled. It was genuine, and he grasped her hand, but his voice sounded strained as he started to speak. It was almost as if it hurt to talk.

"I'll tell her when it's safe. I'm jeopardizing everything by being here, but I couldn't let them arrest you for something you didn't do." He closed his eyes.

"Bennett, what is going on?" Sabrina whispered.

"Nothing you need to worry about. I need you to keep this quiet. I promise it won't be for long." Bennett leaned in and kissed her forehead. "It will all make sense soon."

"Bennett, is this about Grant's involvement with criminals?" Sabrina asked as the man was about to leave.

"I can't say, but it will make sense soon." He disappeared through the curtain.

She didn't know how long she stared after him, but a sense of relief came over her when Sandy and Shadow returned without Aaron. The problem was, how was she supposed to keep this from Harriet? The woman was devastated when she lost her husband. Sabrina didn't know how Harriet got up in the morning.

"I can't believe he's alive," Sabrina whispered, mostly to herself.

"Sabrina, I need to get back with A.J. Shadow is staying here with you, but you can not talk to anyone about what just happened. I'm not sure exactly what's going on, but I know it's classified." Sandy hugged her. "I know it's hard, but get some rest."

With that, Sandy left her alone with Shadow. He stood next to the curtain, peeking out through the small opening. She felt like she was in the middle of a weird dream, but it wasn't, and she didn't know where it would end.

She managed to get a couple of hours of sleep but had no idea how. Between the nurses coming to take her vitals, what seemed like every hour, and the sounds of machines beeping made it impossible to rest, but mostly, she still didn't know anything about Crunch. She was about to ask Shadow if he'd heard anything, but the curtain was yanked open, and Zara appeared.

"He's awake," she practically squealed.

Chapter 27

His head throbbed, and it was as if his brain pushed against his skull. He'd think it was ready to explode if he didn't know better. Everyone told him he was fortunate to be alive. A concussion, smoke inhalation, large bruises across his thighs, and some minor burns didn't seem like a stroke of luck, but at least Sabrina was safe.

When he woke up in ICU, he frantically glanced around for Sabrina. He only settled when his mother told him she was safe and recovering in another room. The doctor came to check him and let him know the scans were clear, but he needed to stay for a few days.

"Zara is gone to see Sabrina and hopefully bring her to see you," his dad said.

Crunch nodded because speaking seemed impossible when his voice sounded like a croak. The doctor said because Crunch inhaled so much smoke, he'd be a little hoarse, but that didn't bother him. His lack of clear memory after the shower was his concern.

"What's with that face, *mon chéri?*" His mother placed a gentle hand on the top of his head.

"I… I don't remember much," Crunch rasped.

"That's not surprising. You smacked your head pretty bad," his father said.

"That lovely young man risked his life to save you. He is now my adopted son." His mother smiled as Shadow walked into the room.

"Hey, brother. You look…alive." Shadow smirked.

"Yeah, where's—" Crunch didn't have time to finish the sentence when Sabrina stepped into the room.

"Hunter," she said as tears filled her eyes.

She went to the side of his bed and reached for him but stopped. The last thing she wanted to do was hurt him, but Crunch grabbed her hand and tugged her into his arms. The only thing that hurt was his head, and now that she was in his arms, the pain seemed to ease.

"I thought… you hit your head and Easton…" she mumbled into his neck.

Knowing what happened to her late fiancée, he could understand why she'd think the worst. It must've been like déjà vu for her. Losing someone was never easy, especially in such a tragic way.

After a few minutes, she pulled back and tried to compose herself as she glanced around the room at his family. She smiled as she wiped the tears from her cheeks.

"I'm sorry, I must look a mess." Sabrina nodded as his dad handed her a box of tissues.

"You look beautiful," Crunch whispered.

"Are you okay? Does your head hurt?" Sabrina cupped the side of his face.

"He's got a head like concrete." Zara hobbled to one of the chairs.

"It's a good thing." Shadow leaned against the wall.

"I'm fine, sweetheart. Just a little headache."

It was a big headache, and his body ached. His throat was sore, and his chest hurt from the smoke, but it was mild compared to how he'd feel if anything happened to Sabrina.

"Does anyone know what happened?" Crunch asked.

"The Fire Commissioner is looking into it, but A.J. believes it was a bomb near the back of the building," Shadow explained.

"Why would someone set a bomb in a dance studio?" Zara asked the same question they were probably all thinking.

"I don't know, but you guys were damn lucky to come out of this with only a couple of injuries." His father wrapped his arm around Crunch's mother.

"What about the second explosion?" Crunch asked.

"All I know is they're still investigating," Shadow replied.

After an hour of holding Sabrina next to him and reassuring her he was fine, he finally convinced her to go with Shadow back to the safehouse. She only agreed because Crunch promised to take the pain medication. When Sabrina left, he lay back against the pillow and closed his eyes.

A hand touching his arm startled him awake. When his eyes opened, he met the dark eyes of a man leaning over him. Crunch was about to demand what the guy was doing there, but a large hand covered Crunch's mouth.

"Don't make a sound." the man mouthed the words.

Crunch didn't feel up to defending himself, but he sure as hell wouldn't let this guy kill him when the man pulled a gun from the back of his pants. Crunch's heart almost jumped out of his chest.

The man lifted the weapon, and Crunch got ready to disarm him, but the guy aimed at the door leading to Crunch's private bathroom. The stranger slowly moved across the room, yanked open the door, and shot twice.

"Threat neutralized," the man spoke into his wrist.

In seconds, several men who looked like soldiers entered the room. Crunch closed his eyes and shook his head. He had to be dreaming because this was like a movie. He was in a hospital, for Christ's sake.

"B.K. is on the way, sir," one of the other men said.

"Who the hell are you people?" Crunch asked.

Two soldiers stepped next to the bathroom door while the guy who first entered handed his weapon to another man. The guy relaxed as he pulled a chair close to the bed.

"There was a hitman here to kill you," the man told Crunch.

"Who was here to kill me, and who the hell are you?" Crunch was pissed.

"I'm Agent Cyril Skiffington with the CSIS," The man said.

"CSIS?" Crunch had heard of it before, but he didn't remember what it was.

"Canadian Security Intelligence Service," Cyril explained.

"Isn't that like the FBI?" Crunch knew NES had worked with them before.

"Yes," Agent Skiffington confirmed.

"Wait? Skiffington? As in Shelby Skiffington?" Crunch remembered where he had seen the man before.

Cyril was the same guy who stopped him at the airport all those years ago. He was older, but it was him. Crunch didn't want to listen to anyone who beat his wife.

"Yes, she's my sister," Cyril sighed.

Sister? Crunch stared at him. If he wasn't the husband rumored to have abused Shelby, why had he confronted Crunch at the airport back then?

"I remember you. You followed me to the airport." Crunch narrowed his eyes.

"Yes, my sister was involved with some bad people. She told me she was going with you to get away from them." Cyril blew out a breath. "She was tired of working undercover."

Shelby? Undercover?

"I know, my sister doesn't look like an agent or act like one. She's retired now," Cyril said.

"What's going on?" Crunch asked.

"Do you know a man named Igor Voznesensky?" Cyril asked.

"Yes." Crunch sat up.

"Do you know what he is?" Cyril crossed his legs in front of him.

"I know what he's suspected of doing," Crunch replied.

"The truth is, he's a contracted killer, and you were the next target." Cyril pulled something out of his pocket. "Do you know this woman?"

Crunch glanced at the phone Cyril held up. There was a picture of a woman he didn't recognize, and he shook his head. He winced as the motion made his head hurt, but Cyril swiped his phone and held it up again.

"What about this woman?" Cyril asked.

Crunch recognized her, but he was wary of saying anything. This guy killed someone and said he was part of Canada's lead agency on national security. Cyril never showed any identification, which made Crunch doubt the guy was legitimate.

"This is important, Mr. Crawford," Cyril pushed.

"How do I know you're not out to hurt these women? I don't know you, and until I speak to—" Crunch was interrupted by a familiar voice.

"He's who he says he is, Crunch." Kurt O'Connor entered the room, followed by Keith and Aaron. "Glad you got here in time, Cyril."

"What the hell is going on?" Crunch asked Kurt.

"Have you heard of VP Con Inc?" Cyril asked.

Crunch flicked his gaze around the room as he tried to remember the company. NES did security for hundreds of businesses over the years, and it would be impossible to remember them all. Still, Keith would know if they'd worked with VP Con Inc.

"No, I don't think so." Crunch glanced at Keith.

"It's a conglomerate that surfaced in the last five years. They're buying property and businesses around the city." Cyril sat back in the chair.

"I don't understand what all this has to do with me or the explosion." Crunch was frustrated.

"When they want the property, there's an offer. If it's refused, they'll make it very difficult for the owners." Kurt handed Crunch a folder. "They've been securing property up and down this road."

Crunch opened the folder and read through the list. All of the businesses on Hamilton Ave. The same road where his mother's studio sat. Over the last year, someone bought a couple of restaurants, a dry cleaner, a corner store, and an office building. They were still operating, but now they were owned by the same company.

"Your mom told us someone was asking to buy her studio," Kurt told him.

"Yes, and I made it clear to the guy she wasn't selling." Crunch tried to keep calm.

"They're subtle in their offers and can be very charming." Cyril almost choked on the last word.

"It's also why we believe you were targeted," Kurt said.

Crunch was pissed but slightly relieved that Sabrina wasn't the one in danger. Grant had to be aware Sabrina knew about his betrayal, and the police would arrest him at some point.

"So, this explosion has nothing to do with Grant?" Crunch blew out a breath.

When nobody spoke, Crunch looked around at the men. None of them would meet his gaze, and he was about to demand answers when another man stalked into the room. The guy waved in two people with a gurney and pointed to the bathroom.

"Clear the scene," the man said with an unmistakable air of authority.

For several minutes, nobody spoke. The only sound was the rustling and grunting from the bathroom. Aaron closed the door behind the gurney as the new visitor turned to Crunch.

"To answer your question, yes, Grant Thornton is tied up with all this, but he is a tiny fish in a hazardous pond," the man said.

"Who are you?" Crunch asked.

"People call me B.K.," he replied.

"That's not ominous at all," Crunch scoffed.

"Like you, I prefer the nickname, but my name is Bennett Thornton." Bennett stood with his hands behind his back.

Crunch opened his mouth and closed it again. This guy was Grant's father, and he was here taking the body of a dead hitman. This guy couldn't be Bennett Thornton because Crunch was pretty sure the guy died.

"I know. I look great for a dead man." Bennett smirked, obviously seeing Crunch's reaction.

"You know, I'm starting to think I hit my head harder than they told me, and all this is a really crazy hallucination." Crunch pulled his hands down over his face.

"You're not hallucinating, Crunch. This is real, and both you and Sabrina are tangled up in this." Keith dropped a hand on Crunch's shoulder.

"We know she didn't shoot Grant, but unfortunately, we don't know who did." Aaron sighed.

"So, I still don't know why CSIS is here and why a dead man is standing in my room." Crunch threw his hands up in the air.

"I'm evidently not dead, but if I hadn't faked my death a year ago, I would be." Bennett lowered his eyes to the floor.

"The CSIS received information there was a hit on Bennett. Whoever wanted him dead knew Grant would take over as CEO. What they didn't know is Bennett is an undercover agent with the agency," Cyril explained.

"It should have been Easton taking over." Bennett took a deep, shaky breath.

"You never know when an accident can happen." Crunch sympathized with the man.

"Easton's death wasn't an accident." Cyril stood up.

Chapter 28

Sabrina sat in the safehouse's living room, her elbows on her knees and her hands pressed against her mouth. She wasn't sure how to feel. The last few days had been one thing after the other, and she couldn't sleep without reliving the explosion.

It was difficult enough to sleep, but Crunch was still in hospital, and she missed him. As soon as the doctor discharged her, she returned to the house. She spent the first hour with her daughter in her arms.

It broke Sabrina's heart when those little eyes looked up and asked her not to go to heaven yet. A year ago, when Charlee asked what happened to Easton, Sabrina told her he was in heaven. She explained he'd had an accident, and God took him to heaven so he wouldn't be in any pain. How else was she supposed to explain it?

After Charlee went to sleep, Sabrina tried to do the same, but her brain wouldn't shut off, and every time she closed her eyes, she could see Crunch and Shadow get thrown from the building. Now she didn't know what to do with herself.

Sabrina slowly stood up and made her way to the window. It was three in the morning, and except for the light in the driveway, it was pitch black. She wasn't sure if she'd sleep without Crunch next to her. Plus, Charlee was spread eagle on the bed, and she didn't want to move her.

"I thought the doctor told you to get some rest when you got home," Shadow said softly.

"Yeah, that's easier said than done." Sabrina sighed.

Apparently, Charlee had deemed Shadow the one who had to stay with them until Crunch came home. Colt was in the second room, and Shadow was supposed to be in the third room. He motioned to the table as he poured them both a cup of tea.

"How's the shoulder?" Sabrina asked as she sat down.

"I've had worse." He joined her at the table.

"You said that at the hospital. Is your job that dangerous?" Sabrina wrapped her hand around the cup.

"I grew up in Alberta. I went to a school where I was the only half-aboriginal student. I was also tall for my age and skinny, and to top it off, my father wasn't in the picture back then. So, you could say I was the butt of everyone's jokes as well as a punching bag for bullies." Shadow sipped his tea.

He spoke as if what he said wasn't awful, but his dark eyes gave him away. Shadow was still angry about his childhood. He was quiet for a while before he gave her a forced smile.

"It made me grow up fast and taught me to work hard to get the hell out of there. When I met Rusty, he changed my life," Shadow said.

"Keith and Emily are amazing," she said.

Shadow nodded.

Sabrina thought the world of the couple and appreciated their kindness. She didn't know where she'd be without them and Crunch, probably married to Grant, living a miserable life.

"You're safe here." Shadow met her eyes.

"I know," she whispered.

"You should get some sleep. Not only for yourself but for your daughter and Crunch." Shadow stood up.

Sabrina took his advice and made her way to the bedroom. When she walked in, Charlee had moved and given Sabrina enough room to crawl in behind her. As soon as Sabrina placed her head on the pillow, Charlee snuggled close. She smiled and closed her eyes as she held her daughter.

She woke to the sound of voices in the other room. Sabrina wasn't sure who it was, but Charlee opened her eyes and grinned.

"It's the Nannies," Charlee squealed excitedly as she jumped out of bed and bolted out of the room.

Sabrina flopped back on the bed and lifted her arm to check the time on her watch. She was surprised to see it was after nine in the morning, which meant she had gotten a few hours of sleep. She dragged herself out of bed, and once dressed, she headed out to the commotion in the kitchen.

"Oh dear, did we wake you?" Alice asked as she poured coffee into a cup and handed it to Sabrina.

"No," Sabrina lied.

"Oh, good. Nanny Betty asked Kathleen and me to drop off some food for all of you. How are you feeling?" Alice handed her a plate with two thick slices of homemade bread, drenched in butter, the way Sabrina liked it.

"My throat is a little sore, but the rest is okay," Sabrina said, holding up her bandaged arm.

Charlee sat at the table with Kathleen, chattering about a sleepover with Scarlett the following weekend, although Sabrina didn't know about it. She questioned if Emily was aware the little girls had plans.

"That's wonderful. Maybe Nanny Betty will send some cookies for it." Kathleen smiled.

"Oh really? I love Nanny Betty. I love you too, Nanny Kathleen, and you too, Nanny Alice." Charlee threw her arms around Kathleen.

"We love you too, dolly," Kathleen said.

Sabrina was concerned about how attached Charlee was becoming to everyone in Hopedale. When everything was safe, she'd return to her apartment, wouldn't she? Suddenly the realization of what happened hit her. The studio was gone. Crunch's family lost everything in the explosion.

She'd overheard Shadow tell Colt the family would need to rebuild the studio because the explosions destroyed the building. Sabrina's heart broke for Crunch's family. Not only did they lose something so dear to them, but they'd also almost lost Crunch. She'd almost lost him.

Her chest tightened with the thought of a world without Crunch in it. When Easton died, she thought she'd never get through the next day but even thinking about a life without Crunch made it hard to breathe. Sabrina had to do something to distract herself from going down that rabbit hole.

By late morning, Sabrina had cleaned the kitchen and played a couple of games with Charlee. She'd tried to call Crunch, but he didn't have his phone. She was desperate to know if he was okay and was about to call the hospital when the front door opened.

Keith walked into the house, followed by Aaron, Kurt, Bennett, and the man he called Skiff. Sabrina wasn't sure why they were there, but from the worried expression on Keith's face.

"Is Crunch okay?" Sabrina tried to sound casual so she wouldn't alarm Charlee.

"He's fine and will be out of the hospital in a couple of days." Aaron gave her a comforting smile.

It was weird, considering he was about to arrest her a few days ago. She still didn't like that Bennett hadn't told Harriet he was alive. Sabrina wasn't sure how the woman would handle that her husband wasn't dead.

"Charlee, guess what?" Keith crouched to talk to her daughter.

"What?" Charlee leaned closer.

"Emily is waiting outside with Scarlett. They're going to the community center to do arts and crafts." Keith grinned.

"They're waiting for me?" Charlee gasped.

"Yep." Keith smiled.

"I gotta get dressed, Mommy. I'll get dressed super fast." Charlee squealed as she tugged Sabrina out of the living room.

Sabrina was at the end of her patience when she finished dressing Charlee. Her daughter was so excited she made it difficult to pin her down. As Charlee left with Emily and Scarlett, Sabrina didn't miss the slight smile on Bennett's face.

When Sabrina met the men in the living room, she felt a knot in her stomach as she watched them go through the papers they'd found in her storage locker. What were they looking for?

"She's a lot like Easton." Bennett met her in the kitchen.

"I know." Sabrina smiled.

"Sabrina, there's something you need to know, and I wanted to be the one to tell you." Bennett motioned toward the table.

Sabrina eased down on one of the kitchen chairs and folded her hands on the table. How much more bad news could she take? It was difficult to control the nervous trembling as Bennett sat at the table with her.

"I know I gave you a difficult time when you and Easton first started dating. I'm sorry for that." Bennett placed his hand on top of hers.

"I appreciate that," Sabrina whispered.

"When I had to disappear, I never thought in a million years I'd have to stay away this long, especially after losing him." Bennett lowered his head and swallowed several times.

"That's why you need to let Harriet know you're alive," Sabrina told him.

"Sabrina, right now, you need to know." Bennett raised his head and met her eyes. "Easton's death wasn't an accident."

The air whooshed out of her lungs, and it was as if it was getting hard to fill them again. She looked at Bennett as if he was speaking another language, and she could see his lips moving, but she couldn't hear what he was saying.

"Wh… What…are you saying… he…" Sabrina couldn't say the word.

"Yes, there's an investigation into his death. The CSIS has several surveillance videos taken from inside my home over the last five years. One of them shows the day Easton died." Bennett's voice cracked.

"Wait…" Sabrina shot to her feet. "You're telling me you have proof Easton was murdered four years ago, and you didn't arrest anyone? Are you kidding me?"

The volume of her voice rose to a place where it caused Keith, Kurt, and Aaron to run into the kitchen. Sabrina shook with anger, and the only thing she could think to do was throw something. She swiped her hand across the table, and the cups flew across the floor and smashed against the wall.

"Sabrina, you need to—" Keith moved toward her.

"Keith, if you tell me to calm down right now, I swear I'll throat punch you." Sabrina narrowed her eyes at the large man.

She'd never been this angry in her entire life. How could law enforcement let Easton's killer walk free for so long? Why did the police not tell her they suspected her fiancée's death wasn't an accident?

Keith stepped back and held his hands up in front of him in surrender. She winced at the way she'd screamed at the man when he was only there to help, but she was enraged. She glanced across the room where Aaron picked up the broken mugs, and she dropped down on the chair.

"I'm sorry, Sabrina. Grant is involved with some treacherous people who'll stop at nothing to get what they want. They probably killed Easton because he was getting close," Bennett explained.

"Did Grant kill Easton?" Sabrina whispered.

"No, but he didn't stop it either," Bennett said.

Sabrina combed her fingers through her hair and took a couple of shaky breaths. She couldn't believe all of this. Easton died because of what Grant was involved with. She may not have shot him, but the way she felt now, she wouldn't hesitate to put a bullet in the bastard.

"What is wrong with him?" she said mostly to herself.

"I wish I knew," Bennett whispered.

"Harriet told me about the day you brought Grant home," Sabrina said as she reached across the table and touched Bennett's arm.

"I honestly believe he found out somehow." Bennett shook his head.

Sabrina didn't know if Grant knew about his parentage, but it didn't matter. Someone who could turn against his family was truly disturbed. She didn't know where things were going, but she was tired of the close calls and the secrets.

"He should be happy he was spared and didn't end up living a terrible life," Sabrina said.

"You would think. I'm not sure what Grant's motives are, but as much as it kills me, I'll have to bring him to justice." Bennett's voice cracked.

Sabrina wouldn't want to be in Bennett's shoes, but Grant deserved to be behind bars if he was involved with the person who almost killed Crunch. She needed to get away from everything and excused herself while the men dug into the papers. She locked the bathroom door and sank into a hot bath.

Over the next couple of days, Sabrina was more and more agitated. They wouldn't let her go to the hospital to see Crunch because they were concerned about her safety.

Thankfully, Keith was going to the hospital to bring Crunch home. Charlee was overjoyed that Crunch wasn't going to be in the hospital anymore and drew several pictures for him.

"Mommy, can we live here forever?" Charlee looked up from her coloring.

What was she supposed to say? The truth was, the house wasn't her home or Crunch's. It was the place they stayed to be safe and couldn't leave until the threat sat behind bars.

"Not forever, sweetie, but we'll be here for a little while," Sabrina said.

"But I love it here. Scarlett says in the wintertime we can go sliding and skating." Charlee stood up on her chair. "She said her daddy makes a big puddle, and then it gets really hard, and we can skate on it. I want to stay," Charlee whined.

"Sweetie, I told you, we're only here for a little while, but when we leave, that doesn't mean you won't see Scarlett again. I'll make sure you get to play with your friend." Sabrina went to her daughter and lifted her into her arms.

"You promise?" Charlee rested her head on Sabrina's shoulder.

"If Mommy doesn't bring you to see Scarlett, I will." Crunch's voice made her spin around.

"Crunch," Charlee squealed.

He smiled and made his way toward them. Before Sabrina could stop her, Charlee leaped out of her arms and wrapped her arms around Crunch's neck. He laughed as she kissed his cheek over and over.

"You're home. You're home." Charlee hugged him.

"I've never had such a wonderful welcome home." Crunch chuckled.

He met Sabrina's gaze and smiled as he reached for her hand. Charlee wiggled until he put her down, and a few seconds later, she handed several drawings to him. He gasped and praised her as he flipped through the pictures. Charlee gazed at Crunch as if he hung the moon and stars, and Sabrina completely understood.

Once Charlee had her fill of Crunch, she wanted to color in the living room and watch a movie. Sabrina settled her daughter at the coffee table and returned to the kitchen, where Crunch leaned against the counter.

"I know Charlee was happy to see me. How about you?" Crunch smiled.

Sabrina moved across the kitchen and wrapped her arms around his neck. She pulled his head down until she could press her lips to his. He sighed into her mouth as she opened up to him. His arms slipped around her, and he pulled her flush against his body.

He kissed her slow as their tongues tangled together in a kiss that seemed like they were trying to make up for the time they'd been apart. When she finally pulled back, she gazed up into his eyes and smiled.

"That was a wonderful welcome home, too," he whispered.

"I'm so glad you're here. I missed you, and I've been climbing the walls here without you." She pressed her forehead against his.

"I missed you too." He sighed.

"It's been such a crazy few days, and Harriet called me to see if she can take Charlee for supper, but I'm terrified to let her go, not to mention I don't know how to keep myself from telling her that Bennett is still alive," Sabrina said.

"Maybe we can invite her here for supper," Crunch suggested.

"I don't know. How can I look Harriett in the eye and not tell her Bennett is alive?" Sabrina rested her cheek against his chest.

"We'll figure out something." Crunch pulled her into his embrace.

Charlee was out like a light by ten that evening, and Sabrina curled up on the couch with Crunch. Soft music played from the television, and a couple of candles sat in the middle of the coffee table. It was the first time she felt somewhat relaxed in weeks.

"Sabrina," Crunch whispered.

"Hmm." She was too relaxed to use actual words.

"There's something I want you to see." He shifted and pulled something out of his pocket. "I didn't think this would survive the explosion."

"What is it?" Sabrina sat up.

He held up his phone, and she gasped at the condition. It looked like she would expect a phone to look after an explosion. The case had chips missing out of the corners, and the glass split diagonally. He smiled when he tapped the screen, and it lit up.

"One of the firefighters found it on the ground and brought it to the hospital. Imagine my shock when I plugged it in, and it worked." Crunch tapped the screen.

"At least you got it back," Sabrina said.

"Sabrina, while I was in the building, I didn't think... well, you know." Crunch handed her the phone. "I made this video for you and my family. I want you to watch it."

She watched him walk out of the living room, but before he made it to the kitchen, he gave her a nervous smile. She held up the phone, hit *play*, and held her breath.

"Sabrina, I'm so sorry I didn't tell you sooner. I don't think I'm getting out of here, and I wanted you to know... I love you."

Her vision blurred with tears as ragged coughs and his raspy voice cracked through the speaker. A soft sob escaped from her throat as his heavy gasps continued, but she couldn't see anything as the video went dark, but his voice still strained to finish his message.

"I'm sorry, Sabrina. I'm sorry, Mom and Dad, I'm not going to get out of here. Zara, take care of..."

He coughed again, but then someone shouted, and she knew it was when Shadow finally found him. Sabrina sobbed as she listened to the moment Shadow saved the man she loved.

"You can take care of them yourself. Let's get you out of here," Shadow's voice sounded muffled.

She listened to some grunts and the unmistakable sound of the wood crackle. When she heard Shadow again, she laughed.

"Come on, twinkle toes. Get up off your arse," Shadow yelled.

The explosion must've jolted the phone enough to stop the video because it ended. Sabrina held the phone to her chest and wiped the tears running down her cheeks.

Crunch was alive in the kitchen but listening to how close he came to losing his life. He probably thought he was about to die and wanted her to know he loved her. He loved her.

"Oh. He loves me," she whispered.

"Yes, he does."

She looked up. Crunch stood in the doorway with his hands in his pockets. His hair was disheveled like he'd run his fingers through it, but his gaze focused entirely on her.

"I heard the video end," he said.

"That was difficult to get through." She blew out a breath. "You… your voice was…the cough."

She couldn't finish. Sabrina stood and dropped the phone on the table as she walked toward him. He didn't move as she stepped in front of him and gazed up into his eyes.

"I didn't think I was—" He stopped when she put her finger against his lips.

"Hunter, I don't know if I would've survived if you didn't get out of that building. I love you so much, and I thank God for angels like Lane." Sabrina smiled.

"I don't know if Shadow would agree he was an angel, but I'm certainly indebted to him for saving my life." Crunch smiled.

Crunch lifted his hands and cupped her face between them. He gazed into her eyes as he lowered his head and softly touched his lips against hers.

"I love you, but there is something you need to know about my past. It may change your mind how you see me," Crunch said with a tremble in his voice.

"I don't think anything could change how I feel about you," Sabrina whispered.

Crunch took her hands in his, but he didn't say anything for several seconds. When he lifted his gaze to meet hers, he blew out a shaky breath before he spoke.

"Okay. I used to be an exotic dancer," Crunch said quickly.

"And?" Sabrina wasn't sure if that was the end of his story.

"That doesn't bother you?" Crunch tucked a piece of her hair behind her ear.

"Why would it bother me? A lot of people do it. As a matter of fact, Pam told me she danced at a club when she lived in Ontario." Sabrina touched his cheek.

Pam told Sabrina about her life before moving back to Newfoundland and settling down with her husband. Sabrina didn't think any less of either of them because there was a time shortly after Easton died she thought about taking a job at one of the gentlemen bars in the city.

"I can imagine you were outstanding." Sabrina smiled.

Crunch smirked as he slipped his hand behind her head and threaded his fingers into her hair. His other arm wrapped around her waist as he covered her lips with his. The kiss was slow and tender, but she craved more. She slipped her arms around his body as his tongue licked across her lower lip as if begging to enter. She opened to him and got lost in the passion.

"I need you, Hunter," she murmured against his lips.

"Sabrina, I want you so much, but Charlee," he whispered.

"She's all tucked in the other room with her teddy." Sabrina smiled. "Stupid me realized a couple of days ago why she kept crawling into bed with me."

"Are you sure?" Crunch kissed down the side of her neck.

"I'm sure." She sighed.

Crunch growled as he pressed her against the wall with his body. Her hands tugged frantically at his shirt, and his tongue slid into her mouth. Sabrina whimpered with resistance when he pulled away long enough to remove his shirt and tug hers off as well. Then he was on her again, kissing her like he needed it to breathe.

She could feel the length of his erection through his jeans, and when he thrust it against her groin, she groaned with need. He cursed into her mouth as he cupped her ass, and she wrapped her legs around his waist. Crunch ground against her throbbing core as he kissed and nipped down the side of her neck.

"Hunter, are you sure you're well… Oh, yes." Her train of thought shifted when he wrapped his lips around one of her breasts.

"I'm perfectly fine to show you how much I love you," Crunch whispered when he raised his head from her breast. "Are you okay?"

Sabrina nodded, and that was all he needed to spin around and carry her into the bedroom. Before he stepped inside, he glanced toward the room where Charlee was sleeping and looked at her.

"I promise, she won't be crawling in with us," Sabrina whispered.

"We can lock the door just in case." Crunch smiled as he placed her back on the floor.

He reached behind him, closed the door, and locked it, his eyes never leaving her as she slipped out of her yoga pants. She stood in front of him with only a thin pair of lace panties. His eyes flared when she stuck her thumbs into the waist of them, then slowly slipped them off.

He popped the button of his jeans and dropped them. He stepped out of them, giving her a full view of his engorged cock because he wasn't wearing underwear. Sabrina bit her lip as she backed toward the bed, and he groaned as he wrapped his fist around his dick.

"I'm so fucking hard for you." He growled.

"I can see that." She crawled up on the bed until she was kneeling in the center.

He stepped next to the bed and beckoned her with his finger to come closer. Sabrina crawled closer until she was kneeling in front of him on the bed. She wrapped her hand around his throbbing erection, and he hissed between his teeth.

"Jesus, your touch sets me on fire," Crunch moaned.

"Touch me," she whispered against his lips.

Chapter 29

It was amazing how two words could make a man practically lose control. When she asked him to touch her, he shook with the need. He cupped the back of her head as he pulled her hand from his cock because the way she stroked him was about to put him over the edge.

Crunch lowered her to the bed as his hand cupped her breast. His lips teased and nipped down her chest to the sweet nipples, pebbling in his hand. Sabrina mewled as his mouth enveloped her tight bud and sucked.

"Yes, Hunter," she murmured.

He nipped at each breast, enjoying the taste of her skin and the sexy sounds coming from her. Her hips thrust up as if begging for attention, and he was more than willing to give her all of his care.

Crunch slipped his hand down over her soft belly to the swollen nub at the top of her sex. She sucked in a breath as his thumb circled it slowly. She was wet, and his finger slipped between her folds.

"So ready for me," he murmured against her breast.

"I want you inside me, Hunter," Sabrina begged.

"Soon, baby." He wanted to make her come with his fingers first.

He dipped his finger into her wet heat, and she moaned as her hips thrust up to meet his hand. He curled his finger inside her as his thumb pressed against her clit. Sabrina gasped, and she fisted his hair with a gentle tug.

"Hunter, Hunter," she moaned.

The sound of his name on her lips as he brought her pleasure was the best aphrodisiac in the world. The more she moaned his name, the harder he became. He felt her start to shudder under him as he brought her to climax.

"Oh, Hunter, yes."

Crunch lifted his head to look down as the aftershocks spasmed through her body. The look of pleasure on her face made him smile, and he slowed his finger inside her. Her eyes were closed as she rode out the last of her orgasm.

When she opened her eyes, she raised her hand to cup his cheek and lifted her head so her lips could meet his. Crunch slipped his tongue into her mouth as he rolled them over and moaned when his cock touched against her wet sex.

"Make love to me, Hunter," she murmured against his lips.

He grabbed his dick and placed the head against the entrance of her pussy. Crunch pushed slowly inside her, causing both of them to groan. The feeling of her inner walls grasping his dick almost sent him over the edge, but he stilled when he was deep inside.

"I love you, Sabrina," Crunch whispered as he gazed into her eyes.

"I love you too, Hunter." Sabrina smiled.

He lowered his head until his lips met hers. Her legs wrapped around his thighs, pulling him closer as she threaded her fingers through his hair. Crunch pulled his hips back and then pushed back into her with a hard thrust. He moaned into her mouth as his groin pressed against hers.

"Fuck," Crunch panted as he pulled back from her lips.

"Don't stop," she begged and pulled his lips back to hers.

Crunch hooked his arm under one of her legs and pulled it up, allowing him to drive deeper inside her. He wanted to go slow and make love to her all night, but his cock throbbed painfully, and he couldn't contain the urge to pump into her until they were both trembling in pleasure.

"Yes," Sabrina hissed.

"I need to go faster, baby." He growled through gritted teeth.

"I need you to go faster." Sabrina wrapped her other leg around his waist.

"I love you," he whispered as he thrust into her over and over.

"Yes, I love you too," she cried out as her pussy squeezed around his cock and her body convulsed in pleasure.

"That's it, baby," Crunch panted as he pumped into her two more times.

His climax hit him like a freight train, and his body shook. He grunted against her neck as his cock jerked inside for what seemed forever. When he finally emptied his last orgasm, he lifted himself on shaky arms to look down at her.

"I think my heart stopped for a minute." Crunch chuckled.

"Mmmm, I think all my bones have become jelly." Sabrina sighed.

Crunch leaned down and brushed his lips against hers. She smiled against his mouth and dragged her nails down his back, making goosebumps erupt on his skin. He lifted his head and rolled onto his back, so she was lying on top of him.

Sabrina's gaze traveled down to his chest, and the smile left her face. When she lifted her head, there was sadness in her eyes. It wasn't the reaction he was looking for after they'd made love.

"What's wrong?" Crunch asked.

"I know you're here, and your injuries will heal, but I keep going back to what could've happened."

"I'm fine, baby. You can't keep thinking like that." Crunch pulled her head down to rest against his chest.

"I know," she whispered.

"I guess it's hard not to think the worst." Crunch kissed the top of her head.

"I'm sorry. I'm kind of ruining the afterglow." She pressed her lips against his chest.

"Baby, nothing could ruin the afterglow of making love to you," he murmured against her hair.

She sighed and snuggled tighter against his chest. He wrapped his arms around her and closed his eyes. It was the most relaxed he'd felt in days, and there was nothing that could ruin his mood.

He found something that could screw up his happy feeling the following day. Grant Thornton. He'd been released from the hospital and was desperately trying to get in touch with Sabrina through her brother, not that Colt would give the asshole any information.

Aaron arrested Grant as he left the hospital. Declan made sure the phony will was investigated and gave the information to his boss. Saul gave Declan the green light to find out how Grant managed to get several bank officials to provide him with access to Easton's accounts.

By the time it was all said and done, the police had charged eight people with various crimes. Grant sat in his house with an ankle monitor until his appearance before the court, which meant he made calls to contact Sabrina.

"Can we get a restraining order against this prick?" Crunch asked Jason.

"I can see if he has any restrictions about contacting Sabrina. If not, I can see about getting a no-contact order," Jason explained when he dropped by.

"I hope he's not bothering Harriet." Sabrina was pacing the kitchen.

"Have you talked to her?" Crunch asked.

"No, and I feel terrible. I don't know how I can look at her and not say anything about Bennett." Sabrina sighed and plopped down on one of the kitchen chairs. "Plus, I kind of lost my phone in the explosion."

"We'll have to rectify that situation, and you'll no longer have to keep things from Harriet." Bennett walked into the kitchen, followed by the woman in question.

Before Sabrina could say anything, Charlee squealed and jumped into her grandmother's waiting arms. Crunch met Sabrina's eyes and could see the uneasiness in her expression. She stood up and made her way toward Harriet.

"Before you go saying how bad you feel, don't. Bennett explained everything to me last night." Harriet smiled.

"After I got yelled at for an hour," Bennett muttered.

"Listen, you're lucky I didn't throw the kettle at you." Harriet glared at her husband.

"Who are you?" Charlee asked, looking at Bennett.

The room went hushed as everyone glanced around the room. Jason decided that was his cue to leave. He was out the door, and nobody spoke until the door slammed shut.

"Charlee, this is your grandfather," Harriet told the little girl.

"Like Scarlett's poppy?" Charlee looked up at Bennett.

"I'm not sure who Scarlett is, but yes, I'm your poppy." Bennett smiled at Charlee.

"Where have you been?" Charlee jumped out of Harriet's arms and wrapped her arms around Bennett's neck.

The man had been quick to catch her and hugged her tightly. Sabrina blinked back tears as she tucked herself under Crunch's arm. The man was clearly overwhelmed with emotion because he could finally hold his granddaughter.

"I've been away working," Bennett said after he cleared his throat.

"Nanny said you were in heaven with my daddy. Is he coming back too?" Charlee's eyes went wide.

Again, everyone was silent until Sabrina broke the quiet. Her voice was soft and shaky as she explained the situation to her daughter in a way the four-year-old could understand.

"No, sweetie. We thought Poppy was in heaven, but he was…" Sabrina met Bennett's eyes.

"He was doing a secret job and forgot to tell us where he was going," Harriet interjected.

"Right." Bennett nodded.

The explanation seemed to appease Charlee, and she dragged Bennett and Harriet into her bedroom to show them where she was sleeping.

Cyril, Keith, and Aaron walked in a couple of minutes later, and from the tense way Keith held his jaw, he was pissed about something. Cyril was on his phone speaking with someone who wasn't giving him the answer he wanted. At least it appeared as if the man was pissed off because he kept throwing his arm in the air while he spoke.

"How the hell can you not find her? I thought you had it all under control. What the hell is wrong with you?" Cyril snapped.

Crunch locked eyes with Keith. Things looked like it wasn't going well, and from the way Cyril's face changed several shades of red, it was obvious whoever was on the phone was probably going to be the recipient of the blow-up about to happen.

"I don't give a damn how you do it. Find her, and find her yesterday. If you don't, don't call me back, and don't bother coming back to work." Cyril yanked the phone down from his ear. "That undercover should've been fired."

"Problem?" Bennett stepped into the kitchen.

"She's out of sight, and we don't know where she's gone," Cyril grumbled.

"Undercover isn't easy, and keeping tabs on someone isn't either. Calm down. It's not like she'll be difficult to find again. She isn't going to leave the province." Bennett leaned against the counter and crossed his arms over his chest.

"Who exactly is it you're looking for?" Sabrina asked.

"A woman—" Cyril stopped when Sabrina gasped.

"You were there that day." Sabrina pointed at Cyril.

"What day? Sabrina?" Crunch wrapped his arm around her.

"I remember. You were in the office with Grant when I arrived. I remember you." Sabrina continued.

Crunch glared at Cyril. The fact he'd been at the Thornton estate before Grant's shooting made Crunch begin to wonder if they could trust the guy. After all, why would he meet with Grant when he was supposed to be investigating Grant's involvement with criminals?

Crunch locked eyes with Keith. From the clenched jaw, it appeared Cyril hadn't filled Keith in on that little bit of information.

"Yes, I was there because Grant believes I'm the one who made his father's death possible," Cyril explained.

"Why didn't you tell me that?" Keith asked.

"You aren't law enforcement, but in case you're wondering, your brother does know," Cyril snapped.

"Bennett, are you sure you can trust him?" Sabrina glared at Cyril.

"I'm a hundred and ten percent sure." Bennett smiled at her.

"So, who are you looking for?" Keith asked.

"She's Mitch Snider's sister. She inherited his estate, but we think she may be the key to finding the guy running this crew. The guy wants what she has." Cyril held up his phone. "This is her picture."

Crunch took the device and stared at the photo. He had no idea why, but the woman looked familiar. Sabrina stood next to him and leaned in to see it. Her hand flew to her mouth, and she gasped at the same time. Crunch realized he knew the woman as well.

"I know her," Sabrina and Crunch said at the same time.

Chapter 30

Sabrina's heart pounded as she stared at the smiling face on Cyril's phone. This woman had spent time with her daughter and helped her when she was down on her luck. Sabrina considered this woman a friend.

"How do you know her?" Cyril asked.

"She befriended Sabrina when she worked for me," Bennett answered for her.

"I can't believe Holly would be involved with something like this." Sabrina shook her head.

"That's what I keep saying, but Cyril doesn't believe it. She may be Snider's sister, but she never had anything to do with him," Bennett grumbled.

"Did you just call her Holly?" Crunch asked.

"Yes, Holly Peddle." Sabrina looked up at him.

"Well, she's a dead ringer for the woman who was supposed to testify against the guy that killed Snider, you know the guy you… neutralized." Crunch pointed at Cyril.

"There's a reason for that." Cyril sighed. "They're sisters."

"Okay, so the stripper and this girl are sisters, and Mitch Snider was their brother. Do I have all this right?" Crunch ran his fingers through his hair.

"Yes." Cyril nodded.

"Their mother worked for me too, and she tried to keep her kids out of that life. Holly kept her hands clean, but Diamond was rebellious, and Mitch was a lost cause." Bennett shook his head.

Sabrina's head was spinning. Holly was her friend, and she'd never said anything about having a sister or a brother. As far as Sabrina knew, Holly never had any family.

"Maybe I can call her," Sabrina suggested. "I mean, we're still in contact, and I did promise to meet her for coffee soon."

"No," Crunch interjected.

"Why not?" Sabrina stared at Crunch.

"What about if she's working with Grant or the people he's involved with?" Crunch shook his head.

"I'm going to call her, not go meet her." Sabrina rolled her eyes.

"Sounds like a good idea. There's no way she'd suspect you." Cyril nodded.

She pulled out the replacement phone she'd picked up and hoped her contacts had downloaded. She scrolled through the list and breathed a sigh of relief when she found it.

She tapped the number and put it on speakerphone. Everyone stood around her as the phone rang several times, and then the voicemail kicked on. Sabrina waited for the beep and then spoke.

"Umm… hi Holly, it's me. I wanted to know if you… wanted to get that coffee. Call me back." Sabrina ended the call and shrugged.

"Hopefully, she'll call back." Bennett sighed.

"I mean, you're with the CSIS. Can't they track her phone and see where she is?" Crunch motioned to Cyril.

"They did, but she doesn't seem to be close by her phone," Cyril said.

"So, if you knew that, why would you let her call the girl?" Crunch threw his arms up in the air.

"Look, it's obvious you don't trust me, but I'm trying to bring some horrible people down. One of those guys used my sister as a punching bag until she finally got away from him. Her undercover work almost killed her, so this is personal to me too." Cyril stepped next to Crunch. "It's not just a job for me."

Sabrina stared at the man who looked as if he was about to burst into tears. He wasn't some hard-nosed cop out to make a name for himself. Cyril wanted to make sure the bad guys got what they deserved.

"I know I look like some of those assholes, and most people take me as a criminal, but it works out for me when I need to go undercover to bring these guys down," Cyril explained.

"I'm sorry," Crunch said.

"Don't be. You're not the first one to distrust me. As a matter of fact, a run-in with Kurt O'Connor twenty years ago had me in cuffs and locked behind bars because he didn't believe I was undercover. It was around Christmas so getting in touch with the powers that be was close to impossible." Cyril chuckled. "Come to think of it, that asshole still hasn't apologized for that."

"I wouldn't hold my breath waiting," Keith returned with a smirk.

"Trust me. I won't." Cyril pulled out his phone and put it to his ear.

Sabrina's heart went out to the man. It must be awful to immerse into a criminal organization and witness the horrendous things people do. She still found it weird to know Bennett was more than a businessman. All the times he'd be gone for weeks at a time, he was helping bring down some of the worst people in the world.

"Are you okay?" Crunch whispered as he put his arm around her shoulders.

"Yes," she answered, but was she really okay?

Sabrina wasn't sure she could accept that her friend Holly was involved in any of this. When she thought about it, Holly never talked about her family. The only time Sabrina asked her about it, Holly told her she didn't have any close people in her life.

"Her apartment is empty, but my agent found her phone and purse inside." Cyril ran a hand over the top of his head.

"Do you think someone took her?" Keith asked.

"What woman do you know who leaves without her purse?" Cyril asked.

"I'll head to the station and put out a missing person report," Aaron told them as he headed out through the door.

Sabrina tried to stay calm and not worry over what could've happened to her friend. The same friend could be involved with the people who attempted to kill her and Crunch. When did her life become such a mess?

Chapter 31

Two days passed, and the police still couldn't find Holly and Diamond. Both women seemed to have vanished off the face of the earth. According to Aaron, Grant was questioned about the women and swore he didn't know where they were.

Crunch stood outside the room where Aaron and Cyril were working on getting as much information out of Grant as they could. The guy certainly didn't look like the cocky bastard who walked into the diner that day.

"I told you, I don't know where Holly is, and I don't have a clue who this other woman is," Grant shouted as he plowed his fingers through his hair.

"All right, then tell me this." Cyril leaned back in the chair. "Who killed your brother?"

Grant's face paled, and his mouth dropped open several times. His eyes widened as he glanced between Cyril and Aaron and his hands tightened into fists.

"I didn't kill him," Grant whispered.

"We know that, but we need to know who was at the top of the stairs." Aaron pushed a tablet across the table.

"How could you cover for someone who killed your brother?" Cyril shook his head.

"He's not my—" Grant stopped. "If I tell you, then I'll be the next one dead. These people…"

"He needs to know I'm alive," Bennett whispered next to Crunch.

"Do you think that's smart?" Crunch asked.

"If he sees these people didn't actually kill me, maybe we can convince him to turn on them." Bennett walked to the door of the room.

Grant's eyes widened, and his mouth dropped open as his face paled. Grant's reaction to his father entering the interrogation room would've been amusing if it weren't such a difficult situation.

"D…Dad," Grant stammered.

"Grant." Bennett walked further into the room.

"You should have known when I told you who I was that I wouldn't have had your father killed," Cyril said.

"I… I didn't… they would've…" Grant stuttered over his words.

"They wanted Easton and me dead so you could take over the business. Then they would control everything, and you helped them." Bennett walked around to stand in front of Grant. "My own son."

"Oh, don't pretend you cared about me. I know I'm not your son." Grant shot to his feet and faced Bennett. "Did you think I was too stupid to figure it out?"

"You may not be my blood, but you're most definitely my son. Your mother and I raised you. We never treated you any different than Easton." Bennett stopped when Grant laughed.

"Bullshit. You gave him everything. I was the oldest, and you gave everything to him to take your little trips. I was the one bringing in money for you, and you didn't give a damn," Grant yelled.

"You were working with the same criminals your mother wanted to keep you from. She gave you up to protect you, but it didn't work. Grant, for the love of God, tell these men what you know." Bennett kept his voice calm.

"My so-called mother gave me away and kept me from knowing my true family. You think you're a powerful man, don't you? You've no idea how little power you got. You'll never bring down these people." Grant smirked. "You're nothing, and I'm done talking. I want a lawyer."

Crunch cursed under his breath and wished he'd stopped Bennett from heading into the room. There was no way Grant would talk now, which meant they were back at square one.

Crunch's phone rang, and he pulled it out of his pocket. He tapped the screen when he saw who was calling.

"Hey, Declan," Crunch said.

"I need to talk to you. Can you… meet me at your house?" Declan asked.

"I'm at the Hopedale Police station right now. Do you want to meet me here?" Crunch asked.

There was silence on the phone for a few minutes. Crunch thought maybe Declan hung up, but the call was still active when he checked the screen.

"Declan?"

"I'm at your place now. I need to show you something. It's important." Declan cleared his throat.

"What's this about?" Crunch glanced into the room where Grant sat.

"I…I have information on… the explosion at your mother's studio." Declan sounded strange.

"I'll be there in ten minutes," Crunch said.

The call ended, and Crunch put his phone back in his pocket as Aaron stepped out of the interrogation room. He looked frustrated and shoved his hand through his hair before speaking.

"You shouldn't have let him come in there," Aaron told Crunch.

"What was I supposed to do? Tie him to a chair?" Crunch retorted.

"Sorry, I know this is important to you." Aaron sighed.

"Look, I need to meet Declan at my place. He has some information on the studio explosion," Crunch said.

"Do you want me to go with you?" Aaron asked.

"No, I'll be fine. Besides, Declan will probably come back here to fill you in too." Crunch headed out of the room.

"Okay, keep your phone on in case we need to get in touch," Aaron shouted after him.

Crunch gave him a thumbs-up as he hurried out of the station. One thing about Hopedale was he could be anywhere in less than a half-hour walk but decided his truck would be faster.

Crunch hadn't been back home since the day he grabbed clothes. The windows were all fixed, and the locks changed. Keith had also made sure the damaged siding was removed and replaced with new pieces. It looked as if nothing had happened.

He pulled into the driveway next to a black SUV. He stepped out of his truck and walked to the passenger side of the other vehicle. Before he got close, someone stepped behind him and placed something against the back of his head.

"Open the back door and get inside. Don't be stupid, or the bullet in this will make a huge hole in your skull. Oh, and hand over your phone," a man's voice rumbled behind him.

Crunch tried to turn around, but the guy pushed the gun harder into the base of his skull. Crunch slipped his hand into his pocket and slowly removed his phone. He held it out and was startled when the guy snatched it out of his hand.

"Do not push me, Mr. Crawford." The man growled as he slammed the phone on the ground.

The man pushed Crunch forward, and Crunch reached for the handle of the SUV. He didn't move to get into the vehicle, but the man behind him shoved him.

"I said get in," the guy ordered. "My boss is very anxious to speak with you."

Crunch slowly stepped into the vehicle and glanced over his shoulder at the man holding the gun. He didn't look familiar, and chances were he was a hired gun for whoever wanted to speak with Crunch. The door to the SUV closed, but a groan behind him caused him to spin around.

"Declan?" Crunch spun around in the seat.

Declan lay across the third row of seats, his arms tied behind him. His face was bloody and bruised, with one of his eyes swollen shut. Crunch reached back and touched the man.

"I'm... sorry... he wouldn't stop..." Declan swallowed. "He kept hitting me."

Crunch eyed the driver and wondered if he had a weapon as well. He didn't want to do something that would get him killed, but as the vehicle sped out of his driveway, Crunch's heart pounded. He didn't know who they were, but he had a feeling he'd find out soon.

Chapter 32

Sabrina sat on the front step of the safehouse and watched Charlee, Scarlett, and her brothers run around after a couple of puppies. Emily sat next to Sabrina, complaining about her husband.

"Like I don't have enough to do with my salon, the kids, and the house. Now he wants to have not one but two puppies. I swear I love the man, but sometimes I want to kick the living shit out of him." Emily sighed.

"They're cute, though." Sabrina smiled.

"I know," Emily grumbled. "I told him he's not going to work until they're trained."

"So why exactly are you here with the kids and puppies, but Keith is somehow absent?" Sabrina chuckled.

"Something about an urgent call." Emily placed her elbows on her knees and rested her chin on her fists.

Sabrina wrapped her arm around the woman and gave her a gentle squeeze. Emily was probably not happy about the dogs, but Keith's company was essential, and if he left for something urgent, it was probably crucial.

"I heard Grant asked for a lawyer," Emily said.

"Who told you that?" Sabrina asked.

"I overheard Keith on the phone." Emily shrugged.

"I guess Hunter is staying at the station until they know more."

Crunch left early that morning when Aaron informed them they would question Grant. She didn't want him to go, but he explained he needed to be involved in the investigation while he could. She hadn't heard from him since, and she assumed they were still asking Grant questions.

Sabrina jumped up when her phone rang inside the house, expecting to see Crunch calling. However, she didn't know the number on the screen, but she didn't want to ignore it. Maybe it could be Holly or Crunch calling from the station. She still hadn't heard from her friend, and the police were still looking for her. Sabrina still couldn't believe she was into anything illegal. Holly was in trouble.

"Hello," Sabrina answered.

"Ms. Burke, I want you to listen carefully." A man's voice echoed through her ear.

"Who is this?" Sabrina demanded.

"That's not important right now. I need you to follow my instructions to the letter," the man said.

"Why should I listen to you?" Sabrina asked.

"I sent you a video. Watch it. I'll wait." The man chuckled.

Sabrina pulled the phone from her ear when she felt it vibrate in her hand. She pulled up the video sent from the same number and hit play. At first, it was dark, but the footage scanned across what looked like a white brick wall. When it stopped, it focused on a dark figure on the floor.

"You see, Ms. Burke, this is the worst that could happen if you don't follow my instructions." The same voice came over the video.

The video zoomed in on the object, and Sabrina gasped when she finally realized what she was looking at. A man lay motionless bloody and bruised. The man was in such bad shape she couldn't recognize if she knew him or not.

"If you don't follow my instructions to the letter," the man said as the video moved again. "Your friend here will meet the same fate."

"Hunter," Sabrina gasped his name.

Crunch sat with his limbs secured to the arms and legs of the chair. His head hung forward, but she could see his chest moving. He was alive.

"What do you want?" Sabrina made her way to the bedroom so Emily wouldn't hear her.

"Your fiancée had something that belonged to me. Since his brother wasn't able to find it, you will. I know you don't want your friend to meet the same fate as Mr. Hill." The man actually laughed.

"My God, that was Declan. You killed an officer of the court." Sabrina kept her voice low.

"He's not dead. Yet. If I don't get what I want, he will wish for death, and so will your friend." The voice wasn't familiar.

"What do you want?" Sabrina peeked out to make sure nobody was listening to her call.

"There is a black case with several jump drives inside. I have reason to believe it is in that safe deposit box," the man said.

"Easton put a safe deposit box in my name, but I don't think––" Sabrina was interrupted when the man shouted at her.

"You better check it," he roared.

"Then what?" Sabrina asked.

"I'll call you in three hours. Make sure you answer," the man demanded.

"Okay," Sabrina whispered.

"Oh, and Ms. Burke?" the man said.

"Yes?" Sabrina swallowed hard.

"Do not tell anyone what you're doing. If you contact the authorities, I'll find out."

The call ended.

Sabrina held the phone in her hand with the video paused on Crunch. He was alive, but who the hell had him, and why didn't she know he was missing?

"Sabrina," Bennett's voice echoed through the house.

She took a deep breath and tried to calm herself. She didn't want to do anything to alert someone. They'd asked questions, and she couldn't put Crunch or Declan in any more danger. The only problem was, how was she going to get to the bank and back in three hours without someone finding out?

"Sabrina," Bennett shouted.

She quickly made her way to the front of the house and stopped when she saw Crunch's parents, Zara, Colt, Keith, Bennett, Harriet, Cyril, and Shadow.

"What's wrong?" Sabrina asked.

"Hunter is missing," Camilla whispered.

"Wh…what?" Sabrina whispered.

Her body trembled, which made it more believable that she was shocked about the news, but the truth was, she was terrified. She held Crunch's and Declan's lives in her hands, and if she failed, she'd lose another man she loved.

"He went to meet Declan Hill, and when A.J. drove by Crunch's house, he was nearly run off the road by a black SUV speeding out of the driveway." Keith's voice was tight.

"His phone was found destroyed on the ground next to his truck," Cyril told her.

She couldn't speak. She knew someone had Crunch, but she wasn't taking a chance with his life. Sabrina needed to get away from the house and make her way to the bank. It would sound easy if she weren't on a property with more security than most government buildings.

"I need to get out of here." Sabrina pushed through the group of people.

"I'll come with you," Colt said.

"No," Sabrina shouted. "I need you to watch Charlee. I'm not going far," Sabrina lied.

"I'll take care of her," Emily said.

"Thanks," Sabrina whispered.

"Are you sure…" Colt began, but she held up her hand, and he stepped back.

Sabrina didn't make it to the door because Keith blocked her path. He stared down at her with narrowed eyes as if he knew she was keeping something from them. When she pressed her lips together and her eyes filled with tears, Keith rested a hand on her shoulder.

"Crunch knows what he's doing, and we'll get him back safe and sound," Keith told her in a low voice.

"Yes, I know," Sabrina whispered and stepped back from him. "I need to take a walk. Please."

Keith nodded and stepped aside so she could leave. Sabrina grabbed her purse off the hook next to the door and practically ran outside. She was putting her life at risk, and for a moment, the thought stopped her. She had a daughter to think about, but Crunch's life was in danger, and if anything happened to her, Charlee would be safe with her brother, Harriet, and Bennett.

She glanced back at the closed door of the house as she dug through her purse, looking for her keys. Her fist closed around her keyring as she hopped in her car. Hopefully, she could get off the property before someone noticed her vehicle was gone.

"I'm going to save you, Hunter." Sabrina started the car and slowly eased away from the house.

She practically held her breath until she was through the security gate. Thankfully, Crunch had told her the code to open it so she could get out without asking anyone to open it. She raced toward St. John's, hoping to make it to the bank before it closed.

Her phone rang several times on the way to the city, but she ignored the calls, knowing they were from her brother and Keith. They probably already had someone chasing her, but she managed to get to the bank and was inside the vault about to open the safety deposit box.

The attendant left her alone, and Sabrina's hand shook as she opened the cover. She sucked in a breath as her eyes fell on the engagement ring from Easton on the top. She shoved it aside and slowly took everything out to find what the man was looking for.

"Where is it?" Sabrina muttered to herself.

Grant didn't know about any of the items in the box because it was never in Easton's name. She'd never mentioned it to Grant or his mother and felt guilty about it for a while but realized it was the only thing Charlee had from her dad.

The only things she saw were boxes with some family jewelry. She dropped down on the chair and blew out a breath to calm her racing heart. It wasn't there, and she wasn't sure where to find it.

"What do I do?" Sabrina muttered.

She stood up and began to put everything back. She smiled as she picked up a black box that contained a necklace Easton gave her on their first anniversary. She opened it and ran her fingers over the large garnet surrounded by diamonds. It was beautiful, but she didn't feel safe keeping in her apartment.

She was about to close the box when she noticed the velvet seemed disturbed at the corner. She gently grabbed the edge and lifted it until it came free. That was where she found it. Three USB drives lay there inside a small clear bag with a tag that said, *evidence*.

"This must be it," Sabrina whispered.

She snatched it out and quickly put everything back inside the safe deposit container. Her hands shook as she locked it again and walked out of the vault. She told the attendant she was finished and waited while he secured the box.

When she got outside, Sabrina sprinted to her car as fast as her legs would go. She thought it was safe when she made it to her vehicle, but someone jumped in beside her. She gasped and hugged her purse in front of her.

"Where are we going?" Shadow asked.

Sabrina stared at him with wide eyes, and her lips pressed tight together. He didn't seem like he was getting out of her car, and she quickly composed herself. She positioned her purse on her lap and started the car.

"I'm going to Hopedale," Sabrina said as calmly as she could.

"So, you decided to sneak off the property to come to the bank and back to Hopedale. Why?" Shadow raised a dark eyebrow.

"I needed to do some banking, and I knew if I said I was going, someone would've told me it wasn't safe," Sabrina lied.

"And they would be right. I also find it hard to believe you would decide to do some banking when you were just told Crunch is missing." Shadow pulled on his seatbelt.

"It's not like it's midnight, and I'm in the middle of a busy city. I needed to distract myself." Sabrina pulled out of the parking spot.

"Where it is easier for someone to disappear and nothing distracts someone from worrying about a person they love," Shadow interjected.

"How did you know where I was?" Sabrina sighed.

"You're carrying a GPS tracker." Shadow chuckled.

"Who the hell put a tracker on me?" She glared at the man next to her.

"Your phone carrier," Shadow deadpanned.

Sabrina rolled her eyes when she realized what he meant. Common sense should tell her they would track her phone. It didn't matter, she had the drives, but now she had to wait for the call. She had no idea how she'd bring him the USBs because it wouldn't be so easy to get away next time.

Chapter 33

Crunch glared at the man standing against the wall on the other side of the room. He didn't know the man, but it wasn't like he was the person in charge. It was clear the guy took orders. He didn't give them.

"Can you at least check on him to see if he's still breathing?" Crunch snapped at the man.

Declan lay in a heap on the floor, and it had been several hours since Crunch heard him groan or saw him move. Crunch asked the guard several times to make sure Declan was alive, but the guy ignored him.

"Look, check his pulse. You don't want to end up charged with killing an officer of the court, would you?" Crunch raised an eyebrow.

"Shut up," the guy spat.

"I'll do that when you tell me if he's still alive," Crunch insisted.

The guy glared at Crunch, then glanced at Declan on the floor. It seemed as if he would ignore Crunch's request, but he rolled his eyes and stalked over to Declan.

The guard poked Declan with his foot but didn't get a response. He pushed Declan over with his foot, causing a small groan from the injured man.

"There, he's alive. Now shut up." The guard stepped back to the door.

"What does your boss want?" Crunch asked.

"I thought you said you'd shut up if I checked him." The guard motioned toward Declan.

"I'd like to know why I'm tied to a chair in some asshole's basement," Crunch spat.

"You'll find out soon enough." The guard smirked and walked out of the room.

Crunch looked around and sighed. The only furniture in the room was the chair, and there wasn't a window. The only way out was the door the guard walked out of and locked with a distinct click.

He glanced toward Declan and wondered if he could get him to wake up enough to help untie him. The asshole who secured him to the chair knew how to make sure Crunch wouldn't escape.

"Lots of experience, I guess," Crunch muttered.

He couldn't even use his feet to push the chair across the ground because his legs were secured high enough that they didn't touch the floor. These guys were professionals, but he was pretty sure if he found a way to topple over in the wooden chair, his weight would probably break one of the arms or legs of the chair.

He started to sway back and forth, but voices outside the room made him still. As they got closer, he heard female voices, and they didn't sound happy.

"Why can't you let us go?" one woman whined.

"Shut up. You're going in here with the rest, so we don't have to worry about you getting away again," the man shouted.

The lock clicked, and the guard pushed two women inside, and one fell to the floor. The other staggered and spun around to glare at the guard as he slammed the door behind them.

"Bastard," the angry female screamed.

"Who are you?" The woman who fell looked up at him.

The other woman he knew immediately and from the way her eyes widened when she saw him, she obviously recognized him. She hurried to help the other woman to her feet before she spoke.

"He's one of the guys who were guarding me when I went to court," Diamond said barely above a whisper.

"You mean when you decided to be an idiot and believe those assholes?" the other woman snapped.

"They were going to hurt you. What was I supposed to do? They already killed Mitch." Diamond choked on her words.

The other woman closed her eyes and blew out a breath. When she opened her eyes again, she turned toward Crunch.

"What's your name?" she asked.

"It's Hunter, but everyone calls me Crunch," Crunch told her.

"I'm Holly, and I'm guessing you know my sister," Holly said as she walked to him and began to work on the ropes around his arms.

"You're Sabrina's friend," Crunch said.

Her head snapped up, and she looked at him in confusion. Diamond wasn't saying a word as she worked on freeing Crunch's legs.

"You know Sabrina?" Holly whispered.

"She's my girlfriend." Crunch smiled.

"She's an amazing person," Holly said as she tugged and pulled on the ropes.

When she finally got one hand loose, he reached across and started pulling at the ropes on his other arm. He wasn't having much luck, and Holly hurried around the chair to help.

"She is," Crunch said.

"Is he dead?" Diamond asked as she glanced at Declan.

"No, but he's hurt bad. I need to check on him," Crunch said as he finally pulled his other hand free.

Diamond managed to free his legs, and he jumped to his feet. He moved to Declan's side and dropped to his knees as he placed a finger against the side of the man's neck. There was a pulse, but that didn't mean he was okay.

"Declan, hey, I need you to open your eyes." Crunch gently tapped the lawyer's cheek.

"Is that Declan… Hill?" Holly gasped.

"Yes," Crunch said without looking up.

"Oh, God. No." Holly hurried to the other side of Declan. "Baby, you have to wake up."

Crunch glanced at Diamond, and for the first time since he met the woman, she looked unsure. It was hard not to feel for her when she stood with her arms wrapped around herself and eyes wide with fear.

"Baby?" Crunch touched Holly's shoulder.

"We're dating," Holly sobbed.

Crunch sat back on his feet and blew out a breath. This had to be a conflict of interest when Declan was in court. It didn't matter because the whole case blew up anyway. Did he know Holly and Diamond were sisters?

"We need to get out of here." Crunch stood up.

"Good luck with that. That's the reason we're in here. Diamond picked the lock on the room we were in. That ape caught us and dragged us back here." Holly lifted Declan's head and placed it in her lap.

"Who is holding us here?" Crunch asked.

"We call him the voice because that's all we've ever heard." Diamond glanced back at the door.

"Diamond, I know what you did. Who had you change your testimony?" Crunch asked.

"I've no idea. I received a couple of phones in the mail with a letter telling me what to do. I never knew who it was." Diamond eased down on the chair.

Crunch pulled his palms down over his face as he tried to figure out a way to get them all out safely and find out who the hell was the puppet master of all this shit. Nigel Greenwood was desperate to have the property, but that didn't explain why Sabrina was a target. The guy was a businessman who did some dirty deals, but was he capable of all this?

"Diamond, do you think you can pick that lock?" Crunch whispered.

"Probably, but that jerk took my bobby pins." Diamond sighed.

"Shit," Crunch grumbled.

Crunch glanced down at Holly and Declan then started to pace. Even if he could get out of the room, Declan was still unconscious. From the way Holly was stroking his hair and whispering soft words to him, Crunch knew she wasn't about to leave without the man. He knew someone in love when he saw it.

"Okay, first we have to get him somewhat mobile." Crunch crouched next to Declan.

"He looks really bad." Diamond stood behind him.

"You may as well stop now. You four are not going anywhere," a voice echoed through the room.

"The voice," Diamond whispered.

"What the hell do you want?" Crunch shot to his feet and looked around for the speaker.

"Your sweet girlfriend is getting it for me. Never thought she was involved, did you?" The male chuckled.

"You're a liar," Holly shouted.

"Believe what you will, but in less than an hour, the sweet Sabrina and I will be on our way to a place where you'll never find us." There was some crackling and then quiet.

"He's planning on taking her." Crunch clenched his teeth.

"Why would he take her?" Holly asked.

"Maybe she is working with him," Diamond suggested.

"She's not," Crunch and Holly said together.

Their conversation was interrupted when Declan groaned, and his eyes fluttered open. At least the one not swollen shut. He blinked several times with his good eye, and when he saw Crunch, he shook his head.

"I'm so… sorry. They have my girlfriend… the guy was going to…." Declan stopped when Holly touched his cheek.

"I'm fine, baby. I'm here." Holly wiped a tear from her cheek.

"Thank fuck," Declan whispered and winced as he sat up.

"Do you know who did this?" Crunch needed to know.

"Two guys I've never met grabbed me outside the courthouse. After they kicked the shit out of me, I was told they had Holly, and I needed to call you, or they'd kill her." Declan winced.

"How badly are you hurt?" Crunch asked.

"I think I got a couple of broken ribs." Declan lifted his shirt and hissed.

Crunch crouched to look closer and cringed at the black and blue marks across the man's body. Crunch wasn't a doctor, but the bruises on Declan looked painful, and internal bleeding could probably be a problem as well.

"Let's get you up on your feet." Crunch carefully tucked his arms under Declan's armpits. "I'm going to count to three and then get you on your feet. It's probably going to hurt like a son of bitch."

"Just get me up," Declan said through clenched teeth.

Holly stood up and held her hands against her mouth as Crunch prepared to pull Declan to his feet. Diamond pushed the chair closer and stepped back.

"Okay, you ready?" Crunch asked.

"Ready," Declan confirmed.

"One, two, three."

Crunch pulled the injured man to his feet, and Declan let out a roar of pain. It was difficult to see someone in so much agony, but as long as the guy could move, he was alive. Declan took some short breaths once he was on his feet, and Diamond pushed the chair over so he could sit.

"Baby, are you okay?" Holly crouched next to him.

"I'm... I'm okay." Declan winced.

"Okay, now we need to figure out how to get out of here," Crunch whispered to himself. "I'm not letting this asshole get close to Sabrina."

Chapter 34

Sabrina kept her mouth shut as she listened to Colt rage at her for disappearing. When they finally arrived back at the house, Keith took her keys and glared at her because her brother didn't give anyone a chance to chastise her.

"I can't believe you would..." Colt went on.

"Enough," Kurt's voice echoed as he stepped into the house, followed by another man.

"But she—" Colt stopped when Kurt held up his hand.

"I know what she did, but yelling isn't going to change anything. Plus, we have another problem." Kurt motioned to the man behind him. "This is Saul Dean. He's the Crown Attorney, and he just informed me that Declan hasn't come back to the office."

"He's missing too," Sabrina blurted out without thinking.

"No, we think he's responsible for all this," Saul said.

"No way," Keith snapped.

"Right now, he's a person of interest," Kurt interjected. "Crunch was going to meet him."

Sabrina wanted to shout that she knew Declan wasn't guilty and was in danger, but she pressed her lips together. She glanced at the time, and her heart felt as if it had stopped. The man said he'd call in three hours, which was more than two hours ago. She needed to get somewhere private to wait for the call.

"I can't listen to anymore. I'm going to lie down." Sabrina spun around and went to her room.

When she closed the door, Sabrina waited to ensure nobody followed behind her. With her ear pressed against the wood, the only thing she could hear was the murmur of the voices from the kitchen. She glanced at her watch again and blew out a breath. There were still fifteen minutes left, and the guy better be prompt.

She sat on the bed with her phone in one hand and her purse in the other. She checked several times to make sure the USB drives still sat inside the zip-up pocket of her bag.

"I'm going to bring you home safe," Sabrina whispered.

She breathed in and out to calm herself, but when the phone vibrated in her hand, it startled her, and she dropped it. Sabrina snatched it up and frantically tapped the screen.

"Hello, hello," Sabrina whispered.

"Ms. Burke," a man said, but he sounded different.

"Who is this?" Sabrina asked.

"I'm an associate of the man you spoke with earlier. He's indisposed at the moment but asked me to contact you. He wants to know if you retrieved the package," the man said.

"Yes, but what am I supposed to do with it?" Sabrina whispered.

"I'll have to speak with him to let him know you have it. He will contact you." The line went dead.

"Damn it. He makes it sound like this is some sort of business transaction," Sabrina muttered.

She dropped her hands into her lap and blinked back the tears forming there. At least she had saved Crunch from getting hurt, but was she being naïve, believing some criminal that he'd release Crunch when he got his drives?

"God, I can't keep this from the police, but..." Sabrina covered her mouth with her hand.

The man said he'd know if she told the police, but she couldn't risk Crunch's life by believing this guy. He may kill Crunch anyway. She needed to tell someone, and she knew who to call.

"Sabrina," Sandy's voice came through the receiver on the second ring.

"I need you to come here to the safehouse... I have to tell you something—" Sabrina stopped. "Please don't tell anyone I called you."

"I'm on the way," Sandy said without any questions.

Sabrina paced the room while she waited for Sandy to arrive, but she was still second-guessing herself. What if she never saw Crunch again? What if somehow the man found out she told Sandy?

"Damn it. What do I do?" Sabrina dropped her face into her hands.

"Sabrina?" Colt walked into the room.

"Please, I need to be alone," Sabrina whimpered.

"Sandy is here. She wants to see you." Colt backed up from the door, and Sandy walked in.

"Oh, honey, everything is going to be okay." Sandy wrapped her arms around Sabrina.

"I'll be out in the living room if you need me." Colt closed the door.

"What's going on?" Sandy whispered.

Sabrina grabbed her purse and pulled out the USB drives. She held them in her fist for several seconds before she inhaled deeply and opened her hand.

"What is this?" Sandy asked, taking it from her.

Sabrina pulled up the message and connected her earbuds before she tapped play. She handed it over to Sandy and waited. Sandy's face didn't show any reaction, but her eyes narrowed as she studied the phone. Sandy dropped the phone on the bed and pulled the earbud out when the video ended.

"When did you get this?"

Sabrina took a deep breath and told Sandy everything in a low voice. She was terrified someone would hear her, but it was as if Sandy lifted the weight of the world off her shoulders.

"Has he called again?" Sandy asked.

"He hasn't, but an associate of his did and said he'd contact me." Sabrina blew out another breath.

"Okay," Sandy said.

Sabrina tried to do what the kidnapper wanted, but deep down, she knew it was best to tell the police. They wouldn't do anything to put Crunch's life in jeopardy. If she didn't tell them, she could lose the love of her life.

"Okay, when he calls back. I want you to ask for proof of life for both Crunch and the lawyer." Sandy stopped. "Keith and A.J. are going to be pissed, but we need to tell them."

"But—" Sabrina stopped when Sandy held up her hand.

"I know what he said, but we need help." Sandy stood up and pulled out her phone.

Sabrina watched her as Sandy tapped furiously on the screen. When she lifted her head, she nodded.

"Keith will be in here when A.J. gets here." Sandy sat next to her and held her hand. "You did the right thing."

"I feel like I may have put him in more danger," Sabrina said.

"Trust me. Crunch knows what he's doing," Sandy assured her.

Her phone rang as Keith and Aaron stepped into the room and closed the door behind them. Sandy put her finger to her lips to tell the men to be quiet as Sabrina tapped the screen and put the phone on speaker.

"Ms. Burke, I'm so glad you were able to get my property," the man said.

"I have it, but I don't know how I'm getting it you," Sabrina said as she looked up at Keith.

He waved his hand to get her to continue. Aaron brought a laptop and handed it to Sandy. She went to the other side of the room and started tapping the keys.

"I'm going to send you some instructions of where to drop the package," the man said.

"I need to know Hunter is okay and Declan," Sabrina exclaimed.

Keith's eyes widened, and Aaron pressed his lips together as he dropped his head back and looked up at the ceiling. They were both pissed, like Sandy said they would be.

"I sent you that video," the man snapped.

"That was hours ago. How do I know you never killed them right after that? I want to know they're both okay," Sabrina demanded.

"Well, Ms. Burke, I'll send you another video with the instructions." The man stopped. "Don't push me because I'll end them if you don't do exactly as I say."

"Okay." Sabrina swallowed.

The phone call ended, and Sabrina couldn't hold back the tears. She looked at Keith and Aaron as they stood behind Sandy. They hadn't said a word to her.

"Well?" Keith snapped.

"The call wasn't long enough." Sandy's shoulders dropped as she lifted her eyes to meet Sabrina.

"You should have told me." Keith pointed at Sabrina.

"Don't raise your voice at her." Sandy shot to her feet.

"He's right. I should've gone to him or A.J. or even Cyril." Sabrina blew out a breath.

"Although my uncle trusts Cyril, I'm still not fully on board with him," Aaron admitted.

Sabrina listened as Sandy, Keith, and Aaron talked about the next step. She stared at her phone, willing the message from the man who had Crunch.

"We'll keep this between us." Keith waved his hand around between the four of them in the room.

"I'll need to put a team together once we get the instructions," Aaron said.

"We'll use the guys from NES. I know none of them are compromised, but we need you to tell us everything from the beginning." Keith leaned against the dresser and crossed his arms over his chest.

Sabrina cleared her throat and began from the moment she got the first call. They listened intently while she spoke. Hopefully, something in her story would help them find Crunch and bring him home.

Chapter 35

Crunch stood next to the door and listened for the sound of anyone coming. It was difficult to tell the time or if it was day or night. He glanced back at the other three people in the room with him and wondered if they would all make it out alive.

He leaned back against the wall and closed his eyes. He pictured Sabrina's beautiful face and tried to hear her voice in his head. She was the reason he was determined to get out of there alive and get back to her.

"Do you think they'll come back with food or bring us to a bathroom?" Holly broke the silence of the room.

"I got the feeling they don't care if we eat. We probably won't make it out of this room," Diamond muttered.

"Shut up, Diamond," Declan snapped.

"What? Isn't that what we're all thinking?" Diamond shouted.

"We're getting out of here alive," Crunch yelled over them.

When he heard the distinct sound of shoes hitting against the concrete outside the room, he held up his hand for the group to be quiet. He listened to see if it was only one person or more.

"Step back from the door," a voice echoed over the speaker.

"They must have a camera in here somewhere," Holly whispered.

Crunch backed away from the door, fully prepared to overpower the man on the other side of the door. Hopefully, it was only one person because Declan, Holly, or Diamond wouldn't be able to overtake anyone.

There was a click of the lock, and the door opened slowly. Crunch was ready to lunge until he saw a gun pointed at him. He stepped in front of the other three as the guard stepped inside.

"Let us out of here," Diamond shouted over Crunch's shoulder.

"I need to take a video of you to send to your woman." The man locked eyes with Crunch.

"What about us?" Diamond asked.

"You need to shut up," the guy snapped.

"Can you at least let us go to the bathroom and get some food?" Crunch asked.

The guy held up his phone for several minutes but didn't say anything. When he dropped his arm, his eyes scanned the four people in the room.

"Move, I need a video of the lawyer too," the guard waved the gun.

"So, nobody wants to know we're alive," Diamond whined.

The guy lifted his phone, pointed at Declan for a few minutes, and then dropped his arm again. He slowly backed out of the room, keeping the gun aimed at Crunch.

"Take them one at a time to the bathroom, and I'll get some food sent." This time, the voice didn't come over the speaker.

Whoever was holding them was outside the door in the dark hallway. The guard nodded and pointed at Diamond. She glanced at Crunch as if to get permission to follow the guard. When he nodded, she headed to the door.

"If you try to escape, I'll blow a hole in your head, understand me?" the guard told Diamond.

"Yes," she whispered.

Before she stepped out of the room, she glanced back over her shoulder at Holly. No matter how cocky Diamond could be, she obviously cared about her sister and seemed reluctant to leave her.

"Can my sister come with me?" Diamond asked the guard. "I promise we won't do anything."

"Fine." The guard waved to Holly.

Both women stepped outside the door, and it slammed closed. Crunch glanced back at Declan. He shifted in the chair and winced as he grabbed his side.

"Do you think they're coming back?" Declan asked.

"Don't you?" Crunch crouched next to the man.

"I trust Holly, but after what happened in court, I don't know about Diamond," Declan admitted.

"All I know is if we don't make a go for it, we probably won't get out of here." Crunch glanced up at the speaker.

It seemed like the women had been gone for a long time. Crunch stepped to the door several times to see if he could hear them. He was beginning to believe they weren't coming back, but then he heard the click of their shoes again.

The door opened, and the guard pushed the two women into the room. He pointed the gun at Declan and motioned to come with him. Crunch and Holly helped him to his feet, and he staggered toward the door.

"Let me go with him," Crunch said.

"I'm not stupid," the guard scoffed.

"I'm not going to do anything. Jesus, the guy can barely walk." Crunch pointed at Declan as he took another unsteady step.

"Don't try anything," the voice echoed over the speaker.

"I value my life and his more than that," Crunch snapped.

The guard nodded, and Crunch carefully held up Declan as they slowly moved out of the room. The guard walked behind them, the gun held securely in his hand. Declan grunted and groaned with every step they took. If the guy had broken ribs, the movement would make the pain worse.

"How far is the bathroom?" Declan asked.

"Just down this hallway," the guard snapped.

Crunch studied the surroundings as they moved through the narrow hallways. He hadn't seen any windows but noticed at least a dozen closed doors. They were clearly in the basement of a building, but there was no hint of which one or even if they were still in the city.

"Stop," the guard said as they came to the end of the hallway.

The guard shoved open a door, and Crunch glanced inside. It was a bathroom with two stalls, a sink, and a flickering light overhead. Crunch helped Declan to one of the stalls, and he nodded as he closed the door.

When Crunch relieved himself, he walked to the sink and glanced at the exit. The guard watched him with narrowed eyes and the gun still firmly in his grasp. It may be his only chance to get them out of there, but he didn't know if the voice was close by watching.

"Fuck," Declan grunted as he pulled open the door of the stall.

"Careful, man." Crunch help Declan to the sink.

"It's getting harder to take a breath," Declan whispered.

"Hey, do you have a first aid kit?" Crunch asked the guard.

"I don't know," the man snapped.

"Can you find one? At least I can help make him comfortable before you figure out what you're going to do to us." Crunch glared at the guard.

"Fine, I'll check, but you're going back to the room first." The guard motioned the gun toward the hallway.

When they arrived back in their prison, the guard slammed the door, and they were left alone again. Crunch cursed under his breath as he watched Declan ease into the chair. He glanced back up at the speaker.

"Declan, I hate to ask, but can I borrow that chair for a few minutes?" Crunch pointed to the speaker.

"Can't you see he's in agony?" Diamond glanced up at the speaker.

"No, it's okay," Declan said as he stood up slowly.

Crunch pulled the chair across the floor and climbed up on it. He carefully reached for the speaker and lifted it off the hook to inspect it. Electronics weren't his strong suit, but if he ripped the wires from the wall, it had to disconnect the thing. He glanced over his shoulder and then gave the thing a hard yank.

"That should bring the voice running," Crunch said as he climbed down off the chair.

"He's going to be pissed." Declan forced a smile.

"Well, I guess I don't have to be sneaky in showing you this." Diamond pulled a cell phone out of her pocket.

"Where did you get that?" Crunch asked.

"Let's say the guard isn't as aware of his pockets as he should be." Diamond handed Crunch the phone.

"You stole his phone?" Holly gasped.

"Yes." Diamond rolled her eyes.

"I never thought I'd say this, but you're a genius." Declan eased down in the chair.

"I know exactly who I can call." Crunch grinned.

Chapter 36

Sabrina sat on the couch in Keith's office, holding her phone tightly in her grasp. She was waiting for the proof of life and instructions from the man who kidnapped Crunch. It seemed as if it was taking forever, and the longer it took, the harder her heart pounded.

"I should have told you right away," Sabrina whispered with a hitch in her voice.

"It's okay. We'll get him home safe and sound." Shadow sat next to her.

Keith suggested they move to the NES building. It was still on his property and away from the crowd, now congregating at the safehouse. Emily took Charlee to a sleepover with Scarlett, and the rest of the group stayed.

She glanced around the large office at the people who worked with the man she loved and knew they would do anything to bring him home. Keith, Shadow, Aaron, Crash, Trunk, Bull, and Sandy sat at a large conference table as they discussed what would happen as soon as she heard from the kidnapper.

When a shrill ring filled the room, Sabrina lifted her phone to check the screen, still black. She shook her head, and disappointment settled in her belly.

"It's mine, but I don't know this number." Sandy held it up so everyone could see the screen.

"Answer it," Keith told her.

Sandy placed the phone on the table and hit the speaker. She glanced up at Keith, and when he nodded, she spoke.

"Hello," Sandy answered.

"Sandy," Crunch's voice echoed through the speaker.

"Hey man, where the hell are you?" Keith practically yelled.

"Look, I'm being held in a basement of some building, and I'm not alone," Crunch said.

"Who's with you?" Aaron asked.

"Declan Hill, Holly Peddle and Diamond Starr. We're all okay, but Declan—" Crunch stopped talking.

"Crunch?" Sandy shouted into the phone.

"Sorry, thought I heard the guard. Anyway, Declan's hurt. Can you trace this phone, Sandy?" Crunch asked.

"Hello, have you met me? Already on it," Sandy replied as she frantically tapped away on the keyboard of her laptop. "Keep the line open as long as you can."

"I'll try." Crunch cleared his throat. "Rusty, how's Sabrina?"

Sabrina shot to her feet and leaned over the phone. She swallowed several times before she could speak without bursting into tears.

"I'm here, Hunter. I'm fine," Sabrina said with a slight crack in her voice. "Are you okay?"

"I'm fine. I'll see you as soon… Shit, gotta go," Crunch whispered, and the call ended.

"Hunter," Sabrina shouted.

"Sandy, please tell me you got his location," Keith asked.

"Hold on," Sandy clicked the keys a few more times and then grinned. "Got him."

"Where is he?" Aaron asked.

"If this is right, he's in the city, but this building is next to the courthouse." Sandy pointed to something on the screen.

"Let's go get him," Sabrina shouted as she headed out of the office.

"Whoa, Sabrina, you're staying here. We can't take a chance." Keith grabbed her arm gently.

"But—" Sabrina looked up at the large man.

"I'm sorry, Sabrina. We don't know who has Crunch, but we know they're dangerous, and we can't save him and keep you out of danger," Aaron told her.

Sabrina glanced around the room, and although she knew they were right, she desperately wanted to be there when they found him. Before she could argue, her phone buzzed, and she glanced down at the screen.

"It's him," Sabrina said.

"Open the text," Keith told her.

The videos attached to the text showed Crunch and Declan in a room. They were alive, but Crunch wasn't wrong when he said Declan was in bad shape.

"Does he have the instructions?" Shadow asked.

Sabrina shook her head, but another text came in from the kidnapper. It gave detailed instructions on where she had to bring the USB drives, and they had two hours to drop them off.

"That's nowhere near the building where I traced the phone," Sandy said.

"Well, I guess we're sending two teams." Aaron held up two fingers.

"I guess I'm going too," Sabrina interjected.

"No," Keith replied.

"This," Sabrina snapped as she held up her phone, "says I'm supposed to bring the drives. If he sees anyone else—" Sabrina stopped when Keith held up his hand.

"We'll have Crunch before that." Keith began to rattle off orders to the people in the room.

"How do you know you'll have him? You don't even know exactly where he is. He could be anywhere." Sabrina grabbed Keith's arm.

"I'm not going to risk your safety. One, Crunch would put my head on a platter, and two, my mother, Aunt Alice, Aunt Cora, Nanny Betty, and my wife would cut my balls off and feed them to my cat." Keith narrowed his eyes.

"Do you trust your team?" Sabrina stood.

"Of course," Aaron said without hesitation.

"Do you trust your guys?" Sabrina looked up at Keith.

"One hundred percent," Keith admitted.

"Then why don't you trust them to keep me safe while I serve as a distraction to this asshole?" Sabrina tilted her head and glared up at him.

"Good try. Trusting our teams isn't the issue. Not trusting the criminals is why you're staying here." Keith walked out of the office.

Sabrina tossed her arms up in the air and growled in frustration. All she could do was sit and watch while several more NES employees, as well as three of the other O'Connor brothers, put a plan together.

"I know it's frustrating, believe me." Sandy sat next to Sabrina. "But they want to keep you safe and get Crunch home safe as well."

"I know," Sabrina sighed.

"And we'll get him home safe," Sandy assured her.

Sabrina swallowed the lump that threatened to strangle her. It was difficult to stand by and trust someone else to bring home the man she loved, but she didn't have a choice.

"What the fuck is he doing here?" Aaron grumbled as he glanced up at the doorway.

Sabrina glanced up. Saul Dean was in a deep discussion with Keith, Kurt, and John O'Connor. They were speaking quietly, but Aaron didn't seem to like being left out of the conversation. John was the chief of police, so he'd be involved with any kind of operations, but Kurt was mayor and technically shouldn't be in the middle of it. It didn't matter that he was formally the chief.

"He still believes Declan instigated all this," James whispered.

James O'Connor was another of the brothers and also a police officer. He was the deputy chief but didn't hesitate when Aaron called him. Crunch was like family to the O'Connor family, and they wouldn't give up until he was home.

"Yes, because I'm sure Declan would take a beating to cover for himself." Nick O'Connor, another brother, and police officer scoffed.

"We don't have time to deal with that asshat. We have less than two hours." Aaron blew out a breath and glanced at his watch.

Sabrina remained quiet as she watched the men and Sandy put together a plan. It was difficult to concentrate on anything because she was terrified, they wouldn't get there in time, and it would cost Crunch his life.

"Are you sure this isn't going to put the victim in danger?" Saul asked as he glanced down at the table.

"It's the best course of action, and if the guy wants the drives dropped off at this area, he's not going to be at the other place." Keith sounded annoyed.

"I hope you have the drives secured in evidence." Saul locked eyes with Aaron.

"I still have them." Sabrina held up the bag with the drives inside.

"Why would you allow her to have access to the evidence?" Saul narrowed his eyes at Aaron.

"She's holding them because I asked her to. I'm going to be going through them." Sandy took the bag from Sabrina's hand.

"Shouldn't they be put into evidence?" Saul snapped.

"With all due respect, Sandy is one of the top analysts in the country, and she has done this for the department more times than I can count," John said.

"This guy kidnapped four people to cover up whatever is on those drives. Sandy will find out what it is. I can guarantee that," Keith interjected.

"Good. Keep me up-to-date." Saul nodded to everyone and then strolled out of the office.

"I hate that guy," Aaron grumbled.

"You and most everyone who ever met him." Kurt chuckled.

Nanny Betty and Kathleen dropped by a few minutes later with food for everyone because they needed nourishment to bring Crunch home safe, according to Nanny Betty. They left after they placed several boxes on the table and left as quickly as they arrived.

An hour later, everyone was gone except for Sandy and Sabrina. Sandy was going through the drives like she'd told the Crown Attorney, and Sabrina was chewing off her nails, waiting for word from Aaron and Keith.

"You know, if you keep doing that, you're going to chew your fingers down to the knuckles." Sandy glanced at Sabrina over the laptop.

"I know. I feel useless." Sabrina dropped her hands down on her lap.

"Come over here and look at this." Sandy shot to her feet.

"What?" Sabrina moved around the table and glanced down at the screen.

"This proves Declan is a victim." Sandy pointed to the screen.

"Oh, God." Sabrina stared at the account name.

"I need to call A.J." Sandy was about to reach for her phone, but it started to ring.

"Don't answer that," a voice echoed in the room.

Sabrina lifted her eyes toward the sound and gasped when she noticed two men standing in the doorway. One held a gun pointed at them, and she recognized him immediately. The other was a stranger.

Sandy's phone stopped, but a few seconds later, it buzzed again. When Sandy started to reach for it, the man shook his head and cocked the gun.

"Don't even think about it. By the time someone comes to check on you, it'll be too late. Turn it off," the man ordered.

"I knew there was a reason I didn't trust you," Sandy muttered under her breath as she picked up the phone and turned it over.

"I'm not concerned with who likes me. All I want is my property and to get rid of anything linking me to all of this. In less than an hour, all of it will be over." Saul Dean narrowed his eyes.

"You're supposed to be an advocate for victims," Sandy snapped.

"It wasn't as lucrative as strip clubs or the property that I've acquired over the years. It's a tough job." Saul sighed.

"I'm sure being a criminal is an arduous occupation," Sandy scoffed.

"It wasn't complicated. Not until Grant screwed up and his brother got his hands on the drives. Grant was supposed to keep track of my finances. He didn't get his smarts from his father." Saul chuckled.

Sabrina took in the man holding a gun and gasped when she saw it. Saul's greying dark brown hair, brown eyes, and olive skin were similar to Grant's and even the long nose with a slight bump. Sabrina gasped.

"You're... Grant's father," Sabrina whispered.

"Ding, ding, ding, give the woman a prize." Saul snickered.

"That's why he wouldn't say anything to the police." Sabrina fisted her hands at her sides.

"He won't be saying much anymore. In about..." Saul glanced at his watch. "Fifteen minutes, he'll be with his mother."

"You're going to kill your own son?" Sabrina gasped.

"No, I already did. It takes some time for the poison to take effect." Saul glanced at the table. "Go grab the drives," Saul told the other man.

"What are you going to do, Saul Dean? Take them and kill us?" Sandy asked, pulling Sabrina behind her.

The other man walked around the table and snatched the USB drives off the table and the other one out of Sandy's laptop. He lifted his eyes and met Sabrina's gaze. The man appeared nervous, but he didn't say a word as he headed back toward Saul.

"I'm not stupid, Mrs. O'Connor. I'm not going to kill you. I'm going to kill the person who did it." Saul quickly aimed his weapon and shot the other man in the chest.

Sabrina screamed as the man grabbed his chest and dropped to the floor. Sandy went to the man to help him, but it was too late. The guy gasped and stopped breathing.

"You see, my story will be that Nigel Greenwood was a terrible human and pushed people out of their businesses so he could take over their property. He did some dreadful things, and right before he shot you two, he admitted to kidnapping your friends. I came back to help, but he turned the gun on me, and I needed to protect myself." Saul smirked as he spun his story.

"You won't get away with this." Sandy backed up until she was in front of Sabrina again.

"I already have." Saul chuckled as he reached behind him and pulled a second weapon out of his pants. "I can't shoot both of you with the gun that killed Nigel. That would look suspicious."

He lifted the gun, and it was as if someone poured a jug of water down over her body. This man was going to kill her and Sandy. Sabrina would never get to hug her little girl ever again or tell Colt how proud he made her. Crunch would never know how much she loved him.

"Oh, don't worry. I'll make this quick and painless." Saul smirked as he slowly lifted his arm.

Sabrina squeezed her eyes shut and waited for the bullet to take her life. She heard a loud pop and then a heavy thud.

Chapter 37

Crunch stood next to the door with his back to the wall, so he was not visible through the door's small window. He knew help was on the way but didn't know if the guard would come to kill them before being rescued.

"Back away from the door," the guard shouted.

"We're not close to the door," Holly called out.

There was a click, and Crunch held the chair over his head as the door slowly opened. The guard stepped inside and lifted a weapon. Before he had a chance to take a second step, Crunch brought the chair down over the man's arm and quickly grabbed him around the neck.

The guy struggled to get free, but Crunch increased the pressure, and the guard passed out from lack of oxygen. Crunch didn't want to kill the guy, but he didn't want him conscious either. Crunch lowered him to the floor and picked up the weapon.

"You killed him," Diamond whispered.

"No, I knocked him out. Come on, let's get out of here," Crunch told them.

He dragged the guard across the room, and the four of them hurried from the room. Crunch locked the door behind him because he didn't want anyone halting their escape. He dropped the key on the floor next to the door and quickly followed Declan, Holly, and Diamond.

Crunch called Sandy's number, but the voicemail cut in after several rings. He cursed and tried again. This time, someone answered but didn't speak.

"Sandy," Crunch said.

She didn't speak, but he could hear people talking. Crunch listened carefully to the conversation. His heart raced when he heard Sabrina's voice, and she sounded terrified.

"Who are you calling?" Declan asked.

"Quiet," Crunch whispered.

He could hear most of what Sandy said, but it wasn't easy to understand the other voice. It was male, but he didn't recognize it. When he heard Sandy say, Saul Dean, he let out a curse under his breath.

"What are you going to do, Saul Dean? Take them and kill us?" Sandy asked, pulling Sabrina behind her.

"I'm not stupid, Mrs. O'Connor. I'm not going to kill you. I'm going to kill the person who did it." Saul said then there was a gunshot.

"Fuck." Crunch gasped.

It took everything ounce of strength to end the call, but he needed to get someone there to help them. He wasn't sure who Saul shot, but he didn't have any loyalty if he killed his accomplice. Crunch called Keith's number.

"Come on, Rusty, answer," Crunch growled through his teeth.

"Hello," Keith answered.

"Sandy and Sabrina are in trouble," Crunch told him.

"They're at the office. Why would you think they're in trouble?" Keith asked.

"I called Sandy. Rusty, it's Saul Dean. He's behind all this." Crunch pushed on a door at the end of the hallway.

"The Crown Attorney?" Keith shouted.

"Yes, get back to the Compound," Crunch ordered.

"We're outside the building where Sandy tracked you," Keith told him.

"We got out of the room, and now we're trying to get out of the building," Crunch told him. "Don't worry about us. You need to get back to save them."

There was a muffled conversation between Keith and someone else, but Crunch couldn't hear it. He saw Holly push on another door, and it opened. They stepped out in an open space that appeared in the middle of a renovation.

"I know where we are," Declan said.

"Where?" Holly asked.

"This is where they're moving the Crown Attorney's office. It's right next to the courthouse." Declan winced as he tried to hurry toward the exit.

"Let's get the hell out of here," Crunch said as he pushed on the door. "It's locked."

"Watch out," Diamond said.

Crunch barely stepped out of the way as she threw a brick through the glass of the door. Crunch kicked out the shattered window, and they stepped through onto the front steps. He glanced up the street and shouted when he saw Keith and Shadow running toward him.

"We got to get back to Hopedale. Now," Crunch yelled.

Chapter 38

Sabrina was on her knees, eyes closed, but no second shot. The only thing she heard was a thud and loud grunt. When she peeped through her fingers, she gasped in surprise.

"We stopped into the bathroom on the way out and heard these guys talking about getting what they came for." Kathleen had a fire extinguisher in her hand.

Sandy tied Saul's hands behind his back with an electrical cord as Kathleen and Nanny Betty came further into the room. Sabrina slowly got to her feet and glanced down at the unconscious man. She grabbed the edge of the table to steady her wobbling legs.

"Are ya all right, dolly?" Nanny Betty wrapped an arm around Sabrina.

"I'm fine." Sabrina didn't hesitate as she wrapped her arms around the older woman and hugged her tightly. "You saved our lives."

"They really did." Sandy stood up and hugged her mother-in-law.

Sabrina was still shaking when Nanny Betty released her. She eased into one of the chairs but jumped to her feet when loud voices echoed from the hallway. It was almost laughable when Cyril and Bennett stepped into the room with guns drawn.

"It's all right, lads. Kathleen knocked dat fella out." Nanny Betty wrapped her arm around Sabrina's waist.

"Are you ladies okay?" Bennett asked.

"We're all fine," Sandy told them. "He's probably going to need a trip to the hospital, but it's too late for that guy."

Cyril had his phone to his ear and barking orders to someone on the other line. Sabrina tried not to focus on the dead body and the unconscious man.

"Sabrina, are you sure you're okay?" Sandy whispered as she crouched in front of her.

"I'm not dead, so I'm more than okay." Sabrina forced a smile.

"I don't care. You should've had some idea this fucker was the head of VP Con," Cyril roared at someone in the corridor.

"I'm sorry, sir, but there were no links to the Crown Attorney," A female answered.

"Let's get you ladies out of here," Bennett said as he motioned toward the doorway.

As Bennett escorted Sabrina and the other women out of the office, Sabrina stumbled when she came face to face with the woman talking to Cyril.

"Vanessa?" Sabrina gasped.

"Ms. Burke," Vanessa replied.

"Do you know she—" Sabrina began but then stopped. "Of course, you were undercover too. For four freaking years. This shit has been going on for four years."

Sabrina shook with rage as she glared at Cyril, but he didn't seem daunted by her change in demeanor. That only pissed her off more, making her want to shake the man until he apologized for screwing with her life.

"Why did you work as a nanny for my daughter if you were supposed to be watching Grant?" Sabrina pointed her finger in Vanessa's face.

"We needed to make sure you weren't involved," Cyril answered.

Sabrina stared at the man with her eyes wide in horror. They thought she was involved with criminals. She didn't know if she could speak after a revelation like that, but Vanessa seemed to have noticed her shock.

"I told them there was no way you were involved the first day I met you." Vanessa's eyes softened. "I do want to apologize for how I treated you."

"Four years," Sabrina whispered.

"Sometimes investigations take longer," Cyril said.

Sabrina shook her head, and Bennett wrapped his arm around her shoulders. He brought them into one of the other offices. He seemed angry, but she didn't ask why because she didn't want to know anything else.

"You'll be more comfortable in here." Bennett nodded.

"Thanks," Sabrina whispered.

They were all quiet, but Sabrina could hear the muffled sounds of the police arriving to take Saul and the man he killed. She wasn't sure how long they'd be there, and someone had died, but her only concern was if Keith and Aaron found Crunch.

She was about to ask Bennett when she remembered something Saul admitted. He'd poisoned Grant, and as pissed as she was at the man for everything he did, he didn't deserve to die.

"Bennett, you've got to get someone to check on Grant." Sabrina shot to her feet.

"Yes, that asshole said he poisoned him. Although, it's probably too late." Sandy glanced at Sabrina.

"Grant is in the hospital, and as far as I know, he's going to survive. I got the call as I was on my way here," Bennett assured them.

"How did you know what was going on?" Sandy asked.

"We got a call from Keith to get over here right away, but apparently, these lovely ladies rescued you." Bennett smiled at Kathleen and Nanny Betty.

Sabrina glanced over at the two women, who looked pretty proud of themselves as they sat on the small sofa. Sabrina shivered at the thought of what could've happened if Kathleen and Nanny Betty hadn't been there. She was about to say something when she heard a couple of angry voices.

"Where are they?" Kurt called from down the hall.

"Kathleen," another voice shouted.

Sabrina recognized the sound of Sean O'Connor as his voice echoed through the building. She'd never heard the man raise his voice at anyone, especially his wife, but both he and Kurt sounded furious.

When they stepped into the room, both men blew out a breath of relief, but the anger on their faces didn't fade. Sean stomped right over to his wife and pulled her up into his arms.

"What the hell were you thinking?" Sean asked with a crack in his voice.

"I was thinking I didn't want that terrible man hurting our daughter-in-law and Sabrina," Kathleen said as she pulled back and looked up at her husband.

"Mudder, are you out of your mind. You're almost ninety years old," Kurt addressed his mother.

"I'm only eighty-eight, and I'm not an invalid, and I was only backing up Kathleen," Nanny Betty snapped.

Sandy seemed to be struggling to hide her smile. Nanny Betty was barely five feet tall and barely a hundred pounds, so the thought of her as back up against a murderous criminal was almost comical, but Sabrina cringed at the thought of what could've happened to both of the incredible women.

"Backup? What were you going to do, scold him to death?" Kurt scoffed.

Sabrina didn't hear her response because when she glanced toward the door, Crunch was standing there. Everyone around her seemed to fade into the background as she slowly stood up with her eyes locked on the man moving toward her.

She held her breath as he came closer, and her eyes blurred with tears when he stepped next to her. She reached out slowly and gently placed her hand against her chest to ensure she wasn't dreaming.

"You're… you're okay," Sabrina cried through the tears streaming down her cheeks.

"I'm okay," he whispered.

Sabrina practically threw herself into his arms, and he held her tightly against him. He was alive, and they were all safe. She tucked her head into his neck and released all the emotion she'd held in for the last little while. It was over, and they could finally live their lives.

Chapter 39

Two weeks passed since Crunch escaped and finally moved back into his house. With all the guilty parties either in jail or dead, Sabrina and Charlee could go back to their apartment. He'd asked her to stay with him, but she told him she needed to get her head around some things.

The media went crazy with the news of Saul Dean and his numerous crimes. The CSIS dug deep into all of Saul's affairs, so he'd end up in jail for a long time. The man killed several people or hired someone to do the job. It was tough to get his head around the fact that someone he knew could be responsible for such horrible things.

The guy who kept Crunch and the others locked in that room admitted he'd been the one to shoot at Sabrina and Crunch. He'd also admitted to trying to hit Crunch with a car and leaving the note on his step. Apparently, Saul blamed Crunch for Sabrina's refusal to marry Grant. The guy had no issues rolling over on the former Crown Attorney and gave the police a list of accomplices working for Saul.

The shareholders of VP Con dissolved the company and liquidated the assets. He didn't care because he was just glad it was all over.

Grant survived the attempt on his life and made a deal to testify against Saul. He would still do time but with a reduced sentence. He also gave the police the information on the lawyer who helped with the fake will. When the police went to arrest Finley, they found him hanging in his garage. He'd committed suicide to avoid going to jail.

The Crown Attorney's office offered Saul's job to Declan, but instead, he joined his old firm and moved into a house with his girlfriend. Diamond and Holly started seeing a therapist to help with their trauma. Both women were shocked to find out who was responsible for their abduction.

Sabrina met with the lawyers to find out what to do about Easton's estate. Grant practically cleared the accounts, but he couldn't sell the house or the building. Easton had already put those properties into Sabrina's name before he died. Sabrina was shocked because Easton had done it without telling her.

Grant finally admitted that the main reason he wanted Sabrina to marry him was so he could trick her into signing the property over to him. Then he could turn it over to VP Con and get paid for it.

Zara suggested both Crunch and Sabrina back out of the ball because of what happened over the last couple of weeks, but Sabrina wouldn't hear of it. They practiced almost every day, and although she was living back in her apartment, they did manage to spend several nights together.

The previous weekend, they'd danced the night away at Hulk's wedding, and as they celebrated the love between Hulk and Caroline, Crunch glanced around the hall. So many happy couples filled the room, and he knew Sabrina was it for him. He wanted to make her his wife and be a father to Charlee.

That was why he invited Colt out for a couple of beers at the pub. Since Sabrina was helping his sister do some preparations for the ball in a week.

Crunch walked into Jack's Place and walked into the pub. As usual, Friday night was busy, and the band on the platform was a group who'd played there before. They were good, but, in his opinion, *Rockin' The Law* was better.

"Hey, Crunch," Ethan 'Ace' Norris said from behind the bar.

Ace worked for NES as a pilot for clients and staff who needed to fly privately. He was also Nick O'Connor's brother-in-law. When Ace wasn't flying, he worked as one of the bartenders for Jack's Pub.

"Hey, Ace." Crunch sat at the bar.

"Bottle or tap?" Ace asked.

"Bottle," Crunch said as he glanced toward the door.

Colt stepped inside and waved to a couple of the regulars he'd gotten to know since coming back and forth to Hopedale. Crunch waved to him, and he headed toward him.

"One for Colt too, Ace," Crunch shouted over the music.

"Nice crowd here tonight," Colt said as he sat down on the barstool next to Crunch.

"Weekends are always busy here." Crunch dropped a twenty on the bar and motioned to a table at the back of the pub.

"Congrats on the new job, by the way," Crunch said.

Keith offered Colt a position with NES as an analyst. The company was growing rapidly, and the computer work was getting too much for the other analyst, Smash and Sandy. Colt was apprehensive until Keith told him what his salary would be.

"Thanks. I was wondering when I officially get my new name." Colt chuckled.

"Got any embarrassing moments in your life?" Crunch smirked.

"None that I'm going to mention." Colt took a sip from his bottle.

Crunch felt nervous about his conversation with Colt. He didn't know what he was supposed to say or ask. He'd asked a couple of his friends how he should approach the subject but asking permission to propose seemed archaic. So, Crunch pulled a black ring box out of his pocket and placed it on the table.

Colt picked it up and opened it. He took the ring out and slipped it on the tip of his pinky finger. Crunch swallowed as Colt studied the piece of jewelry, then placed it back in the box and closed it.

"It's a nice ring, but I'm afraid I don't swing that way." Colt smirked.

"Smartass. I asked you here to get your thoughts on me proposing to your sister," Crunch said as he put the ring box back in his pocket.

"Now I'm heartbroken. Here I thought I was your one and only," Colt teased.

Crunch rolled his eyes and took a long drink of his beer. He took a deep breath before he spoke again.

"I love your sister. I never thought I'd feel this way about anyone, but I want to spend my life with her. I know your parents passed, and you're the only family she has." Crunch met Colt's gaze. "I would like your blessing."

Colt stared for a few seconds and then took a swig of his beer. He held out his hand, and Crunch narrowed his eyes in confusion. Colt wiggled his finger, letting Crunch know he wanted to see the ring again.

He placed the ring box in Colt's hand and sat back in the seat. Colt took out the ring that Zara helped Crunch pick out. His sister was delighted he'd asked her and swore she wouldn't say a word to Sabrina.

The jeweler told him it was a fourteen-carat round diamond ballerina engagement ring. When he heard the ring's description, he didn't even ask to see another. To him, it looked like a snowflake, but he knew it would look stunning on Sabrina's finger.

"I think you're perfect for my sister, and I can't wait to see her face when you slip this on her finger. I know she loves you, and so does Charlee. After everything you've been through, nobody deserves to be happy more than you two." Colt handed him back the ring. "You most certainly have my blessing."

Colt held out his hand, and Crunch shook it. Then he told his future brother-in-law his plan for the proposal. Would she say yes?

Chapter 40

Sabrina smoothed down her dress for the hundredth time as she waited for the introduction. Crunch stepped in front of her and took her hands in his. He looked mouth-watering in his black tuxedo, but her breath caught in her throat when she looked up into his eyes.

"Are you ready for this?" Crunch smiled.

"Sure, I'm about to throw up, but ya, I'm raring to go." Sabrina smirked.

"I'm nervous too, but we got this." Crunch leaned in and whispered in her ear. "Pretend it's only you and me."

Sabrina closed her eyes and sighed as his scent enveloped her. His presence helped calm her jitters and gave her the courage to perform in front of some of the most influential people in the province.

She glanced to the other side of the room and smiled when she saw Bennett and Harriet standing next to the stage as Zara explained how the foundation used the donations. Bennett promised to retire from his undercover work and was in the process of selling his business. They bought a house outside the city not far from

Hopedale and put their estate up for sale. Harriet believed the house had too much bad karma to have a happy life there. Bennett agreed.

Her brother smiled at her from across the room. Sabrina was surprised he attended, but he was thrilled to watch Sabrina and Crunch dance. If only there weren't so many strangers watching them too.

"Thank you again for your generous support," Zara said and then glanced toward Sabrina and Crunch.

Sabrina took a deep breath and nodded to let Zara know she was ready. Well, as prepared as someone about to vomit could be. Crunch took her hands and pulled her to face him.

"I love you. We got this." Crunch gave her a quick kiss.

"I love you too," she whispered.

"Now, I am thrilled to introduce our dancers. They'll be performing an old-fashioned waltz as well as a dance they choreographed themselves. Please put your hands together and welcome my brother Hunter Crawford and Sabrina Burke." Zara waved her hand toward them.

Crunch held her hand as they walked to the middle of the hall and got into position for the first dance. The music started almost immediately, and they glided around the floor like they were the only two people in the room.

Sabrina concentrated on Crunch and relaxed more as they spun around the room. When the first song ended, she was surprised by how fast the dance went. They moved to opposite sides of the room in position for the next song.

When Niall Horan's voice echoed in the room with the seductive lyrics of *"Slow Hands,"* their sexy routine began. Again, she kept her attention on Crunch and enjoyed the flare of arousal in his eyes when he pulled her against him.

She smiled as she spun away from him and reached back for his hand as the song ended. She was confused when he didn't grab it and spin her into his arms like they'd practiced. She turned her head as he dropped down on his knee.

She barely heard the crowd's *oohs* and *awws* when he lifted an open ring box up for her to see. Zara handed her brother the microphone and grinned.

Sabrina covered her mouth with her hands as Crunch cleared his throat and lifted the microphone to speak. She'd never heard a room with over two hundred people become so quiet.

"Sabrina, I look at you here in front of me, and my heart pounds in my chest because I can't believe how lucky I am to know someone so amazing. I look at you, and I see the woman I want to waltz with for the rest of my life. The person I want to Foxtrot through my days and Tango through my nights with." Crunch smiled. "It would make me the happiest man in the world to call you my partner, my wife, my forever. Sabrina, will you be that for me? Will you marry me?"

It was as if everyone around them took in a breath and held it as they waited for her to respond. With the lump in her throat and the tears running down her cheek, she knew getting out any words would be a struggle, but she took the microphone from him and smiled.

"Yes, Hunter. I'll be all those things. Yes, I'll marry you." Her voice cracked.

She dropped the microphone on the floor, causing a loud bang to echo through the hall, but it wasn't nearly as loud as the crowd when Crunch stood up and slipped the ring on her finger.

Sabrina practically jumped into his arms and pressed her lips hard against his. Crunch lifted her off the floor and spun them around while everyone around them cheered and whistled.

"I love you." She threw her head back and shouted as loud as she could.

"I love you too, baby," Crunch replied.

She didn't know if she'd ever be this happy again, but she couldn't wait to tell Charlee about the proposal. Her little girl would be overjoyed since she seemed to think Crunch was Sabrina's prince charming.

Minutes later, they were pried apart by family and friends hugging and congratulating them. Sabrina had her own surprise planned for the evening, and it felt even more right now that Crunch's family were going to be hers as well.

"I'm so happy for you," Zara squealed.

"My son is one lucky guy." Crunch's father kissed her cheek.

"He certainly is," Bennett said as he hugged her.

Sabrina smiled as she glanced around the floor, looking for the microphone she'd dropped. She wanted to announce it while everyone was still close by.

"What are you doing?" Harriet asked.

"I need the microphone," Sabrina told her.

"Got it." Colt smirked as he handed it to her.

She'd told her brother her plans, and he thought it was a great idea. It was something she always wanted, and it would help Crunch's family too.

"Thanks," she mouthed the word to her brother.

She managed to reach for Crunch's hand and tug him toward her. She also waved for Crunch's mother and sister to stand next to her and then brought the microphone to her mouth.

"If I could get everyone's attention for a moment." Sabrina's voice echoed through the speakers.

Everyone in the room quickly quieted as they waited for her to speak. Crunch watched her with curiosity but held her hand as she looked around at her favorite people in the world.

"After everything that has happened over the last several weeks, I'm more than happy to get back to a normal existence. As some of you know, I've been given the deeds to the building where I wanted to open a dance studio." Sabrina reached for Camilla and Zara.

"Camilla, I've looked up to you from the first time my parents brought me to see you dance in New York. I was awed by your talent even at the tender age of six. I followed your career, and when I found out you were in Newfoundland and looking for an instructor all those years ago, I was thrilled when you hired me." Sabrina swallowed the lump forming in her throat.

"I know talent when I see it," Camilla said.

"Thank you. Zara, when you and your mom asked me to help after your injury, I felt alive again for the first time in a long while. I was so devastated when your beautiful studio was destroyed and almost took the life of your son." Sabrina glanced at Crunch.

She cleared her throat and tried to compose herself because even though he was safe and healthy in front of her. It still made her shudder when she thought about what could've happened to him. She took a shaky breath and began to speak again.

"I've decided to offer you both the building to reopen your studio so you can continue to teach the art of dance way into the future. It's perfect and big enough for you to expand." Sabrina smiled.

Camilla stared with wide eyes filled with tears, and Zara had her hands over her mouth as she squealed in surprise. When she glanced at Crunch, he smiled and wrapped his arm around her shoulders.

"Are you serious?" Zara shouted.

"Very." Sabrina grinned.

Camilla hadn't said a word, but she stepped next to Sabrina, took the microphone, and took Sabrina's hand. It made Sabrina a little nervous because Crunch's mother's expression was unreadable as she lifted her hand and spoke.

"I want to thank you, *mon amour*, but I'm afraid we can not accept—" Camilla was interrupted.

"Mom, what are you saying?" Zara gasped, but her mother held up her hand.

"We can not accept unless you agree to be a partner with us." Camilla smiled.

"You don't—" Sabrina began, but Camilla stopped her.

"I started my studio for my children. To pass on to them, and since you're marrying my son, you're family." Camilla handed the microphone to Crunch and pulled Sabrina into a hug.

"I'd be honored to be part of your studio," Sabrina whispered as she hugged her future mother-in-law.

She finally had everything she ever dreamed of for herself and her daughter. One day, she'd look back and know that this was the day she finally got everything she ever dreamed of.

Epilogue

Brent 'Crash' Adams leaned against the bar and smiled as his friend clumsily danced with his new wife in the middle of the dance floor. Hulk may not be the best dancer, but he looked deliriously happy. Bruce 'Hulk' Steel gazed at Caroline as if she hung the moon, and she smiled at him with the same lovesick expression.

"Lucky bastard," Crash muttered under his breath.

"Another one down." Gage 'Smash' Hodder stepped next to him at the bar.

"They're falling fast," Crash said.

As the words left his lips, she walked by, and his heart did that odd flip in his chest. Doctor Allyson Sullivan was the only woman he ever met who could bring him to his knees, but they were only friends. That was the way she wanted it.

At first, he thought it was his job as a security specialist with Newfoundland Elite Security, or NES. The government contracted the accredited company for all security needed for diplomats, politicians, or protection for private citizens. Over the last several years, things had gotten a bit dangerous, and he'd been shot at more than once.

He met Allyson on one of his jobs when her sister needed security. Bethany witnessed a murder, and the police wanted her under protective custody until they arrested the suspect. It was personal for his boss because the women were family friends. Keith 'Rusty' O'Connor didn't hesitate to put two of his staff on them.

Crash spent several weeks with Allyson, and they clicked right away. After Bethany's ordeal was over, he continued a friendship with her, talking and getting to know each other. He thought they were headed in a romantic direction until he tried to kiss her one night. She'd made it clear they were only friends and practically threw him out of the house.

She called to apologize for overreacting the next day and told him she wasn't looking for anything romantic. That was where he remained, the friend zone with a woman who he wanted more than he could ever imagine.

As if she heard his thoughts, their eyes locked. Allyson stopped as he reached back to place his beer bottle on the bar without breaking their gaze. She was beautiful in her gold dress that hung below her knee. It dipped just low enough to give a hint of cleavage, and it was the sexiest damn thing he'd ever seen.

As he stalked toward her, Allyson's smile slipped a little, and when he was in front of her, she tipped her head back to gaze up at him. The twinkle lights around the hall looked like diamonds flickering in her blue eyes. Her auburn hair hung in loose waves over one shoulder and her lips glistened with some sort of gloss. It made it hard to breathe, so he was glad she was a doctor, just in case his heart stopped too.

"Well, don't you look handsome," Allyson shouted over the music.

"Thank you." Crash smiled. "You look stunning."

"Thanks." Allyson folded her hands in front of her.

"Would you like to dance?" Crash held out his hand as the band slowed the tempo of the music.

Allyson glanced over her shoulder and then back to him. Reluctantly, she placed her hand in his, and he escorted her to the dance floor. Crash's heart thudded in his chest as he pulled her into his arms and began to sway to the music slowly.

"Bruce looks so happy." Allyson nodded toward the groom.

"Can't say I blame him. Caroline's an amazing lady, and those boys love him." Crash didn't allow her eyes to move from his. "Love wins out."

Caroline had two sons from a previous relationship who worshiped the ground Hulk walked on. The large man became a complete marshmallow when it came to those two little boys and would do anything for them.

"Yeah, love wins," Allyson said, but he could see sadness cloud her eyes.

"Won't be long before they pop out a few more kids. I know Hulk loves her boys, but Caroline wants more kids. I don't think Hulk will deny her that." Crunch chuckled.

"It's nice that they can have that." Allyson's eyes glistened with unshed tears.

"Hey, what's with that face? It's a wedding. Happy thoughts." Crash crouched so he could look into her eyes.

Crash wrapped his arm around her shoulder and led her out on the patio. When the door closed behind them, he turned to her.

"Ally, what's wrong?" Crash asked.

Allyson shook her head and moved to the railing that encircled the deck of The Rock. Hulk rented the dance club for the reception because it was the only place large enough for guests. Practically the whole town of Hopedale attended to see the happy couple start their life together.

"Sweetheart, talk to me." Crash placed his hands on her shoulders and forced her to face him.

"I'm fine. Weddings… they just… too many memories." Allyson shrugged.

Crash pulled her into his arms, and she rested her cheek against his chest. He closed his eyes as he pressed his lips against the top of her head. It was difficult to think of friendship when the simple act of trying to comfort her made his heart pound.

"I'm sorry. I'm ruining this for you. You should go find your date and enjoy yourself." Allyson pulled back and smoothed her hands across the lapels of his suit.

"I didn't bring a date, Ally." Crash placed his hands over hers.

"Oh," Allyson whispered.

"There's only one woman I wanted to be my date, but that's not possible," Crash said.

"No, it isn't." Allyson sighed.

"Why?" Crash touched her cheek.

Allyson tipped her head back and met his eyes. He knew there could be something between them, but he had no idea why she fought it. When her gaze dropped to his mouth, her tongue flicked out and licked her lower lip.

"Ally," Crash whispered as he lowered his head.

"Brent." Allyson breathed his name.

Crash swallowed as he brushed a kiss lightly against the corner of her mouth. She gasped and lifted her eyes to meet his, but she didn't pull away. She fisted the lapels of his tuxedo and pulled him closer. His mouth crashed against hers, and he slipped his hands around the back of her neck.

For the last eight years, he'd dreamed of kissing her like this, but it was so much better than he'd imagined. The scent of her jasmine perfume and the taste of champagne on her lips was intoxicating. As his mouth moved against hers, he pulled her against his body and ran his tongue across her lower lip.

She threaded her fingers through his hair as her tongue flicked against his. She moaned into his mouth and his rock-hard dick pressed against the zipper of his trousers. He knew she could feel what the kiss was doing to him, what she was doing.

"Opps," a voice squeaked.

Allyson pulled back, and Crash glanced over the top of her head. He bit back a curse when he saw the older woman smiling a few feet from them.

"I am right again," Cora Nightengale singsonged as she linked into her husband's arm.

"You are always right, my dear." Brian, Cora's husband, smiled as they made their way down the steps toward the parking lot.

Keith's aunt was a lovely person, and people adored her, but she was known as Cora the Cupid. She was legendary for her matchmaking and several years earlier told Crash to ask Allyson out. She continued to remind him every chance she got.

Crash would like nothing better than to pursue a relationship with Allyson, but she kept her distance. At least until tonight. Maybe they'd reached a point where she realized they could have more together.

"Shit," Ally muttered under her breath.

Allyson stepped away from him and wrapped her arms around herself. Their moment clearly ended, but Crash knew he couldn't go back to being simply friends after that kiss.

"That shouldn't have happened." Allyson shook her head.

"Why?" Crash stepped closer, but she lifted her hand to stop him.

"We can't... I can't... It won't work... I got to go," Ally stammered and then rushed back into the club.

"Fuck," Crash growled through his teeth.

He had no idea why things wouldn't work between them, but he sure as hell would find out her reasoning. She had to know he'd do anything for her, and if it took some convincing, he'd make her see they belonged together.

About the Author

What does someone say to describe themselves? You could start by saying what others say about you. Scratch that. It doesn't matter what others think about you. So here we go.

First of all, I'm a wife and mother. I'm also a grandmother. That alone would fulfill any woman's life, and to be honest, it does. But.....

I'm also a writer, someone who loves to tell stories of love, suspense, heartache, and of course, happily ever after. For most of my life, I've written those stories for myself. A type of therapy, I suppose. I love the characters I create. They become part of who I am because there's part of me in them.

So... Now that you know this about me. I hope when you read my books and fall in love with them.

You should also know that I'm a Newfoundlander. What is that, you ask? We're a proud people who live on an island off the east coast of Canada. Some people believe Canada ends with Nova Scotia. It doesn't. If you keep going east, there is a beautiful island full of amazing people and magnificent scenery. That is where my stories are set because let's face it. The best stories always come from the places you know and love.

Also, check out

NES Series

O'Connor Brothers Series

O'Connor Girls

O'Connor Prequel

Rhonda Brewer

Keep up to date on all things new.

Follow me on

Facebook
Twitter
Instagram
MeWe
All Author
Bookbub
TikTok

Sign up for my newsletter and never miss another release!

http://www.rhondabrewerauthor.com/talk-to-me

www.ingramcontent.com/pod-product-compliance
Lightning Source LLC
Chambersburg PA
CBHW070347260626
47161CB00001B/51

* 9 7 8 1 9 9 0 2 0 6 0 2 3 *